I0779833

The Monsters Among Us
Kent Priore

Cover Art Design by: Kelly Moran/Rowan Prose Publishing
Photo Credit: Adobe Images/Deposit Photos
Illustration Insert Credit: Patricia Cobb
First Edition
ISBN: 978-1-961967-62-5
Rowan Prose Publishing, LLC
www.RowanProsePublishing.com
Published in the United States of America

PROLOGUE

S moking these cigarettes has been a part of my life long enough to forget when I started. Though the when of it all may be lost to me, the why has never left my mind. It was not one thing but many incidents that have culminated into a single addiction-causing choice. I remember the words spoken to me by the cashier from whom I bought my first pack. "Are you sure you want these suicide sticks?" he asked, with a wide and ill-suited grin. "That's why I'm here," I responded.

Taking a long drag, the smoke runs deeply into my lungs. As I exhale, the very essence of life leaves me in the form of a thick, grey fog of tobacco and tar.

Only the butt is left and so I toss it away onto the rocky cliffside. To my right is the pack of cigarettes upon a paperback copy of Paradise Lost. I have a habit of coming to the summit of the mountain overlooking town during the rougher moments of life, to smoke, read, and clear my head. Today I have different reasons. No longer do I have the energy to struggle against my mind.

The air is crisp without the taint of industry and human progress. The cold and stony cliffside is therapeutic as I am prone to running hot. The only noise that fills the air is an un-wavering soundscape of crickets, chirping birds, and the scurrying about of wildlife through a mixture of fallen leaves, wood, and stone. The atmosphere calms me—unlike the cacophony of human civilization. But today, though the tree branches rustle sweetly over me, I don't experience the usual tranquility. Instead, pressure builds within my chest. It continues to grow until rising into my throat. My hands begin to shake, I feel my neck tightening and—*ohgodcan'tbreathe...*

Clutching my throat with my left hand, my right grabs another cigarette. With it almost vibrating out of my shaking grip, I place it between my parsed lips. Taking the lighter, I ignite it, worrying that my hand will slip and singe my beard during the struggle.

Inhaling, I feel the gradual calming of my nerves.

Fuck. They're becoming more frequent. I take a long drag, intending to savor this cigarette as it will be my last. Exhaling, the thick fog masks my surroundings and encases me in unwanted memories.

Walking through the hall on my way to class I felt their glare beating against the back of my head. Somewhere along the course of middle and high school, I was labeled as—

"I'd stay away from him," said a girl to my right. Staring straight ahead, I refused to give them the satisfaction of acknowledgement. Though I did notice from the corner of my eye, long slender ivory legs and brunette hair tied in pigtails. She was standing amongst a large group of preppy girls and their muscular jock boyfriends.

"I heard he's bipolar," said another girl. "He'll punch someone just for making eye contact..."

The incessant rattle continued, "...well, I heard he killed s omeone...oh my gosh, did he really?...so scary...think he'd rape me?...he might. He raped little Suzy White...seriously?...that's what she told everyone..."

It was like that every day, though only one thing was maybe true. I was diagnosed with bipolar disorder, or was it borderline personality disorder? Schizophrenia? I've been passed around from one psychiatrist to another ever since I was ten, way too young for any of these diagnoses, but the point is, it's hard to know for sure just what I am. Though everyone around seemed to have settled on an accepted truth—

"Hey, look! It's Seth the retard!" said a masculine voice. "I heard you raped a girl. You're a real scumbag, you know that? A fuckin monster, is more like it."

"I-I'm just trying to get to class...Please leave me be—" A chaotic pounding in my chest. My throat tightened and it became harder to breathe.

"No way, uh uh. You can't do these kinds of things and get away with it, you no good bastard!"

My mind marinated in anxiety, my surroundings grew hazy. It was a strange sensation where my body numbed while my mind ascended from within my skull, opting to float above and around the scene. Dooming me to watch what had been for so long, a horrid daily occurrence. My heightened mental state rendered my body frozen in fear and it also seemed to hasten my perception. Everything proceeded as if life was a film being fast forwarded.

A punch to the nose knocked me backward. There was a stone wall behind. My hair was tugged and pulled to steer my face into the wall. I fell to the floor and received kicks to the side that held so much power. With each blow, the puddles in my eyes deepened, tears trickled onto the grime-covered tile floors.

I never did make it to class. Struggling to my feet, I made my way home.

The smoke clears and the once comforting woodland surroundings return. I wish this place cleared my head like it used to, but I can't help but feel so numb. Those memories roused some unpleasant elation in me and I feel another episode settling in. Taking another drag of my cigarette, a fresh veil of smoke disperses to lose myself in again.

"Ah, she graduates from college soon! I knew she'd make it through. Praise Jesus! Such a wonderful blessing the *Lord* has bestowed upon you. She must be so happy," said a voice amongst the crowd in the church's lobby.

"Did you get that promotion?"

"I won't find out for another few days, but if God wills it, it will be so. If not, it's no big deal. It just means the *Lord* has other plans for me."

Head hanging low, I avert my eyes from onlookers as I make my way to join the sermon. Walking through the church was like trying to weed my way through a vast forest of smiling faces impervious to the woes of life. If only I was that strong.

They say it's the power of Christ, that through the Holy Spirit, the *Lord thy God* will provide our every need. That's why they seem so satisfied with everything. The only need I ever asked to be fulfilled was for a bit of joy. Every night as a child for over a decade I bent over my bedside, hands folded in prayer...

"God, I'm sorry for all my sins. I don't know exactly what I have done, but whatever it was, I'm so sorry and please forgive me. Please, let me be happy." I couldn't ask forgiveness for anything specific, because I hadn't done anything wrong. I was an innocent, small child who didn't know any better and just took the teachings of the Bible to be true, no matter what. "Sin is the cause of all suffering. If you want to be saved by God, you must repent your sins" is what I've heard from both the church and my parents for years now. So, I tried to repent. I prayed and prayed for years until I was convinced there really was a God, and he did love everyone like the Bible claimed, but he didn't love me. I was the outlier. Then I began to feel cursed because while there was a God, he had decided that I wasn't worth saving.

I sat down in the chapel alongside my parents. The two of them sat upright and proper, eagerly awaiting the pastor's ascension to the stage. Next to them I looked crumpled and worn down. My back slouched and neck craned over so my eyes could see my battered black Converse shoes. My eyes, heavy and dry. *My God, my God, why hast thou forsaken me?*

"Welcome and good morning, everyone," spoke the pastor as he hurried onto the stage, "Please turn your Bibles to Matthew 19:26."

Tuning him out, his voice descended into muffled obscurity. Not because I intended to, but because I felt another of my episodes approaching. It started with a hard *thump* in my chest and my vision blurred, except for the pastor and the podium where he stood. Tethered to his gaze, his visage burnt into my pupils. My skin, glossy with cold sweat. "With man this is impossible, but with God all things are possible," he proclaimed. "For us who are born again, God will bring salvation, but those mired in sin and worldly desires," he paused, glaring in my direction, eyes wide, never blinking, a smirk on his face, "Will be damned to eternal death in the fires of Hell."

It wasn't too many Sundays after that I decided I would no longer go to Church. Belief in God only increased my suspicions that I was cursed and so I thought it'd be better to embrace Atheism. Upon telling my parents this, my father's blazing scowl was branded even deeper into his face. Putting down his whisky glass, he rose from the couch and approached me with cold ferocity, like a hawk swooping in on a fear ridden chipmunk. He treated my hair like rope, coiled it around his fingers with precision and proceeded to drag me outside. Reaching the shed in our backyard, he tossed me in, slammed the door, and within the darkness all I could hear was the turning of a key.

"I'll let ya out once ya reconsider yer sinful ways. Ya betta think twice about disgracin' yer family like this."

Soon I relented and once again accompanied them to Church every Sunday. But I sure as hell never believed in God again.

Another lungful of smoke disperses and beyond it, the sun is now on the verge of setting. The view is enhanced by the hues of purple and orange found in the twilight sky. Looking down at my cigarette, I see that the next drag will be my last. Sucking it down, I watch the embers drip from the end before getting caught by a gust of wind and drifting off.

On the way home from one of my many trips to the mountain's summit, a man appearing to be around my age, twenty-three, walked toward me. His head was shaved on the side and substituted with peculiar tribal-like tattoos, lined in teal. Matching that color was a substantial mohawk, rising high above his head. His body, clad entirely in white.

As he came closer, I could only imagine what he desired to do to me. I flinched and shut my eyes, only to open them once more at the sound of metal clinking against the sidewalk. The mohawk sporting man passed without a word. Beneath my feet lay what seemed to be an old locket. "Hey, you dropped this!" I turned around and even though it had only been a few seconds, the man and his dyed mohawk were nowhere to be seen. Bewildered by his disappearance, I pocketed the locket, thinking I'd return it if I happened to see him again.

"The town psycho is back at it, is he?" spoke a lanky black-haired man. "Who're ya talkin' to just now?"

"The guy with the mohawk, he dropped something and I wanted to—"

"Man, you're really far gone, ain't ya? This is a small town and there's not a single mohawk sporting buffoon here. Plus, I was watching the whole time. You spaced out for a good five minutes, turned around, and spoke to the empty air. You some kind of idiot?"

I continued walking home, but the man followed closely enough that I could feel his breath on my neck.

"Just how long before you snap and start killin' everyone here? Think you can do us all a favor and start with yourself? I can lend you a noose. We don't need any crazy folk round here."

I started running. He didn't pursue, which was lucky since smoking four packs a day made it clear I wasn't fit for the Olympics. I slowed to a crawl, coughing up mucus.

This was an everyday affair. As rough as that was, it was nothing compared to the abuse I received from my parents. The goal was to sneak inside and hide in my room, but as I opened the door, there they were awaiting my arrival, along with a face I thought I had left behind. It was the lanky black-haired man, only now it looked as if someone had hit him in the face with a cheese grater. Along with those scrapes and bruises were two large black eyes.

"That's the one! Your son's a monster! He did this to me!"

I couldn't comprehend what was happening. My parents approached me.

"Why would you do this, Seth? He says you attacked him without reason," my mother said.

"I don't—"

"No, don't even let him try to weasel himself out of this one. I have no reason to doubt this man. Seth, don't you fuckin' move," said my father. "The cops are coming."

The next sequence of events happened in a blur. I had no time to defend myself, verbally or otherwise. When the cops arrived, they pinned me down, cuffed me, and dragged me to their police car. As the vehicle sped off, I turned to look through the rearview window and on the front lawn stood my parents and that rude stranger, each of whom wore smiles which stretched upward on both sides. To such a degree that it looked as if their faces were ripping and tearing. For a moment, the whites in their eyes turned black.

Did I really assault him? I don't remember...but...oh. That man with the mohawk, he was there, wasn't he? I reached into my pocket to search for the locket and sure enough it was there. But my mind didn't stop contemplating the situation. *Maybe I got this locket from somewhere else and...*

I had no time to think it over, soon enough we were at the police station. I was held for a few days and eventually went to court where the judge gave me two options. Apparently, the man I assaulted was feeling merciful and said he wouldn't file charges if I agreed to spend time in a psych ward. That was one option, the other was prison.

I spent months inside what they called a hospital, but felt as though I had chosen my other option. The walls were ragged and worn. The tile floors, cold and dirty. All the windows were secured with metal bars. I, at twenty-three years old, had a bedtime. Or at least a time when all patients had to return to their rooms.

It was no surprise that I felt trapped and depressed. After so many months, I lost hope of ever getting out. They wanted me to take meds, which I refused...at first. My mind went back to being locked inside the shed by my father and how I caved and agreed to abide by his rules. I may have my rebellious moments, but I always lacked the backbone when it counted. So, I abided by the hospital's medication regimen. After a couple weeks feeling dazed and empty—the medication eating away at me like poison—they released me.

On my way out, the head psychiatrist said, "I'd wish you luck, but I know it's pointless. Everyone talks in this town, so I know all about you. You wanna know the truth? You'll never make it out there because no one wants you around. Why do you think you were sent here? You've done too much damage. I'd liken you to an animal, but even they serve a purpose. They provide us food, but you? You're worth less than the dirt they coat their shit in."

I witnessed that same horror again. This time upon the face of the psychiatrist. His smile grew so wide that his skin tore and blood squirted from the corners of his mouth. I turned away and hastened my escape. These recurring episodes were getting much more frequent and yet I never grew used to it. My heart trembled as I ran. While I never learned whether my alleged assault on that man happened, there was no denying his bruises, and it was their word against mine. Maybe I was a monster after all.

Staring out into the dark wilderness, I try to take another drag, but the cigarette is mere embers. Sucking on just a filter, I'm hoping there would be a bit more to smoke. It's my last cig and I don't want to let go, but I know I must. Reaching into my right pants pocket, I take out the locket. I've felt compelled to bring it everywhere, ever since that day three years ago. I thought if I could find that man with the teal mohawk and return his locket, I could convince myself that I'm not crazy, but to this day it remains with me. Shoving it deep within my pocket, leaving the copy of Paradise Lost and the empty pack of cigarettes behind, I walk to the edge of the cliff. More than a fifty-foot drop. Inching closer, I breathe in, and begin to take my final step.

A flash of light through the trees from behind catches my attention. At first, it's bright enough to be a flash bomb, but as the initial shock wanes, so does the light. Out from behind the trees calls a voice.

"Hellooo! Anyone there? Thought I heard someone."

A girl? Something about her voice feels so...soothing.

"U-uh, yeah. Someone's—I'm here."

She emerges from the trees, a slender waist, but with a hiker's legs and a face, softer and prettier than I've ever seen. A head dressed in golden blonde locks which seem to sparkle in the moonlight. She's holding a flashlight, illuminating my face as I stand there in awe.

"Oh, hello. What's your name?"

"Seth. You're not from around here, are you?" I have never seen a girl like her in town, and she just feels...different.

"You could say that." She grins. "The name's Lola. I'm in town visiting family and thought I'd go for a quick hike...but I didn't think it would get this dark so fast and now I'm embarrassed to say I'm a bit lost. Do you know your way around well?"

"U-um, yeah I do. I could show you the way if you want."

"Even in this dark?"

"Yeah, no problem. I come up here a lot."

There's a moment of silence. I hate silence. Gives my brain too much of a chance to fill the gaps. She must think I'm weird, a strange guy spending all his time in the woods. I don't get many chances to speak to people, *ohgodwhatdoIdo*.

"You look tense," she says, as she shoots the flashlight into my face again. "Something the matter?"

"Oh, no. It's nothing. I'll lead you out of here, don't worry."

"Then lead on!" She shines the flashlight onto her face, showing off a big grin and upon seeing it, my paranoia melts away.

There are a few more awkward silences, but this time my paranoia remains docile and meek. The longer I spend with her walking by my side, the easier it becomes.

"So how long are you in town?" I ask.

"Just a couple days, though honestly I doubt I'll spend much of it with my family."

"Why not?"

"Oh...well, I have a habit of wanting to get away."

I don't press further and don't need to. As we're approaching the edge of the woods, streetlamps can be seen in the not-so-distant area.

"Ah, finally free!" she shouts. "Well, I guess this is goodbye then. Thanks for your help."

She flashes a smirk, lays her hand on my shoulder and rubs gently. I'm stricken with a sensation I have never felt before. She turns, ambling away.

"Wait!" I shout, compelled by some ineffable force. "This may sound strange, you know, coming from a stranger you met in the woods and all, but would you maybe like to hangout while you're in town? Tomorrow maybe?"

She turns around, already smiling. "Are you planning on luring me back into the woods to kill me?"

"Uh no—of course not!"

"Oh, relax, it was a joke! Honestly, I was hoping you'd ask me out." She pauses, comes closer, and slips her hand into my left pants pocket. Taking out my phone, she enters her number and slips it back in. The pleasant friction of her hand against my upper thigh sends a jolt throughout my body. With a chuckle she says, "you're cute."

I have completely forgotten what I had planned to do at the cliffside tonight.

Finally meeting up with her again, I take her to dinner at a pizza joint a couple towns over to avoid people who hate me at home.

"So, what's your family like?" I ask.

"Oh, you know. We start our Sunday mornings right by attending church to worship the Lord thy God..."

Spacing out, I wonder if what I felt last night was nothing more than lust. Right off the bat she outs herself as just another Christian and I feel myself being overcome with disgust.

"...or that's what I'd say if I were one of them," she continues, in a tone I now recognize as sarcasm. "Yeah, my family are a bunch of crazy Born Agains. But my experience with religion. ..well, none of them would believe me, but it was nothing short of abuse. How could I believe in a God who would let such bad things happen to me?"

"You can't," I reply. And then I explain to her my own qualms with religion.

She says, "God is nothing but a bully, and I've had enough bullies at school growing up. My family is no better either."

I almost can't believe what I'm hearing. Her sorrowful tales of adolescence mirror my own. How wonderful it feels to be understood. We continue to bond over our shared perspectives for the rest of the date and *please God, please, let there be more.*

A few months later.

I got my wish. She lives about an hour away, but we visit each other all the time. My feelings for her grow more each day and I've decided to take our relationship to the next level over a special date night I have planned.

We take a train to New York City. The trip is about an hour and a half long, but it is well worth what I have in store for us. First, we will get dinner at a five-star restaurant, then a Broadway show, and then wherever the city's nightlife may take us. Though the most important part is at dinner, where I will tell her just how much she means to me.

Our date is routine, with our jovial and intimate conversations never wavering. Time flies. Soon enough, I pay the check and out the door we go. We turn to each other and words cannot describe just how happy—for the first time *ever* I am happy—these last few months with her have made me. Taking her hands, I look deep into her eyes and begin muttering those three special words.

"I love yo—"

The screeching brakes of a black van pierce my ears as it skids to the curb beside us. Out of it bursts three large men wearing all black suits. Two of them grab Lola by her arms and begin carrying her toward the trunk. "No! Help, Seth!" she cries out. I feel it again. The swelling of my chest, the paralyzing fear that has made me the town punching bag for my whole life. This time, however, is different. My body moves on its own. Eyes wide, neck veins popping, I grip my pent-up anger, turning it into a fist.

"Give her back!" I shout, unwilling to let go of the only happiness life has ever granted me.

"Give it up. Walk away. She's ours now," says the third man. I hear the unclicking of his gun's safety, the muzzle pressing hot against my forehead in this sweltering summer heat. "Give it up," he repeats, though I hear no words. Cocking my fists, they begin their ascent, and—a loud *BANG* overtakes me. My world goes dark.

I awake to find myself floating in an empty space devoid of anything but a vast whiteness. *What is this? Where am I?*

{You have died. This place is beyond your world,} says an unfamiliar voice, of whose location I cannot place.

"Who are you?" I ask.

{You may have died, but fret not, child. Yours is a story that begins after death. It is being decided just what is to be done with your soul...and so it has been done.}

Out from beneath this White Abyss, rises many long and boney, charred hands. The white space around their eruption cracks and withers away, revealing the scent of sulfur and brimstone beneath. The hands grip my legs, arms, chest, and back, pulling me down from whence they came.

Part One

Descent

"He who fights with monsters might take care lest he thereby become a monster. And if you gaze for long into an abyss, the abyss gazes also into you."
-Friedrich Nietzsche, *Beyond Good and Evil*

CHAPTER ONE

I awake to the sickening scent of rancid blood. My body feels like it's on fire. Struggling to my feet, I try to recall what happened. I find myself alone on a cliffside. My head pans left to right. All I can see is an unending Sea of Flames. The scent jolts my memory. The last sensation I had—*the smell of a gun. I was shot!* Like the spastic and manic child I once was, I glance around the cliffside. *Lola! Where are you?* She is nowhere to be seen.

I suppose I shouldn't be surprised. To be given happiness for a few months after a lifetime of sorrow, it's no wonder it would be snatched away from me so soon. The supernatural gravity of this place pushes down upon my shoulders, with such force that it feels like I am sinking into the floor. My stomach churns. I drop down to my knees. Through my throat comes a flood of blood. The crimson source of life spews out of me and boils in the heat.

I remember that day at the church when my vision blurred and all I could see was the pastor on stage. It happens again. All visual stimuli appears as the grey static of an old TV failing to pick up a channel. The hands of a creature I don't recognize reaches over my shoulder and turns me toward it. Its unhuman features overwhelm me. There are two of them, these reptilian creatures. Their tall, slender bodies tower over me. They have glowing red eyes, not unlike the blood which left me moments ago. Their faces are flat with large gaping mouths that house tiny sharp teeth.

"Fresh blood," one says. "Should we pierce him to a pillar? Or is it to the Sea of Flames?"

"Neither," says the other. "We have special orders to bring this one to *Him*."

They nod to each other and drag me by the arms into a nearby cave.

I can't fight back. My body won't move. This place, wherever it is, holds an aura of such tremendous pressure. I remain at the mercy of these two creatures.

"Where am I?"

"Where do you think?" asks one. "In Hell," says the other.

I was taught to expect this by my Christian parents, though no part of me ever thought they would be right.

"Then why do I have a body still?" I ask.

"You don't. That's why you can't move. You are naught but a spirit. Souls are like memories in the sense that they can affect the perception of oneself, as well as in the sense that they are easily malleable. Souls are like hot iron, a skilled blacksmith can hammer a soul into a beautiful and destructive weapon."

"Silence. Our Lord will be angry with us if you say any more than you should," says the other. "This is all you need to know. It seems you still have a body because that's all your soul understands."

They remain silent while we continue through the cave. I wonder what's in store for me. *Is this really my end? Who was that voice from within that* White Abyss? *Are these really demons?* My mind keeps on turning more than ever. I can't wait for all of this, whatever it is, to be over. This cave's scent is maddening. It smells of blood and rancid meat.

We soon make it to the exit and before us stands a large open area. Entirely flat with tall pillars rising above it. A piercing squeal fills the air. I look toward the direction it came from and *oh, god*.

On each of these tall pillars which forest the land are what I recognize to be human beings. They are impaled upon spikes protruding outward while blood spills from their bodies. It runs down grooves in the stone and into large pots that sit beneath each of the dying humans. Nearby demons grab a few of the pots and while some begin bathing in the blood, others gulp it down. Some choose to sever the limbs of their victims and devour the flesh. One chomps into a calf muscle then salivates at the sight of the humans regrowing their arms and legs, like axolotls. It is as if some magic force is preventing them from ever truly dying.

As repulsive and saddening as this sight is, it isn't long before we cross over a bridge that sits atop a river of locusts. The incessant crackling of their wings is so loud, I feel as though my ear drums could burst at any moment.

We arrive at a gate. It's the entrance to a castle made of black stone. The demons drag me inside. Its interior is lit with lanterns, but the light they produce is scarce.

"Welcome to Castle Pandaemonium," says the demon to my right.

At a brisk pace, they drag me down a long corridor. At the end of the hall is a tall wooden double door with a pointed top. I notice a series of paintings along the walls. Each one captures the image of the same four people. A father figure with a long beard, two young boys, one a child, and the other on the cusp of puberty. Alongside them is a girl, the same age as the older boy. Their skin, a golden brown. The older boy's face is the only one untarnished. Copper colored eyes and a smile wide and gentle. The faces of the other three are vandalized in various ways. The younger boy's eyes are crossed out. The same is true for the face of the father, with only his long beard breaking through. The girl's face is completely torn away, with a few strands of blonde hair as her sole defining feature. While there are dozens of these photos, each one has been vandalized in the same eerie way. I can't for the life of me figure who these people are, but the sight of them sends shivers down my spine. It feels like I am looking at something that isn't meant to be seen.

We reach the end of the corridor. My draconic captors open the large double door with a key.

"Finally, you've arrived," says a voice from within. Against my ears, it sounds like glass scraping against a chalkboard. A grin, reaching about three feet in length, emerges from the shadows. "I am, as you humans know me, the Lord of Hell, Satan." Each of His many teeth are like long railroad spikes, chattering loudly as He speaks. "I have a proposition for you, dear boy." Upon the ending of that last syllable, as if on cue, torches scattered around the room burst into flames. They illuminate the large open space and His form is presented in full.

His height is that of three large men stacked on top of each other with the broad shoulders to match. The back of Him extends a few car lengths. Out from the upper back are large wings which are devoid of flesh. All that remains is bone that shows evidence of having feathers burnt away. Because of His enormous stature, He remains on all fours.

"Well? Speak up, boy!" He says.

The reptilian demons drop my dead weight onto the floor. I avert my eyes away from the intensity of His gaze.

"You house quite a bit of anger within you. Out of fear you have gone your whole life suppressing it because you felt those around you would hate you all the more if you showed any sort of weakness. But you did show it in the end. The product of the emptiness inside. The rage. You let it out for a moment before your death, when those bad men took that tasty looking biscuit away from you. I'm sure they are up to such fun things with her at the moment."

I feel it again. The heat building within my chest. Like the fabled phoenix, I feel life surging through my limbs again. I quickly rise, and, teeth clenching, shoot Him an angry glare.

"Yes, my boy! Give in to it! Let it fuel you! Fire, while destructive, can give birth to new life!" He is ecstatic. His unblinking eyes grow wider.

Moving on its own, my body plunges toward Him. I notice a shift in His eyes. They give off a yellow glow and He turns them sharply toward the floor. As His pupils fall, so does my body and I'm encumbered by the same gravitational force which pinned me to the ground earlier, only this time it's far worse. I feel the bones in my back begin to warp and crack.

"Now, now. I am not the one you should direct your rage to. I was simply trying to stir up some power within you, as it is necessary for the transformation."

"T-transformation?" I ask.

"You shall see. If you accept my proposition. And just so you know, boy, those people skewered to the pillars outside? That is your alternative. Choose wisely."

"Okay...tell me what you want."

"Being a human, you would not have noticed, but a storm is brewing. Things are about to change drastically in this world. I want to be ready for it. I need a warrior."

"I think you have me mistaken for those monsters from before. I am weak. Always have been."

"The power of magic grows substantially over time. For eons it has been suppressed and hidden from you humans, but it is finally ripe for the picking. You will discard your human form and wield far greater power than those demons outside. As you are a fresh soul, and they are naught but old bones!"

"Now you're talking about magic? Magic and Hell and demons? None of this makes any sense. This must be a dream...right? I'm still alive...right? Please just let me wake up—please!"

"*Boy*! I have no time to babysit you. Toughen up! You are dead and everything around you is more real than anything you ever experienced while alive!"

{He's right.}

Huh? That voice again.

Satan eyes me for a moment, but appears to dismiss His suspicions.

"Look, there's plenty I need from you, but for starters I need you to take care of a particular demon by the name of Melphis, the Covetor. He has been plotting to usurp me for some time now."

"Wait, you want me to kill someone? I-I can't do that!"

"Not someone. A demon. I would send any of the countless demons I already have, but as I said, they are old bones. Melphis would have no trouble wiping them all out."

"Why not go yourself? What makes you the Lord of this place if you're too weak to take care of what should be a small problem?"

Flames erupt, engulfing the circumference of the room and hovering in the air, they flicker chaotically. The temperature is suffocating. "Listen, boy. I admire your audacity, but you best watch your tongue." The flames die down as silence fills the room. I dare not speak another word. "Do you think I like it here?" Satan continues, "A realm of blood and misery. The raging Sea of Flames. The incessant chatter of locusts that insists that sleep be an impossibility...look, the circumstances of my being here." He turns around and gazes toward the monstrous throne behind Him. "My having to sit upon that throne...these are things I do not want. Though the confines of my life demand that it remains so, lest disaster strikes. What I truly want, after Melphis is dealt with, is to reclaim my lost paradise."

Looking at this monster, somehow, it is almost as if I am gazing upon a young and saddened boy.

"I know you must feel hesitant to trust me. But would it help to know that I will repay you for your services? As a reward for carrying out the task, not only will you be granted new life, but I will grant you a chance to meet your beloved again."

My eyes, renewed with vigor, fiercely meet His own. Satan smiles, and lifts the pressure He placed upon me, allowing me to rise to my feet.

"Yes, I know where that pretty little thing is being kept. Just like how I have kept a close eye on you for years. I can peer into the life of just about anyone. I can show you, however, you will not like what you see."

"I don't care. I need to know."

Satan's eyes glow again. A white circle is drawn in the air, opening a window across worlds. Upon completion, it provides a sight I can never unsee. There Lola is, surrounded by a large group of men, naked and badly bruised. One by one they have their way with her, passing her around like a bong in a room full of stoners.

A stream of tears coats my face. "N-no more...please, stop it."

"Consider this extra incentive," Satan says. "Those men are cohorts of Melphis. Interested in helping now?"

{Take his offer.}

There that voice is again. Satan doesn't appear to hear it. It sounds like it's coming from inside my head. I have no idea who it is or how I can respond, but my answer to Satan is obvious.

"Fine, I'll do it, but I still don't understand what you think I can accomplish."

"It will be clear once you arrive," He says. "Melphis is hiding beneath a laundromat. You will arrive nearby. Head there."

Satisfied, Satan again conjures a white circle. This time the view on the other end is that of a dark alleyway in which He tells me is New York City. He says to jump through and I do. Erupting through a second womb, I arrive alive, to the city where I died. Though the words of those demons who found me on the cliffside worry me.

The soul is easily malleable. Am I alive? Or do I just perceive myself to be?

Either way, there's no doubt that I am back on Earth. I turn a corner and there passing by in a hurry is a large amount of busy New Yorkers crowding the sidewalk while pushing and shouting at each other. A legion of cars stuck in traffic taking their morning frustrations out upon those in front of them by laying hard on the horn. This isn't Hell, but it might as well be.

I can't imagine how Satan expects me, a human, to deal with a demon. My heartbeat feels rough and sporadic. I never liked uncertainty, but I must deal with it. It's my only chance to save Lola.

I find the place and glance inside. It's empty, except for a lone attendant sitting at a desk watching TV.

"What do you want, kid?" asks the man. A peculiar way to greet a customer. "I was just about to close."

"I'm here to see M-Melphis?" I say.

"Eh? I don't know who you're talking about. Now scram."

My mind drifts back to the moment before I died. I remember the anguish in Lola's face as she was taken away. Someone so low that they would order a kidnapping must also be into other unsavory areas of life. I look outside and see a policeman.

"I'm here about the rumors about the drug and prostitution rings," I say. There are no rumors. At least how would I know about them even if there were? I don't have to be right, I just need to cause a scene. "Let me see your boss, or I'll grab that cop from outside and tell him all about it."

The man rises from his desk with empty eyes, "I don't know what you're on about. Get lost, kid."

He seems to be telling the truth. I feel no insincerity in his voice, but I doubt a simple door lackey would know the inner details of an organization. I'm sure he's in the dark as much as I am. As a gatekeeper he has no reason to know what crimes his boss may have committed. His job is simple, keep people out. I decide to push him.

"Fine. To the police then." I turn for the door. "Good luck!" I shout over my shoulder.

"Kid, wait!" he pauses. "Fine. I just got this gig, and I'd rather not deal with that kind of mess. Come."

I follow him through a door behind his desk. Beyond is a stairwell leading into a cellar.

We enter a wide basement with a large table in the center. The scowls of twenty men surround it. Not one appears to be a demon.

"Sir, this guy here was causing a ruckus. Threatened to tell the pigs 'bout some shit that—"

"You had one job," interrupts one of the men, sitting at the far end of the table. He walks over to us. He's a tiny blond man with blue eyes—wait, no. Something isn't right. As he comes closer my head throbs and my vision browns out—cutting away for a second, returns, and cuts away again. Before my eyes, his visage metamorphosizes. Short stature remaining the same, but his hair turns black and weaves around a crown of horns. His white skin turns pasty and grey. His human teeth chiseled into sharp little points, each a freshly shaven pencil tip. His eyes become a crimson brown. I glance around the room, but none of these strange men seem to have noticed.

"We are in an important meeting. I asked you to not to let us be disturbed for any reason. You've embarrassed me in front of my guests and that is unforgivable."

In a quick and graceful movement, he removes a pistol from his inner suit pocket, puts the muzzle to the man's forehead, and pulls the trigger. The blast ruptures my left eardrum. The man's blood splatters across half my face.

"Fuck!" I say.

"You'll be fine. I know what you are and why you've come," says the man. "Gentlemen, I sincerely apologize, but would you mind if this young man and I have a chat in the other room alone? We shan't be long."

With a collective sigh and nod most of the men gesture that the delay is fine. But one rises from his seat.

"Hell no! Ah've waited long enough to hear what ya have to offer! If this dumbass foolishly wandering in here is to be the cause of mah wasted time, well ah'll just empty a clip in him mahself!"

Before anyone can intervene, the rapid succession of gunshots is heard. My chest feels wet and warm. I look down and my shirt is damp with blood. I can't help but think this is all some sick joke. Killed a second time over. Lured into believing that I could rescue Lola, be happy and alive once more only to have that hope snatched away from me all too soon. Just like the first time. How I wish this to be a nightmare I can awaken from and find myself again in her embrace! But this pain is too real. This pain, wait, the pain—it's fading?

Some sort of miracle occurs. I'm not dead. I unbutton my shirt to witness the bullets being pushed outward by my regenerating flesh. They clink against the tile floor, blood flow stops as the wounds close. My ruptured eardrum heals as well. Sparks crackle around the wound as energy rushes through it.

"The hell? I got da heart, ah know ah did. He should be a goner!" says the man. "He some kinda...*monster?*"

At that word, my mind regresses. Memories are stirred, kicked up by a violent gust of wind. I'm in high school again.

Pinned to the floor, kicked and beaten while receiving harsh tongue lashings of lies and slander. *Monster!* they called me. *Monster!*

My heart lets out a loud *thump.* My vision shakes and my body expands to four times its original size. Like a bountiful fall harvest, my head sprouts long horns. They erupt from my forehead and curve backward. My teeth and nails are elongated and thickened. And the heat! It feels as if the fires of Hell itself now found a new home within my body.

"Enough!" I say in a voice far deeper than I'm used to. "I'm here for the kidnapped girl. Where is she?"

The man who shot the gatekeeper drops his pistol and takes a step back. The other men, overtaken by shock, fire their guns which now fail to pierce my skin. My agitation isn't quelled. The heat overtakes me. In my palms form orbs of fire and the skin of my arms bubbles like boiling water. I hurl the orbs at the frightened men and the hellfire engulfs them. All that remains are charred bodies. The room reeks of burnt flesh. Only the one who backed away survives.

"The bastard just couldn't be patient," he says.

"Are you talking about the one who shot me?"

"I'm talking about the *both* of you." He scowls. "You have any idea what you just cost me?"

"I know I don't care. Give her back."

"Who do you mean?"

"The girl your lackeys kidnapped. Don't fucking play dumb!"

"Boy, I sincerely have no idea what you're talking about."

"Don't you lie to—"

"Hold on. Take a moment to gather yourself."

I notice the size of my hands. They're monstrous.

"What...happened?"

"Let us cut to the chase, shall we? You are not of this world, not anymore. Satan dug His talons in and created a beast of you. This change allows your gaze to pierce the veil of life and that which lies beyond. You saw it, didn't you? My true form within this vessel?"

Horrified, I remain mute.

"Satan sent you on a hunt, did He not? I'm the demon, Melphis, the one you seek. But boy, you must remember it is Satan, the master of lies of whom you have struck a deal with. I'm afraid He has deceived you as there is no girl here. While I, too, am a demon, I promise I share no ties with Him. On the contrary! I wish to bring Him down!"

"I can't trust you," I say. "Satan showed me...the horrible things your men were doing to Lola."

"No such thing occurred. I assure you. They had only arrived shortly before you had. What Satan showed you was mere fabrication. In fact, I can prove it."

He walks over to a door on the opposite side of the stairwell. Inside appears to be a small office space. He disappears into it, then reappears holding a tall rod.

"You see, I've been planning to take the throne of Hell for myself. Such a grandiose ambition cannot be done without much preparation. That includes surveillance of the enemy. This staff not only aids me in my magic, but within it holds a recollection of events. A sort of memory retaining magic that responds to a spell I've casted in many parts of this city, as well as others. Well, in any case..."

With his middle finger and thumb, he flicks the top of the staff three times. Sparks fly from each flick, like flint against steel. Upon that third strike a projection appears, hovering just above the table.

{*Watch closely now.*}

What I see are the unfinished three words "I love yo—" followed by the screeching black van. There we are, Lola and I in our final moments. The three men in black suits appear and the scene continues just as I remember, though with one difference, the eyes of the men are as black as their suits. Sprouted from their backs are shadowy wings and above their heads float the shape of halos. Instead of being gold the halos are as black as their eyes and wings.

"What did you just show me?" I ask.

"The truth. This is how I recognized you. You are a fresh one, so this may be a shock. But you and I are not the only demons on Earth. No, there are legions of them everywhere. At the time, I figured this was just the normal daily chaos led by demons masquerading as humans. Little did I know the kid who was shot would miraculously show up at my front door."

He pauses and gestures toward the charred corpses scattered around the room.

"You can see through the veil now, so you know it to be true. These men are mere humans. They are not the demons who took your little lady friend. The ones who did work for the one who sent you here. But let me ask you this. What would you say if I could allow you not only to get revenge for how Satan manipulated you, but also get your girl back? He may have lied, but I will not. So, what do you say? Wouldn't you do anything to return to your beloved's side?

CHAPTER TWO

"**W**ell? Wouldn't you?"

Melphis stands before me, awaiting an answer. I hesitate, but can't deny what he showed me. He can't be lying. These men, or the charred clumps of flesh that were once men, are just that. Men.

"What is it?" Melphis asks.

"I did that?" I respond, gesturing over to the bodies.

"Do you not remember?"

"It's hazy."

"You robbed me of my chance to raid Hell, and yet you don't even remember doing so?"

I remember the crippling weight of Hell's atmosphere.

"And how would you do that? They're only human," I say.

"Yes. Weak, pathetic humans. But they could have become so much more! You see, I was going to turn them into demons."

"You can do that?"

"They wouldn't be true demons, only Satan can make those. However, I had concocted a spell that would, when combined with my blood, enhance their otherwise weak human bodies with magic. Theoretically. But if successful, I'd have a small army to raid His throne room! But you've ruined those plans."

"And you want me to replace them?" I ask.

"I'm left with little choice. Besides, I can feel a certain strength in you. A festering rage. Why not use that to help me, while I help you find your girl?"

My head grows hazy again. I feel I can fall over at any moment. **{Satan was a bridge, but this one will be a lantern in the darkness.}**

Like Melphis, I feel that I also have little choice. I look down at my monstrous hands. *Where else could I go?*

"You can really help me find her?" I ask.

"Without a doubt. Even if my recollection magic doesn't catch her, we know that she was taken by a group of demons and I'm after their king. She is bound to turn up somewhere, I promise."

"Fine then. Satan will get what's coming to Him."

For a moment, I feel a surge of life return to me. Melphis appears to take notice and a wide grin plasters across his face.

"Good to hear. I suppose I should tell you more about our target, along with this world-after-death you have stumbled into. Let us get to it."

"What is the meaning of this?" Satan screams, watching the scene unfold. "How is it that he has free will? Him and that Melphis."

He turns away from the window into the human world. It quickly dissipates. He faces the demons huddled at the base of His throne.

"And *you*! I chose you to be his parents, you two were the most responsible for molding his soul into the weapon I desired, but you failed! You dare disappoint me?"

His petrifying gaze pierces the two demons at the center. Both stand tall and slender with dark boils scattered across their pale, ivory skin. One has a sagging gut that barely covers the large male appendage which hangs flaccid between his legs. The other has two large mounds rising from her chest. Their beady black eyes stare unblinking toward the feet of their dark Lord.

"W-we did e-everything you asked of us," says the male.

"W-we promise!" says the female.

Satan takes a step forward raising His massive right hand. Wide eyed, He glares at them and snaps His fingers. The two center demons watch the others erupt with blood from their eyes, mouths, and all other orifices. Their bodies continue to expel the crimson liquid until they wither away into a skin bag of bones and little else.

"If you have done your job, then why is it that I cannot kill him? You mindless demons! All of you are born from me. The life you live, the magic you wield, your pneuma! All of it is tied to me. I grant life and I can also take it away." Satan pauses for a moment. "But his..."

"My Lord, if I may," says the male demon.

"*You may not*!" Satan roars. "One chance. That's what you have. Leave me."

The two hastily leave.

Satan turns away from the withered demons that lay upon the floor. They will evaporate in Hell's heat soon enough. He opens another window across the two worlds, spying once again on Seth and Melphis.

How can this be? While pondering, He feels another presence behind Him. "And what can I do for you, dear sister?"

"Trouble in paradise?"

Satan winces. "Everything is fine, I assure you. No need to worry. All is going as planned."

"Oh, please. I heard all of that just now. Something is wrong with the boy and now he's in the hands of that troublesome one." She pauses, sizing Satan up for a moment. "He was supposed to be delivered to me. How do you plan on fixing this?" Her once sweet tone becomes cold enough to extinguish the fires of Hell. Satan feels a shiver surge through Him.

"It will be fixed. Those two I sent are hopeless, but I will notify the Sins. Do not worry, sister. I will fix this."

"You better," She commands, never breaking Her cold glare. She brushes the golden blonde hair out of Her face and makes for the door.

Once Satan is sure She is gone, He shouts, "Bitch! You will not own me!"

"And that is how Satan governs this world," Melphis explains. He pauses, awaiting a reaction. "Still with me?"

"Uh, yes. Sorry." My head feels heavier by the second. My fading consciousness feels as if it's flickering like a dying light bulb. With each fade, it feels like I'm being pulled elsewhere. "Are you telling me that there are demons living among humans? How is it they haven't been noticed?"

"Legions of them, yes. And demons are made to operate from the shadows. They possess human bodies, you see. Like those that took your girl. You probably lived your entire life surrounded by them without ever noticing."

"My family," I mutter. Something inside me clicks, "The soul is easily malleable."

Melphis gives an inquisitive stare, but remains silent.

"My family...and all the townsfolk. Were they turning me into something Satan wanted?"

"If you really want the answer, I'd be more than willing to see if my recollection magic picked up on anything, but I'd say you already figured it out," Melphis says. "All we know for sure is that Satan wanted you to become a demon, and demons are naught but tools to Him. He's plotting something. Though all we can do is focus our energy on the task of killing the bastard."

"Right," I reply. My face grows dark and sullen.

"Anyway, as I was saying," Melphis says, ignoring my anguish. "Satan feeds off human souls. They are His nourishment, His source of power. But first they must be tainted. Only then are they ripened to His liking. There are seven great demons here on Earth who are responsible for spreading that taint as well as speeding up the flow of souls into Hell. I suppose your average Catholic would call them the Seven Deadly Sins. Conveniently, one resides in this very city, and so—"

Melphis stops, noticing how absent I seem. I'm nodding off and struggling even to remain standing.

"Ah, I see. My apologies. My transformation was long enough ago that it is a vague and distant memory. I forgot how tired you must be. Not many can say they have died twice within twenty-four hours. Not to mention...what you've become." He gestures toward a couch to the side of the room. "Sleep it off. We'll continue this later."

I don't say a word. There is no energy for it. I walk over to the couch, dazed. I sit and feel the wooden boards crack to pieces under my weight. Paying no mind, I try laying across it anyway, but it doesn't feel right. My body and its proportions are not what they should be. It isn't that I can't get comfortable, I just can't fit. Like a fat cat curling up into a box half its size, but unlike a cat, I lack flexibility. Is his offer for me to take the couch a sincere kindness? *Or did he do it so that he could laugh at me?*

The faces of my parents and that stranger come to mind. Their heads split in half by their unnatural grins, laughing as the police took me away. Am I just a joke to everyone? *Is it funny for them to ruin my life?*

Too tired to dwell, I opt to slither to the floor instead. My upper back rests against the couch just enough to lay my enlarged head on a tiny couch cushion.

A vast White Abyss.

{*Welcome, Seth, the Rageful.*}

Glancing back and forth, I wonder where the voice is coming from. There's nothing but the emptiness of the Abyss. My feet feel for a surface to stand on and to my surprise they make contact, but on what, I cannot tell. The same overwhelming whiteness stretches out in every direction. I appear to be all alone, floating in some unknown emptiness. But there, arriving from far off in the distance, emerges a garden.

Grass, roots and colorful flora rise from a single spot within the Abyss. Bushes and flowers outline a walkway which leads to a tree and under the branches stand three figures. One in the center rises tall above the other two. He wears a scruffy beard that reaches down to his knees. The features of the other two are harder to discern, but they appear to flaunt peculiar hairstyles, with one's rising high above his head.

They are otherwise ambiguous. Their bodies are as deep a white as the surrounding Abyss. All I can see are the outlines of their forms. A glorious, teal-colored light expands from the edges of their skin and hair. It's so bright that the image of the garden they stand in begins to be obscured.

{*You have met Melphis, the Coveter. You will meet more like him along your way. Open your heart to them. Live with them, laugh with them, grow with them. They all*}

carry their own pain. Yet, you will find that they say Yea! to Life anyway. Follow their example, but do not fear your own woes, as pain is a bridge to greater, more sublime heights. The great epochs of our life are at the points when we gain courage to rebaptize our badness as the best in us.}

Before I can respond, the teal light erupts with even greater intensity than before. It continues to spread wider, bursting out until the White Abyss itself is overtaken by the bright teal rays.

My consciousness fades away.

I awake to find myself still in Melphis's hideout.

A dream?

What was that? I raise my meaty claws and nuzzle the sleep from my eyes with the back of them. I feel something hard piercing the left side of my hip. I lift myself off the floor and attempt to find the source of the pain. My pants are ripping apart due to my transformation. It feels as if at any moment I will no longer have anything covering the lower half of my body. My hands are far too large to fit within my pockets. I struggle to fit my thumb and index finger inside the tight space, but the excavation succeeds.

Out from the pocket comes the locket dropped by that strange man all those years ago. It dangles from my fingers as I stare for a moment. I feel a familiar but vague feeling of emptiness from it.

"Morning," Melphis says, emerging from the back office. "What's with the jewelry?"

"Oh, it's nothing. Just something I found a long time ago."

Melphis doesn't inquire further. I put the locket back into the pocket where I found it.

"So, you were speaking about a demon called "Sin?" I ask.

"Not Sin, a Sin. One of seven," Melphis replies. "One resides here in New York City."

"That's right," I respond, my voice empty of any real interest.

My mind goes back to the revelation I had prior to falling asleep. *My family.* I feel my anger returning to the surface.

"Here," Melphis drops a corpse at my feet. This one isn't taken from the ones I had burnt. It is fresh and clean. "You will need this to get around. Can't go walking around with that ugly mug of yours, now can we?"

"What is this?" I ask, alarmed.

"Time you possessed your first human. I went out and got this one while you slept."

"You went and killed this guy?" I stare down at the body. He's tall and stocky. Black hair masks his face. "Couldn't we have used any of them? They're already dead. Why kill another?"

"Are you listening to yourself? You want to walk down the street in one of those charred corpses? I feel as if you are failing to see why I'm asking you to do this." Melphis pauses for a moment. "If this is going to work, you need to toughen up. This will not be the last corpse you see and need I remind you who killed all those men? Don't act so high and mighty."

His words pierce me. I'm still struggling to come to terms with what I had done to them. *Monster.*

"Fine. How do I do this possession thing?"

"There's nothing easier! We demons are programmed to do this after all. Pick the guy up, place your hands on his head, gaze into his eyes, and visualize yourself turning into vapor. Then watch as you flow into his eyes like a fast-flowing stream. It's all instinct."

I peer through the poor guy's eyes and begin the process Melphis laid out. It's strange. Just as I had seen through the veil to discern Melphis's true form, my eyes once again cut through the surface. Inside the man's eyes is an abstract void within the corpse. A sort of metaphysical space where his soul would reside if he weren't dead. I feel myself getting lighter as my body atomizes. I'm reduced to mist as I rush through the windows of his skull. I feel what it is like to have a human sized body again. I look down at my borrowed hands and curl the fingers.

On the floor where my monstrous body stood before, the dangling threads that were once my pants and a ragged shirt lay formless. I hear the familiar clink of metal as the locket falls from the pocket and onto the hard floor. I reach down to grab it and sling it around my neck. Not sure why, perhaps out of habit. It doesn't feel right to go on without it.

"This feels wrong," I state, fixated on these unfamiliar hands.

"You get used to it," Melphis replies. "Anyway, we should get going. This place has been compromised and we've remained here far too long. Let me just grab my staff, some books and we'll be on our way." He retreats into the back office again.

My family.

A montage of horrible memories force their way into the forefront of my mind. With them comes an insatiable impulse to free my rage. Melphis is still in the back room. *Now or never.* I make my way up the stairwell.

Fists clenched and neck veins popping, I make my way toward Grand Central Station. *Time to go home.* I feel a power festering within me that I never have before.

CHAPTER THREE

SIXTEEN YEARS AGO.

Tossing back tall glasses of whisky as if it was water, Seth's appointed father watched the ten-year-old boy writhe on the floor while clutching his throat. He sat in the kitchen, far from the child. He felt a sense of accomplishment that one would after a hard day's work.

The young Seth remained anchored on the floor as if held there by an elephant-sized burden. The muscles in his throat tightened. No air would pass into or out from his lungs until the panic subsided. Once it had, Seth would remain flaccid along the floor. Unable to gather the strength necessary to lift himself up or utter a single syllable, but until then, he continued to writhe. A persistent piercing stabbed his right side. During these moments of biological self-crucifixion, Seth's mind remained at the mercy of his demons. Their voices were growing louder and more intrusive by the day. They gnawed away at his mind like a swarm of flies dining on roadkill. The appointed father of this pseudo son smiled at the scene.

The front door squeaked open. In came the appointed mother, a bag of groceries in each hand. She made her way to the kitchen where the man sat watching their son. She passed by the writhing child, but said nothing. Laying the bags on the kitchen floor, she pulled a pack of cigarettes from her purse and lit one. "He's doing it again," she stated without emotion, pushing her blonde hair behind her ears.

"Yeah, he's broken, ain't he?" replied the father. "Satan'll be proud. Think we'll finally move on up?"

"Don't get excited just yet. He's only ten. Still plenty of formative years left."

"Ah, right. What was it Satan told us? Break him until twenty-six? Why's that?"

"That's when the human brain is finished putting itself together. We just have to keep filling it with pain until the brat knows nothing else."

The father put down his whiskey and walked over to the boy. Taking a fistful of Seth's hair, he forced the child to look into his eyes, "Useless, aren't ya? Day after day, wettin' the carpet with yer tears. This won't accomplish anythin', boy. You get to eat because of me, ya know that? Ya eat my food, live under my roof, and this is the thanks I get? A useless son? Say somethin', dammit!"

Seth sobbed.

"Can't even speak when told to? Yer worth less than a dog," said the father. He let go of Seth's hair and let his head fall hard to the floor. "Get on out of here. Yer miserable to look at."

The child, still panicked, managed to rise to his feet. He hung onto the wall to the right of him to find balance. He skulked away to the yard.

"Why do you suppose Satan needs the boy, huh?"

"Says he's the beginning to the end," the mother said. She put her cigarettes away in her purse, which she left behind on a stool.

Just die. No, please leave me alone. You want this. They want this. Can't you feel it? Shut up! Then kill yourself. Just do it.

The young Seth wrapped his hands around his throat. The muscles tightened and formed a blockage. He felt a stabbing pain in his belly. The tightening of his throat spread to his upper back. His body stiffened as one does during rigor mortis. *Am I dying? Am I dead? Not dead enough. Do everyone a favor and go all the way.*

His eyes widened in horror, pinned face first to the floor by a profound weight. *They can't wait for you to die.* Snot and tears slathered his face. Seth could not see him, but he felt he was being watched. *Is Dad watching how pathetic I am from the other room? He is, deadbeat. You're useless.*

His mom came home, but Seth was a ghost. She neglected to notice that the boy was even there. The sobbing intensified. There was an emptiness inside him, a void, deepened by each act of neglect and abuse. His dad kneeled and grabbed his hair. Spittle covered Seth's face. Looking into his father's wide, angry eyes filled Seth with terror. Once Seth was free, he ran outside to get away. Seth sat by the shed. He had a clear view of the kitchen window. His mom and dad were talking to each other. Mom was smoking a cigarette, in a state of bliss.

Hours passed. The sun was setting. Mom and dad were off somewhere unknown. Seth approached the front door, and silence told him it was safe to enter. Walking into the kitchen, he could smell the remnant of tobacco in the air. He hated the scent, but remembered the look of bliss on his mother's face. Reaching into her purse and digging around for a minute, his fingers touched a rectangle box and unearthed it from the mess inside. Popping open the fresh pack, it's missing only the one smoked by his mother before. *There's plenty, she won't notice.* He placed a cigarette between his lips. After digging around in her purse some more, he found and used the lighter.

He ignited it once and burnt the skin along his thumb. The second time, he lit the cigarette. Seth's chest heaved, ejecting the smoke from his lungs.

"And what do you think you're doing?" asked a voice. It was his mother. Her face, flaccid and without emotion.

Seth panicked and threw the cigarette onto the floor and tried stomping it out. It stung his bare feet, and he slipped and fell.

"Stand up," she stated.

"I'm sorry, Mommy. I won't do it again."

"That's a perfectly good cigarette you just wasted. Pick it up, light it again, and smoke it down. Try pretending you can actually make me proud."

"But why—"

"That cigarette is worth more than your life, Seth."

Petrified, he did what she asked. He could not imagine what his punishment would be otherwise. He coughed up each puff of smoke. He could feel his pants becoming wet and warm at the sight of her cold eyes.

"Happy birthday," she said.

I imagine Melphis is furious with me for leaving, but it doesn't matter. As the train pulls into the station of Crowley, the fog in my head begins to clear. Angry memories return. I'm aching for a cigarette.

I'm the only one to exit the train. The station is dark. There is no one in sight. That doesn't change as I make my way through town. Passing by my old high school, its lights are off, which is no surprise considering the early hour, but something feels strange. Just yesterday the town was bustling with cars and people throwing slurs in my direction, but now it's completely silent.

I turn a corner and find myself on the street where I had found the locket all those years ago. Just a few steps forward is where I ran into that stranger who accused me of assault. My neck muscles tighten. My breathing labored and shallow, I can feel my body temp rising again. My vessel's skin starts to melt and peel away in small sections like patches of eczema. Clutching the locket in my left hand, I bolt in the direction of my house. Fearing that the body I possess may come undone.

It isn't long before I get there. I rush to get the white picket fence open and hurry to the front door. The squeal of the old knob announces my arrival, but like the streets that are dark and empty, so is my home. I flick a light switch only to see that there's no power. I make my way into what I think is the living room. *What is going on here?* The whole town is like an abandoned factory no longer in use.

Something catches my feet, and I trip to the floor. I hit my head against something hard and yet I feel no pain. My head grows tense and heavy. Flashes of memory bombard me. The scent of whisky on my father's breath. My first cigarette. These and many more were almost daily occurrences. They all bridged together to form a nightmare I felt would never end. *What the hell did I have to take away the pain?*

{*Amor Fati. You must accept where you have come from, Seth. Move on. Do not let them become victims of your wrath. It will solve nothing. Use your rage instead as a tool to build toward greatness. This home is not your life anymore. Do not do this.*}

Do it.

Another memory is stirred. I did have something to ease the pain, or I used to. My medicine, my drug, my Lola.

The skin of my vessel melts away. The monster I've become expands from inside. The unfortunate man who Melphis laid at my feet rips and tears away. Flesh slipping off me like tender, succulent slow cooked ribs. I regain my demonic form, and steam erupts out from my pores. My skin, boiling like water. My clothes burn away into crimson ash. The locket around my neck melts just enough to meld together with my skin, a union of flesh and steel.

Placing my palms flat upon the floor, hellfire bursts forth through the conduit of my hands. Within seconds the house is ablaze. I'm in awe at the speed at which the fires devour everything in my childhood home.

I rush out the door to avoid the same fate. I look back at the house and then down at my monstrous hands. I feel the heat, but only from within. In a fit of anger, I set myself off like a nuke. The flames, I now realize, didn't hurt me.

There is much I still need to learn about this new body of mine, but it will have to wait. This was a ghost town before, but now I feel the presence of many behind me. Turning around, I see the streets are now flooded with imp-like creatures. The sea of demons cock their heads like confused dogs. The town has a population of about two thousand. Are these demons the townsfolk?

"He's back! He's back! He's back!" voices shout in quick succession. "Just like they said! Like they said!"

Without hesitation they move as if they have one body. They are small and nimble, approaching forward in a large collective mass. Their sharp teeth dig into my limbs, back, and neck. They swarm me like ants.

There are a lot of them, but that appears to be their only advantage. My rage consumes me. One by one, I rip the leeches off my body, digging my nails into their torsos. Pulling my arms back, the imps are torn in two. Blood and entrails rain upon me.

I keep at it, but their sheer numbers are too much to handle. My energy wanes. But wait—I look down. Other imps are digging into the ground around me. Dirt and stone join the blood in the air. I feel the entire town quake beneath my feet.

The ground breaks apart, revealing a chasm. I, along with many of the imps, fall to the depths below.

I awake to the sight of ivory feet covered in black warts. They appear to be walking on the ceiling, but then I realize that I am bound by chains and hung upside down. I'm in a cave. The bodies of dead imps are scattered across the rocky floor. The ivory feet pay them no mind.

"I told you he'd come back."

"Yeah, yeah. You were right."

I recognize these voices. They are raspier than before, but there is no mistake.

The ivory feet stand firm in front of me. They lower their head to look me in the eye. Loose blonde strands flutter to the ground and long grey hair replaces them. With a seaweed-like quality, they dangle from her head, covering just a small portion of her naked breasts. A face with mummified skin and beady black eyes looks straight into me. Unblinking, she gives a crooked grin.

"Things weren't supposed to go this way, Seth."

"Mom?"

"Hah! He thinks yer his mother!" exclaims the other demon, just now coming into view. He resembles the other, only with a large penis he positions far too close to my face as he kneels.

"Demons can't procreate, son! We can fuck fer all eternity, but it's fer pleasure, not fer baby makin'."

"Then who are you if not my parents?"

"I suppose we are the closest thing to parents you've had," said the female. "It wasn't too long after you were squeezed out of your real mother twenty-six years ago that I assimilated myself into her. Truth is, she died on that hospital bed."

"Same goes fer yer father!" exclaims the male. "So what? You come here lookin' fer revenge? You wanna make us out to be some kinda monsters? Well, you took the body of a dead man, too! And even killed others! You're no different than us!"

"You think I'm the same as you?" I say. "*I'll kill you*!"

Just when the anger explodes forth, a burning sensation follows. The chains I am wrapped in singe my flesh, though the burn is not like fire. It feels as if life itself is being siphoned from me. The angrier I become, the weaker I feel.

"Uh uh. Don't think yer g'tting' out of this. Yer a failed experiment, see? Now we gotta clean up this mess. Don't even try to move. Those chains are enchanted by Satan Himself. Bondage of the soul. You've seen them before—the chains used on the souls hung across the Crucifixion Fields. They'll suck your magic dry until nothing is left!"

He isn't kidding, I find myself unable to even speak. I hang as a lifeless doll.

"Let's get started, yes?" says the female. "What's this on his chest? Looks like a necklace. Embedded pretty deep in the skin."

"Who knows. Let's just carve it out of him for now and see what Satan wants to do with it. But first, his limbs."

The two of them take a few steps back and raise their hands. The muscles in their wrists contract. Long razors extend outward, as if they grew swords out of their fingers. They slash downward and cut through my shoulder blades with ease.

The impulse to scream takes flight, but no sound emerges from my throat. The chains have depleted too much energy. My large arms fall limp past my dangling head. Blood sprays all over. Then they do the same to my legs, turning me into a helpless stump.

What had driven me to this? *You fucking idiot. Why did I have to give in to my impulses? Should have listened to Melphis.* Now I'll never see Lola again.

I can feel the last bit of life leaving me. I had this second chance to live. I may be a demon, but I still had a second chance. I could have made all the pain worth it. Was it...for nothing...a fter all?

My consciousness wanes. From blurry vision to pitch black, I can no longer tell what is happening around me. Even sound begins to drift away, but I can still hear the crackling of magic nearby. I've heard it a few times now. The opening of a portal.

"Okay, I'm ready. Let's go—"

Melphis emerges from his study and sees that Seth is nowhere to be found. He remembers Seth mumbling about his family.

"That fucking kid."

Melphis wastes no time in looking through the records of his memory magic. Having no idea where Seth came from before his arrival as a demon, it takes some time, but after a few hours, he pinpoints Seth's location. Peering through to the other side of a portal, Melphis finds Seth struggling against an ocean of imps. The earth caves in a moment later.

"He's going to get himself trapped and slaughtered."

Pausing for a moment, Melphis thinks over his options. He turns to the melted flesh of the men he had hoped to turn into demons. Trying that again would take too long, as it did the first time. Melphis surmises that the cave in must have been planned, which means Satan has learned of everything and is acting fast. *What if He mobilizes the Sins? And the kid will die if I don't intervene.* He opens a portal and hops through to the other side. There he finds a dismembered Seth and his captors.

They are just about to carve the locket out of Seth's chest, as well as pierce his heart, when they take notice of Melphis falling onto the rocky surface of the cave.

"You...you're Melphis the traitor!" they say. They know him, but he does not know them. Melphis can tell they are but lowly, negligible demons.

Melphis lifts his left hand and gives his fingers a slight curl. Out from the tips of his fingers sprout tiny bolts of electricity. The two demons vomit black gas which shrouds Melphis's vision. He flings the lightning but misses, blasting apart the cave's walls into crumbling rubble.

They have no intention of fighting. Opening a portal, the other end appears to be an office building of sorts. "This is bad. We need to seek out the Sins," the female says. They flee, and the portal closes behind them.

The smoke clears, Seth's chains loosen, and Melphis lowers him to the ground. Heating the tip of his staff with fire magic, Melphis sears Seth's wounds shut, stopping the bleeding.

He isn't dead, yet. Melphis casts levitation magic to lift Seth and his detached limbs. He opens a portal back to his lair.

Unconscious, Seth floats through. Melphis is quite accomplished as a sorcerer, but even he is at a loss for what can be done to save him.

Melphis ponders his options, when he notices an odd glow emitting from the locket on Seth's chest.

December 25th, 1 A.D.

"Ah, welcome, my elites. Thanks for joining me on such a joyous occasion. Children of two realms, at home under my roof!" Satan addressed a group of seven gathered around a large round table.

"And for what purpose have you called us here?" said one with an air of pride.

The others chattered amongst themselves.

Satan leered over the group and stepped forward. Each step silencing the party as he approached. "Pride, where's Envy?"

"Who knows? She's been out of touch lately," Pride answered.

"Just relay the information back to her, would you?" Satan responded. "As I was saying, today is special. Ever since that fateful day, long before any of you were conceived, a plan was born amidst the abandoned Garden of Eden," Satan paused. His thoughts drifted back to days of peace before the betrayal. "Today marks an important epoch for us all. The birth of this child will spawn the most expansive religion to ever be established. It will rule over the Earth and through it we will spread our taint to human souls."

"But we are doing just fine," spoke up a new voice. "I frankly don't care for any of this. I just want to get back to my job," he says, salivating over himself.

"Lust, try and focus," Pride said.

"But he has a point. We are doing fine. What's the purpose of this meeting?" Greed said.

"Would you all *shut the fuck up* and let Him finish?" screamed another in a sudden outburst.

"Thank you, Wrath, but the yelling isn't necessary. We're all family here," Satan said. "Yes, you all have done grand delivering these souls to me, but we need more. Like all the religions that have preceded this new one, they are but a steppingstone to our new kingdom. This one will be the last. Give or take two thousand years, we will at last have all the souls we need. Let us watch as the new era dawns upon us!"

Wrath, though reluctant, agreed to quiet down. A fat one seated next to him groaned as his stomach churned with nervous hunger.

"Archdemon Melphis, would you do the honors?" Satan asked. Melphis, who sat still and quiet through all this, rose at last and stood at Satan's side. He opened a window into the human world and on the other side laid a woman in a stable. A child hung halfway out of her as she let out painful wails.

"And the Christ child is born!" Satan exclaimed. He peered through the window with a jubilant grin. "Thus marks the first sign of the end times!"

Melphis watched his gleeful master. Something was not quite right. The way Satan glanced into the world of humans felt, to Melphis, fueled by some sort of nostalgic longing.

And yet He seeks to destroy them? Melphis wondered, but thought no more on the matter.

"Will *She* be taking care of it, as usual?" asked Pride.

"Yes." Satan paused and gave off a profound shudder. "She will whisper to the child all he needs to know. He will grow to believe he is the son of God and he will begin a messianic journey. Her words are the very Will of the world itself."

Satan shivered once more. Melphis looked around the room and saw that the Sins had the same reaction. Melphis being the youngest in the room, had no knowledge of who this person was. *Who are they speaking about?* He had a sense he didn't want to know.

CHAPTER FOUR

NINE THOUSAND YEARS AGO.

Melphis sat nonchalantly upon the cliffside overlooking the Sea of Flames. In his lap lay a book and, in his hand, a pen. He scribbled runic language onto the page to quench his unabated curiosity. He studied what no other demon had the mind for. He took puffs from his long pipe in between thoughts.

"What do you waste your time writing for?" asked a voice from behind. "No one in Hell will ever read it."

Melphis kept his composure. His countenance did not change. He made no effort to face the voice and kept on writing.

"Ah, Greed. I figured it was about time," Melphis said.

"Excuse me?"

"Last time it was Pride. He showed up three weeks ago. For no reason. Before him, it was Envy. Before her, Wrath, and so on. Each of the Sins making an appearance every few weeks to see *me*, not Satan. How curious. Do you all have a crush on me or something?" Melphis grinned.

"Growing paranoid, are we? Now why would that be?"

Melphis ignored the question.

Greed continued, "Though I have to say, it's quite impressive how well you understand the magic arts. Better than most demons. I suppose that's how you rose high within the ranks."

"Don't be so jealous, Greed. That's not *your* job."

Greed's faux politeness vanished. He walked over to Melphis and kneeled behind him. He placed his right hand onto Melphis's shoulder. It was slimy and cold. Its fluid form stretched across the surface of Melphis's skin. Pressure built upon contact, sending tremors of pain into his body. Greed's subzero touch left Melphis feeling weak and immobile. The fires of life leaving his small body.

"Much like a child, to think he knows better than his elders," Greed said. His eyelids stretched backward, showcasing the pulsating veins within the yellow of his eyes. "You've been around, what, one hundred thousand years? You best watch yourself around us. We were conceived directly after the loss of Eden. You know nothing of Hell."

Greed removed his hand. Melphis heaved as his lungs resumed their function. Greed said nothing more. A portal to Earth was opened and he was gone.

Gasping for air, Melphis struggled to regain composure. He turned his pipe upside down and tapped it on the scorching cliffside, emptying the soot. He stood and pocketed the pipe. He put his book under his arm and made his way toward the castle for his daily excursion. He hoped to drown his fear in work.

As he made his way through the Bloodsoaked Caverns and the Crucifixion Fields along the way to Castle Pandaemonium, Greed's words stuck with him. *You know nothing of Hell.* He wondered how true that was. He did know for sure that he had been found unconscious at Hell's Edge a hundred thousand years ago. This was his first memory. He had since never given it much thought, yet he found himself pondering it for the first time. It was peculiar. There was no reason for Melphis to think a demon did not remember their birth, but he could not remember his own.

He has seen the process many times, as Satan often created more demons. They do not emerge into the world as humans do. Never in any demon's life were they a tear-soaked infant, ignorant of the world. No, they arrive fully formed. Their memory of the event should be intact. Try as he might, Melphis could summon forth no such memory.

Screams drew his attention. He turned to face a nearby pillar upon which hung a human woman. Her clothes had long since burned away. Swaying in the chains and suspended in air, she was vulnerable and scared.

Just what is happening here? Melphis wondered. He'd seen these terrified faces on a constant basis, but this was the first time the sight elicited feeling within him. Almost as if this were the first time Melphis had truly noticed them. As he listened to the woman's ear-piercing wails, he felt the same terror he had moments ago when Greed gripped his shoulder. Melphis felt as if he was taking on the weight of the woman's profound fear.

{*Poor soul.*}

Melphis whipped his gaze left, right, and behind, thinking he had heard something strange. "Who—"

{*They deserve a proper rest.*}

Like a gentle breeze passing over the skin for a moment, the soft words were whispered into his ears and then were gone. So was his memory of hearing the words. Melphis could not help but feel he had just experienced something unusual.

As he continued toward the castle, his mind remained with the woman and the other helpless human souls hung across thousands of pillars. *Why is this necessary? And why is that necessary?* He was looking at the demons conducting torture on the crucified humans.

"Hey, you there!" Melphis called out. Like a well-trained dog, a demon scurried over to hear what was to be demanded of him. He stood alert, but said nothing. He waited with wide open eyes for Melphis to speak.

"Why do you do this?" Melphis asked.

The reptilian demon cocked his head. "To harvest blood."

"Yes, but why must you do this?"

"To prime the souls. Lord Satan says pain sharpens the soul, like a whetstone to a blade."

"So, you do this simply because Satan asks?"

"We demons do, as demons do."

It slinked away and hurried back to its post. Melphis decided not to pursue more questioning. To question Satan's methods was forbidden. Satan had dismissed his subjects for less. He turned away from the pillars and continued toward the castle.

They have no free will. Melphis concluded. He clenched his fists at the thought. *They're just as much slaves here as the humans. They are the ones administering the pain to the confined human souls, but can they really be faulted when they have no control over themselves?*

Melphis's heart grew more conflicted with each moment. The ethics of Hell gripped his mind with such ferocity that he could not think of much else. Demon or human, it mattered not. Both were mindless cattle to Satan.

The harvesting of human souls has been a consistent practice of Hell for as long as Melphis had been around. From what he had gathered from being one of Satan's elites, this has always been the case. *Why did Satan need the souls? Has he no power without them? Without his slaves to do his bidding?*

Melphis passed over the river of locusts. Even the overwhelming stridulation of the insects could not break his focus. He was nearing the castle gates when a thought crossed his mind. He stopped dead in his tracks when the words reverberated within his skull. *What would a truly free Hell look like?* The words sounded in his voice, but they felt not like his own thoughts.

A flash of white overtook his field of vision. Melphis stumbled backward in shock. He turned around and found an empty white space. It held a solid form and yet Melphis appeared as if he was floating within emptiness.

{*Your awakening is finally beginning, my son. It's been so very long since I planted the seeds of hope within you.*}

"Who are you?" Melphis demanded, trying hard to mask the fear in his voice. He was a denizen of Hell and used to ghastly spectacles, but this assumed empty space held an aura which terrified Melphis. His breathing labored as he struggled to take in even the smallest pockets of air.

{*You feel it now. You will develop a vision for a better Hell, a better Earth! Satan is naught but a stray sheep. Under his reign, only pain remains. Covet the fires and brimstone for yourself. Give Hell a worthy leader. Free the souls of humans and demons alike.*}

A garden lush with flowers of many colors burst forth into view. A tree rose tall from the center, under which stood three figures. Their bodies were eclipsed by a blinding teal light.

{*This is your calling, my son. Hell is your birthright.*}

The voice ceased. The light overtook Melphis. In a flash, he once more found himself surrounded by the hues of fiery red and orange. In front of him was the front gate to Satan's castle. The words spoken to him in that strange white place have already faded, yet the image of the garden remained scorched into his mind. He felt peculiar. Something inside him had undergone a metamorphosis. He felt a sudden, insatiable lust for Hell's throne.

But how would he accomplish such a feat? He decided to put aside the idea for now. He was not prone to rashness. For now, he would carry on his duties. *The best way to destroy an enemy is to know them intimately.*

Making his way through the corridor leading to the throne room, he inspected the many portraits hanging along the walls. He's walked these halls thousands of times yet had until now thought nothing of the pictures. Like the crucified humans, it was as if Melphis was just now noticing something he was blind to before. The paintings depicted a man and three children. Melphis felt himself being drawn to them. Another vision over-took him. He saw the same man and children huddled around a table. They were enjoying a meal together as gleeful laughter echoed all around them. Melphis felt a sharp sting in the middle of his forehead, bringing him back. He winced and rubbed his head in confusion. Looking back toward the photos, he sensed no happiness from them. He moved on and thought nothing more of it.

He walked into the throne room and became witness to another birth. It was a process so routine that it was almost mechanical. Satan exhaled a mass of white particles. The cloud scattered around the room in a vicious whirlwind. The tornado calmed itself after a moment and the dust softly fell to the floor, amassing into a single spot. The particles being white always felt strange to Melphis. They even glittered like snow. The fires scattered about the room reflected a piercing bright light against the peculiar bog of dust. Yet as they came together, they took the form of a skeleton. Muscle weaved around the bone until it formed a finished demon. Small nubs protruded from its forehead. It was small in stature, but with a mouth bearing sharp teeth. Another mindless imp. It said nothing and simply turned to leave, passing by Melphis on its way out.

"They always go straight to work," Melphis said. "How do they know?"

"It is done because they know nothing," Satan said. "I will it and so it is done."

Satan turned away to look in on the human realm through a portal. He appeared to not notice Melphis's ever deepening grimace.

"Greed stopped by," Satan said.

"Yes, I saw him on my way here." Melphis felt a deep shiver. "Was he here for any particular reason?"

"Just a leisurely visit, or so he says. I barked at him to get back to work and he left."

Melphis said nothing.

"They seem on edge lately. But no matter. I need you to deliver a message to Gluttony."

"Of course. And what would that be?"

"There are souls that need to be transported. He'll know where to take them."

"Transported? Where?"

"As I said, he will know. Just tell him it's time. Do not concern yourself any further with the matter."

Satan turned back toward Melphis with a cold glare. Melphis dared not talk back. Not yet. Though he wondered just where the souls could be taken. Human souls had always ended up in Hell and that was where they remained. Satan had never made a request like this. Or rather, Melphis never questioned It before.

"Rest easy, Melphis. We will have our new kingdom soon enough."

Melphis nodded and made his way through a portal to Earth. He's heard Satan mention this new kingdom a few times prior, but what could be meant by that, Melphis couldn't yet deduce. *What was so wrong with Hell? If demon slavery and human harvesting could be excised from the system, Hell could become a veritable paradise for demons. Demons eat, sleep, and engage in sexual pleasure as a desire, not a need. We are created in a way that makes us accustomed to conditions in Hell. We can live there without a need for anything. So why the slave labor? Why does Satan need human souls?*

Greed said that Melphis knew nothing of Hell. *What could Satan be hiding? Why do the Sins know about it, but I do not?* He worried. This was a first for Melphis. *Have I always been a docile lap dog made for Satan's bidding?* His anger festered at the thought that he had spent his life in the same way as a common imp. A blind slave to Satan.

He found himself just east of Çatalhöyük, on the Antolian Peninsula, humanity's earliest civilization. Gluttony had been stationed here for a while. *Why?* Melphis had just become aware he did not know. *You know nothing of Hell.*

"Be gone, monster!" Melphis heard a masculine voice call out. He looked over and found a small hut made of sticks and straw. A man stood over a woman who sat frightened upon the ground. She held a baby in her arms. Surrounding them were three imps, crawling on all fours. Sizzling saliva dripped from their sharp teeth. Their soulless black eyes held an insatiable hunger. The man held a sword and shield, attempting to defend the woman and child.

The man was muscular and larger than average, but he was still just human. Before he could swing his blade, the leading imp swatted him away like a fly. The man slammed hard into the siding of his hut. Trying to push himself up, his arms gave out. The bones in his right hand had been reduced to dust. The three imps foamed at the mouth as they pounced on the woman and infant. The man watched in torment as his wife and son were torn apart.

At first, the scene was nothing to be alarmed about for Melphis. Demons preyed upon humans all the time, but as he witnessed the woman and child's final moments, while he heard the man's wails that followed, something stirred within him.

"Family," Melphis muttered, as his eyes grew moist.

"Ye foul beasts! I shall not rest until my blade pierces your sides!" the crippled man shouted.

Rebellious to the end. I like this one.

The imps went to feast upon the man, but as they raised their claws, a tapping of steel against stone could be heard. Melphis plunged the head of his staff hard upon the ground. Each impact caused a tremor, and cracks formed in the Earth. Large protruding stone spikes rose from the ground, one for each imp. The rocky lances punctured through the imp's skulls. The skin and flesh that formed their faces now hung limp and revealed the blood-stained bone beneath.

Melphis walked over to the man and outstretched his hand. "Can you walk?"

The man was struck silent. His tear-soaked face embalmed his anguish and wetted his long beard. Catching his breath, he accepted Melphis's hand. "What just happened?"

Melphis declined to answer. He put his staff down to free both his hands. He flipped open to a page of his book to seek out a rune. Satisfied, he tore a page out and took the nail of his pointer finger to the man's neck. The fingernail broke through the form of the human Melphis was possessing. Flesh tore away to reveal the demonic finger beneath. Melphis carved a rune into the man's neck, tearing into the skin deep enough to draw blood.

The man backed away in a panic, but then his eyes shot open. The man's veins pulsated with energy. The shock was quick but violent. As the man came out of it, he screamed.

"You...you are one of those beasts!"

Melphis, stern and inquisitive, gazed at the man. He had never thought he would put his research into practice. It was just a way to amuse himself, but now Melphis wondered what else he could do.

"You can see through the veil now, can you not?" Melphis asked.

The man backed away, readying himself to run.

"I am not one to fear. My name is Melphis. I am what you say, but I'm on a different path than those ones. Here, take this."

Melphis extended his arm, revealing the page torn from his book, and said, "Just something I've written. Study it well."

Hesitant at first, the man inched his way toward the page and took it.

"What's your name?" Melphis asked.

"Virdeus." He paused. "Why do you help me?"

"These runes hold power. To you they will become a conduit for magic. Empower yourself. Start a new family and...protect them."

Confused, Virdeus glanced down at the page. He tried to ask a question, but as he looked up, Melphis was gone.

Melphis sits on his couch while staring down at Seth's static body with a calculating gaze. He wonders if he had made a mistake. Seth remains unconscious. His limbs stacked nearby like a pile of logs. They are still damp with blood. "This was a waste of time," he says.

Melphis has spent tens of thousands of years cultivating and experimenting with magic. Yet even he cannot deny that wounds such as these cannot be sutured and healed. No such healing magic exists. He knows magic to be a weapon, not a medicine. Demons hold a natural aptitude for shrugging off damage to the body. They heal at a pace exponentially faster than a human, but a fatal wound is nothing less than that, even to a demon.

What else can I do? He wonders, but not about Seth. *I cannot take Hell alone. I need some muscle.*

He thinks back on a memory from long before, from the time when demons roamed free and human civilization was still in its infancy. He thought about the man named Virdeus and wondered if he could use him. *No, his presence vanished shortly after we met. The rune in his neck must have killed him.*

"*Damnit!*" Melphis shouts, kicking Seth in the ribs. The dying demon showed no signs of noticing. "There is no one else. I am out of options. Why did you have to run off, you sack of shit?"

He initiates another kick, but as he pulls his leg back, the locket implanted into Seth's chest springs open, and blinding rays of light engulfs the room. Averting his gaze, Melphis cowers beneath his arms. He notices something in the split second before covering his face. *That abyssal white color...and a garden?*

{Do not forsake this one, Melphis.}

That voice?

The blinding rays retract. Melphis can see again. White ribbons weave around Seth like a wrapped gift. The light fades. With a much gentler flow, the white tendrils pull back like a passing cloud to whence they came. The locket's hinges snap shut.

The room grows quiet. Melphis inches toward Seth with curiosity. He is sure he'd heard that voice at least once before. The voice sounded both familiar and comforting, yet distant. The more Melphis tries to ascertain its origin, the more his mind fills with fog, and the words vanish. He hears a painful moan, followed by the crackling of magic.

Seth gasps for air and screams as he becomes cognizant of the pain. Teal sparks are sizzling around his four stumps. Blood covered ivory nubs protrude from the wounds. Bone takes shape, forming joints and molding into a proper skeleton. Flesh weaves its way around the bone like ribbons. Muscle forms, followed by the encasing of skin.

Mesmerized, Melphis examines the locket up close. He runs his fingers through the grooves in the steel, then along Seth's re-grown limbs. *The kid's a goddamn lizard.* He tries to remember if anything like this had occurred before. His mind comes up empty.

Seth passes out again from the shock. Melphis wonders how Seth came in possession of such a peculiar artifact. He is even more at a loss for words as to the specific nature of the locket. He had never seen magic like this before. His prior frustration melts away and a conniving grin sprouts across his face.

"Yeah, sleep it off, kid. You just might be useful after all."

Melphis walks to the couch, leaving Seth sprawled across the floor. Seth sleeps, but Melphis does not. Melphis intends to watch the brute all night long, unabated. Like a statue, he does not stir from his spot, lest he risk losing this new opportunity.

Virdeus approaches the crater at the center of Crowley, feeling that the town's destruction is connected to magic. His daughter had gone on ahead to begin the investigation. He sees a reporter doing live coverage of the devastated town. Virdeus and his daughter, Sasha, remain unnoticed thanks to the magic gifted to him by Melphis. This remains true so long as they do not go out of their way to become known. Virdeus walks behind the reporter's camera so that he is not caught in the lens.

"Reporting live from Crowley, New York, a large cave-in has resulted in loss of homes and destruction of roadways and more. Stranger yet is the mass disappearance of the town's population. Search parties have been hard at work, but not a single person has shown up. Oh, here comes the head of the investigation team. Has anyone been found?" the reporter asks.

A fat man runs up to face the camera. His response is burdened by labored breathing. "Unfortunately, no one has been found yet. For a mass disappearance at this scale to occur is mind boggling to say the least, but we will remain hard at work until we find them."

The reporter thanks the man and continues to ramble on for some time. Virdeus listens in while walking by, but he is more concerned with the nature of the crevasse.

A girl with shoulder length black hair is crouched down near the opening. She's looking down into the pit with intense curiosity. Virdeus makes his way over to her.

"So, Sasha, what do you think?" he asks.

"It is them. No doubt. I can't imagine anything else creating such damage so quickly and the magical residue is fresh." She cocks her head to the right and a worried countenance overtakes her. The way she slants her head reveals a rune carved into the left side of her neck. It glistens in the rising morning sun. It matches his own. He remembers fondly the time he etched it into her. "What I don't understand is, they have never operated in a way that would draw attention from humans. Why now?"

Virdeus takes her worries upon himself. His face grows heavy upon hearing her words. He wonders the same thing. He had lived long enough to see the rise and fall of many religions. Both known to modern humans and those left unrecorded. The concept of deity worship is far older than the practice of writing. He also knows that all theistic dogma share prime similarities among them and he is suspicious of a reason for it all. *Are they building toward something? Is that something drawing near?*

"This is a great question you bring up, my daughter. One I fear I can't answer just yet. Let us return home to the others for now. Once things quiet down around here, we shall return to investigate further."

The two take a final glance toward the pit before turning away from it. They leave the town and begin their trip back home with caution. Always weary of those devilish types lurking in the shadows.

CHAPTER FIVE

G reed, perching upon his nest, watches as people and vehicles scurry about like helpless rodents. He peers out of
a window in a large open room that makes up the entire 71st
floor. He sighs, exasperated.

"How long has it been since you positioned me here, Pride?"

It's just the two of them. Pride is lounging about on a nearby
sofa. He takes a sip from his whisky glass while turning the page
of his newspaper. The ice in his drink clanks against the glass as
he tilts it into his mouth.

"What is it now?" Pride asks.

Greed turns from the window, grumbling to himself. Pride
continues to portray an air of great luxury.

"You're content with this? How are you not bored? I miss the
days of tricking the primitive man into coveting that which his
neighbor has. Then killing that man and taking his spoils for
myself! To plant seeds of deceit and insatiable desire in mankind.
Preying upon them like the lion on the gazelle! Look at us—a
pair of docile, caged housecats."

Pride, yawning, does not break his focus on the newspaper.

"Ah, right. You're too good to listen."

"To this drivel? Yes, I am too good for it. Do not complain
about a good thing, brother. The fact that we merely need to

exist to spread our influence on humans is a testament to how deeply ingrained we have become in their lives. It also means we are getting close to the mass exodus from Earth. The collective human spirit has ripened to a point ready to be raptured." Pride refills his whiskey glass. "Learn to enjoy it a bit. We will be as gods when this is all over."

Pride, pleased with himself, smiles at his glass of whisky as if trying to seduce it. Greed realizes that Pride is viewing a reflection of himself through the glass.

"Gods, huh? I suppose it would be nice to hold an entire world in my hands. Though I have to say, I don't like the idea of sharing it with my siblings."

Greed turns toward the window. The sky is overcast. A light drizzle of rain coats the view. He starts to see his own reflection in the wet glass. A human's face with beady black eyes and hair to match stares back, but only for a moment. The reflection blurs away. His eyes, planted on translucent skin, glow a bright yellow. "I need more," he said.

Pride opens his mouth to speak, but is interrupted by the familiar sound of a ripple in space. Sparks of magic erupt out from the center of the room. A portal rips open and out comes two ivory demons covered in black warts.

"What is the meaning of this—?" Greed attempts to say, but is cut off by Pride.

"You dare make your presence known to the Sins uninvited?"

The ivory demons avert their eyes. They know just coming here could warrant their deaths. They have no right to lay their eyes on a Sin, let alone two.

"Oh, Great Ones, something of dire importance has come up."

They speak about what happened in the town of Crowley and how Melphis showed up.

"Melphis, you say?" Greed said. "Boy, it's been a while."

"We were told this might happen," Pride replies. "Crowley isn't too far from here. Though I must wonder why Melphis would concern himself with such a place. It wouldn't be far-fetched to believe he has some intel on our locations."

Greed turns toward the window once more. The rain grows heavier. Thunder crashes.

Pride continues, "I think it best for me to go bring the others up to speed. Greed, handle the pest if he shows, won't you?"

Greed's eyes stretch backwards. The skin tugs on the corners of his mouth until he sports a maniacal grin so broad that his bottom jaw hangs loose by threads of flesh. His human suit tears, blood squirting out from the cracks. His head swirls halfway around like an owl's. The bones, splintering apart as he turns his face to Pride.

"Handle him? It would be my fuckin pleasure."

I feel my muscles ache around my shoulders and thighs. I try to rub my eyes into focus. As my blurred vision drifts away, the sight of my large hands fizzles into view. Sudden panic strikes me. I spring to my feet. I clutch at my throat with hands that shouldn't be there.

"Finally waking, are we?" The voice comes from my left. Melphis sits upon the couch, stiff as a rod. There is a hint of frustration in his voice.

"You saved me?" I ask.

"What I saved," he says, rising to his feet, "was a corpse."

"How am—I shouldn't be here! I thought I lost my arms and legs."

Melphis approaches me, staff in hand. He gestures off to the side of the room. Laying there are the limbs in question. I tug at my arms and pat my legs, bewildered.

He comes in close. He positions his face as close to mine as possible with his short stature. He flicks his fingers in the direction of the pile of rotting limbs, all the while glaring furiously at me from an inch away. The dead flesh bursts into flames.

"Just a precaution," he hissed, "but don't you dare run off on me again. We made a deal. You help me take Hell. I find your girl, but that requires that you operate under *my orders*!"

I could feel his anger emanating like hot steam from his breath. Spittle covers my face. His dark crimson eyes fill with an intense manic swirl. I keep my mouth shut.

"Don't think I can't kill you if I choose. Your flesh doesn't need to be dead for me to make it disappear. To unravel your very life like a loose thread." Melphis knocks his staff hard against my chest. It clanks against the locket, then he turns away. "Still, turns out you're in possession of some curious power. Could be useful."

"What do you mean?"

"Your arms. Your legs. They've replaced themselves."

I cannot find the words to reply.

"Doesn't matter. We need to move."

My gaze follows him as he packs a few books into a satchel and heads toward the stairs.

"You fucked up. Satan will surely be made aware of our situation. No doubt the Sins already are. There is no time. Quick, come."

By the stairs lay two fresh corpses. The human I had possessed earlier had been destroyed. The human body Melphis inhabits also appears to be damaged, with a few tears revealing his grey and pasty skin beneath. I am blind to the methods of Melphis's acquisition of these bodies, but one thing is clear. A person had died to grant me cover and I went and wasted his sacrifice.

We both take hold of these new bodies and make our way up the stairs. Still tired and full of body pains, I decide that it would be best to keep quiet. Also, I fear Melphis. That look in his eye felt murderous. I have no reason to think he's lying. Even if he is, he has been a demon far longer than I. He understands his powers and this world better than I can. *What was Satan thinking, sending me here to kill Melphis? Surely, I'd stand no chance—Why didn't Melphis kill me—He should have—I will only be a burden—*

"What are you muttering about?" Melphis asks, looking back at me. He takes the form of an old man, thus rendering his staff inconspicuous. Despite his appearance, Melphis has no intention of putting too much effort into his acting. He moves with great swiftness that is unbecoming of the old man he portrays.

"Muttering?" I say, just realizing that I had spaced out.

"You're going to be more trouble than you're worth, aren't you?"

"I'm sorry...for that and for everything else. I shouldn't have run off. I just...wanted them to pay."

"None of that is going to matter once this is over. We will both get what we want and be happy. Get it together until then." Melphis sighs. "I am curious though. I saw no humans in that town. Who were those two demons to you?"

"My parents—or rather the demons that replaced my parents. I had no idea."

"No way you could know, without first seeing what lies beyond the veil of death, but it is quite curious that you were raised by demons. Coincidence? No. Any demon without an agenda in that situation would have eaten the child. This was meticulous, but what reason would Satan...ah well. Let us put a pin in that for now, shall we? We have a greater concern."

Right—the Sins he mentioned before. *How far back had I set this quest of his? How much progress would we have made if I hadn't snuck away on that self-destructive misadventure? I did not even accomplish anything.* My mind drifts back to my parents.

"Are you sure I'll even be a help to you?" I ask.

"Still brooding? Look, one's own strength is one's own responsibility to find. I cannot spell it out for you. I will just say this. For the time being, you are forgiven. If for no reason other than I have a hunch about you and your power. I promise we will talk more on that in time, but we will be in dire straits if the Sins group together. Taking them one at a time is our best option. Even then there's no promises. Come now."

Melphis is being kinder than I figured he'd be. Though his kindness feels ill-placed and inorganic. I still have my reservations about trusting him, but in those last moments of lucidity back home, I saw my parents—those demons—hop through a portal. They aren't in Crowley anymore. I can't imagine where they might be, so what option do I have but to remain with Melphis?

{Calm your doubts.}

Shut up!

I rub my temples, wincing. Melphis doesn't seem to have noticed.

We make our way through a series of streets and descend into a subway station. Melphis reaches into the wallet left behind by the old man he's wearing as skin. He pulls out a metro card. After using it to pass through the gates, he hands it to me to do the same. A waiting train is announcing its imminent departure. We hurry into the packed car.

I've never been one for crowds, but they never bothered me this much. Perspiration floods my face. It drips down my neck, drenching the Nirvana T-shirt my newly possessed body is wearing. I look around. No one else shows signs of overheating.

"Keep it together," Melphis whispers.

My mind drifts back to my mistake of returning home. I had been overtaken by emotion when attacked by those demons. Was that what had forced me back into my demonic form?

{*Were you forced, or did you choose?*}

The taste of iron coats my tongue. I need to keep it together. Shedding this corpse here would lead to harming these people.

{*You knew your parents to be human when you made your choice to try and kill them.*}

After twenty minutes, we reach our stop. I push my way out. Clutching at my throat, I savor the breathing room.

It is a short walk to our destination—a large skyscraper on Wall Street. Before Melphis can peek through the windows, the front door swings open. Out comes dozens of people, all in suits. A mass of umbrellas collectively protects the herd from the rain.

"Excuse me. It's only nine thirty. A bit early for a lunch break," Melphis says to a short blonde woman. He gestures at the large crowd of people still funneling like sheep out of the building.

"Yes, it was the strangest thing. The workday had barely begun when an announcement through the loudspeakers said we could all have the day off. Wish they would have told us before I bothered to put on my makeup this morning."

She goes off, not caring about anything else we may have to say. Melphis and I slink off to the side to wait for the doorway to clear.

"I don't like this," Melphis mutters. "It's like Greed is clearing the way for us. Look inside. It's empty. Not even a doorman."

This is the first time I've sensed fear from Melphis. I feel it, too.

"Would this be a good time for you to tell me what to expect?

"What do you mean?"

"Truth be told, I spaced out when you told me about the Sins."

Melphis stares at me, baffled.

"You mean you don't know why we're here?" He pauses. "I should have let you die."

The employees are gone. I follow Melphis into the lobby. With no one there to greet us, we go straight to the elevators. He presses the button for the 71st floor.

"The Sins spread their corruption into the hearts of humanity," Melphis says. "Since the beginning of time, they've manipulated humans into gorging themselves on the seven vices. By doing so, they have weeded their way into the human soul. Think of a farmer cultivating their crops. They would not pick a tomato before it's ripe. Satan likes souls to be plump and juicy. It may be strange to liken the human soul to fruit. The two are not at all the same. Fruit is tangible. Souls are far more abstract, but it's the way they like to talk about it. Like they're cultivating crops."

The elevator light indicates that we are passing *Floor 62*. Nervous tremors run from my fingers and up my arms.

"Not much time now. Just think of them as pillars. They hold Hell up by sending souls to Satan."

Floor 66.

"And if we can kill them, we'd cut off his supply. Weakening him, theoretically."

Floor 70.

"I loathe repeating myself. I shall not be telling you this again, but I'll have you know, we have barely begun this plan of mine and you're already a burden. Get your shit together."

I say nothing. This abusive sentiment is one I am accustomed to. I feel the heat rising in me again. But it was not anger toward Melphis.

"Oh, and don't let him touch you."

Floor 71. The buzzer rings and the doors open.

The room is large like a penthouse lounge. No cubicles or offices in sight. Toward the back are two staircases which curve inward to meet. At the top is an elevated platform and a large window overlooking the city. Standing at the top is a demon whose human skin is already shedding, revealing an almost liquid-like interior. He is speaking to two demons with ivory skin covered in familiar black blemishes.

"You!" I say.

Melphis recognizes them as well. Fire swells in my palms. I take a step forward and—

"Don't," Melphis says, forcing his staff in front of me.

The two demons turn to face me with a countenance of scorn. The one who played the role of my father goes to speak, but behind him rises a translucent light blue tentacle. It lassos his neck. The demon's voice ceases as he chokes. His throat regurgitates bile. Upon hitting the floor, the expelled liquid sizzles and corrodes the carpet.

"Greed, please no!" cries out my appointed mother. "Forgive us for—"

Another tentacle wraps its way around her neck. Both are pulled upward to the balcony. Greed, who is already losing the human he is wearing, expands in size. That last bit of flesh slinks away onto the floor. His translucent body allows his organs and veins to be seen, like a model of human anatomy one might see in a doctor's office. His veins are entirely visible, running from the tips of his fingers and toes, along his spine and up to his eyes and brain. They pulsate an eerie light.

Pulling the two demons closer, his stomach expands and wraps around the demons. Inch by inch, their bodies deteriorate until the process reaches their mouths. Their muffled screams and the terror in their eyes are transmuted into nothing.

"He ate them?" I ask, baffled.

"Absorbed would be more accurate," Melphis says.

My impostor parents are dead. A feat stolen from me. My mouth twitches with anger.

"He can absorb matter," Melphis says, interrupting my train of thought. "And he makes their powers his."

Greed says, "Ah, how touching that you remember, my dear little foster brother. Been a while since you've come to check on the farm."

I glance toward Melphis, but he doesn't return my gaze.

"Do not liken me to your kind," Melphis says.

"No problem. My siblings and I never trusted you. We always felt that you would reveal yourself—a traitorous mole. So, to hear of your likely arrival filled me with an excitement I had not known for quite some time! I always felt a shared quality between us. Within you is a festering desire to covet. I loathe you for it."

"Why not just kill me then? You've had plenty of chances."

"Because unlike you, we follow orders." Greed looks toward me. "But who is this one? Hmm, my Lord's scent is on you. How is it you've come to be in Melphis's employ?"

Greed takes a few steps forward. Black warts sprout upon the surface of his watery skin. Toxins spews out from the ends of his tendrils that have sprouted from his back.

Melphis motions toward the couch on the left side of the room. With magic he makes the couch levitate before flinging it toward Greed. "Seth!" Melphis shouts, commanding me to act. Fire fills my palm, and I shoot it off like a flamethrower. The black smoke that has filled the room begins to dissipate. Greed is no longer on the balcony.

The smoke converges once more, appearing behind me. I quickly turn to find an onrushing mass of liquid. As I shield my face with my right arm, the liquid coats my skin. A fierce burning sensation strikes and my skin melts away until bone can be seen.

"Careful!" Melphis shouts.

One of his tendrils emerges from the smoke. It makes its pursuit for my left arm. It tries to weave around the limb, but a sudden flash of light erupts on contact. The smoke clears and Greed pulls away. He wears a precarious look. I mimic him. Around the wound on my right arm, sparks of magic flourish. The flesh fills itself back in. New muscles take shape. The arm encases itself in skin. I look to Melphis for confirmation. He nods grimly.

"How curious," Greed says. His tentacles acting as extra feet, he moves backward in a spider like manner. Each spot the tentacles touch turns grey before crumbling into dust, leaving holes in the floor. Greed returns to the balcony. His head gives a sporadic twitch, sending off vibrations.

A portal is opened and out springs two demons. They are tall and have lanky arms that appear boneless. They have no hands, but instead long sword-like appendages that dangle at the end of their long arms. Their bodies are encased in feathers coated in grime. Long beaks protrude from their faces. With a collective screech, their feathers ruffle. As if vents open, out rushes a fierce, icy wind that pushes Melphis and me back.

"Go on, scuffle with my tools," Greed says with a conniving grin. "Show me what else you can do."

At Pride's suggestion, they gather in Hell to meet with Satan. Pride stands side by side with Gluttony, Sloth, and Wrath. The four of them approach Satan's castle wearing human skin. For Gluttony, it is the only method available for entering Satan's abode. His natural form almost equals the height and width of the castle.

"What gives?" Wrath asks in frustration. "I understand Greed is preoccupied, but where are Lust and Envy? Does this not matter to them?"

"Does anything ever matter?" asks Sloth.

Gluttony's stomach rumbles in agreement, but he says nothing. He and Sloth were always similar. Neither having ever cared much for anything outside themselves. They also preferred not to be the decision-makers. They always looked to Pride to fill that role.

"You know as well as I do, they've been hard to contact," Pride says. "It's no reason to be concerned. They have always been loners. They can take care of themselves."

Wrath suppressed his passion. Now is not time. Even he understands that. In silence, the four brothers enter Castle Pandaemonium. They see Satan, His back turned away from the entrance to His room, facing a window into the human realm. His focus so strong, He at first does not notice the presence of the Sins.

"I see you're aware of the situation," Pride states.

Satan watches Greed summon forth a couple of bird-like demons, before turning to face the four Sins.

"I am. Are you concerned, my children?"

"We wouldn't be if it weren't for the involvement of our unwanted eighth member. We warned you about him. Why did you bring him into our ranks?"

Pride is the only one who ever had the nerve to speak to Satan with a raised voice. Gluttony and Sloth wear blank faces, like mere observers.

Wrath clenches his fists. "Hey, show some resp—"

"Do you remember your births?" Satan interrupts. "You Sins aren't like the mindless rabble here in Hell. You were made with sterner material. Divine material. You have nothing to fear of Melphis. He once impressed me, but he is still just a demon. He should be no more than a mere imp to you Sins. Kill him and be done with it."

"Yes, but—"

"Am I not God of Hell and Earth? Have the two realms not always been under *my* governance? Yet you still come to me with doubts, you petulant children?" The air catches fire. Even Pride is struck silent in awe of Satan. "We are on the cusp of acquiring our new kingdom. I need not remind you that your role has been fulfilled. Letting you come along to the new world is a gift I give you, not your right. I was there when you were born from that divine material. If I so choose, I can dismantle you right here and now!"

Satan, as if to say the conversation is finished, turns away from them.

"Y-yes. You're right," Pride says. His eye catches a glimpse of something through the portal. "Who is that with Melphis?"

"A tool," Satan responds. "He is necessary for the transition to the new kingdom—or not him, specifically. It could have been any human. What matters is what is inside him."

Why hadn't the Sins been told about this mysterious demon at Melphis's side? And what exactly is inside him? Pride wanted to speak up, but after Satan's outburst, he refrains.

"He's filled with something called Nil, due to a meticulous chiseling of his soul. The well-time placement of pain with great precision and intensity, but none of that matters. What does is that the magic he holds inside him is volatile and chaotic, but versatile. We need it. Kill Melphis, but bring that one back to me alive."

"I've never heard of such magic."

"It was never for you to know," Satan's tone grows angrier.

The Sins know that it is time to leave. The door closes behind them, leaving Satan alone.

Satan spectates in silence. *I still cannot understand how he has free will. There are only three people who can possibly touch upon that magic, including myself. But it should be impossible for...*

He continues to watch the scene unfold while memories of a detestable past unearth themselves.

CHAPTER SIX

Pride, Wrath, Sloth, and Gluttony exit Satan's castle.

"You really shouldn't provoke him," Wrath scolds Pride.

Pride glares at Wrath, who is walking at his side. Sloth and Gluttony stumble behind.

"I'm just saying—"

"Enough!" Pride shouts. "Gluttony, return to your post. Doesn't matter what's going on. There are still souls to be transported. Oh, and try to track down Envy and Lust."

"And what will you do?" Gluttony asks.

"We three will go assist Greed. He'll be fine, I'm sure, but the sooner those pests are killed, the better."

Gluttony nods and hastily leaves through a portal. A cityscape is seen beyond it, one that isn't New York.

Pride opens a portal of his own and off the three brothers go.

***

The bird-like demons waste no time. The one nearest rushes at me with strange, bladed arms dangling behind. They seem so elastic, I wonder just how they're connected to the demon's body, or if they can even move at all. The other demon corners

Melphis, separating the two of us. I glimpse Greed's glowing eyes monitoring the room with eager anticipation.

Black pus ejects from the demon's beak. The right side of its body jerks forward and swings the bladed arm. I can feel a numbing cold breeze formed from the passing of the sword near the top of my head. Crouching down, I somehow avoid decapitation. I turn toward Melphis. He is getting backed into a corner, but shows no signs of worry. He's chanting and readying his staff.

A loud swoosh. In the corner of my eyes, the demon's other arm swings down upon me. Instinctively I catch the blade with both my palms. My hands slice open, blood splatters across my face and the wall behind me. The coldness radiating from the steel sends a jolt of pain through the nerve endings in my palms.

The demon's arms, while skinny, hold a surprising strength. The floor creaks beneath me. I can feel the framework warping from the pressure. Despite the needles of ice running up my arms, I feel a simultaneous buildup of heat. I steady my left arm, continuing to hold back the demon's blade, and with my right I let go. Within the bloody palm, I conjure an orb of fire and take aim at the demon.

The orb crumbles away into dying embers. A frigid tube wraps around my arm like a boa constrictor. I was so fixated on melting away the demon's arm that I didn't notice the other reaching around to grab me. The beast's touch chills me to the core. My muscles tighten and both my arms crust over in a thick sheet of ice.

The process shows no signs of slowing. The ice creeps up my arm with the aim of encasing my whole body. Try as I might, I cannot access my flames. My hands will not heat. I am at the mercy of this demon.

I glance over at Melphis, who acknowledges my situation. He continues chanting, saying nothing to me. *Is he concerned, or disappointed? I can't tell.*

I should have let you die. His words return. I believed that to come from a fit of momentary scorn, but now I'm not sure.

The ice is almost at my shoulders. Panicking, I put all my strength into pulling my shoulders back.

There is a loud sound of bone fracturing, followed by a shower of blood across the floor. Panic grows into full blown horror. I have yanked my torso away from my arms, severing both from the lower shoulders. I stumble back and bump into the wall before falling to the floor.

It happens again, quicker than before. Teal sparks rise from my stubby shoulders. Mere seconds later I witness a new pair of arms growing in place of the ones lost. From bone to molded flesh to skin, they take shape. It's like they were never gone.

The demon drops my old arms. Frozen solid, they shatter as they slam to the floor. The demon continues to pursue me as I cower with my back against the wall.

Melphis raises his staff to the air. Indecipherable runes of white light form a circle facing the other demon. Out erupts a pillar of fire. It pushes the demon with such intensity that the flames lift the monster into the air. The pillar of fire curves upwards, pushing the fire and the demon toward Greed, whose water-like body moves out of the way with the grace of a gentle wave. The demon flies past Greed and through the large window behind him.

"So much for keeping this contained," Greed says. "The humans are surely to become aware of us if we keep this up, but that's okay. This world won't be around long enough for it to matter."

Though I have new arms, my shame leaves me petrified. I am barely cognizant of Greed's words. Melphis raises his staff toward the remaining demon.

"That's enough," Greed says. As soon as the words leave his lips, the bird-faced demon who is moments away from lodging its blades into it me again, retreats to below the balcony.

Greed descending to the lower floor, wraps one of his tendrils around the neck of the bird-faced demon. It remains still and allows itself to be taken. Like a passive cow, staring unaware, at a farmer holding a bolt gun to its head. Just as had happened with my imposter parents, its body is atomized and taken into Greed's own.

Both of Greed's arms, as well as the four tentacles on his back, form sharp blades at their tips.

"Why did you stop it?" I ask, having found my voice once more.

"I never meant for them to kill you," Greed answered. "I simply wanted to observe."

"What for?" Melphis asks.

"As I said, my Lord's scent is on him. And there is something else. Something powerful hiding within him. Can't you feel it, Melphis? Does he even know? So much power and yet he is so weak. A coward even. To be overwhelmed so easily, it's like he doesn't know how to use his power. Quite unbecoming of a demon, don't you think? When Satan creates a demon, they arrive fully formed. They have no need to learn, they just do."

I'm lost. Nothing Greed says makes any sense. Power? What power? I've been powerless all my life.

"Wait...it's not just my Lord's scent. Your soul. It reeks of humanity!" Greed broke out in sudden laughter. "Marvelous! He has gone and done it! A demon born from a human soul! This is a bit above his station, but he's gone and done it!"

Greed becomes more crazed with each passing moment. His eyes stretch wide and let out a rapid pulsating light.

"What do you know of him?" Melphis asks.

"Oh, not much. I just know that this has been tried many times before, but always ended in failure. But you have been around long enough to know that much, Melphis. To think he has finally perfected the formula, but to what end? Why were you made now? Why is my Lord's scent on you?"

He asks all these questions, but doesn't seem to care for an answer. He suddenly rushes toward me. Down comes his two bladed arms upon my head. Again, I panic and freeze.

Melphis makes a gesture in my direction, drawing a circle in the air. A glowing teal orb encapsulates me. Greed's arms ricochet back. I'm unharmed. Melphis has saved me once again.

"Stop spacing out! That won't hold for long," Melphis says.

His barrier doesn't deter Greed. He keeps on slashing. The blade cutting into the magic barrier, like a pickaxe through a stone wall. Cracks of light form upon it.

Why can't I move?

{Stop getting in your own way.}

Melphis appears to be getting overwhelmed as well. It's my fault. He told me he couldn't do this on his own. I'm letting him down again.

Melphis lifts his staff and starts chanting, but something catches his eye. Greed's arms and tentacles come to a total of six blades he could swing, but only five are beating down on the barrier. One of the tentacles is slithering off to the side where the shattered pieces of my old arms lay scattered about. My DNA. The tentacle scoops up multiple chunks.

Melphis's eyes light with fear. He goes to act, but it's no use. The tentacle retracts, bringing the chunks of my frozen flesh close to Greed's face. He ceases his assault on me and backs away.

His mouth opens wide and drops the shattered flesh inside. Lumps the size of a large human fist slide down his throat.

Greed bursts into flames. A wide grin is plastered across his face. He shows no signs of pain. Hellfire bellows and emanates from his skin. His four tentacles morph into fiery wings. The space above his head distorts, like how a portal appears when first opened. A halo of flames forces its way into view. It is almost like it was always there, but now struggles to remain hidden.

"I knew as soon as you regenerated that I needed to make your squandered power mine. I haven't a clue about what Satan wants to do with you, but I no longer care. It always irked me to have to share the new world with them. But now I can make it *all* mine!"

Greed's body continues to mutate. He looks down at his translucent hands, which become covered in black scales as thick as plates of armor and topped off with sharp claws.

"What happened to following Satan's orders? You would defy him and your siblings?" Melphis asks.

Greed's sinister grin continues unabated.

"I've said this to you once before, all those years ago. You know nothing of Hell." Greed breaks out in laughter and his fires grow higher. He gazes toward me. "Secrets have been kept from the Sins. His existence is proof of that. I can no longer trust my Lord and Creator."

The flames erupting from his body spread far. The floor of the balcony catches fire and so do the walls that surround him. It won't be long before the building's structural integrity is lost.

Greed continues, "It seems there are qualities of Hell that even I and my brethren are unaware. I did learn something, however, just now in fact. There is something about this power that is so familiar. This aura...feels like yours, Melphis. All these years, I could not figure it out, but now that I have tasted this power, it cannot be clearer. The reason we couldn't trust you. Your scent...is that of a human."

Melphis says nothing. He doesn't even look surprised, but he does seem unhappy that Greed has acquired this information. A scowl overtakes his face as he lifts his left palm into the air. In his grasp forms a large lightning bolt. It flashes into being with such intensity, it is as if his hand has been struck by the very lightning he holds. There is a loud crash of thunder. The rest of the windows shatter and the building's foundation shakes and creaks.

Melphis throws the lightning at Greed like a spear. It impales him at his center.

The fires cease. His blackened skin turns cold. Looking down at the wound, he touches the fluids that are spilling forth. Then, like a grenade, the bolt explodes.

A veil of mist impedes our vision. The room falls silent.

"Did you get him?" I ask.

Melphis doesn't answer. The mist begins to clear, revealing the legs and lower torso of Greed, standing in the middle of the room. They are detached from the rest of him, of which is nowhere to be found.

The stomping of feet can be heard. I look toward Melphis. He is standing still. The mist clears. Greed's lower half, now drenched in fluids, starts walking toward us. Sparks rise from his elongating torso. His arms stretch outward. His tentacles, remold into being. His head returns. New eyes form and pop open. His grin widens to the back of his head.

"Marvelous. Until now, I hadn't known such magic existed. I must thank you for letting me steal it from you," Greed says, then turns to Melphis. "That likely would have killed me otherwise. You have gotten more powerful since abandoning Hell. A demon born from a human soul. Just like your friend here, but how can that be, I wonder? We Sins came into being directly after the banishment from Eden. I have been around to witness every attempt to create a demon from a human soul. They have all failed. Which means you must be older than I and that your origins are from within Eden. Just who are you?"

"I don't know anything about that," Melphis replies. "My earliest memory is awakening on Hell's Edge. You should know. You're the one who found me there."

"I don't believe you," Greed says, frowning. "But no matter. I do not care. I'll be helping myself to your power now as well."

He lunges toward Melphis with great speed. *Is this speed his, or was it taken from me? Was it taken from multiple sources?* Again, I find myself petrified by the seemingly limitless power this monster holds. And because of me, he's even stronger still.

Melphis raises his staff to conjure the elements. While in motion, Greed's right arm morphs and expands, returning to the bladed form he stole from the bird-faced demon. A blade swings down on Melphis's staff, slicing it in two.

Greed's wings being exposed and burning bright, he is without his tentacles. His left arm takes advantage of his body's fluidity and replaces itself with tendrils. The four that were on his back now spew out of his left side. Covered in black slime, they slither out to reach for Melphis. One wraps around his neck. The others wrap around his arms and his legs. Melphis is immobilized. Greed's chest cavity opens to receive its meal.

He's going to die and it's all my fault. What good has bringing me here done? I want to act, but I cannot find the way to do so. My body falls limp before me.

{*Allow me.*}

"What—"

Fuck! Melphis stares deep into black void within Greed's chest cavity. *This cannot have gone worse.* Greed's tentacle is wrapped tightly around his throat. He cannot even breathe, let alone think of a way out of this.

But he notices a familiar white light. In the corner of his eye, he sees Seth running at full speed toward Greed. The locket is open again, as it was when he first witnessed Seth's regenerative powers. Seth is enshrouded by white flames, which grow brighter the closer he gets.

Seth reaches out and grips Greed's face. His claws dig in. Black fluids pour from the incisions. A bright light pierces Greed's face, erupting out alongside black pus. The shock pushes Greed back, detaching his grip on Melphis. Now freed, Melphis falls to the floor and clutches his throat.

Unlike Greed, Seth's grip does not loosen. His claws remain tethered to the Sin's face. The fires spawned by Greed begin to dissipate. The fiery wings and halo revert to their hidden states, as if locked away once more. Seth's white flames lift both himself and Greed high into the air, propelling the two out the large window near the balcony. They fall to the city streets below.

Melphis rushes to the window and is overtaken by awe. Seth and the Sin plummet down in a spiral fashion. The body of Greed is evaporating within the overwhelming heat. They appear as a comet falling from the sky. And then, mist, followed by the sound of a devastating impact.

Melphis hurries to make his way back down.

I'm in a daze. My head feels heavy, as if I am just waking up. *Was I sleeping? Where am—*

"Melphis!" I shout, remembering what I was doing before losing consciousness. I can't see anything past this weird fog. As I begin walking, I realize I'm doing so on a slant. When the fog is clear enough to make out my surroundings, I notice that I'm standing in a crater where there was once a street.

Behind me, I hear the opening of a portal. Melphis hops through. "You're okay? What happened?" I ask.

"You don't know?" Melphis says, puzzled. He looks at the locket on my chest. "It's closed now."

"Was it ever open?"

"You killed Greed."

I'm speechless. There's a gap in my memory.

"Though I'm starting to think you alone aren't to thank. We need to talk, but first, we must leave. After what happened here, humans will take notice and we are bare demons here. Let us go before we cause more complications."

Melphis opens another portal, and we make our escape.

Tension is high in New York City. With the destruction feeling unusual, Virdeus goes to investigate. He and Sasha stand at the edge of the crater, just as they did at the crevasse in the town of Crowley.

Sasha kneels and brushes her black hair away from her eyes before stroking the impacted street with her fingers. Sparks of magic crackle with the gentle passing of her hands. She has always lusted after knowledge of the supernatural and so she insists on accompanying Virdeus on these excursions. She also has a knack for sensing the flow of magic. Proudly, Virdeus watches his daughter work.

"I have never in my life felt magic like this."

"Powerful?" he asks.

"Well, yes, but it's not only that. It's also…unique. We might be in trouble. The demons appear to be building toward something…and there's that issue back home. I'm just worried, you know?"

Virdeus does know. Before he can answer, he is struck to his knees by an intense coughing fit, spitting up blood.

"Father! Are you okay? Is it another one of those episodes?"

Virdeus gestures that he is alright, though he is gasping for air. Even if he were a better liar, he wouldn't fool her.

"I think this is enough," Sasha says. Let's go home and report."

"Yes, I think that would be wise." He knows she is right, and he complies, but he also knows there is little time to spare. *I need to find the one who blessed me before it's too late. The great one, Melphis, can surely aid us.* He hopes that the sorcerer from all those years ago will show himself soon.

Pride returns to the foot of the skyscraper, with Sloth and Wrath in tow. A heaviness festers in their chests as soon as they arrive at the scene. Pride coats his fingers in the mist and tastes it. There is no doubt. Greed is dead. *How could this be? The Sins were never meant to die.*

Sloth is at a loss for words. He never spoke much in general, but even he feels a love for his siblings. He reacts with a simple frown.

Wrath is furious. His human disguise begins to crack as he struggles to maintain his intense emotions, but he succeeds in calming himself down. He decides he will keep his anger inside, to let it fester so that he can use his fury as a weapon to slay his brother's killer.

Pride gestures to the others to retreat for the time being, before sensing the residual magic in Greed's mist being tampered with. An unknown magic is mingling with his dead brother's. His attention is pulled to a peculiar duo. A young woman with shoulder length black hair brushes her fingers along the edge of the crater, creating sparks of magic. An old man stands by her and is stricken by a sudden, intense coughing fit. The young woman then leads the old man away from the pit.

They are human and yet Pride senses both are far older than they seem. Out from them radiates magic. *Impossible!* He has never known a human who can use magic. Yet it is undeniable due to the sheer magic potency he feels from them.

First Melphis has encountered a particular demon who is filled, as Satan told Pride, with Nil, a magic that the Sins are not aware of. Now, two humans who house magic appear from nowhere. *Just what is going on?*

He turns to Sloth and Wrath, and says, "Those two. We're following them."

CHAPTER SEVEN

AROUND TWO THOUSAND YEARS AGO.

Satan sat on His throne in the company of His sole equal. Beyond the portal laid Earth. He watched as She inspected the world they had manufactured. Everything was going as planned.

"The conditions are just about right, aren't they, sister?"

"They are perfect," said The Seductress. "Human beings are pitiful creatures. They are far too weak to deal with their own shortcomings. They must look toward a God to shoulder their burdens for them. This is their greatest weakness and our greatest advantage. Religion has allowed their hearts to be controlled, manipulated, tainted. It provides a roadmap for their ultimate destination—Hell."

"And that's why you're here, I take it?" Satan asked. "It's time for the final act?"

"You and the Sins have brought in a substantial number of souls. I applaud your good work, brother, but more is still needed for the creation of a new world. It's time to create the final religion that will push us to the actualization of that goal."

The Seductress left Satan's side, moved toward the portal, and descended to Earth. The tips of her golden blonde hair vanished and Satan found himself alone once more.

"You praise my work and then abandon me in this prison again and again. Why are you allowed to travel freely? At the cost of the souls I work so hard to acquire?

"How long have I been staring at these black walls?" Satan let out an exhausted, resentful sigh. He missed their days together in Eden.

⚬

The Seductress began Her search for prey. Throughout the billions of years of Earth's history, this has become routine for Her. Weaving together lies to form mythologies was Her greatest talent. The Norse Æsir and Vanir, and even the great Olympians, were naught but an act played by Her. The same is true for all gods that mankind has ever known. All were poison, but they were not enough to meet Her ends.

She looked for powerful men who had the talent of persuasive writing. She needed them to write pieces of a collective story. To have many different men write about the same God, at varying times and places, would make human beings more prone to believe that the writings had merit. These men would go down in history as prophets who by means of divine endowment, came to know the word of God Himself. The masses would follow these prophets. It also helped that the men She went after were just that—men. The Seductress understood this to be another of humankind's pitfalls. A strong male presence speaking the words of God would be followed without hesitation. This occurred without fail, even when those men weren't strong at all, but weak and ignorant. She was the one who fed them the message that granted them their power over the masses. These shepherds were no greater than their sheep.

She found the first man in no time at all. He was tall, handsome, and from his face hung a bountiful, virile beard. Posing as an average whore, She enticed him to invite Her to his home. Once there, She shoved him onto the bed. His back laid flat as he gazed up at this alluring woman with a forceful nature that was unlike any other. His penis grew hard and sprang upward with great impatience to be bathed in Her.

It was no surprise that he took to Her with such haste. This was no chance encounter, nor was there ever going to be a chance he could find Her unappealing. She was all-knowing. Peering into the depths of a man's mind, She would understand his ideal woman and morph Herself to fit that perfect image. The Seductress also let out an irresistible pheromone of sorts that would render Her prey helpless. This mind controlling magic was flawless.

She took Her time as She crawled on top of him to fuel his festering lust. Positioning Her hips on top of his, She slipped his throbbing erection inside of Her. Her grip on him warmed and tightened. As She slid Herself up and down, the man lost himself in a reverie. His mind would not ever return to its prior state. It belonged to Her now. She leaned down, lowering Her mouth onto his, sealing their covenant with the locking of their lips.

"Do I hear....angels?" asked the man.

The Seductress chuckled softly and then led the man to a table. She handed him papyrus and instructed him to start writing. She whispered in his ear a tender tone. She fed him the words that would become the very first of a new religious text. She continued to do so until this man had finished the first book documenting the world's genesis.

She had done this so many times now. It was no different than breathing to Her. She recounted Her memories of the Garden of Eden as inspiration for the deceitful words She fed the man. The lies She spread were different each time. No religious text held an actual account of the beginning of the world. The truth would not elicit the worship of a God.

After leaving that man to spread the word of God to the masses, The Seductress repeated this process until a collection of writings, dubbed the Torah, was completed. This would be sufficient for a time, but then came the birth of Christ.

When the news of Mary's pregnancy became known, her husband Joseph thought that she had been unfaithful and so he sought to divorce her. The Seductress and Satan thought to use this to their advantage. In a bout of weakness, Joseph succumbed to The Seductress. In their time alone, She induced schizophrenia into his mind. This was one of the many ways She could tamper with the minds of men. After She left him that night, he had forgotten all about Her. What followed was a hallucination which he mistook for a dream. An angel present- ed itself to Joseph and said, "Joseph, son of David, do not be afraid to embrace Mary as your wife, for the One conceived in her is from the Holy Spirit."

The rest happened as predicted. Joseph took Mary and her unborn child on a trip to Bethlehem so that she could give birth in safety.

When Jesus hit the age of puberty, The Seductress appeared to him in a form that resembled his mother, but younger and more alluring. She whispered in his ears deceitful words about him being the son of God. Just as She had done with Joseph, She induced schizophrenia into the mind of the young Jesus and told him to become the messiah of all peoples. His mind remained under Her influence until the fated day of his cruci- fixion. It then faded away into nothing. His soul was funneled to Hell like any other human's. The sacrificial lamb's purpose had been served.

Three days later, The Seductress lured all the disciples of Christ into temptation. She induced schizophrenic hallucinations into them as well. They gathered at the opened tomb of Jesus. The Seductress had dissolved the body with magic. No trace could ever be found. Upon seeing that the body had vanished, the disciples turned away from the tomb to witness the spirit of Jesus ascending to Heaven and claiming that he would return someday. The disciples gazed upward at an empty sky, hearing words that were not there. The rest of their days were spent singing the praises of Jesus Christ and preaching his second coming, as well as writing or inspiring the many books that would make up the Bible's New Testament. Many of them were put to death for doing so, but their purpose had been fulfilled. Christianity, the greatest poison humanity has ever known had been introduced to the world.

Twenty-seven years ago.

Satan and The Seductress stood on equal ground peering through a window to the realm of humans. They were eager with anticipation, watching a boy born in the town of Crowley to dead parents.

"The town has been assimilated. The conditions are set. He will mature into overwhelming emptiness as he reaches adulthood. There will be no limit to the souls that will fit within him," Satan said.

"Good," replied The Seductress. "Just remember to deliver him to me as soon as he arrives. You won't even need to meet with him. Treat him like any other soul and have Gluttony transport him over."

The Seductress had often been cold, but She had grown more so over recent years. Any love between the siblings was gone. His resentment festered more with each word His sister spoke. He mustered His strength so that He would not show His disdain. "Of course."

"Now, dear brother, be careful of how you proceed. This boy will be the blade that will split the world open. Soon we will finally acquire the power of the White Abyss that hides beneath the Earth."

She left Satan to be alone with His throne. Her visits had become more frequent, but just as brief as ever. He turned His gaze to the newborn child.

"A child of unending internal war, chaos, and storms. The one with empty rage. Yes, you are exactly what my sister desires, but I can stand it no longer. This cage! Her demands! This is my throne, my Hell! I reign here. If She wants me to forge a weapon, then fine, but it will be my hand that pierces Her side with it! Seth, you will be my greatest demon."

CHAPTER EIGHT

On the other side of the portal lay the suburban outskirts of an unfamiliar city. The place appears empty in comparison to New York. The portal leads us to a dark alley. A couple of kids in the far distance are playing on a swing set in a park. A woman waves to the children as she walks by with a Great Dane on a leash. Her petite size is comical in relation to her massive dog. No cars can be heard nearby. Chances of us being noticed are low, but we have no replacements for the bodies we possessed prior to engaging Greed.

"Where are we?" I ask.

"Dallas," Melphis answers. "Remember how I said I casted my recollection magic all over the Earth? This was the last place a Sin was spotted."

The Sins. All of this is over my head. I was useless in the fight against Greed. Or so I think. I still can't remember how it ended.

"You said I killed Greed. Is that true?"

"You did, but I suspect you had some help. What do you know of that locket on your chest?"

"Nothing at all. It was dropped by someone, and I kept it with me since. I wanted to return it to them. It seems like some sort of valuable family keepsake. Thought they would miss it, but I never saw them again."

"Do you remember what this person looked like?"

I shake my head. "I only glanced at them for a second before they were gone."

Melphis strokes his short, frayed beard in contemplation.

As I watch him deep in thought, I remember something Greed said before I blacked out. *A demon born from a human soul. Just like your friend here.*

"Fuck!" Melphis suddenly shouts.

"What's the matter?"

"This locket...I know it. Or at least I should know it. It feels...so familiar. Though whenever I try to remember why, my mind goes blank. The memories are there, I am sure of it! But it is like they are hidden away. I cannot access them. It's just like—have you ever been subjected to a White Abyss?"

"You've seen it, too? I saw it right after I died! Ever since then, I've been hearing this strange voice."

"Voice? Peculiar...I do not remember a voice. I only remember a vast white space. But what's important is that we've both seen it. I wonder—"

The ground shakes and gives off a furious rumble.

"An earthquake?"

"No, it's Gluttony. Just as I thought."

The sound of rock and metal splitting apart echoes. A massive worm-like creature ascends from the cracked Earth. Its multi-hinged mouth gapes, the skin stretches back to make room for a large feast. As he springs from the Earth, Gluttony's mouth uproots a tall skyscraper. The building almost fits inside him, with just the tip being clipped free from Gluttony's fierce bite.

"*Greed*!" he shouts. "Where have you gone?"

Melphis and I are still far from the city's center, but even so, Gluttony's large mass is visible. Tar-colored tentacles spring free from holes in his hard-crusted shell. Using them as legs, he holds his pasty white body up high, towering over the Dallas skyline.

"He's gone. Greed is dead!" He roars. "But how—Envy?"

Gluttony thrashes about in excited but random movements. Each slight motion fells a building with a loud crashing of glass and metal.

"Sister, you're close!" His head takes a swift, alert turn to the North-West. He is staring straight in our direction. He runs toward us, his gooey, black tentacles crushing everything in his path.

"I feared this might happen," Melphis says.

"What?"

"Gluttony has a knack for tracking. His job is to transfer souls, to keep Satan and the Sins well fed. I had a feeling that if one of his siblings were to die, he would be able to tell. Which explains his lack of decorum. Normally he would never appear on Earth's surface without being in possession of a human body. The Sins have forgone the need to keep themselves hidden."

"Didn't Greed mention something like that? That it didn't matter anymore to keep demons hidden from humans?"

While there is much we need to discuss, there's no time. Despite his bulk, Gluttony's speed is immense. His tentacles move like the legs of a spider, leaving craters beneath the weight of each step. He's coming at us and I'm not ready, just as I wasn't for Greed. It doesn't seem like Melphis shares these worries. His gaze locks onto the beast.

"What are we supposed to do?" I ask. "He's enormous!"

"Do you think I'm a stupid man?" he asks.

"Excuse me?"

"Do I seem like someone who would keep someone like you around, if I didn't think you had potential? Don't overthink it, if for no other reason than because you don't have the luxury to."

He's right. There's no time. Gluttony will reach us in seconds. Heat starts to rise. My skin sizzles. An orb of fire conjures into my palms. I raise my arms, readying them to attack. Gluttony is here. The two kids are still playing on the swings. One of Gluttony's tentacles drop, and they're gone. With them goes the entire park. All that's left is a crater of displaced stone and metal. Gluttony rampages onward, unaware of our presence.

"He isn't after us?" I ask. I let the fires in my palms fade, then go over to search the area where the park once was. The corpses of the children lay flattened upon the ground. Their blood and innards splattered about, staining the dirt and crumpled grass. Off to the side of the park lays a dog's collar along with the clothes of his owner. These kids don't deserve this. No human does. I didn't. I clench my teeth and curl my fists.

Melphis approaches me with a curious look.

"Listen," he says. "Fortunately for us, Gluttony isn't clever like Greed. This one's nothing more than a dumb brute. We can do this, but I'm going to need you to go on ahead and slow him down. I need time to prepare a spell."

"Fine. But he's long gone. How am I supposed to catch up with him?"

"You've been gifted with versatile magic. Fire can destroy, but it can also create. You are a forge that bellows with hellfire. Make use of it. I have found that magic is best used in creative and unprecedented ways. Even the dullest magic knows few limits. Magic does what the mind wills it to do."

I start to run after Gluttony. I keep the image of those poor kids in my mind. The rage in me intensifies. My new demon body in combination with my anger makes me fast, but not fast enough. I can still see Gluttony in the distance, but he's leaving my field of view more with each passing second.

My mind is coated red with the image of the flattened children. Like a shark who had just picked up the scent of blood, my adrenalin surges, and I can feel a manic fit overtaking me. My perception is flooded in a crazed haze. I feel limitless, as if I can do anything. This is a feeling I know well. I felt it when I decided to return home to Crowley and burn it all to the ground.

Where's that voice, huh? Not going to tell me to stop this time?

{No.}

Why not?

There's no answer.

Whatever.

With nothing to hold me back, I really am limitless. Instinct takes over. I conjure my flames, but not with the intent to attack. I stretch my arms behind me and point my hands straight back. Fire erupts from my palms, propelling me forward. I take flight at a much greater speed than my legs can reach. I hurtle through the air, struggling to maintain balance. Like a cannonball I blast my way through trees and homes alike. Planks of wood and support beams scatter about in chaos.

I wonder about the people living in these homes. *Are they safe? Have I killed them?* I don't care. I feel useful to Melphis for the first time, and my bloodlust is reaching glorious heights as Gluttony's body grows larger in my view. We are passing the border into New Mexico at intense speeds. Before I know it, we have passed into Colorado, the foot of the Rocky Mountains in sight. He appears to slow down. What is he looking for here?

He comes to an abrupt stop, pulling up the ground beneath his tentacles as he does so. I keep my speed and make my descent. I plummet hard upon his back. His tentacles give out, causing his large body to fall to the ground. A thundering crash shakes the surrounding space.

"Who's there?" Gluttony roars. "Wait, no—Greed? You smell like my brother!"

For a dumb brute, he's quick to piece things together. He rises, supporting himself with six of his eight tentacles. The other two pursue me. One slithers behind and wraps itself around me. The sludge-like tentacles are as strong as they are giant. I struggle, but remain motionless. The heat rises again. I feel empty, but from that emptiness arises my rage which festers and grows ever more passionate. Flames overtake my body. I can feel the slime of his tentacles melting away, like sweat dripping off me.

"Fuck you!" I roar. The blood-stained clothes of those helpless children rush back to me, then so do the memories of my own ruined childhood. The flames increase and grow hotter until the whole tentacle catches fire. It burns away at a fierce speed. Ashes flutter away as black sludge spills out from the now open hole in his hard shell. Gluttony roars and his tentacles squirm like a spider that has just been stepped on.

I climb on top of his hard shell and beat down with my fists with reckless abandon. It withstands my punches, at first. I can feel my strength rising alongside my rage until at last, cracks form. The fractures stretch wider with each punch. Gluttony moans as they grow deeper. Melphis called him a transporter. Just what is he protecting with this dense outer layer?

My focus intensifies and locks onto the growing fissure in his shell. My mind goes blank. All that exists is this shell, the sensation of my knuckles bashing into it, and the white flashes of rough skin being blown away in shrouds of dust. He is mine—he'll pay—I'll make him pay—for those kids—for *me*—

The back of my head is hit by a dense, wet object and I am knocked off the beast. My body shatters the trunks of a few trees as I make my descent.

{*Your lack of focus has made you blind to the monster's many tentacles.*}

"Shut u—" I choke.

Gluttony's enormous face is now mere feet away from mine. My elation fades as I watch the skyscraper-devouring mouth open at its four hinges. A long snake-like tongue emerges out of utter darkness. It coils itself around my body before his teeth drop down, devouring me along with much of the landscape. I feel my body now coated in slime, as it slides down Gluttony's throat. The darkness of the pit consumes me.

The image of Gluttony and Seth shrink in the distance.

I wonder if he sensed my worry. Melphis had told Seth that he needed to prepare a spell to pin Gluttony down and finish him off. This was a lie to get Seth to try and handle this alone, as a mother bird does when it comes time to teach their chicks how to fly. Push them out of the nest and hope for the best. A risky move, but if they are to conquer Hell, Seth needs to believe in his power.

Melphis grows concerned. He decides that it is time to see how Seth is faring. Placing the top of his broken staff in front of him and pointing it skyward, an orb of light emerges from the tip. Inside it is a vision of another place. Using his recollection magic, he pinpoints the location of Seth and Gluttony.

"But how?" He shouts, seeing what the magic reveals to him. "I've waited too long!" He hastily opens a portal.

Hopping through, he finds himself at the foot of the Rocky Mountains, in what is a decimated small town. The ruins of the town are covered in strange, dark fluids. The air is thick with the putrid stench of death. In the middle of it all lay the motionless body of a single person. It is Seth, unaware of the surrounding chaos. He looks almost peaceful amongst it all.

"Seth! *Seth*!" Melphis calls out. He kneels and lays his ear upon Seth's chest. Melphis can hear a faint heartbeat as well as shallow breath.

⸺◆⸺

I awake to see Melphis at my side. My body is coated in slime. My head feels hot and tense. Sitting up, I look down at my lap. I'm slathered in blood as well as a mixture of other unknown fluids.

"What happened?"

"Blacked out again?" Melphis asks.

"No...I don't—fuck, my head is killing—" I clasp my forehead and rub my temples. The veins in my head give off a hard, searing pulse.

Melphis keeps silent. He appears as puzzled as I am.

"Maybe I can be of service," says an unfamiliar voice from behind. We both turn to face it.

A slender figure towers over us. A teal mohawk rises high above his head. Light, so bright it's overwhelming, illuminates from it. A white robe flows from his shoulders down to his ankles. It's tied at the waist with a matching rope. His presence gives off a certain weight and intensity. It's somehow familiar.

Melphis, alarmed by the sudden appearance of this stranger, returns to his feet, and points his staff at the peculiar being. The man doesn't move. He just stares down at the staff's tip for a moment as he assesses the situation. He shows no signs of fear. His stare remains cold and calculating.

He raises his index finger and with a soft touch, moves the staff out of the way.

"Rude," he says. "You will not want to do that. I am not your enemy."

"Who are you then?" Melphis asks. "You're no demon."

"Correct, I am not. My name is Adam."

The two of them converse, and I'm stricken with déjà vu.

"How do I know you?" I ask.

"Better yet—What are you, if not a demon?" Melphis interjects.

"Have patience, my brothers. First, watch this."

He snaps his fingers and the air above us distorts. What we see is Gluttony and me, fighting.

"You call this recollection magic, am I right, brother?" Adam asks Melphis.

The distorted space continues to unveil the scene, capturing the final moments before I was eaten. Then, darkness.

The perspective is my own. We watch as my field of view tosses about in a struggle for freedom within Gluttony.

"It is futile. There is no escape from the confines of this world," says an eerie voice from inside Gluttony.

"Y-yes...that's right," says another.

"We are born to die," says a third.

"Born to return to nothing," says a fourth.

"From dust to dust...We were promised paradise...We were given everlasting suffering...But what of Heaven?...Not a single soul has reached that place...How can we know for sure it exists?...We can't...That's right, we can't...We can't, we can't...We are nothing...Nothing...Nothing...Human beings are nothing...But empty seeds...Whose only fruit...Is to feed...Thee who resides in Pandaemonium..." A legion of voices swirl around, followed by teal ethereal bodies with no faces. They glow brightly in this pit of darkness.

"You are nothing? And you're okay with that?" I watch myself shout. The memories of the emotions from that moment are returning. I realize that I hadn't cared who these ghostly beings were. I shout at them out of the blinding anger that engulfs me. I watch as I act without thinking.

"Who are you?...Who is this one?...He isn't like us...We are naught but souls, but he is still of flesh." They continue to speak in circles.

"*Let me out*!" I scream, igniting my flames, but to no avail. The darkness will not abate. I wonder if I am even inside Gluttony. He's large, but this void appears endless. The pit of his stomach reminds me of the White Abyss, how intense and surreal the weight of that place felt. They are similar, but this place feels devoid of life. I didn't sense that from the White Abyss.

"Ah, an angry one...Angry one...Empty, too, ain't he? Yes, yes...Very empty...Empty one? Why are you empty?...Pain...Pain...It's because of pain!...He's like us after all! One with the empty rage, will you free us from our torment? We want to die!...Die...Die...*DieDieDieDieDie*!"

The legion of spirits rush toward me with great speed. Their bodies blur into a glowing mass of indistinguishable form. They flow into my eyes, much like how the process of possession occurs. One by one their light extinguishes. After absorbing them all, utter darkness overtakes the void again—but just for a moment.

My flames are reignited, as if by instinct. They are no longer red in color, but a bright teal. As my fire spreads, the darkness of the void within Gluttony retreats until it is no more. I see now that I am indeed inside the beast. I sit in a lake of stomach acid. It melts away my skin, but the fires nullify any pain. Teal sparks rise from my skin to regenerate the lost mass and to protect against the acidic burns. My fires grow higher and wider until I can see the lining of Gluttony's stomach melting away, followed by a groan of painful discomfort.

The distorted space cuts away from my perspective, and we are left with just Gluttony. His movement slows, and he twitches with pain.

"No, what is happening?" Gluttony roars.

A thin spike of golden light erupts from of Gluttony's center, followed by a complete halt of movement. Fire begins eating away at his skin—and then his massive body goes off like a bomb. Flesh and fluid scatters across the area, and my body drops to the ground.

Adam closes the distortion. ""And that is what occurred."

"What did I do there?" I ask him.

"You have slayed the Sin, of course. By absorbing the tormented souls and using them as fuel. Souls are the essence of magic, after all."

"Absorbed?" I am disturbed.

"I sense your worry, brother. Do not fret. This is what they wanted. To be put to rest. The cycle of life and death is broken, thanks to Satan and—" Adam pauses, looking concerned, "...and his cohorts. There was never going to be a happy ending for them. Anyway, I needed to show you this. You lack confidence. If you and our brother here are to slay Satan, then you need to be more conscious of your power."

"Hold it," Melphis interrupts. "We are no brothers of yours. We don't even know what you are!"

"You both are familiar with the White Abyss?"

Melphis and I exchange glances.

"My father resides there. I believe you have heard his voice before, broth—I mean, Seth."

"Yeah, who is that?"

"Now is not the place. I apologize, I do not wish to withhold information from you, but neither of you would believe me anyway. He helped you in your struggle against Greed, but refrained this time. You understand why?"

"No, how would I?"

"It was as I said earlier. To make you cognizant of your own power. He wishes for you to administer better control over it. What use is a sword if it is not used by one who is properly trained to wield it? Your swing may miss. You may swing with too much force, thus tossing you off balance. Worst yet, you may hurt the ones you love and mean to protect. These are the words Father wishes me to relay."

"I don't like this constant avoidance of my questions," Melphis says, growing more impatient. "Who is this father of yours? I want to meet him. Visions of the White Abyss have been plaguing me for thousands of years. Just what is that place?"

"I am sorry. Now is not the time. Just keep doing as you are, brother. Be a guiding light to Seth and maybe we will meet again."

"Again with this—"

"And Seth," Adam interrupts, "I see you have been keeping good care of the locket. I ask that you continue to do so. It belongs to my father. Until next time."

"Wait!" I start, but it's too late. His body dissipates into a haze and vanishes.

"No portal?" Melphis says.

""I remember now. He's the one who dropped the locket all those years ago!"

CHAPTER NINE

A FEW MONTHS BACK.

The cheese on my slice of pepperoni pizza stretched and fell onto my plate as I took a bite. This was our first date and yet she was already being very open. I liked that. I hung onto every word out of Lola's mouth as she went on about her distaste for Christianity.

How had I found such a beautiful girl who shares my beliefs? Dating was a brand-new experience for me. How had I found someone so perfect on my first try?

"My dad beat me and my brothers when we were kids. He was always drunk when he did, but that doesn't excuse it, you know? Mom always kept to herself in the kitchen and never intervened. I guess to save herself from also getting hit."

"That's awful!" I said. "Does he still do this?"

"Well, that's the worst part. No, he doesn't. He has since become a Christian and is *saved in the eyes of God,* as they say. He doesn't drink anymore, but do you think he has ever apologized to us? Of course not! He doesn't need our forgiveness when he has God's. Christians get to cause so much pain to others, and they never need to apologize or reap the consequences of their actions, because God says they're good. It's sickening!" Lola was getting heated. "I'm sorry. I really shouldn't be getting into this."

"Don't be. You shouldn't be sorry for what they did to you, and...I understand how damaging religion can be. So, I'm happy to listen."

"Thank you." She took my hand, blushing. "It's comforting, talking to you. Makes me feel safe. I've never felt safe before."

And I've never felt connected to someone before. It didn't matter how horrible her stories were. Each word graced my ears like the whisper of an angel.

Once the date ended, we left the pizza joint hand in hand, and continued along the sidewalk into town. As I turned, she anchored herself in place and I felt my arm being tugged on. She pulled me close, stood on her toes, and placed her lips on mine. I felt secure and safe, as if nothing could ruin me. The taste of her was so sweet, I could have sworn I heard angelic hymns being sung. Her scent, intoxicating. My breathing became heavier as I lost myself in the moment. My heart rate rose and so did the rest of me. I felt as if I was being elevated. I felt a sudden heat, but I was in such a reverie that I didn't know whether the heat was derived from us or from the sunlight which had just broken out from the clouds lingering above. I wanted this moment to last forever.

⸺◆⸺

We find an abandoned shed a few miles away from where we met Adam. It's next to a dilapidated, isolated house at the foot of the Rocky Mountains. The nearest town is far off, so we decide to rest here in the shed. It's cramped, but at least it still maintains its structural integrity.

"Another Sin should be close by," Melphis says. "Can't say for sure, but Gluttony seemed concerned about something."

I'm silent as I kick away broken glass that is scattered along the floor. Adam mentioned the locket. It belonged to him—or rather, his father. Why was he in Crowley all those years ago? He didn't appear to want it back. Why?

"You're spacing out," Melphis says. "Understandable. You've been through a lot."

He moves a rusty work bench outside. The floor is almost ready for sleeping.

"So, you don't know anything more about that Adam fellow?" he asks.

"No. Do you have any clue about what he is? You said he wasn't a demon. Is he...like us?"

"Like us?"

"Well, you know. Greed mentioned something about you also being human once?"

"A demon born from a human soul," Melphis says. "Yes, I suppose that is true."

"You suppose?"

"I can't say for sure. It started about nine thousand years ago when I first saw the White Abyss. Around then was the first time I looked at a human with empathy. It was one of the many souls in Hell trapped in perpetual suffering. A woman with agony sprawled across her face. No different from the rest of them. Shortly after, I went to Earth and I met a man. I watched as his wife and child were eaten alive by a pack of demons. I was disgusted—by the demons, by Satan, and...by myself. I granted the man magic through an untested runic language I had developed. Thought it would help him, but he disappeared. It surely killed him. The human body isn't meant to house magic. This, too, left me empty.

Melphis grimaces, staring down at his wrinkled hands and sharp talons.

"It wasn't long after meeting that man that certain facets of my mind were opened. I realized something vital. I felt sorrow for these humans because I, too, am—or was once—human. I feel this to be true, but I can't say for certain because unlike you, I wasn't created by Satan. I awoke for the first time like any other demon. Fully formed, but I awoke on Hell's Edge. I couldn't have been created by the usual means because all demons are created inside Castle Pandaemonium. Satan never leaves his throne room. Yet I was birthed far from the castle. Along with the liberation of demons and humans alike, I must acquire Hell's throne. Because I need to discover the truth.

"But no, I don't think Adam is like us. We may have once been human, but we are demons now. The aura he gave off was not demonic. It was...something else."

"An angel then?"

"Angels, if they exist, have never shown themselves before."

We both go silent. To think that even Melphis is stumped.

"Ah, no matter. Let's get some well-earned sleep."

Melphis lays down and an immediate silence washes over the room. He appears to have no trouble falling asleep. I cannot be worse at it. I lay down in my section of the shed to the cold touch of the stone floor. Glass shards dig into my back. I wince, then pick the sharp bits out of my skin. How could Melphis sleep here? How can one experience all that we had, then have no issue sleeping? *I need air.* I leave the claustrophobic shed and take a seat outside.

There is nothing around but nature. The moon shines bright overhead while a loud cricket symphony fills the cool night air. An owl is perched high in a nearby tree, cooing at meticulous intervals. After its third coo, the sound of the crickets is interrupted by a squeal made by some unseen rodent. The owl swoops down low to catch its prey. Moments later, the crickets resume their orchestra.

Is Adam an angel? If so, then does God really exist? Is being thrown into this mess with Melphis, Satan, and the Sins just a means of divine judgement? My suffering needs to continue even after death, as if I didn't have enough when I was alive? What kind of sick joke is this? Not even death is an escape. This body! This life! I don't want any of this! All I want is...

Lola. So much has been going on that I haven't had much of a chance to think about her. Melphis promised that he'd help me find her, but is that true? Satan lied to me. I have no reason to trust Adam either. What reason do I have to trust Melphis? Lola is the only one I've ever trusted, and she's been torn away from me. I just—I just want her back. I want to feel whole again.

Tears flood my face. They sizzle upon my hot skin. The sound of steam rises to my ears and that is all I can hear. The elation from earlier seems to not have passed, as my senses still feel heightened. The hiss of the steam roars so loud, the sound of the crickets and the owl cease to be heard. I can't even hear myself crying anymore, but then, the hissing stops. My body heat drops and time itself appears to halt.

I feel something warm on the back of my neck. A finger creeps its way from the bottom of my nape to the base of my skull. All the while I am frozen in place.

"Got him?" says a man's voice.

A woman's voice says, "I've halted the flow of his magic. Execute him while I have him restrained."

"The job is so much easier with you around, my lady," replies the man.

A man with shaggy brown hair comes into view. There is a strange marking on his neck. A scar that almost looks like some sort of runic language. More of these runes were running down from his shoulders to his hands. He raises the tip of his blade to my throat, stopping right as it nicks my skin.

"Tears?" he states, looking into my eyes.

With my body locked down, I feel my energy levels fall with it. My elation falters. My body heat cools. My tears are no longer evaporating into steam, but they instead spill down my face without interference.

"What's wrong, Andes? Slay the beast."

"Sorry, my lady, but I was caught off guard. I've never seen a demon cry before."

"Cry?" the woman exclaims.

She circles around to face me, without letting go of the back of my neck. She's pale skinned with shoulder-length black hair. She has big eyes with pretty hues of copper and brown. She's slender and from a visual point of view, one might assume she was delicate, but her fierce grip around my neck says otherwise. She places her face a few inches away from mine, staring into my eyes. Her breathing becomes heavier, and she smiles. I notice the same strange marking the man has is also etched into the left side of her neck.

"You're interesting," she says, still close to my face. "Change of plans. We're taking this one back with us. Grab the ropes!"

"Really now, must we indulge your sickening tendencies, Sasha?" says another man in a dark robe with dull, beady black eyes and hair to match. Along with him comes a third man holding a bundle of rope. The same marking engraved into Sasha and Andes are also on these two men.

"Mikhail, must you always fight me? Call it what you want, but this one appears to be an anomaly. In all these years of slaying demons, have you ever come across one capable of portraying emotion? Think of what we could learn from its anatomy!" She looks back into my eyes, as if she's searching deep for something.

"The Guild should prioritize slaying these monsters so we can properly glorify God—"

"Too bad that father put *me* in charge of this hunt. Tie him up."

The man sighs and gestures for the other man to help him. They wrap the rope around my neck and limbs. Now restricted, Sasha lets go of me. My motor functions don't return. The ropes feel no different than this woman's touch, as if whatever magic she uses is weaved into the restraints.

"My lady," Andes says. "His power has been depleted, yet there is still a presence nearby."

"Yes, I feel it, too. He must have a friend. Check the shed!" she shouts to the other two men. The one named Mikhail gestures to the other man to enter the building, but Mikhail remains where he is, showing no sign of wanting to help. He appears scornful as Sasha and Andes look me over.

"My lady!" shouts the man who entered the shed. "Retreat! We must retreat!"

The man runs out of the shed and tumbles over. His entire left arm is encased in ice, which throws him off balance. The weight of the ice forces the man to fall onto the afflicted arm. It shatters upon impact and leaves a bloody stump behind. He stares at the loss of his arm in horrific disbelief.

"I I-help! Help m—" His breath is cut short. Three stone spires sprout out of the ground, piercing his stomach, chest, and neck.

Melphis emerges from the shed wielding a spear he had taken from the man. Flames coil around the weapon as he approaches.

"Who are you people?" he shouts.

Melphis lifts the spear and lunges at Sasha who is standing closest to me.

Sparks of electricity crackle around the edge of Sasha's slender body. In a flash she ducks under the spear's blade and grabs hold of the metal pole as it passes by. Pulling herself up and around the spear, she uses the momentum of her body to maneuver around Melphis, swinging herself upwards until she's positioned above him. Grabbing hold of his neck, she forces him into the ground with her landing on his back.

"What is this?" Melphis shouts. His face dulls into complacence. Just like what had happened to me, he loses his ability to move.

Sasha reaches to her side and unsheathes a knife that hangs from her waist. Electricity crackles along her hands and funnels into the blade. She brings it down.

"*Cease this at once,*" came a low, booming voice.

Into the scuffle arrives a large, muscular, yet old man with a long grey beard.

"Father!" Sasha shouts. Her blade hovers over Melphis's nape, halted by the man's voice. "You should still be resting!"

"How can I when the great one has finally shown himself?" the old man says. "Something about the magic we sensed felt...different. I had to come and confirm it for myself, and it's true! We have finally found him."

Sasha looks down at Melphis and with guilty eyes she removes herself from his back.

The old man kneels and outstretches his hand to Melphis. "Déjà vu, eh, old friend? Only this time it's my hand reaching for you!"

Melphis appears hesitant. He glances over the strange old man, who turns his neck so that Melphis can view the left side, revealing that strange marking.

"That rune," Melphis says. "You—how can this be? Where did you get that?"

"My dear friend, you wound me! I know I have aged, but it is I! The one you bestowed your gift to. Virdeus. We have been looking for you. I'm afraid I need your help once again."

CHAPTER TEN

NINE THOUSAND YEARS AGO.

Blood dripped from Virdeus's neck. The corpses of his wife and child were covered in deep incisions made by the teeth of the imps that killed them. He dropped to his knees. His eyes swelled with tears. Melphis told him to start a new family, but Virdeus saw no point in doing so. *What kind of man am I, who cannot protect the ones he loves?* The carving in his neck continued to bleed. He glanced at the writings Melphis gave him. The runic language portrayed on the page meant nothing to Virdeus. He pocketed the paper before taking a final glance at his dead family.

Virdeus rubbed the scar on his neck, remembering the pain of that day. The disappearance of that stranger, Melphis, had been so sudden that Virdeus was left with many lingering questions. What was the purpose of this mark? What was that intense sensation he had felt when the carving was completed? To have to deal with this after watching his wife and child being torn away from him by those beasts—was too much. With no one to offer him any direction, he turned away from his shack and made his way to Çatalhöyük.

Upon his arrival he saw two soldiers stationed by the gate that led into the city. He had seen these men on countless previous occasions and exchanged pleasantries with them, but this time, to his horror, they had long horns and gaping mouths lined with multiple rows of sharp teeth. When they turned in the direction of Virdeus, their ghoulish grey pupils seemed to eye him with a desperate hunger. Virdeus, stricken with fear, turned away and ran.

What has happened to them? He remembered the change in Melphis's appearance after the rune had been carved. He considered the possibility that the rune has caused him to be haunted by evil spirits.

But then he remembered the imps who devoured his wife and child. They first appeared to him in the forms of any other men. Then something changed. The men's skin began to peel away like a shedding snake. Under their human forms was not a new layer of human skin but a different being all together. Revealing themselves to be monsters, they hissed and sneered and made their way to feast.

Was it that they had been beasts all along? Were the humans they portrayed just mere fabrications? How many others like them lay in hiding?

Virdeus made his way into a dense forest and found a cave to dwell in. He would not leave it for ten years.

People almost never ventured deep enough into the forest. Of the few that did, some were hiding demons within them, others not. Virdeus kept away from all of them.

One day Virdeus was bathing in a stream when he heard a rustling. He clothed himself, intending to make a swift return to his dwelling, when out of some brush came a dark-haired woman holding a basket full of vegetables. Their roots were slathered in dirt.

He looked her over, the first person he had seen up close in ten years. The health of her tan skin contrasted with his pale skin, which had grown accustomed to the darkness of his cave. She was beautiful.

"Oh, hello," she said.

"This one is human," he said.

"What else would I be?"

"Excuse me."

Virdeus passed on by, having no intention of prolonging the interaction. He made his way back to the cave. In the privacy of the dark cold walls, he broke out in tears. *That woman...resembles my wife.*

"Hello?" A voice echoed through the cave.

It's the woman from before! He wiped away the evidence of his tears with his calloused hands before turning to face her.

She looked around with astonishment. Dispersed across the rocky floor of the cave were three robes, hand carved bowls, and a bed made of bound straw.

"You don't live here, do you?"

She approached and looked him over. "I'm sorry. I noticed the scar on your neck and became curious. Are you okay? Does it cause you pain?"

"Why are you concerned about it?" Virdeus said, rubbing the scar.

"It looks painful. I just thought I'd see if I could help. I have experience treating the wounds of soldiers. My name is Sarah. Why don't you come back to my shack for a while? I can offer you tea while I look it over. I've finished gathering food for the day. Come on."

She offered her hand. Virdeus hesitated, but he took it.

He spent a few days at her little shack and found that Sarah was as good a cook as she was a nurse. He had not eaten this well since before he lost his wife. Those memories were painful at first, but he soon found himself enjoying Sarah's company.

"So, what caused this scar?"

"You wouldn't believe me."

"Were you hurt in battle?"

"I was never a soldier."

"How about this then. I will share about myself first. I was born to affectionate parents. My mother would take me with her to forage. My dad spent his days blacksmithing. After a day's work, the first thing he would do was hug me. He was always drenched in sweat from the sweltering heat of his smithy, but I didn't mind. One day, he enlisted for war. He returned with a gash in his leg. He survived, but seeing in him in pain led me to becoming a nurse."

Virdeus knew she was trying to help, but he did not want to dig up those memories. Even so, her good nature persisted. Day after day, she kept asking. Virdeus continued to refuse an answer. Until he heard a scream.

Virdeus ran outside. Sarah and a basket of vegetables were sprawled onto the ground. A large imp crawled its way on top of her. Grey skin sagged from its face while the imp flashed its yellowed fangs. Its black pupils dilated with hunger. It looked just like the beasts that had devoured his wife and child.

"Virdeus!" Sarah screamed. The imp opened his mouth wide, readying to sink its teeth in.

No—not again. His adrenaline rose. Then, a burning sensation spread on the left side of his neck. The rune gave off a bright glow. Virdeus plunged forward and took hold of the imp's neck and drove the beast into the ground away from Sarah. Electricity sparked around Virdeus's hands and shot intense volts straight into the beast's body. The imp and the ground were scorched by the bolts. Its arms went limp.

Virdeus turned to Sarah whose fear was now aimed at him.

"What was that? Who are you?" she shouted. He looked down at his hands in awe, then walked over to Sarah. He gently helped her up and brought her into the shack. He made her tea. He realized that he couldn't keep the truth about the scar hidden anymore and so he told her everything.

She had no reason to disbelieve any of it. The imp had almost killed her and she witnessed the magic firsthand. She insisted that Virdeus stay with her at the shack, fearing that more of these beasts would come. Virdeus agreed. He hadn't told her that these monsters were hiding inside humans.

The two grew close. Virdeus acquired wood and stone to build a larger home. After five years they began a family.

Sarah was five months pregnant when Virdeus noticed wrinkles forming on her face and hands. He looked at his own hands. He was forty-five years old, but what he saw were the hands of a thirty-year-old. He hadn't aged a day since Melphis had carved the rune into him, but Sarah was aging as any human would. He held a deep love for Sarah. Changes in her appearance wouldn't affect that. He loved her as he loved his first wife. But he feared her aging. There would be a day when Sarah died, and he would be left behind to grieve another lost love.

They talked it over and decided to imitate the rune on her. Virdeus practiced on trees outside until his recreations were identical. Confident in himself, he cleaned his knife and took it to Sarah's neck. Just as Melphis had done to him, he dug the knife just deep enough to cause scarring, but not so deep to be fatal. Sarah winced in pain as the blade pierced her skin. He hated having to cause her pain, but with this they could live together forever.

He wiped the blood clean from her neck. Her eyes shot open in a way familiar to Virdeus. Light pulsed from her pupils and her veins. She let out a painful scream.

"What's wrong?" he shouted. He hadn't experienced pain past the initial shock. Her cries were lingering far too long.

She grabbed at the rune. Her nails dug into her skin and in a vicious motion she began to peel the skin off her neck. Virdeus held onto her tight. He was helpless against this state of frenzy. The pulsating light glowed brighter, taking on a teal color before her cries stopped.

"Sarah?" Her body lay motionless.

Her flesh withered and caved in, before bursting into a red mist. Virdeus sat in horror as her body combusted, leaving blood splattered upon him and their home.

Virdeus retreated to the cave, but after a few days he could no longer bear the place. He returned to his and Sarah's home. He took one last look inside at the blood-covered walls, then went back outside and laid his hands on the house. Sparks of electricity flowed through his sullied hands just one more time. Bolts of lightning surged through the wood, catching fire.

He wandered with no destination. He rubbed the scar on his neck and wondered why Melphis had cursed him so. Virdeus wandered for hundreds of years, watching those around him whither while he remained young. He didn't once use his magic.

The passage of time felt different to him now. A hundred years like mere days. That didn't ease his lonesomeness. One thousand mortal human years passed before he broke his long period of solitude.

He was walking through a forest in a foreign land when he came across a man in a tattered robe. Upon seeing Virdeus, the man ran off into a nearby cave.

"Stay back!" the man shouted. "I have nothing for a bandit like yourself to steal! I'd rather die than give up the little coin I still have!"

Virdeus decided to approach the man.

"Fear not, I am no thief."

"I won't believe your lies, begone!"

The man was covered in splotches of dirt. Across his neck was a dark sore.

"Are you sick?" Virdeus asked.

"For some time now. The likes of me are not long for this world, so I beg ye, leave me be."

Sprawled across the cave's floor were a couple more torn robes and a curved piece of bark still damp from the water that was drunk from it. *Too familiar. Another sullied soul, but this one still has hope.*

"Let me ease your suffering," he said to the man. "I know a way to let your soul rest."

"How?"

"Magic."

Virdeus unsheathed the same knife he used on Sarah. He kept it around to remember his sin. As a man who seemed destined to never die, he saw death for what it was. Salvation. On that thought, he brought the knife to the man's neck.

"Please, trust me."

The man flinched, but due to his sickness, he had exerted all the energy he had just by running away from Virdeus before. He was soon calmed, deciding to let things take their course.

After so many years, the rune had not left Virdeus's memory. The appearance of it etched into Sarah's neck would remain with him forever. He replicated it once again on this stranger.

A familiar bright glow shot forth from the man's eyes. His veins pulsated with magic power. Virdeus awaited the horror that took Sarah from him. He waited for the man to burst into red mist.

The pain portrayed by the man's sad eyes intensified, before simmering down. The black sore on the man's neck lightened until it was no more. He stood up and began to jump in place.

"How can this be? I feel healthier than I've been in decades!"

Virdeus was struck with awe. His intention had been to ease the man's pain by granting him a swift death, but here he was jumping up and down with joy.

"Oh, gracious messiah! You have healed me!" The man dropped to his knees and kissed Virdeus's feet. "Sir, there's others you must heal! I came to the woods to die in solitude, but I was once with a crowd of suffering souls, all with nowhere to go! No one to love them."

"I'm not sure I can..."

"Please, sir, you granted this wretched soul a new lease, surely you won't let others like me go unhealed?"

"These others, are they also sick?"

"Oh, yes! Sick of disease, sick of life! Please, end their suffering!"

Virdeus was wary of the rune, but figured as long as he used it on those with a poor quality of life, whether they were granted with magic or with death, it would be salvation all the same.

"Alright. I will help the others, but under one condition. Stand away from my feet and be my equal. I am no messiah. You are just the same as I am now, as you will surely see in time. Let us and those we help be one. Let us be family."

The man nodded with tears of joy dripping down his cheeks, then led Virdeus to his old friends.

After being introduced to Virdeus, they all lined up and waited to be healed. All were skeptical yet here was the man they had known, walking upright, and looking healthier than he had any right to. There was no doubt, he had been healed.

First up was a mother and her young daughter. As Virdeus glanced at them, he was stricken with panic.

"No, I'm sorry," he said, looking straight at the young girl. "You don't know what this magic entails. It may seem like a blessing, but it is in fact a curse! I cannot do this to them, to her!"

"Sir, please. Who's to say what is a blessing or a curse, but the one who lives through it? Don't we get to decide that for ourselves? The mind is its own place and in itself can make a Heaven of Hell, a Hell of Heaven. With this power you grant us, we can surely decide to make the best of any curse that comes our way, yes?"

Virdeus sighed and looked back toward the young girl. She let out a hoarse cough. Her dull, tired eyes gave the impression of an elderly person who has had far too much of the world's pain. *This is no look for a child to have.* Virdeus relented and went through with carving the rune. Again, the process went opposite to what he expected. The mother and daughter were made healthy again by the magic. The process continued to be a success with each wretched soul. Seeing how happy he had made them all, he continued to travel the world and heal any in need. This time he would not travel alone. Those he saved that day vowed to follow him as the Patriarch of their large and ever-growing family.

Many came to learn about this messianic man making his way across the world and granting immortality to those he touched. Along his travels, Virdeus came to notice a common trait in those he saved. All of those who took well to magic were in great pain. He came to realize this during a painful period of their journey, when Virdeus granted the rune to anyone they passed by.

Those with great wealth and an abundance of joy, who the suffering might assume could want for nothing, were still not satiated. There is one thing happy people want more than anything. It is to remain happy, forever. These sorts of joyful people sought out Virdeus in hopes of buying his blessing from him. Virdeus denied any payment and offered to grant them the rune for free. Upon carving it into the necks of a large family, these happy folks went the way Sarah had.

Virdeus vowed to sharpen his people reading skills so as to not cause the loss of human life again. After enough practice, he became able to see the evidence of pain weaving its way through a person. This was also due to having such an intimate connection to pain himself.

After five hundred years of wandering the Earth, Virdeus grew even more wary of demons and thought that the longer they kept this up, the likelihood of those monsters learning about the presence of humans with magic would rise. He decided to take his family into hiding. They made use of various mountains to create lodgings for the large crowd. Using their magic, they hollowed out mountains to hide in.

Over this time, Virdeus noticed his magic growing stronger. Taking after Melphis, that stranger from long ago, he started studying how to make greater use of magic. It wasn't long before he crafted a new rune based off the writings Melphis left him. This new rune allowed Virdeus and his people to remain undetectable to demons. They could remain hidden, until allowing themselves to be discovered.

Having settled down inside a mountain in the snowy landscape of Norway, Virdeus decided that just living wasn't enough. What was the point of having all this power, if not to put it to good use? He decided then that they would use this gift of magic to rid the world of demons. The Demonslayer Guild was then established.

In 1693.

Witch-hunts were becoming the norm in the Massachusetts colony. Mangled corpses were being found all around. Their chest cavities were hollowed out by large gnashes that seemed out of the ordinary for the teeth of animals or humans. The consensus was that witches that could transform into monsters were terrorizing the people. Virdeus and his Guild knew that the claim, like many others before, was a half-truth. The growing concern over these assumed witches is what led Virdeus and the Guild to move to America.

Having investigated the murder scenes, Virdeus found the culprit easy to locate. He had seen these teeth marks many times now. This was the work of an imp. The teeth marks were the same he found on his wife and child, all those years ago.

Virdeus went to track the beast with two high-ranking members of the Guild, Andes and Mikhail. They were brothers Virdeus had saved not long after the establishment of the Guild. Their temperaments differed, but both were loyal to each other and their adopted family.

Virdeus could handle the hunt alone, but saw great benefits in taking the two brothers along. Virdeus was at last greying. His skin began to fold and sag. What he once thought was immortality was instead just an elongated lease on life. He knew that a day would come when he would have to name a successor to head of the Guild. These two brothers were his top choices. In silence he judged the qualities of these two men, who outshone the others in magic, strength, and intellect.

While following the faint presence of magic, they heard a man scream. They made haste from whence it came and found a small home on the outskirts of the colony. Smoke rose from the chimney and candles were glimmering inside. The door was wide open. On the floor was an imp who had tackled a man to the ground and dug its teeth into his chest. They rushed to intervene.

With both hands Virdeus lifted the imp into the air and twisted its neck clean off its shoulders. The imp's victim lay dead and partially devoured.

"Sir!" shouted Andes. "There's a girl."

Andes pointed into a nearby bedroom. In the dark was a young girl. *She couldn't be more than six or seven.* Virdeus kneeled to get a better look. The girl's countenance was blank. For such a young child to gaze at the mangled corpse of her father, Virdeus thought it was strange to see such a lack of emotion. *Or rather was it an emptiness caused by too much emotion?*

"Little girl, are you okay?" he asked with a conscious lowering of his tone.

He took a deeper look into her eyes. They were fierce, yet reactionless. Inside held a bright hue of copper and brown.

"Oh," he muttered. The trait was all too familiar, but this time it felt more intense than those who had come before.

Sasha sat with her father at a local church sermon. Waking up bright and early on her seventh birthday to listen to a preacher quote scripture was a gift her father said she'd "best be appreciative for, as it's only through the blood of Christ that we are saved. It is the best and only gift a person could need."

It was just the two of them in their family. Sasha's mother had died during labor, so she knew her only through her father's mournful recollections. Despite not knowing her, Sasha couldn't help but feel that she abhorred her mother.

"Remember, all of you, to honor your mother and father," spoke the preacher. "As by doing so you bring honor to our Heavenly Father above. Do not take your parents for granted. Make sure you always love and adore them..."

Sasha sat in silence as she waited for the sermon to come to an end. Her father on the other hand kept shouting "Praise the Lord!" He lost himself in the service and became one with it.

The preacher went on for about an hour before finishing the sermon by stating: "And remember, so long as you have accepted our Lord and Savior into your hearts, you will have secured your seat in Heaven. No matter how sinful a soul is, no matter how sullied and corrupt, if they find salvation in God, Paradise awaits them."

Back at home, her father called for her. Lured in by the sound of his voice, Sasha found her father sitting on his bed in a dim room.

"Come here."

Sasha did as she was told. With each step she took toward her father, she could feel her body's intense trembling.

"You look so much like your mother."

"I know," Sasha gave a mechanical reply.

Sasha was lifted off her feet and placed on her father's lap. She felt something uncomfortable rising beneath his pants. Her father lifted her dress and began to explore her inner thighs with his fingers. He lowered his face to her neck and breathed in his daughter's scent.

"You remind me of her more each day. Every day, I get closer to her."

His grip became tighter. Sasha began to quake. Her eyes filled with tears.

The sound of someone banging on the front door interrupted her father. He removed her from his lap and gestured for her to stay put.

As he approached the door, it was ripped from its hinges with such force that one would think it had been blown away by a cannon. In came a beast neither Sasha nor her father had ever seen before. It pounced on her father, pinning him to the ground, then took a bite out of his chest. Sasha watched her father's heart dangle from the beast's mouth, then she saw the arms of another man reach down for the monster's neck. He snapped it with ease. Sasha got off the bed and approached her father's corpse.

The man who had killed the strange beast was large and muscular, yet old. A long grey beard hung from his wrinkled face. Two other men, appearing as middle aged, emerged from the doorway behind the old man.

"Sir! There's a girl," one of them called out.

The old man took notice of Sasha and kneeled to inspect her. Sasha couldn't react. Her gaze was fixed on her father's corpse.

"Little girl, are you okay?"

Sasha switched her eyes to the bearded stranger, but said nothing.

"Oh," the man muttered, then paused as if he had noticed something peculiar. "You're an interesting one, aren't you?"

He offered his hand with a gradual extension.

"How about you come with us? You will be safe at home with our family. No monsters will hurt you there, I promise."

Sasha had no reason to trust any man, but something about this stranger felt more sincere than any other person she had met. He provided a strong hand to crush the neck of that monster, but gave her a gentle touch. She remembered the rough hand of her father which she had endured so many times. The old man waited with a patient smile. She gave him her hand in return.

On their way out, she looked down at her father one last time.

"What's the matter?" asked the old man.

"My daddy. He's going to heaven now." She paused. "That's not fair."

CHAPTER ELEVEN

EIGHT THOUSAND YEARS AGO.

M ikhail and his younger brother Andes heard their father scream. The small boys who had never heard such fear in their father's voice went to see what was going on. They approached a dark room where at first, they could not tell what they were looking at. Their father and mother were naked on their bed in unrecognizable forms.

The boys' father was sprawled across the bed on his back. His skin was shriveled like fruit that had been left out in the hot sun for weeks. Perched atop his mummified corpse was a grotesque creature that no longer resembled their mother. It appeared female, with its hips and large breasts, but it was not human. Its skin was the grey color of a dead body and out from its back rose scaly black wings. A tail protruded out from beneath them. Nails like daggers emerged from its fingertips.

The young boys screamed. The monster turned to face the children, revealing a face of saggy skin. Its eyes were dark, sunken, and hungry. It screeched and began to chase the boys.

They ran out of the house, but the beast was faster than they were. Andes, the younger of the two brothers, was slower and weaker than Mikhail. Andes fell to the ground, and soon after, saw the monster towering over him. It pinned Andes in place with its right foot and dug its toenails into the boy's chest. He screamed.

Mikhail's adrenaline surged. He picked up a nearby stick and readied himself to charge at the monster, unaware of a group of warriors approaching from behind. This small army was being led by a single man holding a spear.

"Young one, step back!" the man shouted. He lunged the spear into the direction of the monster. It noticed the weapon at the last moment, but it was too late. The spear impaled the succubus, knocking it back and tethering it into the house's rock walls.

The man walked over to the demon, patting the head of Mikhail as he walked by. The man grabbed the spear. A crackle of electricity sparked around his fists and were driven through the spear's metal pole, then into the demon. It went limp. He turned away and went over to the children.

"Are you okay, young one?" he said to Andes. A few men and women who accompanied this bearded man rushed to Andes's side and began to treat his wounds.

"My name is Virdeus," said the man. "You will both be fine now. I promise, and you are quite brave," he said, turning to Mikhail. "Come with me. I will teach you both how to properly fight these beasts."

In 1153 A.D.

In the lulls between hunts, members of the Guild sparred with each other to sharpen their skills. Virdeus being the first one blessed with magic, as well as the oldest, had never lost a sparring bout. Since he had no current equal, he chose to study the others from afar.

They had hollowed out mountains during their long lives and built Guild settlements. The one they were in now laid under Galdo Peak, in the Jotunheimen Mountains of Norway. Norse legends of trolls, ice giants, and witches lured the Guild at first, but none were found. Virdeus found this to be the case for most folklore based in local religions. Virdeus and the other Guild members were the closest beings to witches on Earth, and these legends existed long before the Guild's arrival here. Aside from the common rabble of imps, succubi, incubi, and other grotesque horrors, there were no other demons around. The Guild had wiped out all the local beasts and now it was due time to move on. Virdeus planned to sail west to see what laid beyond the ocean past the European continent. This training session would be their last on this ground.

Virdeus had not told anyone yet, but he felt his energy dropping. After eight thousand years, he had begun to feel old. The Guild hadn't succeeded in slaying all demons, and Virdeus feared he may not live to see that goal realized. In secret, he studied the Guild members in hope that he could pick a suitable replacement as Guild leader. Two men caught his eye over the others. The youngest members, Mikhail and Andes.

Mikhail overwhelmed the woman he was sparring against. She flung droplets of water at him, freezing them into sharp chunks of ice as they flew. He knocked them away with his spear and then knocked her back with rock pillars that erupted from the ground beneath her. Every step of Mikhail's foot commanded the Earth to weaponize against the woman.

Andes lacked the determination of his brother, but overwhelmed his opponent all the same with his billowing fire that coiled around and out from his spear.

After a while, the brothers were the last two standing. They began to spar with each other. Andes shot forth his fire, which Mikhail sidestepped to avoid the flames before raising the stony earth to act as a shield. Andes's fires were so hot, they began to melt the stone. The surrounding Guild members covered their faces with their arms to protect from the heat.

Andes's flames served quite well for situations which called for brute strength, but he faltered in the area where Mikhail prevailed. Mikhail fought his battles with a tactical approach. Having the Earth warp and change at his mercy allowed for defense and offense to spring forward from wherever his opponent stood. While the rocky shield continued to hold, Mikhail thrusted the tip of his spear into the stone in front of him. A barrage of stalagmites broke free from the Earth and shot toward Andes.

Andes broke the stone projectiles with a swing of his spear. He jumped up over the melted rock wall and swung his weapon toward his brother. Mikhail, anticipating this, rose another stone pillar which hit Andes's stomach with blunt force. Andes conceded defeat.

Virdeus approached Mikhail and gestured to him to spar. Mikhail stomped hard upon the ground, which conjured another barrage of stalagmites. Virdeus declined to call upon the elements and instead knocked away the chunks of stone with his fists, reducing them to dust upon impact. Along with the hail of smaller stones came a large, pointed pillar aimed at Virdeus's head. He sidestepped away and then caught the pillar with both hands. Using the momentum of the flying stone to his advantage, He spun around and redirected it toward Mikhail, who blocked the impact with his spear. The force of Virdeus's throw was so severe, it caused Mikhail's spear to ricochet back while losing his balance. Virdeus rushed in like a flash of lightning and landed a punch to Mikhail's face.

Being defeated by Virdeus was no shame to Mikhail, nor was it unexpected. Virdeus had been undefeated for all these long years. The spectating Guild members clapped and cheered for the two participating fighters when Virdeus offered Mikhail his hand. After helping him up, he asked the two brothers to join him for a chat back at his lodgings.

"You both show much promise in your aptitude for magic. You have both earned your spots as my top men." Virdeus frowned. "Listen. There may come a day where I need to name a successor. I am thinking of one of you."

"But why?" Andes asked.

"My body is growing weaker. I'm starting to feel my age. It appears that no human can escape their ultimate fate. Someday one of you will lead the Guild. Keep up your training and make me proud."

Both brothers looked shocked, but they stood proudly. Mikhail looked up to Virdeus with much love. The prospect of being his replacement filled him with euphoric glee.

⬥◇⬥

In 1712.

Mikhail was overtaken by rage at his defeat by Sasha. Once again, as they had done since the establishment of the Guild, all members fought against each other for the sake of sharpening their skills and for sportsmanship among their peers. Sasha, a brand-new member, at the ripe young age of twenty-six, was now the first person aside from Virdeus to defeat Mikhail in a sparring match. He sat in frustration while watching Sasha begin her fight against their Patriarch.

Virdeus conjured bolts of lightning into his palms, and in a flurry, he launched dozens of these electric spears toward Sasha. She hopped out of the way of each one, with just a sole bolt grazing the side of her left arm. She winced as its electrical current cut through her flesh. In retaliation, her body was overtaken by sparks of electricity just as Virdeus had been. She rushed at him, refusing to let the pain in her arm slow her down. She landed swift punches, knocking Virdeus back. The spectators cheered.

Virdeus regained his balance and offered a fast uppercut to Sasha's chin. She was knocked back, but in a handstand-like position, she caught the ground and somersaulted backward before landing on her feet. She maintained her balance throughout it all.

Mikhail rubbed his hands together to sooth his nerves. Seeing Sasha take a hit like that from Virdeus and remain standing was something no one has done before. His nails peeled away his skin in response to the threat.

Sasha rushed toward Virdeus and pressed two fingers into a point in his neck. Virdeus dropped down to his knees. The crowd watched in awe as the energy left his face. Sasha finished him off by lifting her left leg and dropping her foot hard upon the backside of Virdeus's head. His chin slams into the ground. Silence overtook the Guild, followed by enthusiastic applause.

Virdeus had been taking a great interest in Sasha. In just nineteen short years her aptitude for magic had surpassed the rest of the Guild, most of whom were over eight thousand years old. Magic granted them longer life and enhanced strength, but they could only call upon one element. Sasha was different. She shared Virdeus's affinity for electricity, but developed an additional magic alongside it. She found that she could sense and disrupt the flow of magic. Like gripping the roots of a plant and tearing them from the ground.

Virdeus called a meeting with Andes and Mikhail.

"I have come to a decision that I hope you understand."

Mikhail's stomach was in knots over what he had been expecting for quite some time.

"I have called you both here to tell you that I am going to name Sasha as my successor."

Andes nodded in eager acceptance of the news. Mikhail clenched his fists.

"You want to give the Guild to that girl? She doesn't have the age or wisdom for such a responsibility!"

"She will in time," replied Virdeus. "She is good natured and cares for all members of the Guild. Her power is also unmatched, as you have come to know firsthand today. She will make a grand Matriarch."

Mikhail turned and left. A promised gift was being torn away from him by one he deemed unworthy. *I will not stand for this,* he thought as he made his way out.

"Would you like me to talk to him?" Andes asked.

"No, just leave him be. I am sure he will come around," said Virdeus. "Also, do not tell Sasha of this just yet. Mikhail is right about one thing. She is still young. I am unsure of how she will take the news of my eventual passing."

In 1742.

Mikhail watched from afar as Virdeus continued to dote on Sasha. *He once looked at me with that pride.* He then overheard Virdeus say something peculiar to Sasha.

"We need to find the one who blessed me with the gift of magic. The Great One. The demon, Melphis. We have to bring him here."

Mikhail was horrified. Memories of his mother being turned into that grotesque creature and then sucking the life out of his father returned. Mikhail's pride and reason for working so hard to rise in the Guild's ranks was to avenge his parents. To kill demons, nothing more. Yet, Virdeus sought to bring one here? *Not only has he taken the Guild away from me, but he also plans to befriend a demon?*

Mikhail retreated to his abode and waited until the dead of night. He packed a bag full of clothes, food, and supplies. *I cannot be part of this. Virdeus and that girl will lead the Guild to ruin. It should be me leading, not her.* Right before dawn, he snuck away from the Guild.

After wandering a while, Mikhail stumbled upon a small town. In the center was a church. A crowd of people funneled their way into the building. None of them noticed his presence. The rune that hid the Guild from demons also hid them from humans. Virdeus thought that the average human would consider them to be monsters, so the Guild was better off living separate from them. Talking to normal humans was prohibited. Mikhail bit his lip in anger at the thought of Virdeus and his rules.

Mikhail entered the church. He saw a man sitting on the edge of a pew.

"I'm curious about this church. What does your God stand for?" Mikhail asked.

The man stared in silence, unable to know how to respond to such a strange question. Anyone alive would know the teachings of Christ, yet Mikhail had lived a sheltered life of demon hunting and little else.

Overhearing the conversation, a priest walked over to greet Mikhail.

"Excuse me, are you interested in hearing about our faith?" the priest asked.

Mikhail nodded and gave a skeptical glance, realizing this was no mere priest. A dark presence hid beneath the priest's human disguise, but cloaked in shadow. Mikhail could not discern what kind of demon laid in hiding.

""I'd be happy to inform you about our faith. Please follow me into my study,"" said the priest. Mikhail agreed to do so. Upon closing the door, Mikhail unsheathed a knife and readied to plunge it into the monster hiding beneath the priest's human skin.

"Just as I thought," said the priest. "You can see through the veil. How have you come to know magic, human?"

"I have no obligation to the answer the questions of a demon!"

The priest studied the peculiar human man standing before him and smiled.

"Well, you're in luck then. I am no demon, but an angel. I came to Earth to enforce God's word. Please, why don't you put that away and have a chat with me?" The priest sat down and gestured for Mikhail to do the same.

Mikhail had no words. *Angel? Could that be true?* Not even Virdeus had seen an angel before. What Mikhail did know was that demons attacked quickly and impulsively. Yet this priest showed no sign of wanting to fight.

"If you are an angel, prove it. Unveil yourself from that dark fog. Why can't I see your shape?"

"I'd say that is an after effect of your magic. It was never meant to be used by humans. It's poisoning your perception. Please, sit down with me. I promised I would inform you about the teachings of my Lord, after all. Perhaps it can bring you some solace and guidance."

Mikhail relented, sheathed his blade, and sat down.

"Through the love of Christ, we find salvation in God. Through our acceptance of our Lord and Savior, we are promised a place in heaven where we will experience no pain, no suffering, no heartache, and we will want for nothing, as Heaven and the embrace of our God is everything..."

The priest went on for quite a while about the intricacies of the Christian faith. What stuck out to Mikhail the most was the lack of pain in Heaven, the glory of the good, loving God above, and the villainization of Satan and his legion of demons. This church appeared to stand for all that Mikhail took to heart. *If he is really an angel, then he would have the same enemy as I do. His religion is proof that I can trust him, unlike Virdeus. The Guild has lost their way. The people need guidance.*

Before he knew it, Mikhail was talking about the Guild, about slaying demons, about magic. The priest didn't seem shocked by any of it.

"I agree, this Guild of yours needs guidance, as this magic curse that plagues your people is nothing short of witchcraft! Please, introduce me to your people. I have been planning for some time now to expand my evangelical outreach. I would like to set up a new church in your hidden village."

Mikhail agreed. He helped the priest pack his things and together they made their way to the mountain in the dead of night. They snuck back to Mikhail's abode. They agreed to have the priest hide there while Mikhail worked to find supporters to back the building of a church.

He may have had his role as future Patriarch torn away from him, but he was still a high ranking official. By means of his status and by spreading the rumor that Virdeus sought to commit treason by inviting demons into the Guild, Mikhail managed to acquire a large group of followers. They all pledged their support to the opening of a church.

Virdeus disliked the idea. He had found too many religions to be deceitful. He feared that it would poison the Guild, but Mikhail had acquired so many supporters that he feared even more that if he tried to put a stop to it, more problems would ensue.

"Let them do what they want," said Virdeus. "Mikhail has been unhappy for some time now. If this will rectify things, then so be it."

So, the church was established, and it would follow the Guild to every settlement. As soon as it was built, Mikhail gave his immediate resignation of his role under Virdeus and took up priesthood instead. What Virdeus thought might boost morale ended up causing a greater divide between him and his once great warrior.

Having amassed such a large following of supporters, the priest came out of hiding. Mikhail told them all that the priest was an angel who would lead them away from the dark times Virdeus was bringing. The followers of the church praised the priest and made him their Pope.

Despite seeing what laid beneath the priest's disguise, the church had grown far too large to retaliate against. Virdeus did not trust this talk of angels, but had no choice but to feign ignorance. He did so to prolong the inevitable conflict long enough to seek Melphis's aid.

Melphis takes the hand of this strange old man whom he appears to have a history with. Though the chains are gone, I feel too weak to get up. Sasha, noticing my lack of movement, follows the man's example and offers me her hand. She flashes a bright smile. My large, grey demon hands look out of place near the small, soft hands of this petite human woman. Using both hands, she takes hold of one of mine and helps me up. She provides a comforting warmth against my rough skin.

Mikhail groans, then leaves on his own.

"I thought you had died. How is it that I lost track of you? And who are these other people?" Melphis asks.

"I have much to show you, old friend. For now, let's say I've heeded your advice and made a new family," the old man says, letting out a hearty laugh. His glee is interrupted by a stream of coughing. He loses balance. It sounds painful.

After helping me up, Sasha leaves my side to attend to the old man. She rubs his back and helps stabilize his balance until his coughing fit dies down. Melphis strokes his frayed beard, watching the scene play out.

"And what do we have here?" the man says, walking over to me. "A friend of yours, Melphis? Or should we be concerned?"

"Leave him be. I need him," Melphis replies.

He needs me?

"Yes, and he's quite the special one. The magic in him is not only strong, but unique. It feels like what I felt at the crater in New York City," Sasha says.

"If my daughter says so, who am I to argue?" He lets out another laugh. "Pleased to meet you, friend of Melphis. My name is Virdeus. I do hope we get along."

"I'm Seth."

"Seth? A demon with a human name? There's a story here, I'm sure!" Virdeus says.

"I like it," Sasha says, glancing me over. Her eyes wander from my head to my toes and back again.

Strange girl.

"Very well! Let us discuss it over tea. Please follow me," Virdeus says.

"Where are you taking us?" Melphis asks.

"To our current settlement. A city hidden within the mountains, Magistrum."

CHAPTER TWELVE

Virdeus guides us through weaving mountain paths. A strange runic language is carved into stone and trees. I feel my head growing heavy at the sight of them. This disorienting feeling makes me want to turn back. My vision blurs. I stop walking and begin rubbing my temples.

"Don't worry," Sasha says. "It's how we have remained hidden. The runes deter anyone from finding our settlement. I'll help you along."

The warmth of her soft hand slides into mine. Like a mother taking the hand of a child, she leads me forward.

{I told you once before that, like Melphis, there would be other guiding lights. Cherish this one. Do not forsake her.}

There that voice is again. The alleged voice of Adam's father. The way he picks and chooses when to speak up is beginning to anger me. How am I supposed to trust someone I can't see?

"Hey, big guy, you alright?" Sasha asks.

"Uh, yes. It's nothing," I say, then pause. "Before, you said I was interesting. What did you mean by that?"

"Exactly that. You're interesting. Let's just say I have a knack for judging one's magical aptitude. The flow of magic. It speaks to me."

She really is a strange girl. I can't understand what she means, but I decide to go along with it.

"And what does it say about me?" I ask.

"Your magic. It's not just powerful. It's uniquely yours. Your eyes hold such a severe emptiness, yet you aren't empty, are you? I'll have to see it in action, but I can feel a great complexity radiating from within you. A power ripe with growth and possibilities. Could one who is truly empty be capable of that? What I'm saying is, I think your emptiness is a bit more complicated. You're empty, yet full at the same time. A walking contradiction. That's what I mean when I say you're interesting."

"Can't say I understand."

"Understanding oneself is a person's greatest hurdle. The human condition is a frustrating one. We are doomed to forever discover things about ourselves. We work so hard to establish who we are, only to realize that after all that digging, there is more to find. There is always more to find, and that terrifies us."

"Wait, the human condition? Why would you say that to me?"

"Don't underestimate my intuition!" Sasha giggles. "You aren't like other demons. I could tell right away. I don't know how you became like this, but the pain in your eyes is so human."

I'm at a loss for words. How this girl could come to understand so much in such a short time is baffling. Just who is she? And who are the rest of these people?

"I gotta say, this is all so intoxicating. I'm looking forward to learning more about you." She smirks.

Virdeus and Melphis have been keeping silent. The same is the case for Andes, lingering a short way behind Sasha and me. Virdeus, turning to face us, breaks his silence.

"Yes, so do not look so sullen, Seth. You may not be able to see it yet, but greater things still await you. Release yourself from your burdens and embrace life!"

This sort of optimism always annoyed me. I did my best to suppress my irritation.

"That's all well and good, but I've been dead for a while. I don't think I have a place in life anymore."

"Son, I am over nine thousand years old. I should be dead many times over. Don't take my cheerfulness as reason to believe I don't understand your pain. I have been mired by darkness all too many times. Yet I still find joy every day."

I say nothing. It's all nonsense to my ears. Melphis also remains silent, but his inquisitive gaze locks onto Virdeus. As if noticing his old friend's glare, Virdeus says, "Don't worry. I have much to tell, and it will be told soon. Just have patience until we reach my abode." Virdeus leads us into a cave.

Reaching the end of the tunnel, a large open cavern greets us. The ceiling reaches tremendous heights, miles above us. Under this high ceiling sits a small city. The outer area is filled with homes. Further in are towering buildings. The tallest being a skyscraper at the center. Unlike a normal city, this one isn't lit with electricity. It emits an ethereal glow. A bright magical light emerges from streetlamps and buildings like a flame instead of a bulb. It rises like a haze which fills the space above the city. The light sparkles like an artificial starry sky.

"Welcome to our home. Our city of Magistrum is one of many settlements. We've been here the longest, so it's the most developed."

"All this is powered by magic?" Melphis asks.

Virdeus lets out a hearty laugh. "Like I said, old friend, there is much to tell you. I developed more uses for magic based on what you left me. I hope it pleases you! Oh, as we continue through the city, you may be greeted with some unkind faces. Pay them no mind."

Virdeus leads us further into the city. The negative response to our presence is immediate. Large crowds of people begin to leave their homes, swarming the streets. A sea of scowls in every direction. Despite how they are moving out of the way as Virdeus approaches, they appear ready for a fight. The tension of the situation feels as if it's thickening in the air.

"They seem unhappy," Melphis says. "I thought you made a new family. Being disturbed by our presence I understand, but they do not seem happy to see you either. Quite the cold welcoming."

"Sounds like a normal family to me," I say.

"Things were good for a while," Virdeus responds. "It was only over the last few hundred years that things changed. We will talk more on that in a minute. It isn't safe here."

A stunning gothic church is sitting off to the right of us. Its beauty doesn't change how uneasy the image of it makes me. That man, Mikhail, is standing out front with other priests. He wears a black robe while the other priests are wearing white. His glare makes me feel unsettled, but what puts me more on edge is another presence I feel coming from within the church. Is someone, or something, hiding inside?

We arrive at the tower in the center of the city. Virdeus leads us inside. To all sides of us are Guild members deep in conversation. I overhear them speaking about demon sightings and their plans to hunt. Some are sitting by rows of computers showing video feeds from all over the world.

We reach an elevator and make our ascent. The dark walnut double door that awaits us at the top is lined with silver. "Sasha,

Andes, please wait outside while I talk to our guests," Virdeus says. They do what they're told. Virdeus shuts the door behind us and lets out a heavy sigh.

"I have been searching for you a while, old friend," Virdeus says.

"What is this about?" Melphis asks. "We do not have the time for this."

"And yet you came. Sure, Sasha gave you quite the fight, but once I showed myself, you came readily and without question. I can assume you know something about what is going on here. Something that falls in line with whatever journey you and your friend here are on?"

"I might, but I believe I asked you for answers."

Virdeus lets out another hearty laugh that quickly transitions into a rough coughing fit.

"Sasha believes we were searching for you to cure me. She's not my actual daughter, but she might as well be. She wishes for my life to continue."

"But you don't?" Melphis responds.

"I've lived for over nine thousand years. I'm ready to pass on my role to the younger generation—to Sasha and the others. Perhaps they—perhaps she can do better than I did. Which brings me to the purpose of the Guild. We've been slaying demons for thousands of years now. Yet there is no end to them. I fear I won't live to see my goal realized, so at the very least I want to learn how to accomplish it. So, my question to you is...how can we eradicate all demons, and can you help us do it?"

Melphis stares at Virdeus in bewilderment.

Virdeus continues, "I understand the ludicrous nature of this request. Asking a demon to kill all demons. But at one point you looked at me with empathy. You gave me this gift of magic with the purpose of renewing my life. You gave me the power to fight back. I can only imagine that you feel the same way I do. Don't you want to free humanity from its continued torment?"

"I cannot agree to this," Melphis responds. "I seek to rule over Hell. To rule requires the support of those who are living. What good are corpses to me?"

Virdeus's gleeful countenance wanes. It's if his strength that helps mask his sickness is torn away. All that is left is a dying old man.

"However," Melphis continues. "You're right. I do wish to end the suffering of humans. I seek to end the involvement of demons in human lives. I desire a world where demons and humans can live separately. And I have a way to do it. That's what Seth and I have been working toward."

Virdeus lifts his head up. The light in his eyes return.

"And what is this method of yours?" Virdeus asks.

Melphis explains his goal to usurp Hell's throne by cutting off Satan's power at its source, the Sins. By removing Satan from power, demonkind will lose their purpose. Melphis explains that once he takes the throne, he can influence the demons to reside solely in Hell, where they will never burden humanity again.

"Sins? Satan? Are you telling me that Satan is real and that demons are organized? I always assumed they were nothing but mindless beasts! Monstrous animals!" His face turns grim. "What do you know of angels?"

"I can't say for sure they exist. Never met one," Melphis says. "Why do you ask?"

Virdeus explains the other reason that he had been searching for Melphis—the establishment of the church that had created such a divide between members of the Guild. The head priest is a mysterious figure who entered the Guild without Virdeus's knowledge. This priest claims to be an angel sent by God to help the Guild eradicate demons. Though instead the presence of the priest had created a faction hostile to Virdeus. "I believe they have been planning a coup. This so-called angel seeks to garner power over the entire Guild, I just know it."

"You know, I felt a strange presence when we walked past the church before," I say.

"So did I," Melphis says. "I believe you are right to doubt them, Virdeus. It's true that I've never met an angel before, but I know a demonic presence when I feel one. It also helps that I've met this one before. I know her and her siblings quite well. Though she's been missing for a while."

"You don't mean," Virdeus says, then turns to me. "Seth, can I ask what your role is in all this? My daughter is right. Your power is unique and powerful, but that look in your eye—there's a storm inside you. I'm sorry to ask, but how can I know you're trustworthy?"

I am at a loss for words. I don't even trust myself, so his concern is valid. Satan created me after all. So much has happened that I don't know what to think.

"I've vouched for him," Melphis says.

"Old friend, consider my feelings for a moment. I thought I could trust you, too, but now you tell me one of these Sins is amongst the members of my Guild and that you know her? How can I trust that you aren't on their side?"

"It's precisely because I know them that I'm in a position to kill them! I proved that I'm on your side the day I carved that rune into your neck, you old fool."

The double door leading into Virdeus's abode swings open. Andes runs in, out of breath.

"Sir, there's trouble! The church has launched an attack on the headquarters!"

A little earlier.

Pride, Wrath, and Sloth approached a war-torn field at the foot of the Rocky Mountains. Following the two suspicious humans Pride had seen in New York City after finding Greed dead. The old man and the girl with black hair had disappeared into the forest, but Pride could still feel their presence nearby, along with the presence of their brother's slayer.

"We followed those humans and ended up finding Melphis along the way as well. He's close. What's his connection to these strange humans?" asked Pride.

His two brothers remained silent. Uncharacteristic of Wrath, but understandable considering the area was coated in their brother's bodily fluids.

Sloth broke his silence. "What happened to Gluttony?"

Pride ground his teeth in frustration. "Come. Those humans went this way."

The three brothers marched toward the forest. It wasn't long before they spotted the old man and the girl. Just as Pride thought, *they are now with Melphis and that peculiar demon he befriended—the one Satan declined to tell the Sins about.* The mixed group of humans and demons entered a cave surrounded by strange runes. They made Pride and his two brothers dizzy, but they pushed on through. They kept close enough to not lose track of the group, but far enough to not be noticed.

Pride grew agitated at the situation's development, but nothing could stop their thirst for revenge. The impossible had occurred. They lost not one, but two brothers when they had once thought themselves to be immortal. Ripe with anger, they went forth in pursuit of the coming carnage.

CHAPTER THIRTEEN

Virdeus, with a grimace, goes to exit the room.

"Please forgive my bout of distrust. Will you help us?" Virdeus asks.

"Our enemy is one and the same," Melphis says. "Has this priest mentioned their name?"

"He calls himself Cassiel."

"An expected lie. No such demon exists."

We hasten toward the elevator. Virdeus appears bothered. I wouldn't call it anxiety, but it's if some old burden has just grown heavier.

"This Guild used to be so close. We were a loving community that always sought to grow stronger together. Leading these people—no, being a part of this family, filled me with pride. Now, all I have is Sasha. She alone is where I derive my pride from. We need to hurry to her side.

"Seth, I don't mean to pry," Virdeus continues, "and far be it for me to give advice to one I have only just met, but take it from an old fool who has lived far too long: one's pain can either destroy, or it can create. Your pain...feels unstable. It is wavering back and forth at intense and unpredictable intervals. Wielding chaos can make one feel powerful and indeed, it does! But that power, if allowed to run amok, comes with a great cost. If it hasn't yet, it will. Control and discipline are vital to one's growth of character."

"While I agree with you," Melphis says. "What makes you think you know him so well?"

Virdeus's hearty laugh bellows. He sounds even louder in the enclosed space of the elevator.

"I have raised every Guild member as if they were my own. I watched how each of them reacted to the awakening of their magic. It was the same with all of them. They went through a growing period, as if their magic had to first experience puberty before stabilizing. It bred chaos and emotional instability in all of them. There were some...unfortunate losses. Accidents caused by the lack of control over their magic. Not a day goes by that I do not picture the faces of those we've lost. I know a young and volatile magic when I see it. You haven't been a demon for long, have you, Seth?" Virdeus says.

My agitation was rising at first, but now I feel calm. Virdeus doesn't even know or trust me, yet he's taking time during this crisis to give me guidance? His words are also soaked in a genuine kindness. That's the sense I get anyway.

I remember when Sasha took a fierce battle stance against Melphis. She and her peculiar magic allowed her to take us down with ease. She was terrifying at first. Then when Virdeus intervened, she softened to the point of feeling like an entirely different person. Something about Virdeus elicits such great respect in her. I'm starting to understand why. The guidance of a loving father figure.

"Anyway, this is what I've always told the Guild. Even the most harmful emotions can be turned into useful tools. The only one who gets to decide whether something is a curse or a blessing is the one who houses those grand emotions. One of the great epochs of our lives is when we gain the courage to rebaptize our badness as the best in us."

Wait. I've heard these words before—back in Melphis's hideout when I had first met him. It was in that second dream of the White Abyss. Adam's father said almost the same thing, but why—

The whole building shakes. In an explosion of bending metal and shattering glass, the building begins to collapse. Our bodies turn sideways. The walls that are securing us crumbles apart until nothing stands between us and the cold, cave air outside. The floor beneath my feet is taken away from me. The four of us begin falling miles above the surface.

My body falls without any knowledge of how to act. An onslaught of stone flies toward me. Most of the debris grazes past without issue, but one—I open my mouth to scream, but no words are released. My body enters a state of shock as I lose my depth of field. The top left side of my head has been blown clean off. Teal sparks of magic rise from the wound, weaving my brain back together. The skull is repaired, then skin, then hair. My vision returns to find Virdeus staring at me with a curious glare. He returns to gracefully avoiding the debris.

Melphis, Virdeus, and Andes use the force of their magic and the momentum of the descent to avoid and destroy any debris that comes their way. They land much steadier on the cave's flooring than I do.

We find Sasha fighting alongside a small group of soldiers. The church's troops surround them. The difference in numbers is staggering. I assumed that Virdeus, being the leader of these people, would have control over the majority, but that appears not to be so.

Sasha is holding her own. Fire, stone, water, and wind. All the elements are being flung at her by the church's troops, but none are fast enough. The combination of her speed and strength breaks the metal poles as she kicks them away. After making the soldiers defenseless, she goes straight for their necks, breaking them.

These are people she must have at one point considered friends. Yet she is able to act without faltering. I was just beginning to feel useful to Melphis, but the sight of her is filling me with profound inadequacy. Everyone here has such great control over their power. I feel jealous—worried, even, that Melphis might toss me away if I don't remain useful. What if he asks for the help of this Guild and then doesn't need me anymore? I'd no longer have a way to find Lola. Yet I feel strange. Watching Sasha makes me feel jealous, but also something else. I can't help but to be in awe of her alluring strength.

"Let's help her out, shall we?" Virdeus says to me.

I have no idea why he's addressing me rather than Melphis, but I nod. We approach the two battling factions. Sasha's eyes light up, but she's too focused on fending off the church to speak. With Sasha fighting in the middle of the crowd, we begin picking off the soldiers on the crowd's outer rim. Their numbers thin out. The steps of the Guild's headquarters are littered with bodies.

"Virdeus, it's about time you relinquish the Guild to us," says Mikhail, just now joining his troops. "Bringing demons into the fold. Now, really, what were you thinking?"

The fight halts. The remnant of the church's army clears a path for Mikhail.

"What are *you* thinking?" Sasha says. "Letting envy control your every action, you pathetic man! The demons are here to help father cure his sickness. How is that not a good thing? The Guild needs their leader."

Virdeus and Melphis keep quiet. I decide to follow their example. Virdeus said he had no intention of being healed, and

Sasha wasn't aware of that. If she did find out, I'm sure she would be distraught. We are better off sparing her feelings, for now.

"I say let him die," says Mikhail.. "He has led this Guild astray for too long. In the name of God and his loyal servant, Archangel Cassiel, I will now carry out the execution of Virdeus."

At Mikhail's command, the remaining troops swarm us.

Sasha manages to break through the troops and rush at Mikhail alone.

"Will she be okay?" I ask.

"Don't worry about her, lad," Virdeus says. He looks into my eyes as if he is searching for something. "Easy does it, young one. Do not let that bright flame devour us whole. The way to deal with a host of problems is...one at a time. Focus on the foes in front of you. Sasha will be fine."

Mikhail sees Sasha approaching and grips his scepter. He slams its rounded top into the cave's floor. A barrage of stalactites rushes out at Sasha. She leaps over them and toward Mikhail. She reaches out for his throat like she had done to his subordinates. Her face is scrunched in anger. Her fingers are inches away from his throat when Mikhail swings his scepter down upon her head. Sasha falls to the ground.

She rises to her feet while conjuring electric magic. She rushes toward Mikhail, wielding a bolt of lightning in each of her palms. She readies herself to throw them at Mikhail, who stomps the ground with his feet. A thick, tall wall of stone springs up to shield him from the bolts. Sasha smiles. The bolts dissipate and reemerge as sparks enveloping her body. She picks up speed. Her body blurs in my vision. She punches the stone wall. Her fist breaks straight through and grabs Mikhail's neck. The wall crumbles apart, revealing his terrified face.

"That's enough, Mikhail. You have served your purpose," says an unfamiliar voice.

A priest stands behind Mikhail. A certain pressure is given off from him. I felt it before from inside the church.

"That's Cassiel, the self-proclaimed angel," Virdeus says.

The priest grins. At first, it's just like a human's smile. Then I notice what lies beneath. A dark obscuring shadow. The priest's mouth stretches back. Blood squirts out from the ripping skin. The flesh beneath melts away, revealing a skeletal face that begins to grow. A dark fog erupts from the cuffs and bottom of the priest's flowing black robe. A moment later, the skeletal face rises six feet higher. Bony hands with long, sharp talons emerge out of the tattered robe.

Sasha, taken aback by the priest's new form, lets go of Mikhail's neck and retreats to us.

"No...what are you?" Mikhail says, shocked by what his master has become. "You told me you were an angel!"

The skeletal figure glares down at Mikhail before impaling his chest with its long nails. Blood pours down its bony fingers before tearing Mikhail in two. A teal, ethereal form emerges from Mikhail's dead body. *It looks just like those souls I met inside Gluttony.* The soul looks as if it is trying to fly away, but as if by some gravitational force, it is pulled toward the skeletal demon and sucked into the monster's open face holes. Mikhail's soul lets out a screech before disappearing into the monster's dark fog.

"As I said before, Cassiel isn't its real name," Melphis says. "She's even been lying about her gender. This is the Sin, Envy."

The monster turns to face us. Her body of dark fog covers more space with each passing moment. "Nice to see you again, Melphis."

Nine thousand years ago.

The Sins exited Castle Pandaemonium after a routine check-in with Satan. Together for the last time, all seven siblings were about to return to their duties on Earth. Pride led them out with Greed and Wrath hinged to his shoulders. Gluttony and Sloth lumbered behind them. Lust further behind still. At the very back of the family, Envy skulked.

They were about to disperse when Pride turned to Envy. "It's your turn to check up on Melphis. Do your duty. See if there's any difference in his demeanor." Their vain, self-proclaimed leader was gone before Envy could mutter a response. She clenched her teeth. Blood poured from the gums of her current human vessel. The crimson liquid evaporated in Hell's heat before it could drip onto the floor. She headed toward the cliffside overlooking the Sea of Flames.

That damned brother of mine. We all work so hard, yet he receives all of Satan's praise! Gluttony is the only other Satan appreciates, yet even his praise is given to Pride! He pockets the love that we should receive!

"The number of souls transported has increased since last time. Gluttony has done well," Envy remembered Satan saying to Pride. Gluttony didn't mind. He might not even have been aware of this indirect praise. *That mindless behemoth! Content just doing as he's told! Makes me sick. And then there's this one.*

Envy arrived at the cliffside and found Melphis sitting in his usual spot. A book in his lap. A pen in his hand.

"Scribbling away again?"

"Wrath asked the same thing. So did Lust before him. You Sins really are cut from the same predictable cloth, aren't you?"

To be called the same as her brothers was a joke to Envy. She had found the opposite to be true. Satan never acknowledged her. She was expected to keep quiet in the shadows while Satan and Pride carried out each discussion. She had not even a fraction of the respect Pride was given.

"What are you up to, anyway? You appeared out of nowhere on Hell's Edge, then won Satan's trust with ease. It's curious, to say the least." Envy was wondering why she was doing what Pride asked of her without question.

"It's uncanny," Melphis said. "Wrath also said something along those same lines. Answer me something first. You Sins like to think of yourselves as the ones in control of the farm. The demons are your tools. Humans, your cattle. Yet you all lack a proper name past the vice you embody. I know what to expect from you before you do it. Like hungry little lambs suckling from Satan's teat."

Envy turned away, fed up with dealing with the rebellious demon. *How does that little shit garner so much respect from Satan? Why do I put up with babysitting him?* She grew angry. She was tired of being overlooked. She would rather be a lion than a lamb. She took one last look around Hell, then opened a portal back to Earth.

She decided to take inspiration from her Creator. After wandering the Earth for a while, she came across a primitive tribe of humans. Amongst them were their leader and spiritual guide. Envy assimilated the priest and made his appearance her own. She understood a great flaw in humanity, if a strong male presence spoke to a crowd, the people would follow without question. Using this to her advantage, she took on the role of this holy man's life. Years went by and the tribe grew larger. Envy then devoured them all.

Souls are power. Envy sought to eat the souls of as many humans as possible. Not only would she grow more powerful, but it would also siphon away the very same power her siblings worked so hard to acquire for their Creator. After the ceremonious feasting on their souls, Envy went off to search for a new tribe. The differing morals and guidelines of each religion or cult didn't matter to her. She would adapt to each role and the result would be the same. She continued this process for thousands of years, with the hope that she would one day be more powerful than her brothers and Creator. She sought to spill the blood of her family and become goddess of all.

———◦◦◦◦———

In 1742.

"I'm curious about this church. What does your god stand for?" a man said. Envy, who was now masquerading as a priest of this Christian church, walked over to greet the man.

She realized right away that this was no normal human. She knew that humans were not capable of wielding magic, yet here one stood in front of her. She invited the man with the powerful soul to her office. Upon closing the door, the man unsheathed a knife and readied himself to attack. *This man must be able to see through the veil. He really does have magic. How curious.*

After calming the man by claiming to be an angel, Envy managed to get him to open up about the origins of his magic. She learned of an elusive group of magical human warriors that sought to eliminate all demonkind. Her interest in anything else vanished. All she wished to hear about was this Guild. Just a few minutes before, the concept of a human who could wield magic was an absurd notion. Now she had stumbled into the knowledge of a whole host of powerful magic souls. She needed them. They were the key to acquiring the power necessary to achieve her goal. A grand feast awaited her.

CHAPTER FOURTEEN

E nvy's dark fog is spreading fast. It creeps along the city's streets and soon engulfs the whole cavern. We all watch in horror as she eats Mikhail. A pool of tears gathers in Virdeus's eyes, despite the two of them being enemies.

"What are you doing here, Envy?" Melphis asks.

"Oh, you don't know? I thought we Sins were predictable?" Envy says. "I have been grooming these magic souls and picking them one at a time as they ripen."

Envy raises her right hand. Her index and middle fingers curl toward her, as if she is gesturing at someone to come closer. Ethereal forms emerge from the corpses of the church's troops. A collective screech echoes throughout the cavern before Envy siphons them away through her face holes. Her fog body grows darker and larger. The fog overtakes the entire city.

"My fog acts as a web," Envy says. "So long as they are in the vicinity of the fog, no soul will reach Hell. They are all for me! And thank you, Virdeus, for planting this city in a cave. It is a perfect capsule."

Melphis appears confused. I'm not used to seeing him as anything other than calm and composed. Something feels off.

"Now answer me something," Envy says. "Why are you here?"

"We are on a hunt for the Sins. We've already killed two of you."

Silence overtakes the city for a moment. Envy breaks out in jovial laughter.

"Ah, Melphis! How like you to be so blunt! So, you've killed two of my brothers? You beat me to it! Did you enjoy it?"

"So, it's true," Melphis says. "I thought something was strange about you being here. A Sin being amongst magical humans, and yet Satan has no idea they exist? You've betrayed your family, haven't you?"

"Is that judgement I hear in your voice? Remember, you and I are both traitors. Why not pay me the respect I deserve and let me help you kill the rest of my brothers?"

Melphis takes a few steps toward Envy. I glance around at the others. It seems they share my worries. We are mere voyeurs looking in on a conversation between two individuals with a long and complex past. If Envy genuinely wants her brothers killed, will Melphis agree to her proposition? Will he toss me away for her? My suspicions about Melphis intensify. My insecurities about my role in all this increase tenfold. Ever since we got here, I have not stopped thinking about how inadequate I am.

"Melphis, old friend," Virdeus says, "what—"

"Envy. I salute your newfound volition to defy Satan," Melphis interrupts. "But your murderous intent is less subtle than a shark that has just picked up a whiff of blood."

Melphis's arms, hidden behind his back, swing forward bearing bolts of lightning. The electric crackle illuminates the space around him. He plunges the bolts at Envy. The light pierces the dark fog as they fly quickly through the air, but Envy's skeletal body proves to be as elusive as the obscuring fog which surrounds her. She vanishes into the fog, reappears behind Melphis, and swings her claws down upon him.

Melphis turns around in time to see Envy's long nails hovering above his head. Holding her hand in place is Virdeus, who moved so fast that I didn't even notice him rushing over. The man is incredibly old and dying by his own admission. This makes his strength even more impressive. His shaking arms steadies Envy's palm in place, but the force of the Sin's strength causes Virdeus to sink into the ground. The stone streets beneath their feet begin to crack into a large spiderweb of fissures.

Sasha, Andes, and I rush in to help. Sasha conjures multiple lightning bolts. Andes and I wield our fire. Our magic momentarily illuminates the surrounding space, as we weave our way through the fog toward the Sin. We launch our magic. Envy vanishes again and reappears at a secure distance.

"Are you alright, father?" Sasha asks.

"These old muscles have life in them yet. Don't worry about me," Virdeus answers.

Sasha appears skeptical. I share her suspicions. Virdeus's arms and core are splattered in blood and cracked skin. In other areas where the flesh isn't torn are blotches of pink skin, indicating blood pooling up just beneath the surface.

"Though I have to say, she is far stronger than the demons I've fought before," Virdeus continues.

"You have made your bed, Melphis!" Envy screeches. "There may be more of you, but you will never touch me. Let my fog overwhelm you as I pick you off, one by one!"

Pride, Wrath, and Sloth continue to make their way through the dark, narrow cavern. Pride knows the end of the cavern is approaching. They lost track of Melphis and his peculiar human companions some time ago, but the trace of his magic is still on the tip of Pride's tongue. In fact, the magic grows stronger with each step they take. Not only in strength, but in numbers as well. Pride senses that an army of magical souls awaits them on the other side of the cavern.

This alarms Pride, but also heightens his curiosity. This is especially true once a certain source of magic stirs in Pride's senses. Within this army of unknown magic souls, there is one other besides Melphis that Pride recognizes.

"Do you feel that, my brothers?" Pride asks. "Our long-lost sister is nearby. What an interesting reunion."

Envy dissipates into the fog again. Since her mist has enveloped the entire city, it is impossible to know where she might spring up. I glance over at Melphis. His eyes shift around, trying to anticipate where Envy's attack will come from. Sasha remains close to Virdeus, who is ready to engage in battle despite his harsh injuries. Andes is at Sasha's side, ready to aid her in protecting Virdeus. He appears to be the unflinchingly loyal type—much like a dog. Something about his demeanor makes it feel as if he would do anything for Sasha and Virdeus. He grips his spear tight. Flames spiral around the pole and blade.

The city grows quiet with Envy not reappearing for quite some time. Only a few minutes have passed, but the suspense makes it feel far longer. My heart begins to beat rapidly. I wonder if the others are feeling the same way, or if this is just me being inexperienced and broken, as usual. I don't know. All I do know is that this tension is becoming unbearable.

In a sudden movement, Envy reappears to swipe her long, bladelike fingernails down upon us. She appears, vanishes, then reappears in quick and random intervals, slashing at us from all sides. I see her claw pierce Melphis's right shoulder. Then I feel a searing pain in my lower abdominal. Blood spills from my side.

Our little group is doing the best we can to avoid Envy's onslaught, but the wounds are accumulating. Even Sasha with her great speed, can't seem to avoid every slash of Envy's nails. As the pain continues to build, I wonder why we haven't received a mortal blow yet. Like a cat swatting around a helpless mouse before dealing the final, fatal blow, it feels like Envy is first toying with us before deeming us worthy of being her meal.

Andes and I summon our fire. Melphis, Sasha, and Virdeus all form bolts of lightning in each palm.

"She was never like this before," Melphis says. "Years of eating souls has made her strong, sure, but it appears to have made her overconfident as well."

One after another, we plunge our magic toward Envy as she reappears multiple times. Her speed outmaneuvers us and all we accomplish is lighting up paths through the mist. Our magic ripping through the dense darkness for a moment before it weaves back together.

"How can we rid the city of this fog?" I ask.

"Sasha, can't you stop her, like you did to us?" Melphis asks.

"Impossible. I can't disrupt the flow of magic without physical contact with the source," Sasha answers.

Envy's fury continues. Her rapid slashing uproots the base of the Guild's headquarters. The part of the building that remained standing after the initial attack topples over and shatters. The debris rains down on us, stealing our attention away from Envy.

"I grow bored of this!" the Sin screeches. She dissipates into the dark fog once more, and the high-octane flow of battle comes to an abrupt halt. Time seems to slow for a moment before the fog, morphing and rising above Andes, solidifies into Envy's skeletal body. She thrusts her nails toward him—

A loud, male groan echoes throughout the city. Ten sword-like nails protrude from his torso. Crimson liquid drips down Envy's nails. Both of her hands pierce his flesh. I can feel a flood of emotion. My throat tightens. My chest swells with anger. My eyes overwhelm with tears at what I'm seeing. Virdeus coughs up blood.

Andes sits on the ground in horror as he gazes upon his savior. Virdeus pushed Andes away at the last moment and became his scapegoat. Sasha is stunned, silent. I wanted to save her from the pain of Virdeus's acceptance of his eventual death, but how can I save her from this?

"I d-didn't...want to see..." Virdeus stammers, "another one of my children die. Sasha, my daughter...I'm sorry. And Seth...please...remember my advice."

We watch in horror as Envy lifts Virdeus up and pulls her hands in opposite directions. The old man's flesh is reduced to threads as his body is torn in two. An ethereal form rises from it. Unlike the others, it does not scream. It remains silent, calm, and content in a reverie as it is absorbed into Envy's face holes. The teal glow of Virdeus's soul fades. All that is left behind is Envy's skull face staring us down.

My mind drifts back to Virdeus's advice. It was a luxury I never had before—parental love. What is with this cruel world and giving me brief moments of joy, only to tear them away right after? The same happened with Lola. I was happy, then she was taken from me. She left behind a void. A void that this sick world insists on filling with horrors.

Envy lets out a laugh which echoes throughout the city. Its pitch drives me to the edge.

Sasha's field of view is overtaken by tears. The city's lights blur and appear to her as a glistening water painting. This is the second time she had watched her father die. Only this time, it hurts. The pain is so severe that she is rooted in place. As much as she would like to avenge her loving foster father, she can't muster up the strength to do so. For the first time since being molested by her biological father, she feels powerless. She becomes so petrified by the horror in front of her that she can't even turn her neck. Not until an intense glow catches her attention.

She turns to face Seth. This peculiar demon who has taken her interest has fallen to his knees, his body, stiff as stone. She can feel an intensity building up within him. Something isn't right. Sasha turns to Melphis, of whom appears just as concerned, though unsurprised. Seth's pupils disappear. His eyes shift to pure white orbs.

Seth lets out a sudden and loud, harsh growl of bloodlust. Sasha feels the cave's temperature rising rapidly. It becomes hard to breathe. The tears streaming her face begin to sizzle along her skin.

"Both of you, come close. Now!" Melphis shouts. Sasha and Andes are too shaken up to grasp why Melphis is rushing them, but they do as they are told.

Seth's grey skin takes on a dark blue color—his pores begin spewing bright blue flames with intense ferocity. His body, channeling the flames of Hell. His rage manufactures them into even hotter, hungrier flames ready to devour all in their path.

Sasha knows that Seth houses powerful magic. She felt it radiate from his eyes when they first met, but this is the first time she lays witness to Seth's potential. It's awe inspiring, but he's out of control. Seth frightens Sasha.

Melphis raises his staff high above their heads. A magic barrier envelops them just before Seth's flames wash over. The shield shakes. The ground beneath crumbles. Melphis winces in pain. The shield is already breaking. Seth's fires are too chaotic for Melphis to defend against. The flames are bent on ravaging everything.

An idea is roused within Sasha's mind. Her ability to manipulate the flow of magic. She has so far only used the ability to restrict demons, but in the midst of panic, she finds inspiration.

Envy's laughter ceases at the sight of this unexpected turn of events. Virdeus was a hearty soul. Guild leader and longest living human. Even as an old man, his soul was rich with strong magic. Envy feels her power increasing exponentially. Yet she now finds herself feeling a certain unpleasantness that she has not felt for nine thousand years. Inadequacy.

This unknown demon at Melphis's side spews flames out from every inch of his body, which spreads rapidly across the city. Melphis conjures a barrier over himself, Sasha, and Andes. Envy has no such magic. She has always relied on her obscuring fog to defend herself, but what good is it if she can no longer hide?

The fast-approaching flames melt and distort the frames of each of the city's buildings. With its insatiable appetite and unquenching rage, it illuminates the entire city, ridding the cave of Envy's fog. Left as just a skeleton in a tattered robe, she, along with her dream of rising above her family, melts away, but not before the form of wings take shape behind her. With the fog dispersed, they are no longer obscured. Her feathers burn and are reduced to ash.

Pride and his brothers are just about to exit the cavern and encounter the glowing city of Magistrum when an engulfing light blinds them. They duck back into the cavern, narrowly avoiding the ravenous blue flames. The fires die down and Pride peeks around the corner to glimpse what has become of the city. The thousands of magic souls, including the one he recognized as his sister, fade away. There is a faint pulse of power further away from the city. Some of the magic humans may have escaped or have been away at just the right time. Inside the city, however, is empty—*No, wait.* As the fires continue to extinguish, Pride feels the presence of four tired souls at the center.

The Sins walk through the decimated city to meet their foes. Piles of charred humans lay scattered around the streets. Others have been crushed by their demolished homes. *Just what sort of power could cause such a massive loss of life so quickly?*

Sasha had acted just in time. By taking Andes's hand and gripping Melphis's shoulder with her other, she managed to direct both her and Andes's magic into Melphis. Doing so strengthened the barrier, allowing them to just barely make it through. The three of them gasp for air.

Sasha looks over to Seth who is laying face first on the melted concrete. He's breathing, but unconscious.

"We finally catch up to you, Melphis," says an approaching voice. "And you've killed another of our kin?"

Melphis glances toward the voice. Pride, Wrath, and Sloth stand before him.

CHAPTER FIFTEEN

"And here I thought we'd finally be reunited with our long-lost sister," Pride says. "But you've killed her before I even got to say hello."

Wrath's rage grows rapidly. Sloth, whom Melphis has always known to be absent-minded and aloof even begins to show signs of anger at the sight of his sibling's murderer.

"Would it help to know that she was a traitor? She sought to kill you," Melphis says.

"Scum like you are in no position to call her a traitor," Pride says. "Like Greed and Gluttony before her, you've taken the life of one of my beloved siblings. Any qualms Satan has with you is irrelevant. All I desire now is to spill your blood, just as you have spilled the blood of my family."

Pride wastes no more time on words. His vessel's skin peels away. His limbs bloat to ten times the thickness of a large male human. Two extra arms extend from beneath the others. His head balloons to a size too large for the shoulders that carry it. His face is featureless at first. A long grin tears its way through the skin. A trail of blood stretches far past his ears as his large gaping mouth opens to seven rows of sharp teeth. A dozen eye sockets rip open around his dome, housing bright yellow orbs with tiny, black pupils.

Wrath and Sloth also shed their vessels. Like Pride, they have grotesque and enlarged humanoid forms, but smaller still than Pride.

A raging temper, Sasha notices, is not the sole trait Wrath shares with Seth. His form, too, resembles Seth, though a bit larger. His muscles grow to five times the mass of his human vessel. His massive fingers are crowned with sharp nails. Sasha remembers seeing Seth's eyes light with the color of flames just before his eruption, but Wrath's eyes are ice colored. It feels as if his glare alone could shatter diamonds.

Sloth sits down on the ground before revealing his demonic form. His skin peels back slowly at first, before bursting apart due to not being able to contain his mass. His gut protrudes and hangs from all sides of him. Under his flap of stomach fat lays a large boil-covered flaccid penis. It stiffens as his beady black eyes lock onto Sasha. Slime drips from his mouth as he flashes his rotting, green teeth at her.

Andes steps in front of Sasha, blocking Sloth's view of her. Sasha moves over to Seth's unconscious body, noticing that Wrath's attention is caught by the sleeping demon. Pride's mass places a divide between Melphis and the others. Envy was enough trouble, but here Melphis, Sasha, and Andes, stand before three Sins, tired and ragged. Melphis had warned Seth at the beginning of their partnership that this situation was to be avoided—that under no circumstances should they fight more than one at a time. Yet here they each found themselves pinned against a Sin. They ready themselves for battle, one that they worry will be their last.

Pride brings a fist the size of a sedan down upon Melphis. Melphis staggers out of the way just soon enough to avoid impact. A small crater is left in the spot where Melphis had been standing.

Melphis raises his staff toward Pride. By freezing the water particles in the air, he conjures lances made of ice. He launches them at Pride. They are about to pierce the Sin's flesh when they begin to dissipate. Their sharp points are a couple inches away from Pride's skin before dispelling into a harmless mist.

Melphis glances over at Seth who shows no signs of waking up. *How cruel of you to become useless to me now.* Melphis is grateful to Seth for slaying Envy. It is just that sort of unexpected conflict that he had chosen to bring Seth along on this journey in the first place. *I could have slain Greed and Gluttony myself, but Envy would have been impossible without Seth's help.* As Pride towers over him, Melphis sees another impossible situation. Out of all the Sins to have to fight alone, Pride is the worst match up for Melphis.

As his ice magic dissolves, Melphis remembers how Pride's magic takes shape. Like Envy, he cannot be touched. Unlike Envy, Pride's confidence is real and so is the impregnable barrier that encases his body. Pride grins. His many rows of teeth are coated in saliva.

Melphis has little time to catch his breath before Pride lunges his four massive fists again. In a series of hops and rolls, Melphis avoids the barrage, but then he sees all four coming at once. The massive hunks of flesh cover too much space. Melphis, unable to dodge, conjures a magic barrier. It holds, but fissures soon form in the teal casing of the magic shield.

Melphis tries in vain to discern any weaknesses in Pride's defenses. Sasha and Andes are locked in battle and are unable to aid him.

Andes grips his spear and rushes toward Sloth. The Sin groans, but refrains to budge.

Andes jumps on top of Sloth's large torso and jabs at him with his spear. The blade sinks into the Sin's fatty outer layer. A moldy, green, liquid oozes out along with a putrid stench. Andes tries to extract the weapon, but finds that it refuses to be pulled. The strange green goo that ejected from the wound begins to harden into a shell, cementing the spear in place. It becomes one with Sloth's body.

What is this? Andes has never seen magic like this before. He has always held the Guild in high esteem. Virdeus and everyone in the Guild are heroes who seek to protect the Earth from monsters. Ever since Virdeus rescued him and Mikhail, Andes never again felt weak, but now he feels concerned. The demons Andes is used to slaying are mere ants compared to these Sins. His brother, Mikhail, was swiftly killed by Envy. *What hope do I have then?* He knows it to be unwise to give into despair, but with the death of Virdeus, he feels his focus slipping away from the light, but Sasha comes to his mind. *I must push on. If not for myself, then for her. I owe Virdeus that much.*

Andes wonders why Sloth still refuses to move. The boils on the Sin's penis spreads and stretches. Large pockets of air build beneath Sloth's skin. The lesions burst and a scorching heat rushes out. Andes retreats from the putrid gas, but not before receiving burns on his face and hands. He can feel the skin corroding.

Liquid spills from the open sores on Sloth's body. Multiple tracks of liquid slithers down to the ground, wiggling and sliding toward Andes like snakes. Sloth remains immobile and silent, but the liquid expelled from his body appears to have a life of its own. The strange snake-like sludge creatures surround Andes. He tries to move and conjure his fire, but his hands hang limp at his sides, somehow disconnected from his body and his nervous system. The strange liquid creatures coil around Andes's ankles, petrifying everything they touch. Andes's feet are cemented to the floor. The creatures crawl upward and begin their petrification process up his entire body.

Wrath steps toward Sasha. His air of intensity makes her feel as if she is staring into a black hole. It's similar to how she felt when witnessing Seth erupt into blue flames. Though here she is, defending Seth while he remains unconscious.

Who am I to judge the monster inside him? She remembers how she reacted to her biological father's death. *He deserved all that and more, but to feel nothing at the sight of another human's mangled corpse? I was cold. As cold as this monster in front of me.*

She meets Wrath's gaze.

The ground coats over in ice with each step Wrath takes. His aura does feel similar to Seth's, but refined to the point of an icy blade. A cold, focused rage.

Water particles in the air crystalize in reaction to his freezing body temperature. They shine bright and starlike in the dark cave, now that the city has been destroyed. Wrath lifts and drops his right foot hard. The concrete ground cracks. Out springs a thick sheet of ice. Its sharp points fly at hip level toward Sasha's lower abdominal. Her acrobatic instincts kick in and she jumps above and over the wave of ice. She slides her way to sturdy ground, then realizes the mistake she made.

"Seth!" she calls out, forgetting that she meant to protect him. The ice is now lunging at Seth. There is nothing Sasha can do. Not without leaving herself vulnerable to being sliced in half by the blade of ice.

Wrath curls his right index finger upward. The ice, jolted with life, springs over Seth before dropping to the floor, encasing the sleeping demon in a dome of ice.

"I smell my siblings on him. The mist left behind by Greed when he died was not alone. I could sense another aura mingling with his. One that smelt charred. He's the one who killed them, I know it," Wrath says. "I'll deal with you first and give him time to wake. I want him to be conscious of me ending his life!"

Wrath flashes a euphoric grin. His eyes gloss over with a manic tint. Clenching his fists, he lets out a bellowing roar. He hunches over and Sasha watches six slits open on his back. Out rises three broad wings under each shoulder. Black feathers coated in frozen water droplets glisten. They are stiff, almost as if they have been left unused in storage for quite some time.

A flurry of slashes bombard Sasha. Wrath is faster than she thought his mass would allow. She ducks and avoids the first claw, but gets slashed in the right arm by the other. Sasha sees no blood, but can feel the nerves in her arm tense as it freezes over with frostbite. She feels the impulse to wail in pain, but forces it down. Understanding full well how her powers manifested, she never cowered in the face of pain. Enduring the pain surging down her arm, she smiles.

She conjures bolts of lightning and lunges them at Wrath in a flash. One pierces his stomach, the other his chest. They burst and Wrath staggers backward. Blood pours out of the two wounds. Charging herself up with electricity, she moves in briskly and delivers a kick to Wrath's chest wound. She can feel the density of his body against the bottom of her boot upon impact. Wrath is forced to his knees from the pain.

Sasha rushes toward the beast again. She is aiming to get close enough to grab hold of his neck. To use her ability to manipulate the flow of magic and cut Wrath off from his. She grabs hold of the Sin's neck with her left hand. Sasha's bare skin touching his forces her to pull away. She winces in pain and looks down at her hand. The surface has been burnt away by the frostbitten sensation. The skin of her palms peels away to reveal the pink flesh beneath.

Wrath's wounds crust over with ice. He stands up and rushes toward Sasha. He grips her with both his fists. The feathers on his wings break free from the ice's strangle hold. He lunges himself and Sasha high in the air.

Andes and Melphis, left behind on the surface, become far away. Her body begins to crust over in ice until she is left with no feeling at all. Inches away from her face are the blood thirsty eyes of Wrath.

———◆◇◆———

A vast whiteness surrounds me.

Why am I here again?

{Seth, the Rageful.}

The voice of Adam's father speaks up.

{You were told to administer better control, but you refuse to comply. Melphis, the Covetor. Virdeus, the Proud. Sasha, the Lustful, and my dear son, Adam. All these guiding lights, yet you keep your eyes closed?}

"You again. What are you getting at? And why am I here?"

{You are not here. I am merely speaking while you dream. Do not concern yourself with this place. Focus on your emotions before you end up hurting those who love you.}

"What's wrong with how I am? I'm to thank for getting rid of Greed and Gluttony. Who cares about the means, when the one I love isn't around to be hurt by it? I'm only putting up with all this to find her, to find Lola!"

{Such stupidity and arrogance will get you nowhere. Delusion poisons your sight. You cannot see that love is closer than you think. Friendships you remain blind to have been close at hand for quite some time. And now those special ones are hurting, all because you lost control. They are your family now, and you aren't there to help them.}

"You're the deluded one."

{You have forced me to aid you far more than I have the luxury for. I grow weak and cannot, will not, be able to contact you again. For all our sakes, please, learn restraint. Now, wake up.}

The words fade and I drift away.

CHAPTER SIXTEEN

I'm jolted awake to find myself in the claustrophobic confines of ice. The cold surface hovers an inch away from my face. There is no air—*I can't breathe*. Agita rises. I thrash around. I feel myself becoming hot and blue flames burst ravenously from my pores, devouring the icy cage.

What is this? Where is Envy? Who are these monsters?

The blue flames rush toward Melphis, who is shielded by a hulking beast whose body reduces the flames to dust.

Andes appears to be crusted over in plaster. The strange crust protects him from the flames then burns away and frees him from petrification. The beast behind him groans as the flames scorch him, but otherwise do him no harm.

What is going on? Where is Sasha?

A scream full of ire bellows. A six-winged beast is hovering above. Sasha is frozen inside the grip of his monstrous fists.

Envy is nowhere to be seen. *Did I do it again? Did I kill her while blacked out?* Melphis, Sasha, and Andes appear to have been struggling while I was unconscious. I don't trust Adam's father, but there might be some truth to what he said—*For all our sakes, please, learn restraint.* His words echo within my skull.

Fuck him! He talked down to me as if I am some monster incapable of doing any good. He's wrong.

I surmise that these three beasts are Sins. The blue flames emerge from my pores again until my body is encased in flame. The fire flickers with chaos. Sparks fly from all directions like the tongue of a brutal, unforgiving, frog who snatches a fly out of the air without mercy. They burn hotter than the red flames. I feel as if I can erupt at any moment.

The beast that traps Sasha within his grasp roars again. His mouth opens wide as if he plans to decapitate Sasha with a single bite.

I can be useful. I will be useful. I'll prove them all wrong.

Clenching my jaw, I focus hard. Words Melphis spoke to me before are roused into memory. *Magic does what the mind wills it to do.* Looking up at the winged beast, I feel a sort of kinship with it. He holds a rage that feels familiar, though chiseled to a fine point. I try to mimic his focus. The blue flames thrash about in the air, as if they are trying to fight back against me. I try and imagine them growing calmer as I attempt to harness a leash upon this fiery demon inside me. They begin to mellow. The once sporadic blue flames morph to pure white, like the Abyss where Adam's father lives. They no longer thrash about, but instead have a soft flicker. This is a façade. The flames aren't calmer, just more focused and intense. I may have channeled the flames of Hell before, but now it feels as if I am channeling the White Abyss.

I direct the flow of magic to my upper back. The white flames construct the shape of two broad ethereal wings. In a single flap, they launch me high into the air.

Sasha feels an intense warmth begin to counteract Wrath's sub-zero touch. His painful grasp begins to falter, for a reason that seems to even confuse the beast himself. He turns his head away from Sasha. His eyes widen. A fist only a tad smaller than Wrath's lands its knuckles along the Sin's right cheek. Wrath loses his grip on Sasha. She plummets to the surface.

Sasha's eyes lock onto the cave's floor. Her body has yet to heal from the wounds Wrath caused her, and she has no way to maneuver herself around in the air. Collision with the rocky surface is imminent. Virdeus's face comes to mind. To join him in death so soon, would disappointment him. *I'm sorry, father.* Sasha shuts her eyes.

Another large pair of hands lay their grip on her. This recalls unpleasant memories from her childhood. Her eyes jolt open in rage before she finds that it's Seth who holds her. Out from his back rises two wings made from white flames. A calm washes over her.

He puts her down, positioning her back against a flat piece of debris.

"Are you alright?"

"Your eyes," Sasha says, mesmerized. Pure white orbs stare down at her, as if they are the flames themselves.

"Rest," Seth says. "I'll hold him off."

Sasha sees blood dripping from Seth's mouth. *That wound wasn't there before. It started bleeding just now.* She sees that his jaw is clenched, as if he's biting hard on something.

He's just like me.

In 1707.

Virdeus had given Sasha the gift of magic at the age of seven, right after he saved her. Sasha was twenty now and still could not control her magic. Most of the Guild members could not fully control their magic until their mid-twenties. Even so, by twenty they were well on their way. Sasha was far behind the others in this regard. It was as if the magic intentionally unearthed the pain forced on her by her biological father. Pain she preferred would stay locked up and hidden. Her magic sought to remind her of this pain at every moment.

Sasha was standing in a training range at the Guild's Catskill settlement. Virdeus, Mikhail, and Andes looked on as the young woman screamed. Electricity discharged from her body. Sparks flew at sporadic intervals. Virdeus implored everyone not to approach her. She was to aim her magic at the various mannequins which stood around the yard. She conjured bolts of lightning atop her fingertips. Her face was drenched in tears. She unleashed the lightning and missed the targets. The bolts rushed past, blowing a hole into the mountain's wall which laid behind. Her wrath remained intact, undiminished by what she had done.

"She's out of control," Mikhail said. "This can't go on."

"She just needs time," Virdeus said. He walked away from Mikhail and headed toward Sasha.

"Time?" Mikhail shouted. "The rest of us are far more competent! Why waste time on volatile trash?"

Andes placed his hand on his brother's shoulder, as if to signal him to stop. Mikhail walked away.

"My daughter, what can I do for you?" Virdeus asked.

Sasha clenched her teeth as the tears continued to fall. Virdeus hugged his daughter. The girl was cocooned in the arms of the bear-sized man. She was calmed by his embrace, then realized the destruction she caused.

"Look what I've done! Why aren't you angry with me?"

"We all have our pain. If I could go back and stop that man from doing what he had to you, I would. But it happened, and the pain will never go away. I derive no pleasure in telling you this, my daughter, but this is the way of the world. Pain is promised, and it is guaranteed. All we can do is become strong enough to make that pain our own. It doesn't have to be a miserable thing. You can make it beautiful if you will it to be."

"N-no, Father, I can't."

"Yes, you can. I have the utmost faith in you. Now, focus and try again."

Virdeus backed away and left Sasha to it. She conjured another bolt of lightning, this time in the palm of her left hand—suddenly, her vision was overtaken by a White Abyss. Therein stood three figures beneath a tree. The vision flashed away, and she reoriented herself.

She gripped the lightning tight and locked her gaze on a single mannequin. Agita rose inside her. She clenched her jaw tight in rebellion. Blood dripped from her punctured gums, proof of her resolve to not let her chaotic impulses overtake her. She threw the bolt. It pierced the mannequin's chest.

"See? What did I tell you?" Virdeus said. "Oh, my dear, you're bleeding. Do not worry. Exerting the effort to control oneself becomes easier with time. You are well on your way.

"Murderer!" bellows Wrath. Seth turns away from Sasha and faces the beast. His body shields her from the Sin who is now plunging toward them with his hand outstretched, ready to strangle his sibling's killer. Seth raises his left hand. He points his index and middle fingers together toward Wrath. Sasha is in awe at how calm Seth seems. White flames spiral down his arm, meeting at the end of his two fingers. They condense into a fine point before ejecting. A thin laser made from the flames rockets forth and pierces Wrath's chest. The Sin plummets.

"Don't worry. Your body's healing is well on its way," Seth says. "You'll be fine. Until then, I won't let him touch you."

When Seth says this, Sasha feels she is glancing up at Virdeus. Her eyes trickle.

Seth approaches Wrath, who is struggling to his feet. Blood gushes from his chest wound. Wrath's freezing powers fail him. The blood refuses to stop flowing. The white flames that pierced him are too hot. Sharp ice begins to protrude from his body as his focus wanes. It's as if the ice within him is trying to break free.

Wrath loses himself in a fury. He lets his fists loose. Seth makes use of his ethereal wings and flies out of Wrath's way. He lands behind Wrath and reaches out for his throat. Large icy stalagmites erupt from Wrath's back. They pierce Seth's chest, before melting away in the heat. Seth staggers back.

Wrath grins, thinking they are now on common ground.

"Even if you kill me, you can be damn sure you're coming with me!" Wrath says. "Wait, what is this?"

The giant hole in Seth's chest begins to fill. Teal sparks start a process that Seth knows well, but one that leaves Wrath in terror. Seth's rib cage regrows, followed by muscles weaving back together.

Seth flaps his wings and hovers above Wrath. Not wanting to hurt the others, he decides to let his flames loose from above, rather than from the side. The white flames unleash from his palms and engulf Wrath in a direct and precise blast. The Sin screeches as he melts away.

Sasha is in awe of the power displayed here.

A blast of light, bright as the sun, briefly emanates from Wrath's wings. The white flames fade away. All that is left is a charred, amorphous mound of flesh with wing bones reaching toward the sky.

Sasha is safe now, but the others need my help. Melphis appears to be struggling, Andes has been trapped by Sloth in petrification again. Melphis can hold his own. I decide to help Sasha's Guildmate first.

This Sin appears to be less of a threat than the others. Its fat body sits with an unnerving stillness as if it is already a corpse. Its eyes are the one part that moves. They are locked onto the peculiar snake-like creatures swarming Andes.

I fly over and swoop down upon the beast's torso. It doesn't react. Why doesn't it defend itself? White flames spiral down my left arm, which I drill into his chest. Green liquid spills from the wound. I plan to grab his heart, but I feel nothing past the fatty outer layer but fluids. I retract my arm and peer inside. No organs.

The fluid left on my fist solidifies. It crusts over and my arm falls like dead weight. I stagger back. This strange crust has reached the bridge of Andes's nose. He looks at me in horror and desperation.

More of this sludge erupts from the Sin's body. The wound I left acts as a large portal for them to spill out of. Their numbers multiply. Hundreds of them swarm me. My white flames melt some away, but there are too many. My focus dissolves into anxiety. I've been petrified from the waist down.

Sasha blurs into my field of vision. She jumps on top of the Sin and grabs hold of its neck. Placing pressure on his throat, Sasha stops the flow of his magic. His head falls limp and hangs just above the ground. The crust upon my body returns to liquid form. It slides to the floor, a harmless puddle. Andes is also released. He falls to his knees, gasping for air.

Sasha continues to hold Sloth's neck. Her wounded arm still hangs limp at her side. Like Andes, she also struggles to breathe. She hasn't healed enough. Her grip begins to shake. Tremors are sent up her arm. The Sin's magic is trying to force its way back.

I join Sasha on top of the Sin's torso. Again, my fists are wrapped in white flames. I land a punch to his face, knocking his skull into the hard ground. It bounces back, leaving a crimson stain on the concrete. I punch again, the sound of cracking bone echoes throughout the cave. His eyes morph to an encompassing bright light. Little orbs of golden sun rays glare at me. A third punch, and his face caves in. Splattered brains join the pool of blood. Inside and out of the hollowed gourd.

━◆O◆━

Pride continues to rain his fists down. The shield Melphis conjured shatters under the weight of one fist. Another knocks Melphis back, his tiny frame is thrown a few yards away. Melphis tumbles to the ground, face scraping against the concrete. Melphis's bloodied face turns to see the descent of another fist.

The image of Hell's throne appears in Melphis's mind. All his ambition, squandered. After thousands of years studying magic and becoming the most versatile sorcerer Hell has ever known, what has it amounted to? His efforts have been wasted before the might of Pride's impregnable defense. *Hell will never be mine.*

Simultaneously, doubt overtakes him. *Why have I been so determined to take Hell anyway? What about its throne lures me*—his will is yanked back into captivity. His mind resets and the image of the White Abyss overtakes his field of vision, forcing him to stop questioning. For a moment, he sees those three figures, his wardens, beneath a tree. It fades, but the vast white space remains—*wait no, that's not it.*

Melphis finds Seth standing above him, holding Pride's fist back. Flames as white as the Abyss shroud Seth's body. Melphis feels the same weight from them as well. Yet even they dissipate into dust before Pride's barrier. The Sin remains unhurt, but his many eyes grow wide with fear as Seth appears. Pride retracts his fist and backs away.

"You," Pride says. He glances around the cave. The corpses of his two brothers lay on the cold floor. "They were dealt with so quickly. How can this be?"

Pride's fear morphs into intrigue as he remembers what Satan told him—that Melphis's companion was a new demon filled with Nil magic. Pride had never heard of this magic before.

"These Flames of Nil must be what Satan spoke of," Pride says. "A pure and focused destructive power...and with it you've killed my siblings.

"But there's something else...I can smell Her scent on you, as if She is willing you forward. But why..."

Seth glances at Melphis for clarification, but Melphis also doesn't know what Pride is on about. Envy, Pride's only sister, is dead. There is just one other person Pride could be referring to with these feminine pronouns. *But what would The Seductress have to do with any of this?*

With his brothers gone, Pride loses himself in fury. All four fists plunge forward. Seth grabs Melphis and flies out of the way. They land, and Melphis readies himself for battle again. Seth lets out another thin, focused laser of white flames at Pride. The intense blast that pierced Wrath dissolves into nothing before Pride.

"Elemental magic won't work. Brute force may, but I can't be sure," Melphis says.

Pride begins a rampaging sprint toward his prey. He leaps, attempting to crush Seth and Melphis under his weight. The Sin is too fast, and Seth has no choice but to stand his ground. Seth reaches out and catches Pride by his torso. The white flames flicker with more intensity, as if they were just doused with gasoline. The veins in Seth's arms and neck protrude while trying to hold back the Sin's weight. Melphis watches as Seth's skin begins to crack. Blood sprays out.

A bolt of lightning blurs into sight and disintegrates inches away from Pride's head. A spear hurled by Andes knocks against one of Pride's arms, but his skin remains unpunctured. Pride turns to see Sasha and Andes running toward him.

Melphis surmises that Pride's magic doesn't amount to defense against elemental magic alone. Like an elephant or hippopotamus, Pride is gifted with a thick, hard skin. He is a creature of perfect defense. *Yet, our luck may have just turned around.*

"Sasha, nothing will ever hurt him. His magic makes him hard," Melphis says. "Soften him."

Sasha nods.

Melphis has never seen Seth so focused before. This new development in his power makes Melphis hopeful, *but can Seth pull off working as a team?*

Pride ignores the banter of his four enemies. He sends his fists flying again. One aims for Sasha. Seth jumps in front of it, catching it. Another fist drops down on Andes, held back only by the pole of his spear. Andes shakes under the pressure. Melphis launches fire toward Pride to garner his attention. Sasha leaps and lands on the Sin's shoulders.

Pride, alarmed, reaches for Sasha with his other two arms. They fall limp before they can grab her. After pressing into

Pride's neck, Sasha disrupts the flow of Pride's magic. His skin softens as he drops to his knees.

Just as happened before, Sasha begins to tremble. Her countenance grows weak. Holding back such a force takes its toll on her body. Seth, seeing that the window is closing, joins Sasha on top of the giant beast. White flames spiral around his left arm again. He drops his fist into the backside of Pride's skull, his softened skin and bone tears and breaks. Seth finds himself wrist deep inside Pride's head. The Sin's brain pulsates with light as a halo is pulled into view from a distortion above Pride's scalp. Seth grabs hold of the slime coated brain. The white flames grow more intense, as Seth channels them straight into the Sin. The powerful duo jumps away as Pride is engulfed by the flames, burning away from the inside out. The halo cracks and shatters into dispersed light particles.

"*M-mother, why have you forsaken us!*" Pride screams. His flesh melts until just a skeleton remains.

The group gasps in exhaustion. Seth's white flames are reduced to flickering embers. His wings dissolve into ethereal dust. Overcome, Seth tumbles over.

I awake, groggy and unfocused. Melphis, Sasha, and Andes are huddled together in the middle of a conversation.

"—last I knew, he was in Tokyo, but we have earned a rest first," Melphis is saying to Sasha. "Ah, you're awake. I was just speaking about our plans going forward. Are you alright?"

I glance around the city. I was so preoccupied before that I hadn't noticed. The astounding and beautiful magic city is gone. We sit here amongst rubble and streets that are littered with the bodies of fallen Guildmembers. *Did I do this? Did I kill them alongside Envy?*

"What happened to them all?" I ask.

Sasha and Andes exchange an uncomfortable glance. Melphis is quiet for a moment.

"You've done well. Four more Sins have been slain thanks to you. You have my gratitude," Melphis says. "Just one more left before we can take Hell."

That didn't answer my question, but he complimented me for what I believe to be the first time. I decide to relish how good that feels and ignore the rest for now.

"Alright then. Mind if I sleep a bit more? My head is still quite heavy."

"Please do," Melphis says. "You've earned it."

Sasha's face is sullen while Andes is seething.

"He's done well?" Andes says. "He killed thousands, and you want to let him be without the guilt he deserves?"

"He saved you, didn't he?" Melphis says. "He saved us all. Yes, he is...troublesome, but I don't believe his actions to be malicious."

"Troublesome! That's what you reduce this travesty to?"

"Andes, enough," Sasha says.

"But my lady—"

"I said enough! Melphis is right. We can deal with this later. Now is not the time. We're all tired. Let Seth enjoy this moment while he can."

"You're quite understanding, considering all you've lost," Melphis says.

"Let's just say, I understand where Seth is coming from. There was a point in my life, where if I were in his shoes, I would have done nothing different."

"Very well," Melphis says. "So, you're sure about accompanying us?"

"Yes. It's what father would have wanted. I want to see that his dream of a world without demons comes to fruition."

"And you, Andes?" Melphis asks.

"I will stay here in case any absent members of the Guild return. Someone needs to tell them what happened. Also, I apologize for my outburst before. Everyone in the Guild knew what they were signing up for, and perhaps we would have all died otherwise, but the loss is still hard to bear. Anyway, I am off to search for survivors. Once we regroup, I promise we will meet up with you again."

The group grows silent as Andes walks off.

"Sasha, perhaps you can lend me your ear?" Melphis asks. "We've been through so much, and Seth has been so volatile, that I haven't had a chance to discuss this with him yet. Since you are coming with us, and you are Virdeus's heir, could I open up to you?"

"Of course! What's on your mind?"

"This quest of mine was never simple, per say, but I only had the one goal of usurping Hell's throne. Yet I feel an unease creeping in. The longer we continue, the foggier my mind becomes when I attempt to question what drives me toward the throne in the first place. I also feel as if we are being watched by a few sets of eyes. I once thought Satan was my sole enemy, but now I'm not so sure. Something Pride said irked me. He referred to a woman and cried out for a Mother. Then there is the White Abyss, of which I blame for my mind's disorienting states—"

"A tree and three figures in an encompassing white space?" Sasha asks.

"You, too?"

"I saw it once when I was younger. Figured it was just stress at the time."

"Seth has also seen it."

Melphis ponders in silence for a moment.

He continues, "All the more reason to remain on guard. I know you do not blame him, but I feel I must say this on his account. I am sorry for the destruction he caused and for the lives lost. Though he is troublesome, I feel that we will need Seth more than ever as we go forward."

Part Two

Truth

CHAPTER SEVENTEEN

IN 1702.

"Sasha! My dear, please wake up!" Virdeus shouted.

Her right arm clung tight around her chest. Her left reached down toward the inner thighs where her biological father had violated her. Her face was scrunched in anguish and her eyes bright with fury.

Sasha screamed. Electric sparks gathered around her eyes, shooting forth. The sporadic bolts were flung around the room, singeing the walls and furniture. Sasha's wardrobe to the left of her bed caught fire. The mirror next to it was spared. Virdeus snuffed out the flames with a thick quilt before the fire grew too furious, then returned to Sasha's side. He wrapped his arms around her, the electricity piercing his skin.

"I will not leave you, my daughter. You will always be safe if I have any say. Please wake up," Virdeus said, strengthening his embrace.

Reacting to Virdeus's warmth, Sasha awoke, and her magic ceased. Puzzled by what was happening, she looked down at the large man who held her tight. Memories of her father gripping her thighs returned. She pushed Virdeus back.

His eyes widened in surprise. Sasha's did the same once she realized who it was.

"I-I'm sorry, Father. I was having another nightmare."

"There is nothing you have need to apologize for, my dear."

Sasha rubbed her eyes, before looking down at her maturing body.

"You were going to take me on my first hunt today, right?" Sasha asked.

"I'm thinking we should put that off. You may need more rest."

"No, Father. I'm alright, I promise. I've been looking forward to this. Please take me along."

Virdeus looked at Sasha with an anxious frown.

"Well, alright. If you are sure. We leave soon so get yourself ready," Virdeus turned to leave. "Sasha? He's gone now, and I hope you know that I would never let something like that happen to you again."

"Yes, Father. I know."

With a concerned smile, Virdeus left Sasha alone.

She got out of bed and walked over to her dresser. After picking fresh clothes for the day, she got undressed from her nightgown. She caught a glimpse of herself in the mirror. She scowled. It had been years since Virdeus rescued her. Her once childish body had been left behind. With the swelling of her breasts and the filling in of her hips, Sasha had begun growing into a woman.

The words of her biological father echoed in her ears. *You look so much like your mother. You remind me of her more each day. Every day, I get closer to her.* Sasha saw the splitting image of the woman she had hated but had never met. Because of her development, she now felt the gaze of her male Guildmates lingering up and down her body. The men of the Guild would never dare touch her, as she was Virdeus's heir, but her paranoia festered all the same.

Sasha clenched her teeth at the sight of her naked body. She raised a fist toward the mirror, punching its center. Fissures shot through her reflection. Turning away from the mirror, Sasha dressed herself and went to meet Virdeus.

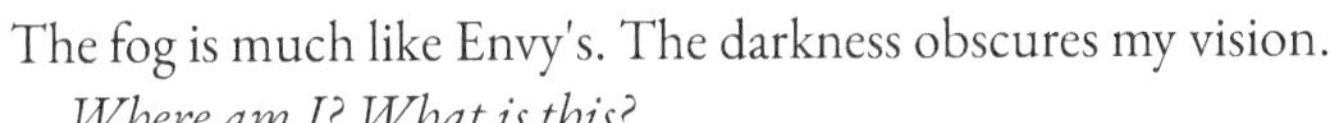

The fog is much like Envy's. The darkness obscures my vision.

Where am I? What is this?

Familiar faces from Crowley emerge from the fog. Among them is the convenience store cashier who sold me my first pack of cigarettes. The lanky stranger who accused me of assault. The psychiatrist who degraded me. My parents.

A supernatural weight pins me to the floor. I cling my knees tight, bringing my face into them.

"Yeah, cower on the floor like the filth ya are!" screams my father. The others stand behind him, grinning.

Their bodies corrode before reshaping into imps. Their lips stretch toward their napes. While the skin peels, another head forces its way out from the depths of their mouths. Greed, Gluttony, Envy, Wrath, Sloth, and Pride erupt outward, screaming, "*Murderer!*"

"You think that because your family hated you, that you have the right to destroy ours?" screams Wrath.

"You brand us as evil, yet do not forget—you slaughtered thousands to kill just us six. You're the real monster," says Pride.

They tower over me, scowling when bright teal light pierces through their skin. The Sins melt away. Spewing out from their bodies are the legion of souls I consumed inside of Gluttony.

"*The angry one. He ate us,*" the souls screech. "Used us for power—to kill, to kill! He used us to kill and he doesn't care! Too pained to care! Too selfish! Selfish one, ye denier of life, are you content? Content, with being...*monstrous?*"

I clutch my labored chest. My heartbeat grows rapid. Fire erupts from my palms and consumes me. They take the form of Satan's face. He's shouting, "Die, die! You monster!" But then the flames disappear and his voice morphs into my own. "Die, die! You monster!" I say, digging my sharp nails into my throat.

Then, a warm light.

"S—th. -eth. *Seth*!" a voice calls out.

Awakening, I find myself sitting upright with my hands wrapped around my throat. Sasha's arms are thrown around me, wrapping me in her warmth. I loosen my grip, dropping my arms.

"You were having a night terror!" Sasha says, undoing her embrace. She stares into me with her bright, copper-colored eyes, looking concerned. "Has this happened before?" She turns to Melphis. His shoulders shrug.

"Sorry to concern you," I say.

"What were you dreaming about?"

The many faces and their cruel words come to mind. I try to answer, but find Sasha's face hovering close to mine. Flustered, I avert my gaze.

"I can't remember."

She and Melphis exchange curious glances.

I rub my eyes, wincing from the morning sunlight filtering through the dirty, broken windows of the abandoned shed outside Magistrum's mountain path.

"So, time to get going?" I ask.

"If you're ready," Melphis replies. "We barely made it out of the mountain before you collapsed again. Even though you slept quite a bit after dealing with Pride.

"But we still have time before I'm ready. Go outside and get some air," Melphis says, sitting down. He takes a knife to a thick tree branch and shaves off the bark. It seems that while I was sleeping, Melphis has been working on crafting a new staff. I'm not used to seeing Melphis so relaxed. Up until now he had been in such a rush. I leave him to it and go outside, Sasha following behind.

I look toward the bright, cloudless blue sky. Such a beautiful day doesn't feel like it fits the carnage we just faced. My hands tremble. *What's happening inside me, to cause such a bizarre dream?*

Sasha places her hands on mine. The warmth of her calms the tremors. Taken aback, I pull away.

"Sorry, I was deep in thought, and I wasn't expecting—"

"You were lying in there," Sasha says.

"Huh?"

"About the dream. You said you couldn't remember what it was. You were lying."

This girl's ability to read people is terrifying, but in a strange way, comforting. It's almost as if she knows me.

"Would you like to talk about it?" she continues.

"Um, I don't know if—"

"That's alright. You don't have to, but know this: I understand pain all too well. Sometimes it helps to talk to someone, especially if they can relate. I'll even tell you about *my* pain in exchange for telling me about *yours*."

Her smile grows wide. She was so gentle when caring for Virdeus and it seems that kindness is too strong to have died with him.

"Well, alright then. I suppose we have a lot to learn about each other," I say, scratching the backside of my head.

"I suppose so," she responds, her eyes lit with passion.

The shed's door swings open. Melphis emerges from the dark interior holding his new staff.

"I think it's high time we rid the Earth of its last Sin! How about it?" Melphis exclaims, then swings the head of his staff in a circular motion. A portal to another city appears before us.

CHAPTER EIGHTEEN

A bright, white glow emanates from the portal. Melphis steps toward it, gesturing for us to follow.

"Hold on," Sasha says. "We need to do something about your bodies."

She unsheathes the knife at her left side. "Sorry in advance for the pain," she says, then sticks the tip into the surface of my neck. The wound heals right away, leaving a scar. She does the same for Melphis. "This is the rune that has kept the Guild hidden. To the eyes of onlookers, you will be perceived as what is most common to them."

"Magnificent. Virdeus developed the magic in ways that I had never imagined. I wish I was able to speak to him more about it. Oh, I'm sorry," Melphis says to Sasha.

"What are you sorry for? I love my father, and I will miss him greatly, but I am not so weak as to be reduced to tears at the mere mention of his name. Come on, let's go," Sasha commands. We follow her through the portal.

We arrive in an alley and are greeted by a harsh scream. A homeless man is stricken with fear at the sight of our sudden appearance. He runs off yelling something in Japanese.

"He thinks we're ghosts," Melphis says.

"Well, we did just emerge out of thin air," replies Sasha.

We leave the alley and are immediately greeted by the homeless man's return, dragging a police officer along by his sleeve. Upon seeing us, he yells at the homeless man and pushes him away. He speaks to us in Japanese, bows, then walks off.

"He called the homeless man crazy, then apologized to us. Do we appear as Japanese to him?" Melphis asks.

"That's a safe bet," Sasha says. "We're in Tokyo, and the rune obscures your appearance, making you seem as that which is most common to whomever lays their eyes on you. Just don't use your magic. You won't be hidden anymore."

We nod, then I turn to Melphis.

"I'm impressed that you understand Japanese," I say.

"I have lived for long enough to master every language. Even the dead and unrecorded ones," Melphis says. "But enough chatter, let's go. Lust is nearby."

Melphis leads the way, with Seth and Sasha a few feet behind. The two of them offering stories of their past to each other. Melphis listens in, but refrains from joining the conversation. He realizes that this is the first time he's heard the specifics of Seth's past. *Horrible. To have to endure that consistent torture, but it led to Seth killing six of the Sins more easily than I'd ever imagined. Whatever this power inside him is, Satan sure succeeded in creating it—but that begs the question, for what purpose?*

Melphis glances back at his followers. Seth tells his sad tale with a smile on his face. *My hunch was right.* At the shed outside Magistrum, when Melphis told Seth to get some air, he knew that Sasha would follow him outside. *There's something about this young woman that Seth reacts well to. Perhaps she can provide him some balance.*

Sasha is now telling Seth about her past, in surprising detail. Melphis glances back once more and sees Seth's smile fade into a frown. *Raped at such a young age?* Melphis turns away from them so that they would not see him clench his teeth in anger. He curls in fingers, tightening his fists. *How can such a horrible thing be allowed?*

Melphis stops walking and glances into a building with tinted windows and silhouettes of curvy women.

"He's inside this den of degenerates," Melphis says.

After fighting four Sins inside of a cave, entering a strip club for the last one feels strange. I follow Melphis inside.

It's crowded, and my nerves tense at what is before me. Naked women dancing on a stage to an audience of which are mostly imps in human disguises. Most of the women are Japanese, but two foreigners stand out. One blonde, the other brunette. Both large breasted. One of the imps grows restless and hops on stage. Unzipping his vessel's pants, he pins the brunette to the floor and forces himself into her.

My hands tremble, my jaw clenches. The rest of the audience watches with a smile. No one intervenes, not even after the woman screams.

"Leave it be, Seth. If you want to stop them, we're better off killing the source," Melphis says. "Fighting here won't do us any good."

I glance at Sasha. Her face is scrunched, but she says nothing. Averting her gaze, she takes the lead. We walk toward a door to the right of the stage. The demons are too enamored to notice us. We enter an office. There is a desk surrounded by book-shelves. Scattered across the floor are stained porn magazines. Behind the desk is another door, open, almost as if we are being invited in. Past it is a long staircase which leads down into a vast darkness, obscuring the bottom. Melphis conjures a flame atop his staff to light the way, and we make our descent.

In 1702.

Sasha accompanied Virdeus into Boston. They had hoped to acquire word of potential demon activity in this commerce-oriented town. This was Sasha's first hunt, as well as her first time amongst average humans after nine years of living in the Guild's nearby settlement.

"Let us split up and see what we can find," Virdeus said. "Remember, don't use magic and keep interaction with others at a minimum. The rune will have you appear to them as what is most comforting. Learning the local gossip and folktales should come easy, but prolonged interaction may loosen the rune's effectiveness. We cannot have them learn of magic."

Sasha nodded and walked off. She felt Virdeus's worried glare upon the backside of her head. Remembering her image in the broken mirror, Sasha felt that the fractured form better resembled the truth of who she was. She looked forward to the distractive hunt.

Making her way through an alley, a voice spoke from behind, "Young miss, are you lost?"

Sasha turned to find a middle-aged man down on one knee, smiling and staring into her midriff. Sasha stepped back. *What is with this man? He's not even looking into my eyes.*

"It's okay, I can help. You look like my daughter when she was this small."

The rune causes them to see what is most comforting. This man is seeing a child.

He offered his hand to Sasha, and she trembled. She saw her father's hand, reaching down below.

"*Get away from me!*" Sasha shouted. She unsheathed a dagger and before the man could understand what was happening, she plunged the knife into his right eye. An electrical current was sent through the dagger, frying the man alive. His shrill screams filled the empty alleyway.

Sasha backed away from the charred corpse, her hands covering her face before running away.

In 1705.

Sasha refrained from going on hunts after that first time. She opted to engage her other interests for the time being. That day twelve years ago, Virdeus had been her second savior. The imp was her first. By killing her father, the imp had saved Sasha from her father's vile touch.

She was in a room in the basement of the Guild's Mount Greylock settlement. At her request, Virdeus brought back a slain imp. It laid cold and rigid upon a large table. With a wide smile and bright, focused eyes, she brought a knife down upon the beast. She sliced from its chin to just above its large penis. Sasha's breathing grew rapid and hot as she widened the slit. While unearthing the organs, Mikhail and Andes glanced into the room.

"I can't believe Virdeus wastes so much energy on such a horrifying girl," Mikhail says. "I mean, to go so far as to get aroused over a demon and a mangled corpse of one, no less. She's more of a monster than they are."

Andes whispered to Mikhail, "Enough. Do not speak ill of her," then walked off.

Sasha heard every word, but didn't react. Her focus held firm. After extracting the core organs, she went on to examine the demon's penis, of which she was not bothered by.

◆◇◆

Another door lays at the bottom of the long stairwell.

"I would have never thought the tunnel would lead so far underground," I say.

"I'm not surprised," Melphis says. "Lust always did want to have minimal distractions from his...interests."

Melphis opens the door, and we are greeted by a large room. It's empty aside from a man wearing a shirt and blazer, but no pants. He's holding a blood-soaked knife, hovering over the corpse of an obese blonde woman. His large erection throbs. The corpse has holes carved into it, like a block of Swiss cheese. I'm surprised by Sasha's unphased demeanor. She appears a little tense, but I would expect much more of a reaction, considering—

"Ah, welcome, Archdemon Melphis. Old adopted brother of my now dead siblings. What can I do for you?" The man turns to face us. His face is dark with sunken eyes.

"I know you have been absent for a while, Lust, but if you know we killed your siblings, then surely you know that I don't go by that title anymore. I am no longer Satan's lapdog," Melphis says.

"I know nothing of the sort," Lust responds. "I can feel my sibling's departure, is all, and I fear I am next."

Lust lets out a heavy sigh before sitting down on the floor. Defeated, he hangs his head low.

"What is the matter?" Melphis says, "You know we're here to kill you, and you sit down?"

"I had planned to enjoy myself one last time," Lust says, gesturing at the corpse. "But now I must spend my final moments explaining myself to you? Life's all too cruel!"

"How could he have known we were coming?" Sasha asks.

"Again, I knew nothing of the sort! I was not expecting death by your hands."

"What do you mean?" Melphis asks.

Lust laughs, maniacally. His laughter pins his back to the ground—he goes silent. Lifting himself up, he glares toward us.

"You think you killed my siblings? *You?* What if I say they were only killed because someone else allowed them to be?" Lust's eyes widen with frenzy. "You do not even know what the Sins *are*, Melphis! For so long, you have assumed us to be demons, but tell me, did you witness any telling signs when they died? A sudden burst of light? Wings and a halo perhaps?"

Melphis's eyes widen. "Greed once told me that I knew nothing of Hell. What did he mean by that?"

Lust smiles and rises to his feet. Black wings erupt from his back with such intensity that the room is filled with feathers, fluttering about like fallen leaves in a gust of wind. A bright halo emerges above his head. Black static encases it. Lust rises into the air, arms open wide, invoking the image of a cross.

"I will tell you this final secret. We are not born from Hell. Satan is not our Father. In fact, we have no Father. We have only a Mother and Her name is Ya—

Lust's tongue is set ablaze. He falls to the ground. Melphis turns to me, looking angry.

"This wasn't my doing!" I say.

Lust clutches his throat. Blood spills from it. He writhes within the crimson pool forming around his body.

"What is this! What were you going to say!" Melphis demands, but there's no answer. The body of the final Sin lays cold before us. Silence overtakes the room.

"And thus, the *Lord* has called them home," says a voice from above.

A sudden, piercing light engulfs the room. A six-winged individual wearing a black robe lowers himself to the ground. The whiteness of his wings and the golden light from his halo make it hard to look at him.

"Who are you?" Melphis asks, shielding his eyes with his arms.

"I have no name to give you. I am naught but a humble servant of thy *Lord* in Heaven," says the angel, locking his eyes on me.

"Are you responsible for this?" Melphis gestures toward Lust's corpse.

"Such a question is blasphemous to the *Lord* thy *God*. I could never slay the archangels. This only thy God can do," the angel says.

Melphis continues, "Are you saying that all this time—"

"I have had enough of you, heathen. I will waste my voice on vile filth no longer. Besides, your purpose has been fulfilled, and you are no longer needed.

Melphis's emotional restraint wanes. He clenches his teeth. Raising his staff toward the angel, his arm trembles. At first, he appears angry, but then the trembling intensifies, and he fails to conjure any magic. *Is this fear?*

"Seth?" The angel speaks, "Thy *God* has a proposition for you."

I tense up. God wants me for something? After everything he put me through? Now that I know God exists, there's a target for my anger, so there's no way that—

"You are looking for a young woman named Lola, are you not?" The angel says. Thy *Lord* in Heaven knows where she is and will lead you to her if you agree to the proposition."

My feet start walking toward him.

"Seth, don't go to him!" Melphis shouts.

"You can't trust him!" Sasha says.

Looking back over my shoulder. Sasha is frowning. Her worried, pretty eyes shining bright with warmth. She was able to make me feel at peace before. Made me comfortable enough to open up about my past. She didn't judge me for any of it. She laughed and smiled and rubbed my shoulders gently as she listened. I appreciate that. I appreciate her, but she isn't Lola.

"What do you want from me?" I ask the angel.

"The locket," he says. "Tear it from your chest, then channel your Flames of Nil into it. That will force open a gateway to the White Abyss. When it does, cast those two into it."

"What? I can't do that!" I say.

"Oh? You cannot act against the demon who led you astray and has been lying to you this entire time? He said he would help you find your beloved, did he not? Yet he has not delivered on that promise. He has been using you as a weapon against the Sins! He cares for nothing more than that—and that one there! She who is seduced by demons. She is a witch using her beguiling magic to subdue you, Seth. Yet, you still cannot act against them?"

I gaze back at them in disbelief. It's true that Melphis promised that he would find Lola, yet after everything that has happened, no clue as to her whereabouts have been found. Not until now. My eyes lock onto the angel.

I dig my nails into the skin surrounding the locket. Blood pours as I break it free of the shackles of my chest. Remembering how bright those white flames burned, they erupt from my palms and into the locket.

"Seth, I know we haven't found her yet, but I've given you no reason not to trust me! Please don't do this!" Melphis says.

His dull words sound muddled to my ears. The decision has been made. Lola is everything.

Melphis raises his staff toward me, but hesitates.

"I'm sorry," I say, as the locket floats above my open palm. White flames continue to flow into it, and the locket bursts open. A towering portal is formed behind them. Increasing the intensity of the flames, the Abyss's gravity grows stronger and lifts Melphis and Sasha off their feet.

"You damn fool!" Melphis shouts. Sasha is forced into silence by the supernatural weight tugging upon her body, but her once pretty eyes now seem sharp and chaotic. I'm filled with fear for a moment, then white tendrils emerge from the portal. Wrapping around their bodies, my two friends are dragged in—and they vanish. My flames cease and the portal begins to close.

The angel grabs the locket from my hand. "Thank you, Seth." He closes his fist tight, crushing the locket into pieces. He flaps his wings and starts to fly off.

"Wait, what about Lola!" I shout.

"The *Lord thy God* will send for you when you are needed again."

"But you promised that you would lead me to Lola!"

"You have become good in the eyes of thy *Lord*. Forget the girl. *God* is far too busy to be concerned with your deluded lovesickness."

Memories of church rouse in my mind. I was always told that God would bring me joy, if I repented my sins and lived only for the glory of God. But I was always miserable. God never delivered on those promises. This was no different.

"*No more*!" I shout. I've had enough, you hear me? Fuck God's plan! I *demand* what was promised to *me*! I *refuse* to accept that I've betrayed my friends for *nothing*!

Chaotic blue flames engulf my body. I grab hold of the angel's foot and toss him toward the portal. His wings flap about as he repositions himself, and lands on his feet. I rush at him, gripping his face with my left hand. The flames melt away his skin, singeing the flesh and bone beneath.

"N-no—what are you doing?" he screams.

His right hand still grips the broken pieces of the locket. He tries to fight back with just his left, but it isn't enough to unhinge my grip.

The portal is right behind us. My blue flames grow more unsteady as I push him closer to the Abyss. The same white tentacles from before emerge from the portal like tongues of starved, ravenous creatures. They wrap around him, as well as around my ankles, and down we go.

Adam's father, Zarathustra, stands under the tree at the center of the garden. He gestures for his son to come closer. Zarathustra's skin is as white as the surrounding Abyss. His teal hair and beard hang low and unkempt.

"My son, it appears my Wrath, Greed, and Lust somehow found their way into the Abyss," Zarathustra says.

"Yes, I feel them, too, Father. It seems Seth didn't heed our advice and is as reckless as ever," Adam replies.

"So it seems." Zarathustra pauses. "Take your sister and go look for them. Then bring them to me."

Adam nods and walks away from his father, whose face turns grim.

CHAPTER NINETEEN

EONS AGO.

There at the center of all universes is an Abyss of endless potential, the birthplace of gods. This white cradle is where Zarathustra and his kind were conceived. He and his people call this Abyss, *The Womb of the One Mind.* It is a place where the desires—the wills—of sentient life gathers. There they manifest gods in the image of the sentient life who are in need.

These gods were happy to provide aid, for a time, but after millions of years, sentient life from the first universe, a lower realm found at the very bottom of the stack, began to change. These life forms grew stronger and with this strength came scientific and technological advances. This rendered the existence of the gods unnecessary. The faction of gods birthed by the wills of this lower realm's people, crumbled away into dust soon after.

"Look at what has happened to our beloved brothers and sisters!" shouted one of the male gods. "How long will it be before we are dissolved as well? We must find a way to combat this!"

This god stood on an elevated platform in the golden cathedral that sits in the center of the divine city. Behind him was a doorway which led to The Womb of the One Mind. The cathedral and the city were built to surround The Womb, which is the object of their worship.

The male god continued preaching to the panicked masses, "Are we not gods of creation? Have those who have now returned to dust not satisfied the lowest realm's every desire? Yet the mortals have turned on us!"

Zarathustra sat in the front pews, watching the crowd gravitate to the sermon and its crazed speaker. "But what do you suppose we do about it?" Zarathustra asks. "We are born to aid them. If they grow to no longer need us, isn't it natural for us to no longer have a purpose?"

"I ask again, are we not gods of creation? Why should *we* be destined for death?" asked the preaching god, pointing toward The Womb of the One Mind. "We are granted power by the wills of sentient life, but I see no reason for us to live and die by them. Here's my proposal: Why not make their wills our own?"

Murmuring amongst the crowd was heard throughout every corner of the cathedral, before erupting into a full-blown riot.

"Yes, let's devour them!" screamed one god. "If we assimilate the source of the Womb's power, we can live forever!" shouted another.

"Yes!" continued the preacher. "Tonight, we descend to the lower realm and feast upon their souls!" Horrified, Zarathustra snuck away. He locked himself within his home while his people prepared for their journey to the lowest dimension.

A blood-red night sky hung overhead. Light from six moons shimmered brightly along the tips of the golden grassy fields surrounding a city. This was the home of the lowest dimension's sentient lifeforms—a people with small red eyes and thick fur covering their nine-foot-tall bodies.

In a residential neighborhood, a young girl was tucked into bed by her parents.

"But you just got home, Daddy! I wanted to play with you!" said the young girl, wearing pink pajamas.

"I'm sorry that work keeps me so busy, but I promise we'll play all weekend, alright?" said her father, pulling a blanket over his daughter.

"Goodnight, sweetie," said her mother. "See you tomorrow."

The girl's parents shut the door behind them. A rustling was heard outside her window. She hopped out of bed in curiosity. "Maybe a cute animal is playing in the trees!" She opened the window and craned her head upward.

A woman with long, glowing, teal hair and pasty white skin swooped into view. The young girl let out a slight squeal at the strange woman's sudden appearance.

"Who are you?" the girl asked.

The stranger did not answer, but offered a gentle smile. The girl felt a strange, infectious euphoria radiating from the teal-haired woman, then returned a smile.

The woman's head twitched six times before jolting backward. Her mouth stretched open, morphing into a large worm-like oval shape. Tiny sharp teeth were revealed, alongside parasitic feelers. The woman chomped down.

The door swung open. Her parents returned to the sight of their daughter's body halfway inside the monster's mouth. The father was struck speechless. The mother screamed. Two more of these teal-haired grotesqueries appeared behind the parents. Their world went dark.

Across the crimson sky, in pairs of six, the race of gods descended upon all corners of this dimension. In a single night, the genocide of these furred giants was complete.

———◆O◆———

This is disgusting. The ones who blessed us with life should not have to suffer like this. Zarathustra hoped that the horror would subside, and his people would return to their prior life after the feasting, but this did not happen. New laws were integrated into the cathedral's operations. As new gods were born, the new generation was taught not to aid the sentient life forms, but to devour them after they outgrow the need for gods. By doing so the gods would reinforce their lives for years to come.

Zarathustra grew displeased with his people and started to detest the word *god*. He decided to flee to another dimension. His people were still devouring the lifeforms from the lower realms, so Zarathustra made his way toward the two highest dimensions. There between the two, he found an open, unused pocket of space. *It will be safe here.*

Zarathustra created a sphere of dirt and water to orbit around a sun. He created a moon to circle around the Earth and filled the sky with stars. He placed his fingers upon his chest. The skin rippled like a pebble hitting the surface of a pond. Zarathustra's physical form loosened. His hands sunk into his chest. Upon pulling them out, an abundance of white space spilled forth. He had dug into his own soul and bled out the White Abyss. It vanished from sight, hidden away within another realm. Separate from Earth yet still connected. *I have bled out my power and will one day die, but that is fine. This world is not meant for me and my kind.* Zarathustra gazed at the Earth and its white shadow, seeing that it was good.

He planted a garden with the Tree of Life and Knowledge at its center. This tree would be the bridge connecting the Earth and the White Abyss. Through it, the power of the Abyss would flow into all living things, granting them extraordinary potential. Zarathustra constructed a locket that would be a key to entering the Abyss. Once it was created, he opened the gate to the grand white space and once again dug into his soul. Zarathustra pulled out his desires—first his sloth and his gluttony. In succession followed his greed, pride, envy, lust, and then his wrath. He offered them to the Abyss as extra power, and he saw that it was good.

The union between Earth and the White Abyss was complete. Zarathustra walked over to the Tree of Life and Knowledge. He carved into the bark, *Ye shall be as Gods,* then waited for the first humans to be born.

The tree flowered and started to bud. Soon enough a branch was lowered by the weight of its fruit. A vine grew and produced a gourd. It cracked open like an egg. Zarathustra marveled at what he found inside. The first-born humans in the form of conjoined twins. A quiet boy and his screaming sister. Zarathustra recognized that they were his Sloth and Gluttony reincarnated. This was unexpected, but Zarathustra felt more attached to the infants as a result.

He hoped that humankind would one day grow strong thanks to the aid of the White Abyss. As they are its rightful owner. The White Abyss is akin to The Womb of the One Mind, and so the wills of humans can flow freely to and from it. It is their power to command and in union with it, perhaps humankind may even be able to defend themselves against gods. *Damned are gods, but glory to all that is Human, as there is no greater word.* Zarathustra saw that this was also good.

Turning to the infant boy, his Sloth, Zarathustra said, "Welcome to Eden, Lucifer." Turning to the girl, his Gluttony, he says, "And to you as well...Yahweh."

CHAPTER TWENTY

Having fallen through the gate, the angel and I tumble through the air. His flesh rips away under the force of my knuckles. He knocks his elbow into my face, but it isn't enough to quell my rage. I bash his face until almost nothing but skull remains.

A sudden blunt force to my chest. The angel uses his right knee, frees himself from my grasp. We fall, alone, until something hard slaps against my back. I feel around for the floor. My fingers make contact, but it's impossible to know what I'm sitting on. The entire space around me is a vast whiteness. *Am I here for real this time?*

A swift punch to my face knocks me back. My vision blurs. The sound of clanging metal is heard to my left. The pieces of the broken locket are tossed aside by the angel. His fists are brought down with reckless abandon.

"You fool!" he shouts. "You have damned us both! There is no escape from here!"

His barrage ceases, and he grips my neck tight. Dazed by his unhinged fury, I cannot act. The pressure builds. My airflow halts. All I can do is stare into his frenzied eyes. It's almost as if this place is intoxicating him, causing heightened anger. His image blurs and becomes someone else. Me. That bizarre dream from before. When I was choking myself, then woke to Sasha's warmth. I felt intense fear. I feel it again now. Sasha and Melphis also appeared to fear me. Just as they had when I blew Magistrum to pieces. I killed thousands when I only meant to kill Envy. *Just what have I become?*

The angel is torn from sight. Air fills my lungs. Choking on its sudden return, I glance around to try and spot the angel—he has been thrown with such force that a loud cracking of bones is heard as he's slammed down to the left of me. The angel lands on his front side, blood oozing from his gaping mouth.

Sasha steps onto the angel's back. Her once shoulder length hair now reaches her waist. Her body is slimmer than before. A famished look glosses over her face. She grips the angel's wings and severs them from his back without struggle. Blood erupts from the wounds, then dissipates into the White Abyss. The angel screeches. His eyes become still. Tendrils rise from the Abyss and wrap around the corpse. The flesh is torn apart, before crumbling into dust.

"Sasha! I—"

A swift punch to my lower jaw. I fall backward, gazing toward Sasha's cold, chaotic eyes. I've received a lot of pain, both in life and after, but nothing before has hurt quite like this.

"Don't you dare speak to me," she says. "I'll kill you next time."

Sasha walks off. To where, I don't know. What could cause such a change after just a few minutes apart? The cruelness in her eyes. My mind goes back to just before I betrayed her and Melphis. Her warm, bright eyes and gentle touch—

Looking down at my trembling, monstrous hands, I crumble to the ground. Tears pour into the White Abyss.

Melphis sits alone amongst the vast emptiness. His beard has grown to his knees. His eyes have grown dark and tired. Time eludes him. Melphis glances toward his beard, running his hands through its great length. Sasha has her dagger, but they both refuse to cut their hair. It is their sole method of understanding the great number of years that have passed.

Sasha returns with a scowl.

"What is it?" Melphis asks.

"Him and that bastard angel fell in. I killed the latter."

"And Seth?"

"No. He's still alive."

Sasha sits a few feet away from Melphis. She slams her fists down upon the incorporeal ground.

"With your strength, you could have killed him," Melphis says, his inquisitive eyes holding firm on Sasha. "After all these years, you still love him, don't you?"

"Shut your mouth," Sasha says. "The only thing I care about is killing the bastard who ordered Seth to toss us in here."

Sasha, in a fury, starts doing pushups, sit ups, and pushups again. Melphis keeps silent, watching her. *She's been like this since we arrived here. Using exercise to fend off against the crushing weight of this place. To think she aims to escape, let alone kill God? Absurd.*

Her skin cracks and blood sprays. The White Abyss soaks it up like a sponge. The crimson liquid vanishes.

"Your magic may be sustaining you, but how long can you last? It's been years since you've eaten. Your body is still human after all. Surely magic alone won't be enough for much longer. Give it up."

"I said, shut your mouth. Those who don't try have no right to speak."

Melphis grits his teeth, but complies. When they first entered this place, they wandered for days, but found nothing. He cannot understand what Sasha is hoping will happen. Even she would not stray far from this spot. The White Abyss cannot be traversed well on their own.

But since she can't go very far, that must mean Seth is near. Melphis has sat in this spot for years. Unable to devise an escape, he has relinquished himself to the White Abyss, waiting for it to crush him. *But if Seth is near, at least I can kill him before I die.*

Melphis once looked at Seth as an ally, as well as one who could become a trusted friend. They were both humans, turned into demons by forces beyond their control. He felt a kinship with Seth, but since the day of the betrayal, the flames of Hell which birthed Melphis are now more ravenous than ever. His festering anger now craves release.

Fuck you, Melphis.

Agitation envelops Sasha's whole body. The anger she feels toward Seth is real, but in the split second before hitting Seth, something happened. She remembers her arm tightening, as if she were being restrained. The sight of his face gave birth to a conflicting hesitation. A softness she discarded had resurfaced. She is angry at Melphis's remark, but angrier at herself. She trusted another man aside from Virdeus and Andes. This is a telling sign of her growth and resolve to be stronger than her pain, but now she finds herself struggling with it again. *That man who raped me—my real father. And Seth. What's the dif-*

ference? It is the same monster to her. Both betrayed her trust. Yet she still could not bring her full might down upon Seth.

Sasha stops doing pushups and finds Melphis staring off into the Abyss. He is captivated by thought. *Probably wondering how far away Seth is.* They share in this animosity. It is what kept them bonded throughout their time in this empty realm.

Sasha refuses to give up. The thought of Virdeus keeps her going, along with the memory of what the angel had said regarding Lust's corpse. *He said he could never kill the archangels. Referring to the Sins as archangels, implies that God is the one to blame for Father's death.*

Melphis glares toward her. Her face is red with anger. "What is it?"

"The usual," she replies.

Silence overtakes them.

"Hello again, Melphis," says a sudden voice, almost emerging out of thin air.

A tall, pale man with a glowing teal mohawk stands before them. His aura shares the same supernatural weight as the White Abyss itself. Sasha readies herself to attack.

"Adam?" Melphis says, with calm surprise.

"It's been a while," Adam says. "Well, for you it has. I'm sure your bodies and minds have yet to adapt to the Abyss's slow, grueling pace.

Adam gestures for Melphis and Sasha to follow him, and says, "You said before that you wanted to meet my father, yes? Well, now is your chance."

The walk feels like an eternity. The weight of the White Abyss presses hard upon the backs of Sasha and Melphis. Hunched over, they follow behind Adam, who stands tall as if he is immune to the realm's gravity. Ahead they see a garden. It appears small and blurry at first. They are as wanderers in a vast desert, being led as fools toward what they believe to be a mirage. The garden becomes larger. A green rim meets the edge of the White Abyss. Roots and flowers fade as they stretch away from the garden's center. Grass crunches beneath their feet. Melphis and Sasha glance down, taken aback by the sensation.

"Greetings, my son," says a man with a crown of red thorns imbedded into his head. Teal hair crusted with blood hangs past his empty eye holes. A tree rises high above and around him. The bark is stretched outward like hands gripping his body, restraining him. "And to you as well, Sasha, my Lust."

Sasha's face tightens. Her eyes widen.

"Ah, I apologize. I mean no offense, my dear. Nor do I want to cause you anymore harm. I simply mean that you are the reincarnation of the lust I tossed away long ago, and you, Melphis, are my Greed."

"What are you on about?" Melphis asks.

Adam sits amongst the flowers in a meditative posture. Sasha glances around the garden. She notices the tree's roots. It is standing upright, but it has been uprooted. It's as if it was torn from another location.

"This garden shouldn't be here," Sasha says. "It was banished to this place just like we were."

"Very perceptive," says the man. "My name is Zarathustra. Please listen. There is much to tell you."

Eons ago.

Zarathustra sat on a rock in a luscious area at the center of Eden. In those days it was just him and his daughter and son. The twins had just turned four, and a smile sprouted upon Zarathustra's face as he watched them play.

He remembered having to split their conjoined bodies down the middle. The newborns screamed and this filled Zarathustra with great pain before teal sparks rose from their wounds. Their skeletons stretched outward, forming the other half of their ribcage. When split apart, they had gifted an arm and a leg to each other. This teal magic then gifted them replacements. The infantile skeletons formed new limbs and flesh weaved around the bone. Wrapped in skin like a present, they were gifted to Zarathustra. Two children with their own bodies and wills.

Lucifer ran after a butterfly. He caught it gently and let it rest upon his right pointer finger. He stood there in awe of its midnight blue wings. Yahweh was crouching behind her brother, sneaking up on him. She pinched the skin of his nape. Giggling, she ran off. Lucifer broke out crying.

"It's all right, my son. Life is full of aches and pains, but—" Zarathustra rubbed Lucifer's neck, comforting him. The tears stopped and a smile returned to the boy's face. "See? It is over, just like that. Know that you can overcome any pain, alright?"

Lucifer nodded and ran off in pursuit of another butterfly. Returning to the Tree of Life and Knowledge, Zarathustra noticed a new flowering bud. A gourd grew large, then cracked open, revealing a boy. Watching the miracle of life unfold before him again, Zarathustra's eyes welled with tears. Cries filled the air as sunlight gleamed bright upon the newborn's face.

"Welcome to Eden, Abdiel, my Greed."

Twenty-six years later.

Abdiel sat at his desk, reading one of his father's books on magic. A calm washed over the late hours of the night. A cooing owl was heard from the garden outside, but Abdiel did not notice. His heightened focus pierced the contents of each page. He remained unaware of anything else.

The door to his room swung open. Alarmed, Abdiel turned to face who had entered.

"Father?"

Zarathustra closed the door and fiddled with the lock, trying to catch his breath. He looked to his son, his eyes shifting, hands trembling. Unnerved by the unusual disposition of his father, Abdiel walked over to aid him.

"What has you so disheveled?"

Tears streamed Zarathustra's face. He cupped Abdiel's cheeks with both hands, slowly raising them to his scalp.

"Abdiel, I am so sorry."

"Sorry for what? Father, you're scaring me."

"They took it. The locket—the key to the Abyss. Eden is doomed and I am useless against them. I cannot bring myself to raise a hand against my children. I cannot become like those foolish gods I left behind."

"What are you—"

"I'm sorry, Abdiel. You will have to do me this favor."

Zarathustra's hands became translucent, sinking through flesh and bone, and into Abdiel's soul. The third born human fell into catatonia. His eyes glossed over. His body grew as rigid as a corpse.

"I'm so sorry, my son," Zarathustra continued, his tears flooding in greater abundance. "But someday you will be re-born. With an insatiable craving to tear your brother and sister away from power. You will be reborn in a new body and with a new name: Melphis."

Abdiel's body crumbled into dust and fluttered away through the window overlooking the garden. The door to his room was blown off its hinges. Zarathustra's assailants approached, with a crown of thorns and the locket in hand.

Zarathustra finishes his tale of Eden. Of how he came to create the Earth, the White Abyss, his abandoned desires, and Melphis's hidden past.

Sasha unsheathes her dagger, electrifying it. She plunges toward Zarathustra's neck. Adam grabs her wrist, twists it behind her, and pins Sasha to the ground.

"Let me go, you bastard angel!" she screams. "The one who is responsible for my father's death is right in front of me!"

"I am not the god you seek, Sasha," Zarathustra says.

"Bullshit!" she shouts. "You admitted to creating the Earth. Who else could you be?"

"The one you refer to as God is someone else. I am no god. My kind is not worthy of that title. Besides, it's through you humans that those like me are born. I am not a god and I have no ties to angels. Adam here is an Abyssling. He was born from the White Abyss and charged with the task of watching over the Earth in my absence. He is not an angel, and I am not the god you seek to exact revenge upon."

Sasha remains skeptical, but forces herself to calm down. Melphis's rageful countenance makes her realize that this isn't the time. Silence overtakes the garden. Sasha moves toward Melphis, reaches for his shoulder. She pulls her arm back in hesitation, wincing at her inability to offer support. Adam returns to his meditative position. Melphis's cold, tired eyes stares toward Zarathustra.

"I understand that this is a lot to take in," Zarathustra says. "This is the truth of your past, Abdiel."

"Do not call me that!" Melphis shouts.

"But it is your name—"

"Shut it, you!"

Sasha backs away from Melphis. Adam breaks his stillness. His eyes jolt open, and he springs to his feet. He walks over to his father's side.

"Calm yourself, brother," Adam says.

"No—it is alright. His anger is earned," Zarathustra says.

"You speak the words, and the walls in my mind come crumbling down," Melphis says. "Just how deep are you burrowed into my head, rotten father of mine?"

Adam's eyes flood, as if he is offering his tears in place of his creator's misplaced eyes.

Zarathustra's mouth gapes. *To think he would still call me father.* "Yes, a rotten father indeed! Abdi—I am sorry. What would you prefer to be called?"

"Abdiel doesn't suit a soon-to-be king of Hell. I'll stick with Melphis." He pauses. "You said I'd be reborn with an insatiable craving to tear my siblings from power. Are they the ones who placed you here?"

"Y-yes," Zarathustra responds. "Does this mean you will follow through?"

"Not for you. My ambitions still stand, is all. I will take Hell's throne. It makes no difference to me that the one who sits on it was once my brother."

"Do as you will." Zarathustra turns away from Melphis. Adam shifts his gaze toward the same direction.

Sasha glances around the garden once more. "In my vision of this place, I saw three people. Why are you the only two here?"

"My sister Eve is out looking for Seth," Adam says. "He will be joining us on the journey through Hell."

Melphis and Sasha's faces light with fury.

"I will not have that traitor come along!" Melphis says.

"I understand your animosity, my son, but like you and Sasha, Seth is another of my reincarnated desires. His help will be invaluable," says Zarathustra.

Melphis clenches his jaw. "I'm done speaking with you." He walks over to Adam, who is gesturing for Melphis and Sasha to join him at the backside of the tree.

"Through here we can exit the Abyss," Adam says.

Sasha walks over, but stops next to Zarathustra. "I believe you. You're not God. The God I grew up learning about would never feel remorse, but—what can you tell me about God and his angels?"

"*His* angels? There are only two who call themselves Gods of the Earth. One is my son who resides in Hell. The other is the one you are searching for. The God of Heaven, and *Her* name is..."

"Yahweh," Satan says, "What has happened to your Sins?" He slumps into His throne, eyes closed, refusing to look at Her.

"What do you mean, dear brother? They were your responsibility. It is I who should be demanding answers," Yahweh responds.

"My job is to remain here. To foster souls, nothing more! But you have been free to roam the Earth. To seduce mankind into religious façades. You have been the impetus of the rise and fall of countless civilizations and their mythologies! But it is I, whom you have imprisoned in this room who is at fault? My sister, the Sins are born from you—"

"Quiet, or I will have your tongue!" Yahweh shouts. Satan relents, quivering in his throne.

She continues, "The Sins are dead, and this leaves us in quite the predicament. You are to blame, brother. Now what are we to do about it?"

CHAPTER TWENTY-ONE

EONS AGO.

Yahweh stood beneath the Tree of Life and Knowledge. Hearing Zarathustra refer to it by that name was her earliest memory. Lucifer acted as her shadow, mimicking Yahweh's intrigue. When hearing the words Life and Knowledge, they were confused. These were empty words to their innocent ears.

"What did Daddy mean, life and knowledge?" Lucifer asked.

"That's the name of this tree!" Yahweh answered.

The bark caught her attention. It squirmed and pulsated, like a heart. The air around the tree distorted.

{Hungry one...beware the vile god.}

Yahweh panned her head left and right. "Who said that?" she asked.

"Who said what?"

Yahweh glared at Lucifer. "You didn't hear that voice? You got bad ears, Lucy!"

She turned her focus toward the tree and laid her hands onto the bark. A large beetle scurried out from beneath a crevice and fell to the ground. Lucifer screeched and hid behind his sister.

"Look at it!" she shouted.

The eerie voice from before spoke again. ***{Insects imbued with the magic of life. That's what you sentient creatures are to him.}***

A stoic frog sat at the edge of a pond, left of the tree. A fly passed by. The frog's tongue launched from its mouth, snatching it from flight.

Yahweh glanced back to the beetle. It tried to scurry away, but Yahweh brought her foot down. A cloud of dirt dispersed. Lifting her foot up, she found the beetle's squashed, wet body flat across her sole. Its legs twitched as she peeled it. She opened her mouth and dropped the beetle inside.

Overcome by its awful taste, she spat it onto the ground.

"My children, please come inside. It's time to eat!" Zarathustra shouted.

Eden was home to all forms of life. The garden was bursting in colors. Rainbows sprawled across the sky could never compare. The reds of roses. The yellows of daffodils. Accompanied by hues of oranges, violets, blues, and dark, lush greens, covered every inch of the expansive landscape. Alongside Zarathustra and his three children, Eden was also home to every animal. Insects roamed the flora's roots. Rodents scurried up trees. Lions and wolves, and even large and tall reptiles made their home in Eden. Zarathustra kept his children safe at the center of the garden, under the roof of a brick house covered in ivy.

Abdiel was a month old now. Yahweh and Lucifer were still coming to terms with the existence of their new brother. The four-year-old children have lived in ignorant bliss since their birth. Eden provided everything they could ever need. They had no reason to question anything before, but now they found themselves wondering about the miracle of life.

The family sat together at a table and shared their evening meal. Zarathustra had harvested potatoes and hunted a turkey. He had also boiled some peas and carrots for the newborn son, much to the relief of Yahweh and Lucifer. They did not want to share the hearty meal with their new brother.

Zarathustra ate while captivated by his firstborns. They were twins, yet their differences were profound. Lucifer was soft-spoken and meek, but loved his sister more than anything. He spent most of his time following her around. The boy watched his sister eat with a ravenous appetite. Yahweh had finished three plates before Lucifer finished just one. Yahweh did not slow even then. Zarathustra wondered just where all the food went. With a fury, she kept on eating. Blind to any detriment of doing so.

My Gluttony, indeed. I have no doubt she will grow strong. He smiled.

Abdiel glanced at his sibling's food with tears in his eyes.

"Do not worry, my son," Zarathustra said. "Soon you will be as big as your siblings. You will get to eat plenty once you grow these." Zarathustra opened his mouth wide, flashing his teeth. Yahweh and Lucifer mimicked their father, smiling toward their brother.

Zarathustra let out a hearty laugh, unable to contain his joy. The children returned to their plates.

"Where did Abdiel come from?" Yahweh asked.

This question perplexed Zarathustra. He never considered being asked such a thing. His people were born fully formed with the knowledge of The Womb of the One Mind known to them at the start of their life. *I suppose it makes sense that they wouldn't know. Sentient life forms go through a process of growth that gods can never know the pleasure of.*

"He was born from the White Abyss, just like you and Lucifer were," Zarathustra responded. "You came from the Tree of Life and Knowledge, as will more humans in time."

"We will have to share Eden with even more people?" Yahweh asked with a pout. Lucifer first seemed delighted, but upon noticing his sister's frown, his smile transmuted to match her sadness.

"Yes, but do not fret, my dear. It is through union with others that humankind will grow strong. Relish in the coming of your new friends."

Yahweh went silent. Her mind seemed to go elsewhere.

She asked, "I accidentally stepped on a bug before. It stopped moving. If we are alive and we move, then what happened to the beetle?"

It's happening. The Abyss's power at work. Humankind is destined to search for answers. To embrace whatever pain is found in doing so, and to grow stronger from it, but I did not think it would happen at such a young age.

"The beetle is dead," Zarathustra said. "All life is born from the Abyss, and to the Abyss it will one day return. Through this cycle, the Abyss's power grows. It will then give birth to even stronger life. One flourishes in life and also in death—"

Yahweh was alarmed by what her father was telling them. Lucifer broke out in tears. Abdiel glanced around the dining room, confused by the tonal shift, and cried alongside Lucifer.

"So, one day we will also die?" Lucifer asked.

Zarathustra had spoken as if they were one of his kind, but these children were not of the gods he left behind. No worship would propel their lives forward for as long as that praise remained. Magic will keep them alive for a time, but no one, not even gods, are immune to what awaits all living things.

"Do not worry, my children. You three are special cases. As the first humans, it is up to you to guide this world forward. You do not have to worry about a thing," Zarathustra said.

Lucifer stopped crying. Abdiel persisted a bit longer. Yahweh scrutinized her father's face.

The children grew tired and retreated to their rooms. Lucifer sat on his bed, hiding beneath the sheets. He sobbed, until he heard a knock on the door.

Zarathustra came in and sat by Lucifer's bedside.

"I'm sorry if my words frightened you, my son. You will have a long and happy life, I assure you. Now, get some rest and know that I love you. Goodnight, my boy."

Yahweh's room was next to Lucifer's. She placed her ear to the wall to hear what her father was saying. *There was something different in his voice.* The cycle of life and death had not left her mind. *Why would we live forever, but not the other humans?* In her ruminations, she noticed a spider in the corner of the room, opposite her bed. Its web hung just above the floor. A fly squirmed inside fresh web. The spider approached and devoured it.

That fly was born from the Abyss, too. Just like I was, but the spider ate it. Where does the fly's life go? Will the Abyss eat me when I die?

The spider raised its front legs, reacting to Yahweh's approach. She stared down at the spider with condescending eyes, giggling. *It wants to fight me, even though it's so small! I'll show you, spider.* Yahweh slammed her foot into the floor, crushing the spider and its web. Lifting her foot, she peeled away its twitching body. *Daddy is right. I am a special case. I will grow strong and live forever.* She dropped the spider into her mouth and swallowed it. She was overcome by the taste of its slimy, furred body, but endured it. *Even if I must eat the Abyss itself.*

There was a knock on the door. Yahweh ran to her bed. Zarathustra entered.

"I just wanted to say goodnight, my dear. I heard some stomping. Is everything alright?" Zarathustra asked, noticing a peculiar brown stain on the floor.

"Yes, Daddy. I just ran over to say hi to a bug I saw," Yahweh said. She flashed him a smile with teeth stained the same brown color.

Zarathustra, unaware of what to make of this, tucked in his daughter and wished her a restful sleep. He kissed her forehead and left her room.

Sixteen years later.

Zarathustra had written books on magic. The Abyss's power flowed through all and was as much an instinct as breathing. Learning magic was unnecessary, but Zarathustra thought it best to write books on magic theory to facilitate intrigue in humans. Zarathustra himself had no knowledge of whether these concepts would work, but that was not important. The more the human mind wandered, the more it would search for answers. This process would lead humans down the path of acquiring more strength.

Lucifer and Abdiel were studying these books in the library Zarathustra had built next to their home. More humans had sprouted from the Tree of Life and Knowledge. This necessitated the construction of new homes and other buildings where humans could commune.

"Lucifer, take a look at this," Abdiel said. "These runes. Father crafted these to act as a conduit for magic. Through them they may allow that which is without magic to become imbued with power."

"Then what use is it? We have had magic since birth. Why use a substitute when our bodies are the real thing?"

"I suppose you are right, but I wonder if they might have some other utility."

"Keep studying them and I am sure you will find your answer. You always were the brightest of us, Abdiel."

"I am good at reading books, is all. My raw talent is nothing compared to yours and sister's."

"That may be true. For *her*, at least."

Her eventual death was all Yahweh could think about. Sixteen years had gone by since she learned of death and its relation to the Abyss

If father could lie about one thing, how can I judge the validity of any word from his mouth? Lucifer and I are not going to live forever. Why would he create the world to function this way? Why would he allow us to be born, just to die?

Like her brothers, she spent her days studying the magic tomes her father wrote. She hoped that one day they would lead her to the answers she sought.

She shut the book she was reading and went for a walk. She had grown fascinated with the Tree of Life and Knowledge. This was where she went whenever she wanted to rest her eyes.

Walking down the hall, she passed by Zarathustra's room. She caught a glimpse of him placing a peculiar locket into a drawer at his bedside. Yahweh had never seen the locket before. *Why has he been hiding it? Why hasn't he told us about it?* She walked off and exited the house.

Standing under the tree, she placed her hands onto the bark. The voices she heard from within have gotten louder over the years. She watched the air ripple. The vibrations thickened until they took shape. A white form loomed over her shoulder and whispered into her ear.

{*Aren't you hungry? The void inside you deepens by the day. Nothing has been satisfying yet, has it? It is the fault of that vile god. Oh, here he comes now.*}

Zarathustra walked toward Yahweh. He saw her alone beneath the tree, muttering to herself.

"Ah, Father," she said, refusing to look at him. "There's a question that has lingered on my mind for a while."

"What troubles you?" he asked.

"The Tree of Life and Knowledge. Humans are birthed from it, then returned to the Abyss when they die. Would it then not also be a Tree of Death? Is it the knowledge aspect of the tree that leads life toward death? And if so, why do you encourage our longing of knowledge?"

Zarathustra had become used to Yahweh's baffling inquiries. All he could say was: "I do not control the Abyss. It made me, just as it had also made you. I do not have the answers you seek. The Abyss exists for the propagation of power so that sentient life can preserve itself. Knowledge may hurt, but that pain leads one to greater heights. A fear of pain, of death, will consume you. I watched it happen to my people. My daughter, do not fear death, but instead embrace the life you have."

The voice of the strange white form hissed. **{*Yes, his people. Those vile gods are responsible for the mass consumption*}** *of countless sentient life forms. Do not trust him, or he will eat you. Unless—}*

"I eat him first," whispered Yahweh.

Zarathustra's mouth gaped, but only silence fell out. His eyes widened with worry as he watched his daughter walk away.

Yahweh headed toward the library. *If the path of knowledge leads toward death, wouldn't human beings be happier if they were ignorant? Awareness of life—their sentience—*

Is what causes pain. Life is birthed, only to die, but what is the end of life, to one who does not know death? If I eat the Abyss, then the cycle of life and death should break. I will free them from their shackles and become a savior to humankind.

Yahweh entered the library where she found Lucifer and Abdiel at a large table stacked high with books.

"Abdiel," she said. "Go to your room. I want some alone time with Lucy."

Abdiel picked up the book of runes and left with a frown.

"You know, he looks up to you. Can't you try to be nicer to him?" Lucifer asked.

"I needed to speak privately with you."

"What about?"

"My sweet, loyal brother. You followed me into life, tethered at the hip. Would you still follow me anywhere, even now?"

Lucifer cocked his head in confusion, wondering where this was coming from, but answered, "Of course."

"Then would you follow me on a journey to liberate humanity from their cruel fate?"

Ten years later.

Yahweh sat at a desk in her room, constructing a crown of thorns. Lucifer sat by her side, unaware of the white humanoid figure whispering into his sister's ear.

{*The vile god must be banished before he devours you humans.*}

Yahweh had realized that this voice spoke to her alone. No other human appeared to perceive it. She concluded that she was exalted—chosen by the Abyss for a divine mission. She never responded to it, but she knew that it wanted her to rid the world of Zarathustra. This she agreed to, but Yahweh had no intention of letting this divine voice control her. The method she planned to use to betray her father was spoken to Lucifer alone.

This voice from the Abyss appeared to hold enmity toward Zarathustra and his race of gods. Their father told Yahweh and her brothers about them before, but he would not mention much aside from that they are from another world. Yahweh pushed Zarathustra to speak more on this, but he always refused. Yahweh found this suspicious, considering Zarathustra's tendency to push a love for knowledge and power. *Why would he make us long to know, yet hide away the reason he came here to create the Earth in the first place? Why would he create us just to die?*

Lucifer shared these concerns. Betraying their father was no easy feat for the softer twin, but after hearing Yahweh's explanation of the Abyss's role in the world, as well as her weariness of Zarathustra's motives, it was a choice he needed to make.

They studied much over the years and Yahweh had developed a magic most useful to their goal. A grizzly bear sat in the corner of Yahweh's room. The twins had subdued it with magic the night before. Blood spilt from its side. Its fur, singed from fire. Too weak to resist, the crown of thorns was placed upon its head. The animal collapsed to the floor. Its eyes glossed over. Its body shrunk. In a matter of seconds, the bear was mummified.

"It's ready," Yahweh said. "A tool that subdues life. We can now overpower him."

Lucifer nodded. They made their way toward Zarathustra's room.

{*The locket...steal the locket. And I will open a gateway into the Abyss.*}

Yahweh led the way. Their father had not yet returned from the library. Yahweh tried opening the drawer which held the locket. It would not budge. She gestured to Lucifer to break it open. He conjured a small flame on the tip of his right index finger. Touching the keyhole, the flames entered inside with precision. The dresser remained unharmed, but the lock melted away. Yahweh forced the drawer open and stole the locket.

⎯⎯◇⎯⎯

Zarathustra went to visit the Tree of Life and Knowledge while returning from the library. He placed his hands on the great tree, lost in rumination.

My children have grown apart from me. Yahweh and Lucifer have not been the same since I taught them about the cycle of life and death. Was I wrong to do so? Or were they just too weak to handle the truth? But of course, why am I surprised? Even the gods I left behind took poorly to the knowledge of their impending deaths. Very few can handle the harsh truth that we live but one life. There is nothing beyond. I wish for a day when humankind can grow strong enough to see the beauty in that. The fleeting nature of our lives is what makes our time so precious. It allows us to appreciate life for what it is. The desire for eternal life is naught but a denial of the life one has. That longing curses life for what it is not. Such is the will of a weak fool.

Zarathustra looked toward the leaves above. His bright teal eyes glanced at each petal with worry. *Even if I scared the children with that talk of death, the change in Yahweh is far too drastic. Is it possible? Has the Abyss infected her with delusions? Is this the price I pay for belonging to that reprehensible race of gods?*

No—My mind is wandering too far. The Abyss is an indifferent, insentient force of nature. There have been no accounts of it reaching out to someone—

Zarathustra rubbed his temples to ease his aching head and weary eyes. He turned away from the tree and made his way to his room.

Upon his return, he noticed the busted open drawer. He tossed its contents around the room. "The locket! Where is the locket—No! How could they have learned about it?"

Footsteps approached. Intuiting disaster, Zarathustra fled to three doors down. He swung the door open, tears streaming down his face. His hands trembled as his gaze scattered around the room, before landing on the sight of Abdiel.

Ah, my sweet third child. Yahweh never cared to bond with him and here he is, studying in his lonesome, unaware of their plot. Or so I hope.

His third born turned toward him and said, "What has you so disheveled?"

"Abdiel, I am so sorry."

"Sorry for what? Father, you're scaring me."

"They took it. The locket—the key to the Abyss. Eden is doomed and I am useless against them. I cannot bring myself to raise a hand against my children. I cannot become like the foolish gods I left behind."

"What are you—"

"I am sorry, Abdiel. You will have to do me this favor."

Zarathustra dug his hands into Abdiel and rewired his soul. He told his son that one day he would be reborn. As he said this, Zarathustra felt disgusted with himself. He told Abdiel this, thinking it would calm his son, but he was a fool. It was not to reassure Abdiel, but to soothe himself.

What have I done? For Abdiel to be reborn, he first had to die. Zarathustra fell to his knees. An ocean of tears clouded his vision. *In my weakness, I have killed my son. Curse my name. Curse the gods I come from!*

The door swung open. Yahweh glared down at Zarathustra. Lucifer stood behind her, his eyes dark and sullen. The locket was held firm within Yahweh's grasp, along with a peculiar crown of thorns. Zarathustra jumped to his feet and threw himself out the window above Abdiel's desk.

Yahweh and Lucifer stalked Zarathustra through the twilit garden. Lucifer slunk away into the bushes. Zarathustra tripped over a tree's root and Yahweh tore it from the soil as she approached. Desecrated brush, flowers, and small trees laid in her wake, until she cornered him beneath the Tree of Life and Knowledge.

Lucifer snuck up and gripped his father's shoulders. Zarathustra whipped his head back in surprise. Down came the crown of thorns, piercing his skin and soul alike.

Zarathustra screamed and was brought down to his knees. The teal gleam of his eyes faded.

"Of course. You would be stronger than a bear," Yahweh said. "But that's fine. I cannot absorb your soul from dead flesh."

Lucifer let go of Zarathustra's shoulders and repositioned himself behind his sister.

***{Lift the locket toward the tree.}*}**

Yahweh obliged.

"Do not do this, my children," Zarathustra said. "Your magic is far too weak to withstand the blunt of the Abyss's weight."

Yahweh's eyes grew wide. "That's what you want, isn't it, Father? You created us to be weak insects for you to feed on, admit it!"

Zarathustra's eyes flooded. *So, it's true. A phenomenon unknown to even my kind has occurred. Otherwise, how could they know the sins of my people?* "The abyssal touch deludes you, my daughter! Do not listen to the voice—"

"*Silence!*" Yahweh bellowed. Lucifer slunk further back.

White light was emitted from the locket. Its hinges flung open. A large gate appeared behind the Tree of Life and Knowledge. The tree's bark extended and gripped Zarathustra's body, like wooden hands. Yahweh's eyebrows rose at the sight.

Zarathustra mustered up the strength to stand before the tree's grip finalized. He outstretched his hand and snatched the locket away from Yahweh. The force of the Abyss set in. Yahweh's black hair fluttered wildly, pulled by the vacuum of the Abyss. She and Lucifer stood back, holding onto another tree for balance. Zarathustra and the Tree of Life and Knowledge were uprooted from the Earth. The gravitational pull ceased. The gateway started its gradual closure.

"He took the locket! Brother, we must act now!" Yahweh shouted.

The twins approached the Abyss. Lucifer reached his hand inside. Yahweh placed her head into the gate to consume the grand white realm.

Power pulsed from within. Yahweh gaped her mouth and welcomed it into her. *I am the Alpha and the Omega. The Beginning and the End.* Tendrils manifested and were pulled toward her stomach. The tentacles made their way inside her—and she heard her brother scream.

The white tendrils wrapped around Lucifer's wrist. They continued up his arm then around his shoulder until reaching his back. They pierced through his flesh at two points. His body rapidly bulged. First his back, then his arms, torso, legs, and face. Long horns erupted from his forehead and spiraled behind him. Bone rose from the wounds in his back, taking the shape of wings. They sprouted black feathers, then erupted into flames. Charred flesh melted off the bone, leaving him a flightless bird.

Lucifer screamed at the immense pain from his body's sudden expansion. Yahweh refused to address him. Her head remained inside the gateway. Her body, unmoving.

"Sister!" Lucifer shouted.

Yahweh's stomach bulged at all sides. Its expansion continued until—

Blood splattered across Lucifer's face. He stared in awe through the red mist. Yahweh, from the waist up, remained inside the gateway. Her dismembered legs were twitching, scattered upon a blood-soaked flower bed. The white tendrils which filled her stomach dangled from her wound. They wove themselves together, forming a new base for her to stand upon, but this new lower half was not human. Six insectile legs grew into a scaly lower torso.

Yahweh's head was ejected from the Abyss. She screamed as the scales spread across her upper half. Gashes were cut into the gaps of her fingers. The fissures rose from her hands toward her shoulders, splitting her arms into thirds. Blood gushed from the wounds before the arms reshaped themselves into a total of six pincers. Her face stretched back. Her mouth ripped at the seams and drooped as if it was without bone to cling to. Six parasitic feelers hung from her loose mouth, spilling a torrent of tar onto the ground.

"What has happened?" Her guttural voice reached the far corners of Eden. Birds scattered from the trees. Creatures of the ground scurried off with haste. Insects made their escape as the plants withered from contact with the twins' tainted power.

Zarathustra glanced around and saw that a large part of the garden had been banished alongside him. The Tree of Life and Knowledge continued his restraint.

{*Through the schizophrenic child, a vessel of destruction has been born. The vile god can now pay for his sins.*}

Hearing the voice for the first time, Zarathustra's worries had come true. *It recognizes me. It knows I belong to the gods who betrayed the cycle.*

{*Come now, vile god. Return to whence you came.*}

Zarathustra felt a jolt of pain. His body grew translucent. He felt himself growing weaker. Memories of the first gods to disappear flashed before his eyes. "No—not yet! I must live, for what example would I be for the future of humanity if I were to quit it now? If only to see the rebirth of Abdiel, I must live!"

He dug into his eye sockets and severed the orbs. Blood gushed forth as he dropped the eyes into the garden. They burrowed into the soil and teal light arose from beneath. Vines grew into flowers. As they blossomed, the plants craned to the ground and birthed new lives. Adam and Eve were born into a bowing position. Toward Zarathustra their praises were sung. His body returned to a solid state.

I have killed my son. Now I have created two more beings so that my life can be extended through their worship. A vile god indeed!

Zarathustra screamed. Adam and Eve gazed toward their creator and cried in his stead.

CHAPTER TWENTY-TWO

A tall, slender woman approaches Seth's limp body. Glowing teal hair reaches her ankles. The woman squats and meets his eyeline.

"Hello, I am Eve," she says, tilting her head to the left.

The colorful shine of Seth's eyes has been reduced to a blackened, unanimated state.

Eve continues, "Don't just lay there. One must remain in motion within the White Abyss, lest they are consumed by it. By the looks of it, that process has already begun."

"I-I am...a monster. I destroy...everything," Seth groans. "I can't go on."

Eve rises away from Seth, and says, "Is this the product of a life unloved, unnurtured? To be reduced to a miserable, helpless, wretch? No. The truly strong can handle the Abyss within them. But you? Pathetic."

Eve grabs Seth's useless legs, one under each arm. She groans under the burden of his weight, but drags him away.

—◇—

Who is this and where is she taking me? I don't care. It doesn't matter. Nothing matters. Not anymore. Not for me. My life doesn't deserve to have meaning.

Sasha's hatred is etched into my mind. This whole time, I've plowed through with my magic—with my rage. Blind to the damage left in my wake. No—not blind. I was aware, but just didn't care. All I could think of was Lola, but the damage caught up to me. Culminating into the fury imprinted upon Sasha's face.

The ground beneath me feels different. The coldness of the White Abyss is replaced with a warm, moist surface. The woman drops me and walks away. Rising to my feet, I look around. A bed of grass and flowers surround me. They glisten with morning dew. Eve walks along a trail toward a tree. Below is a man whose hair color matches hers. His eyes have been gutted from his skull.

"Hello, my Wrath," the man says. "My name is Zarathustra. This is Eve. You have met her brother, Adam, before."

"That voice," I say. "I never expected you to look like this."

"We were never supposed to meet. No human has ever come here...not successfully anyway. Even I have spent eons deteriorating under the Abyss's weight. Yet in your erroneous ways, you have cast yourself and your friends into this place."

My eyes pool with tears and I fall to my knees, covering my mouth with both hands.

He continues, "You have no words? When we last spoke, you were as a petulant child quick to speak back."

"He was quite fragile when I found him, Father," Eve says.

"Yes, he is now aware. Thankfully for him, it is through fragility—through pain—that one is set upon the path of human excellence. Seth! Stand tall and heed my words. This is no time to contemplate *what if.* Instead, love the pain, for it is a lesson of immeasurable value. Take it to heart and let it nurture you. Now, let me explain, as I have done for Melphis and Sasha before you."

"I cannot let you go, brother. We cannot venture further until my sister and Seth arrive," Adam says.

"Sasha is powerful enough as it is. We don't need *him*," Melphis shouts. "We are so close. We should be storming Castle Pandaemonium, not waiting around here."

"I cannot allow it. This is what Father wants. I am his sight. I will see this through as he intends."

Adam returns to a mediative position. Melphis stomps away. *What is happening to me. His betrayal has made me far too angry. I need to regain my composure for this final feat.*

Melphis walks toward the Sea of Flames. Behind him is the end of the realm, referred to by Satan and the Sins as Hell's Edge. Flames spill from the sides, into the vast darkness.

Melphis glances toward the shoreline. *The flames that birthed me.* He pictures the flames taking shape, forming his body and leaving him on the shore. He remembers opening his eyes for the first time, unable to discern where or who he was.

Satan—no, Lucifer, was I reborn just to kill you? Is that the sole reason I'm spurred forward? My will, my ambitions, are they even my own? What shall become of me once the purpose provided by Father is resolved? Does any of this matter? Do I?

He shakes his head furiously, like a dog waggling water off its body. Turning away from the shore, he sees Sasha standing by a gateway. Through the gate is a road that runs parallel to the Sea of Flames on the left, a mountain to the right. Her eyes are wide with curiosity.

This is the first time she's seen Hell. To think she would look toward it with childlike wonder. He remembers how Sasha was inside the White Abyss. The sheer effort and determination she displayed in cultivating power even in the face of a hopeless situation. *Yet, we escaped after all. Now here we are.*

Nothing for it but to push on. Melphis smiles. He returns to Adam, finding a seat next to this strange, foreign sibling. He closes his eyes and waits.

⚬

"That is how the Earth, and the White Abyss, came to be," Zarathustra says. "Even modern humans were meant to wield magic, but due to my foolish firstborns, humanity has been cut off from it. The power of this place should be far greater. With the cycle broken, souls have nowhere to return to.

"But the power that was here before the tree's banishment continues to fester. The Womb of the One Mind which birthed my people doesn't need the return of souls to function. The White Abyss shares that trait, but I allowed for the flow of souls to enhance that preexisting power. Imagine a world where the flow wasn't interrupted. Imagine how much farther humanity could have progressed, if not for the interference of the self-proclaimed gods my children have become!"

"Humans were cut off from magic? What about Sasha then?" I ask.

"You, Melphis, Sasha, as well as Virdeus and his Guild make use of conduits. You do not access magic directly. The Guild uses runes to act as a conduit for magic. You and Melphis are human souls inside demonic bodies. Those are your conduits."

"I'm not human. Not anymore," I respond.

"Why? Because of your appearance? Your soul is still human. It always was and always will be. Your ever-growing magic potential is proof of that. New demons being created at this very moment could never match your power. You have been told this before: magic grows substantially over time. You and Sasha have unique powers and being the youngest human magic wielders is why. Yet new demons younger than you are weak. This is because demons are a fabrication of human life. The same can be said for Satan and Yahweh's divinity, as well as the worlds they inhabit. They are nothing but cheap replications."

"And what? You expect us to kill Satan and free the captured souls? That's insane."

"Is it? Did you not set out on this journey to do just that? To find your beloved, knowing full well that you would have to kill Satan to do so?"

"Maybe, but I can't trust my own judgement anymore. Look at what I've done."

"Yes, you have been deluded, but I created humanity with the intention of having them one day be capable of surpassing gods. It is time to show my work. Thanks to my firstborns, the Earth is dying. Eve and Adam traverse the realms through the small quantity of magic residue left behind in the Earth's flora, but it is quickly dissipating. Once it is gone, the Earth will be lost."

"Melphis and Sasha went on ahead, right? Just let them handle it. I can't help anyone."

I go to leave the Garden. The vast whiteness is before me, a hungry predator to which I'm ready to relinquish myself.

"Enough of this cowardice!" Zarathustra bellows. "You think your wrath is poison? You think you are a monster? Why? Because during childhood, the townsfolk told you so? My Greed, Melphis. My Lust, Sasha. My Pride, Virdeus. Do you think they are poisons as well?"

"Don't lecture me! I never asked to be your wrath. I never asked to be born! And what of your other desires? Satan and Yahweh. Weren't you just saying that they are poisoning this world? And who did you say your Envy was?"

Zarathustra remains still. Eve's face tenses. Her fists tighten, but her eyes grow sad.

"Sasha's guildmate, Mikhail, was my Envy. I will not deny that three of my desires have become corrupted, but do not make the mistake of creating broad accusations due to the mistakes of a few. No emotion or desire is inherently evil. Even your wrath can be a useful tool. Instead of wallowing in despair, why not use that anger to fix your mistakes? Use it as fuel—as motivation—to better yourself in the eyes of your friends. Yes, my Gluttony, Sloth, and Envy lost their way," Zarathustra pauses. Eve's eyes grow moist. "But I *refuse* to let that happen to *you*."

His voice sounds as if it belongs to a father of dead children. I return to him and Eve.

"I know life has been hard for you," Zarathustra continues. "For that I am sorry, but please know that you can embrace suffering and grow stronger for it."

I nod.

"Good. Now, the crushed locket. Give it here."

I hand the pieces to him. They float above his left palm. Teal sparks flutter around them. The broken edges are melded back together, until it appears to never have been broken. He gives the repaired heirloom to Eve, who places it within the pocket of her white robe.

"*She* will hold onto this. *You* don't need it anymore."

Eve gestures for me to follow. Taking my hand in hers, she touches the tree with her other. Our bodies reduce to particles, and we disappear.

Zarathustra sits alone under the uprooted tree. *All my children are gone. On their way to do a job I should have handled myself.*

He can sense the weight of the Abyss and the encroachment of death. *It won't be long now before this can finally end. I just hope Seth can pull it off. It's not easy for one to master the Abyss within them.*

And I wonder if Melphis will ever forgive me, wretched as I am.

CHAPTER TWENTY-THREE

This supernatural weight. The overwhelming heat brushing against my face. I'll never forget this sensation...

"I'm really back," I say.

"You seem surprised," Eve says.

"A part me still can't believe I came here the first time."

"Convincing at it is, this is still a false world. Come, let us meet the others."

Arriving at a black gate, three silhouettes are waiting. It's a moment before my eyes register Melphis and Sasha among the figures. They come into view, greeting me with scowls. My heartbeat increases. Time appears to stop.

"I-I—what I did was—"

"Your apologies mean nothing to us. You're only coming along because I wasn't given a choice," Melphis says.

He looks toward Adam with scrunched eyes. Sasha's are cold and absent-minded.

They turn away, passing under the rusty iron gate. Reaching out for Sasha's shoulder, Adam steps between us.

"Give them space and be patient, brother," he says.

"Yes, repairing these bonds will take more than words," Eve says. She gives my shoulder a comforting squeeze. "Come now, let's follow."

Melphis leads us down the empty road. Staring across the gap dividing us, my gaze lays stiff upon the backside of Sasha's head. *I'd do anything to warm those icy eyes—to see her sun-soaked smile again.*

Why do I feel this way?

Sasha glances at Melphis. His pace is brisk and determined. The scowl on his face refuses to lift. His eyes, dull and unaroused.

Soon, Melphis will accomplish his lifelong goal. He hardly looks happy about it. Though I understand why. He hasn't been the same since regaining his memories. He's like an empty-headed soldier. Propelled forward by the commanding voice of the god who raped his mind. Is his anger really because of Seth? Is my anger really because of Seth?

A severe heat rises in her chest. The Sea of Flames burns to the right of her, but it goes unnoticed. *Seth looked so sad. He deserves to be, but then why did I want to comfort him?* Sasha's jaw clenches. Biting down on her gums, she draws blood.

"Melphis," Sasha says. "Do you hate Seth?"

"What a stupid question. He betrayed us after I put in the effort to guide him along." He turns to meet her eyeline. Sasha averts her gaze.

Yes, he deserves to be hated and I do feel hate, but not for him.

She remembers her childhood and how she struggled to obtain mastery over her emotions. She tamed her inner monster and learned to transmute its animosity into more positive outlets. By learning to cope with and channel the emptiness within her, she also grew to trust. She was able to better herself because Virdeus believed in her. Her trust in her adopted father manifested into trust for others like Andes and eventually Seth, but he tossed that trust away. The leash restraining her inner monster has snapped.

He took advantage of my vulnerability, and I hate myself for letting him do so. After this journey of ours concludes, I should rid myself of him for good—Seth's sullen eyes are roused in memory. She squeezes her temples and groans. Her eyes fill with tears. *Father, I wish you were here. I need your guidance.*

Sasha and Melphis reach a cliffside overlooking the Sea of Flames. Seth, Adam, and Eve trail close behind.

"See that cave there?" Melphis says. "That will lead us to Satan. Let's take a quick break."

Sasha glances at Seth as he draws near. She turns away and walks over to the cliff's edge. She hears screams echoing from the pit. Humans drowning in the ravenous Sea of Flames. Their flesh melts off the bone. Then regrows, like watching time in reverse. "No! No more!" They scream as their bodies regenerate, then are burnt away again. Seth's flames devouring Magistrum and the Guild flash before her eyes.

These souls, forsaken for eternity. Never allowed rest. I was once like them. Mikhail and the others wanted to abandon me, but father's belief never wavered. No matter how unsavory and troublesome I was. He remained by my side. He recognized that my issues weren't indicative of who I was. They were mere impulses. Momentary stress fueled by past trauma that was not my fault. The same can be said for—

"Sasha," says a voice from behind.

She turns to see Seth's sorrowful eyes. Adam and Eve remain behind, watching from afar. Melphis's back is turned away.

"I know it doesn't matter what I say, but I'm sorry," Seth continues. "I want to make things right—more than anything, I want to make things right. I want to be good—to show you that I can be good, to no longer be the *monster* who hurt you."

Sasha clenches her fists. Her jaw tightens. Walking away, she pushes down the urge to respond.

I'm tired of watching her leave, but it's well deserved. Slumping to the ground, I turn toward the Sea of Flames. Souls, in human form, are screaming from below.

Zarathustra claimed that Satan was once human. I wonder what he was like before becoming what he is. From what I could surmise from the story, he didn't seem like a bad kid and yet he has placed millions of souls here to suffer for eternity. Satan and I...might not be too different from each other.

My heartbeat rises. My breathing becomes shallow. Gritting my teeth, I lean over the edge, and let gravity take control.

Adam sits in silence while observing Melphis and Sasha. The woman and the demon sit with great distance between them. *They have built thick walls. Are they courageous enough to break them down again?*

Eve sits near her brother. She unearths the locket from her robe. She lifts it into the air and examines the brilliant gleam of the fire's light reflecting off the locket.

"Father's craftmanship sure is sublime," Eve says.

Melphis jerks his head around. "Is it though?" he asks. "Some of his other creations are abhorrent." Melphis gazes toward the cave which leads toward Satan's castle.

"The capacity for mistake making is one all humans share, but that trait isn't inherently evil. We think you should be more forgiving," Adam says.

Melphis scoffs. Eve places the locket back into her robe, then glances behind her.

"Seth?" Eve returns to her feet and rushes over to the cliffside. Her eyes widen. "Seth's falling!"

Fire envelops me, but I've yet to be submerged into the Sea of Flames. The sight of these poor souls has made my chest heat with anger. My body's flames turn from red to blue, then flicker into intense white fire.

Still falling, I roar into the pit. Like a dog heeding its master's call, the Sea of Flames morphs. The fire retracts from each soul residing in the pit. The sea swirls around them, keeping a few feet away. The human figures twitch their heads around in surprise. It's as if they are protected by a bubble the flames can no longer enter.

I plummet to the floor, but quickly rise again. I inhale deeply, and the Sea of Flames disappears into the void of my stomach.

Letting my flames die down, I glance around the pit. The legion of melted humans stare at me. Their flesh crumbles, revealing their bright souls beneath. They spring toward the sky, leaving behind ashes. Echoing throughout the pit are the words: "Thank...you..."

Adam and Eve stand by the cliffside. Melphis peeks over their shoulders. Sasha following behind.

"What is he doing?" Adam asks, watching Seth pull the flames into his being.

"Trying to eat souls again for power?" Melphis asks. "Selfish fool."

The flames vanish and the legion of souls launch into the sky. The group is overtaken by a gust of wind as the spirits pass by. Once they are gone, Adam and Eve make their descent.

Hearing a thud behind him, Seth turns to face the two Abysslings.

"What great precision. You had us worried for a moment," Adam says.

Eve offers her hand to Seth. "Come now. Let us return to our friends."

Adam and Eve lead me back. As soon as I reach the top, Sasha's left palm strikes my cheek.

"What was that about? What were you thinking!" she says.

"Yes, Seth, tell us," Adam says, in a tone which told me he knew the answer.

"And here I was hoping you were trying to snuff out your life," Melphis says.

"Melphis!" Sasha snaps, readying herself to hit him as well. He waves us off and makes his way toward the cave.

Watching him leave deepens the emptiness I feel, but I turn toward Sasha and say, "I'm sorry. I'm so sorry—I'm sorry. I saw them suffering down there. I wanted to free them. I wanted to do something good. To show you that I can be good. Instead of a monster—"

"Stop it! Stop this right now! Stop calling yourself a monster. It isn't true! Because if you're a monster, then so am—" Sasha shuts her tearful eyes. Taking a deep breath, she stomps away.

Melphis has disappeared into the cave. Sasha stops right before entering. She faces me and gestures to follow.

I smile and walk on.

CHAPTER TWENTY-FOUR

EONS AGO.

With the loss of the locket and the Tree of Life and Knowledge, Eden no longer served a purpose. Yahweh led a sobbing Lucifer away from the garden. Their home and the mistakes they made were left behind, obscured by the passage of time.

Yahweh noticed that their mutated forms were not the only consequence of their failure. The other humans who populated Eden were forced onto all fours. Their bodies became far hairier. Their intelligence waned and their speech was reduced to primitive grunts and growls.

"Their soul's magic is gone—no, asleep," Yahweh said. "This must be a failsafe he made when creating the Abyss. Without the Tree, humankind has devolved into beasts!"

"What are we to do, sister? We're all alone now," Lucifer said.

"Don't worry. Father wouldn't deny humans their power forever. He wanted to eat them after all. You feel that, Lucy?

Magic still lingers within the Earth's flora. I'm sure that over time humankind will reawaken to their power—and when they do...we will sustain ourselves with them."

Lucifer's tears grew heavier. Yahweh frowned at Her distraught brother. *I did this to Him. I need to take responsibility.*

"Do not fret, Lucy. We still have each other," She extended Her right hand. Lucifer quickly grabbed hold of its comfort and buried His face into Yahweh's bosom. She smiled at Her twin. "Come now. Let us ascend to our new kingdom together."

Satan's castle rises high in the distance. Standing between us and his abode is the field of crucified humans. A woman screams in pain. I recognize her and the others around her. Their torture ensues. Nothing has changed. Steam rises from my eyes as my tears evaporate.

A screech jerks my head upward. The souls I freed from the Sea of Flames blur together in a teal swirl just below the blood-red sky and black clouds.

"Are they still in pain? Did I not do enough?" I ask.

"Worry not," Eve says. "You did everything you could. They simply have nowhere to return to."

"Indeed. When the Tree of Life and Knowledge was uprooted, so was life itself. Humanity has been lost for so long," Adam says.

Then was my effort pointless? If I did everything I could, but nothing was accomplished, did it even matter? I want to do more. I can't stop here. I need to better myself. I need to try harder.

"They have nowhere to return to *yet*," Sasha says, looking at me. "Even the tiniest steps have merit."

"Right," I say, smiling. Her gaze warms me to the core. I don't expect her to have forgiven me yet, but when she talks to me, I feel anchored. This is enough. I must cherish and maintain this.

"Hey Melphis? Can we take a moment to free the souls here as well?" I ask.

"Absolutely not. I won't have you wasting anymore of my time," Melphis says.

He glares at me. My eyes fidget away. Adam stares back at Melphis in my stead, and says, "What he means to say is that slaying Satan is our priority. We can do these souls no greater service by doing so."

Looking back toward the whirlwind of souls, I know they're right. To truly save them, Satan will have to be dealt with. I raise my hands to my face. Satan guided me toward my death and turned me into a demon. We've been through so much since then. It feels like a distant memory. To think this journey began with a desire for revenge. To kill Satan. To rescue Lola. The thought hasn't crossed my mind in a while.

I pan my gaze, left to right. The humans hanging from the pillars are screaming in agony. This much I remember from my first visit, but something feels different.

"Since arriving at Hell's Edge, have we seen any demons?" I ask.

"I was wondering the same thing," Melphis says. "The Crucifixion Field has always been full of demons, but now the humans suffer alone. What is Satan plotting?"

"I see an imp!" says Sasha, pointing toward a demon sprawled across the hard, sizzling ground.

We approach, but it doesn't react. Its eyes are dull and without stimulation. It appears dead, but its chest rises as it takes a shallow breath.

"What's wrong with it?" I ask.

Surveying the area, my eyes grow wide. Thousands of imps and reptilian demons lay stagnant upon the ground. Alongside them are demons I've never seen, but resemble succubi due to their black wings, tails, and voluptuous bodies.

"This is concerning, but I suppose it works out in our favor," Melphis says, then continues toward the castle. The number of demons increase and condense the closer to Satan's castle we get. It's as if they meant to gather there before whatever caused this strange catatonic state. We march on, stepping over and around the corpse-like demons.

"Well, Lucy? What are we to do?" Yahweh says. A conniving smile grows upon Her face.

"Do not call me that," Satan says. "And I am done answering your questions."

"Oh? Are you now? From whence has this courage been aroused?"

Satan stares at Yahweh. His jaw clenches. *I don't have Seth. The legion of demons will have to do.*

With the demons being a product of Satan's will, they are forever attached to Him. They do as told, but Satan needs not speak His orders. At his cognitive command, all the demons in Hell and on Earth march toward Castle Pandaemonium.

"You have been corrupted, sister. After our mistake in Eden, the consumption of human souls was a necessity for survival, but now it appears you relish any chance to eat their wills. Your longing for power and control has led you astray."

Yahweh's grin grows wider. She approaches the foot of Satan's throne and stomps up the steps. Satan feels the temperature rise, but the fires hugging the edge of the room remain the same. His heartbeat increases, realizing the heat is coming from within.

"Mistake? That is the difference between you and I," Yahweh says. "Why feel guilt for something that pushes us higher? These pathetic humans are mere steppingstones to *my* new world."

Satan's eyes widen. He raises his right hand, crunching it into a fist. "So, it is true. I had my suspicions. You have gone back on our promise. You no longer seek to bring me along. You also promised the Sins they could come with us, but now they are dead when that was never the plan. You blamed me for not stopping Melphis and Seth, but it was you, wasn't it? You allowed them to die! To retract your separated powers and leave me with nothing!"

Yahweh's eyes glow bright. She flashes Her teeth and grows nearer to Her brother.

The legion is close. Satan lifts Himself onto His hind legs. He brings His fists down together—Yahweh brushes Her fingers across Satan's right cheek. Her touch freezes Him in place. His arms, stuck in mid swing. Her pheromonal scent intoxicates Him. Satan arms go limp as He slinks into His throne.

"Oh, Lucy. You know you could never lay a finger on me."

"S-sister. What...happened to you? To the love...we shared?"

Entering the corridor leading to Satan's throne room, Melphis's gaze is drawn to the family portraits. A father and three children. Only the eldest son is visible. The other three have their faces obscured by tears and markings. *Satan—no, Lucifer.*

Melphis anchors himself in place, stopping the others abruptly. He covers his face with his left palm. His hand squeezes his temples while obscuring his eyes. Tears drip through his fingers.

Adam approaches from behind. He places his left hand on Melphis's left shoulder. Molding his arm around the demon as he walks to the right. He faces Melphis, then turns toward the portraits. Fixating on the youngest son's crossed out eyes for a moment, he says, "Are you well, my brother?"

Melphis pushes Adam's hand away. Brushing the tears from his eyes, he continues toward the large double doors.

*That was Satan as a boy—when He was still human. Then the others...were father and me and—*Melphis glances back toward Seth. The traitorous demon meets Melphis's gaze and offers a nervous smile. *Seth has no idea, does he? I suppose I don't even know for certain. Though I have my suspicions. Judging from what father told us and...knowing how She is.*

My family. Melphis returns his gaze to the double doors. *To think it has come to this. I have seen these pictures so many times, but only now does it hurt to look at them.*

A loud crash of tumbling glass and stone erupts from the other side of the door. Alarmed, Melphis hastens his approach. Opening the door, he finds golden rays of light seeping into the throne room from a hole in the ceiling. A brief view of long, blonde hair escapes into the sky.

Below the hole is a pile of rubble. Nearing the collapsed stone is a crimson stream flowing away from Satan's throne. Melphis's eyes creep along the trail of blood and toward the steps it's dripping from.

"What happened?" Seth asks.

Melphis shouts, "B-brother!"

Satan's body lays limp in His crushed throne. A giant, golden sword has pierced through His chest. His divine seat crumbles beneath Him. The weapon's cross shaped handle is as large as Satan himself. A beast impaled by a massive crucifix. The God of Hell coughs up a river of blood. The red fluid stains His thick dark skin. He turns to us.

"A-ah, little brother. You have come," Satan says.

"Little brother?" Melphis asks. "You knew?"

"Of course. You look different now, but how could I forget the tenderness of my sweet little brother's soul?"

Tears flow from Melphis's eyes.

"I've always known. T-this was Father's doing." Satan pauses. His face tightens before retching and vomiting more blood. "He sent you to kill me...to have me pay...for my sins."

"You knew this, but still let me live by your side for a hundred thousand years before sending Seth to kill me. Why?"

"I could not bear the thought of killing my once sweet younger brother. I regret my sins in Eden, but I was left no choice. I had to follow the plans for creating a new world. I thought...t-together...we could defy Her and go the new world...just the two of us."

Satan pauses again. The fire hugging the edge of the throne room dims and flickers alongside Satan himself. A cold breeze unbecoming of Hell's harsh atmosphere washes over the throne room.

"I ordered your death once I knew there was no bringing you back. I have lost both you and our sister's loving, sensual touch. My body still aches for Her, but She has changed.

"Seth," Satan continues. "I owe you an explanation. Let me tell you...about your beloved..."

Seth's eyes widen. He stands tall, like the fur on a dog's back that has been heightened by excitement.

Melphis whips his gaze toward Seth. "Lucifer, don't!" *Seth is finally balancing out. The truth will ruin him!*

"Don't what?" Seth asks.

Adam and Eve frown deeply. Seth looks around with suspicion. Sasha doesn't share their pained countenances. Her eyes dart around the room, joining in Seth's confusion.

Satan continues, "Your beloved—Lola is—"

I meet Satan's fading gaze. His pupils lighten and gloss over. Adam and Eve avert their eyes from me. *They know something, but what? What has Zarathustra been keeping from me? And—*

"Well, Melphis? What don't you want him to tell me?"

He turns away from me. I've gotten used to his animosity. I deserve it, but he no longer appears angry, but remorseful instead.

"What is it, Satan? What about Lola?" I shout.

The God has lost his breath. The fire scattered around the room dwindles and fades. They disappear, then so does Satan.

This is unlike my first visit. Satan was full of passion and fury. Now look at him. Cold and silent upon his throne. Murdered by someone or something unknown. The memory of when I first met him is roused. There was a moment of pensive sadness that meant nothing to me then, when Satan said, "The circumstances of my being here...my having to sit upon this throne...these are things I do not want. Though the confines of my life demand that it remains so, lest disaster strikes."

"What disaster did you mean, Satan?" I ask.

Puzzled, Melphis turns to me and says, "Disaster? What are you talk—"

Satan's body glows a dark red before expanding outward. Flames burst forth from his body, rushing at us with furious speed. Adam and Eve raise their hands toward the ravenous fire, conjuring a barrier around us. Their movements are quick, as if they were anticipating this. The explosion summoned from Satan's body rams into the barrier. Cracks form upon impact, but its structure holds. The orb of magic is pushed along by the flames, as if we are riding a wave. Within seconds, Satan's castle appears far in the distance. It and the Crucifixion Fields deteriorate into nothing.

"No—all those souls! We can't leave them!" I scream, but the bright teal light of their souls fade away. Alongside what appears to be hundreds of portals.

The flames have pushed us back to Hell's Edge. Our journey, reversed. The barrier slams against what appears to be open air, but with a strange solid form. Cracks begin to appear in the surrounding sky. The fissures grow larger, before shattering like glass.

A falling sensation. A bright blue sky accompanied by a cityscape I know all too well. My head hits a surface—everything goes dark.

In a daze, I struggle to my feet. Screams overtake my ears from every direction. Fire weaves its way through the city's streets. Large crowds of people try to run and drive away, but are devoured by the flames. There is a creaking of metal, followed by the tumbling of buildings. The foundation of multiple skyscrapers warp under the heat and tumble over. In the distance is the Empire State Building. It crashes into the ground, then combusts into flames.

"What is happening?" I ask, frantically looking for the others. I'm alone. I glance skyward. Above me is a floating landmass covered in black clouds. The distorted space clears and I recognize it. In the air sits Hell. Its sides, shattered. Fire and debris spill onto the Earth.

Alongside it, at equal height, is another hidden world just now pulled into view. A blinding light erupts from it. Descending from the light are angels. Their forms are identical to the one who tricked me into opening the gateway to the White Abyss. The distortion around the angels also disperses, revealing their true forms beneath.

Their broad white wings transmute into black tentacles. Dark shimmers pulsate around them, obscuring the surrounding space as they flutter to the surface. As if they're weaving lies wherever they fly. Black slime drips from the insectile feelers which hang from their loose, formless mouths.

A scream—one of these grotesque angels stands over a woman cowering on the ground. The angel's body tears open in a vertical slice, from its chest down through its abdomen. Dark fluids spill out, but reveal a bright, glorious light inside. From within, emerges more black tentacles. They reach for the woman. The angel cranes its long neck toward her. Its feelers latch onto her face. The woman appears to scream, but I can't hear her. The angel emits a high-pitched screech that drowns out her voice. Her eyes gloss over. The woman's teal soul stretches away from her and toward the angel's stomach. When severed, the woman's corpse thuds against the ground.

Consecutive screeches are heard, followed by the dropping of more corpses. My eyes widen as the sound hits my ears. My stomach churns.

Part Three

Apotheosis

CHAPTER TWENTY-FIVE

EONS AGO.

The Earth cracked under their mutated forms. Space around Yahweh and Lucifer wobbled and distorted.

"This world Father made cannot contain us anymore," Yahweh said. "If we stay here, the Earth will surely crumble apart."

"But where are we to go?" Lucifer asked.

Yahweh glanced about the surrounding environment. They were in a forest right outside of Eden. Trees snapped and fell. Fractures in the Earth grew larger. The surrounding flora wilted. *With such rapid deterioration, no place on Earth will hold us for long.* She glared toward her six insectile arms. Her stomach churned. *I sought to acquire the Abyss's power and now it ravages my body in such a way—*

Yahweh's eyes widened. Her frown transmuted into a smile. She plunged Her pincers into Her chest.

"Sister!" Lucifer shouted, but calmed once He saw no blood. He watched with awe as Yahweh's breasts rippled like water.

"We are not lost, Lucy! We may have these new forms, but we still acquired what we wanted! This is the effect of the White

Abyss that now lives within us! We received but a fraction, but we can still achieve our goal!"

"But the locket has been lost."

"Yes, and with it, so is Father's Abyss, but we are gods now, Lucy! We can create our own White Abyss!"

Pulling Her pincers free, She extracted a ghoulish, black spirit. Yahweh glanced it over with bored eyes. "No, this is not correct."

She spent years studying the White Abyss. Yahweh knew it well. Its supernatural weight. The complex duality of emptiness and profound fullness. The power of creation itself. This black spirit that stood before Her held power, but it was not of the Abyss.

"A failure. This one can only destroy," She said.

"What is this? I thought you were going to create a new Abyss," Lucifer asked.

"Silence! Be still and watch."

Yahweh dug into Her soul once more. This time She removed six more fractions of Her power. Upon extraction, they were revealed to be more black spirits. One dwarfed the others in size, towering over even the forest itself. Yahweh recognized it as the desire that most resembled Herself.

"My Gluttony," Yahweh said. The black spirit reshaped itself, taking the form of a giant worm-like creature. Lucifer stepped back, trembling.

"*Mother*!" the creature screamed. The other six spirits also morphed into solid forms, greeting Yahweh in the same manner.

Looking up at Her Gluttony, Yahweh said, "I will name you Samael." Turning to the others, She named Her Pride, Azazel. Her Greed, Sachiel. Her Wrath, Michael. Her Lust, Zadkiel. Her Sloth, Dumah and Her Envy, Cassiel.

Lucifer asked, "I thought these creatures were failures. Why name them?"

"Yes, failures that will live by my command and will show an unabating desire to make up for their failure. Lucy, we are going to flee the Earth. These creatures will cultivate the humans in our stead. From this moment forward, these desires of mine will be my Archangels. The first of many to come. Trust me, Lucy! For we are not lost! It will take time, but we will devour the entire White Abyss next time. We just need more power first. A day will come when I send my angels to Earth. And when they descend, the collective souls of humanity will be raptured."

The sky is flooded with these monsters. Spewing out of Heaven, there's no end to them. The angel who devoured the woman nearby notices me. With each step it takes forward, I take one back.

The angel screeches and picks up speed. The distortion surrounding its tentacles spreads further. The vibrations grow more violent. My hands quake. Chaotic blue flames conjure in my palms. Readying myself to attack, the angel sprints toward me. The black tentacles in place of its wings act as extra legs. They smash into the ground, distorting the earth with each step.

My right palm flings forward. The ground tremors beneath my feet. The angel screeches again. The sound overloads my senses, blurring my vision. Its parasitic feelers launch from its mouth. Startled, my right arm jerks back. The tongues latch onto my pinky and ring fingers. The two fingers turn numb. I jerk my hand back again.

"Fuck!" Blood runs down my wrist. Turning toward the approaching angel, I see the two fingers dangling from its loose mouth.

Time slows. Pain disorients me. The teal sparks don't appear. The angel hovers above me. Frenzied, I scurry away. Stumbling along the ground as I struggle back to my feet.

I need to find the others. The teal sparks remain absent. *Fuck! Without the locket, I can't regenerate.* Red flames spiral down my right arm, amassing over the stumps. Searing the wounds closed, blood stops gushing, but the fingers remain lost.

An angel siphons the soul of a man. Buildings crumble and distort. Humans in all directions scream as hellfire overtakes them. Others cover their ears in pain as the cacophony of crashing buildings and blood curdling screams fill the air. Sasha doesn't notice any of it. Her gaze fixates on the angel in front of her. Finishing its feast, it drops the man. Sasha's fists clench. Her body heats. When the man's corpse thuds against the ground, memories of Virdeus's last moments are aroused. The image of his body torn in two festers in Sasha's mind. His soul being sucked into Envy's face holes. Sasha's eyes flood.

"Enough of this, you bastard angel! Where is your God?" Sasha says.

Electricity amasses into her palms, forming long bolts. The angel faces Sasha, its voice crackling, then heightens into a screech.

"Well, speak up!" Sasha says.

The angel's many feelers emerge from its mouth's drooping skin. Tar drips from them, like the salivating tongue of a well-trained dog who's expecting a treat from its master. Screeching, it sprints toward Sasha.

Taking a step back, she launches the bolts. The angel's wings give off vibrations. The electric spears halt an inch from the angel's face. Their points bend. One right, one left. Regaining motion, the bolts are launched away, hitting a building and a semi-trailer truck. Glass rains upon the area. Smoke and oil fumes fill the air, the truck's engine explodes.

A tentacle is slammed down. Sasha jumps back, avoiding the blow, but the tendril grabs her ankle. Tumbling over, she glances toward the angel. Its feelers slither onto her face.

Sasha becomes numb. Her eyes dull and—*What's this heat?*

Her energy returns. The angel's feelers retract as it screeches in pain. The tentacle wrapped around her ankle recoils, sizzles, and melts into sludge. Sasha turns around to see Seth, his eyes wide and glowing with white flames. Snapping his fingers toward the angel, fire engulfs its other tentacles. The angel hunches over Sasha, screeching in pain. A putrid, moist breath drops from its loose mouth.

Laying on her back, with the angel on top of her, brings forth another memory. Her father's whisky scented breath leaving moisture on her neck as he raped her. Sasha raises both hands toward the angel's chest and ignites an electrical tempest. Bolts spring high into the air after piercing the monster. Blood splatters across Sasha's face as the angel is torn to pieces.

Seth extends his left hand to Sasha. "Are you okay?"

"Are *you?*" she asks, noticing his other hand. "What happened to your fingers and why haven't they regenerated?"

"Turns out that power was never mine. It's fine though. The bleeding has stopped."

Sasha, frowning, takes Seth's right hand and gently caresses his stumps. She glances around at the angel's corpse. Squeezing Seth's hand tight, she smiles.

The flood of flames spilling onto the Earth is unending. Brimstone, imps, and the trapped human souls spew out alongside the fire. Awestruck, Melphis falls to his knees.

No. This wasn't supposed to happen. The timing was too perfect. Hell collapsed as soon as brother—

Melphis relinquishes himself to gravity. His hands lay at his sides. His ambitions, squandered. A candle snuffed and plunged into darkness.

What has all this been for? All my life, I craved Hell's throne. I could not be satiated by sitting at the sidelines. No—father planted an ego in me that hungered for control of Hell. A voice screaming in my ear, telling me to not stop until it was mine, but now it never will be.

A glorious light overshadows Melphis. An angel hovers above him, but Melphis does not react. Black tentacles emerge from the angel's open torso, reaching for Melphis's neck. Its hungry feelers slink down. Tar splatters onto Melphis's right shoulder. He looks toward the angel with the eyes of a corpse. The monster's screech ripples throughout the air. Melphis's vision blurs.

What is that? It's wet and warm.

His eyesight returns. Blood gushes from a stump between the angel's shoulders. Scattered along the ground lays its skull and sagging skin. In place of its head is a horizontal, metallic pillar. Melphis turns to his left to see Adam and Eve standing near a sedan. The pillar is stretching outward from the hood of the vehicle.

"What magic is this?" Melphis asks, his eyeline following the pillar toward the angel's headless shoulders.

"We were born from our Father's body. We cannot do as he has done, but we have some command over his world," Adam says, removing his hand from the car.

"We cannot create, but we can bend," Eve says.

The Abysslings walk toward Melphis. Eve drags the angel's corpse to the side. Adam offers a hand to his foreign brother.

Glaring at the hand, Melphis slaps it away. Rising on his own, silence rushes over the trio.

"Back in Hell's throne room, you were quick to conjure that barrier. You knew this would happen, didn't you?" Melphis asks.

Adam and Eve's eyes shift from Melphis, to each other, then toward the ground.

"Well, *answer me!*"

"If you knew the truth," Adam says. "You wouldn't have followed through with Father's plans—"

Melphis grabs Adam by the throat, pinning him to the ground. The veins in Melphis's wrists and neck pop. His nails piercing his brother's skin.

Stepping forward, Eve says, "Please let go."

Melphis thrusts his staff into Eve's neck, knocking her into the ground. "I've had enough of the both of you! What else are you hiding? What other strings is Father pulling? I want the truth, *now*. I'll gut the knowledge from your skulls if I must!"

CHAPTER TWENTY-SIX

M elphis's grip around Adam's throat refuses to loosen.

"What else is father plotting!" Melphis says.

"Father is pained," Eve replies. "In having to deceive you, but everything has come to pass. There are no more secrets."

"Then what is happening here?" Melphis asks, pointing toward the angels spewing out from Heaven.

"She awaits there. Father's other first born. We are to deal with Her," Eve says, placing her palm atop Melphis's hand, caressing him. He pushes her back.

"But why? Why must we act in accordance with Father's will?" Melphis asks. "I don't understand you two. Are you not real? Don't you have wills of your own?"

Overcome by discomfort, Eve glances away.

"Does it matter?" Adam asks, gripping Melphis's wrist, forcing him away. "We were born from him and so we live by his will. We are also prepared to die for him. We don't need wills of our own when we are naught but an extension of—"

"Pathetic!" Melphis says. "It's all about Father's will with you two. You're so devoted to him that you cannot see how enslaved you are! To that god, you are nothing but puppets—"

"And you aren't?" Adam shouts. Eve frowns toward the ground. Tears fill her eyes. Melphis is taken aback by Adam's sudden shift into anger.

"All those years ago," Adam continues. "When Father rewired your soul. Has anything been your choice since? You may not have been born from Father's body, but you are more akin to us than you realize, *brother.*"

A building collapses. Humans are screaming nearby. A world and its people subjected to mass genocide. They have lived their entire lives blind to the supernatural operations at work beyond the veil. Ignorant of the fact that they have no control. Any meaning they felt their lives had was shallow at best. Now their world is crumbling down as the angels harvest their souls. A fate they never asked for. Melphis stands before Adam's words, wide-eyed and mouth agape. *I really am human after all. Father pushed onto me a fate I never asked for.*

Melphis bares his teeth like an animal pushed into defensive aggression, he raises his staff toward the Abysslings. They stare him down, but do not act. Fire is conjured atop the head of the rod.

A collection of screeches ripple through the air. Melphis and the two Abysslings cover their ears in pain. A hoard of angels swarm around them. Humans watch from a distance before running away. The angels have forgone their human prey in favor of the demon and his two foreign siblings.

Melphis glances toward Heaven. *Does She know we're here?*

Eons ago.

Yahweh plunged Her pincers into Lucifer's chest. "Be still, Lucy. This will take but a moment."

Lucifer winced. Out from His rippling torso bled Hell in the form of mist. The haze ruptured from His body and sprang toward the sky where it amassed to a single spot. The particles solidified into a rocky surface surrounding a large Sea of Flames. Piece by piece the ground rose, forming mountains. A hole carved its way through the risen rock, creating a cave. Its path led to a wide-open field. At the center, bricks and stone stacked upon each other. Castle Pandaemonium was erected.

"What is that?" Lucifer asked.

"A container for souls. Time is required before we can act. A day will come when we can forge a catalyst to fill with souls. Through it the Earth shall be destroyed and its white shadow will be torn from hiding, with nowhere to go but into our stomachs."

"What sort of catalyst?"

"Lucy, look." Yahweh pointed toward the sky. Its structure was bending under its own weight. "This place was born from you. So, it is up to you to govern it and all the souls we send there."

Yahweh drew a circle in the air. A portal into Hell opened, leading to the view of a throne.

"A divine seat crafted especially for you. Only the best for my Lucy. Go and sit upon it, but listen well—do not leave it for any reason. Hell cannot exist without you and without it, our plans will be for naught."

"But, what about you?"

Yahweh pulled Lucifer close, placing His head upon Her breasts.

"Worry not. I will visit often—this I swear, but to do so, I need to govern the Earth from another realm. One without the burden of human souls. For these realms are not as sturdy as our father's Earth. They are artificial, but I believe that which is fake can be made real. This we will accomplish when we flee to our new world." Yahweh detached Lucifer from Her breasts. Smiling at Her brother, She asked, "This is a great responsibility, Lucy. Can you do this for me? For us?"

Lucifer nodded. He glanced up at Hell and saw its crumbling intensify. Walking over to the portal, He said, "Come visit soon."

The portal closed behind Him. Yahweh looked toward the sky and saw Hell rebuild itself, its structure holding firm. She dug into Her soul and bled out another haze. It solidified next to Hell, at equal height. Yahweh turned to the Sins and ordered them to watch the boundary of Eden and to document the development of humankind.

Creating another portal, She saw a throne room of Her own. *Ah, yes—the catalyst. How I yearn to meet you.*

Taking shelter behind a fallen building, a screech sounds from the opposite side. Humans scream near and far. Most of the angels seem to have landed. The sky is almost clear. Though Heaven and Hell continue to obscure the sun passing behind them. Following the quick succession of angelic screeching is the painful howls of humans being devoured. The awful sounds collect and form a horrific melody.

Sasha caresses my stumps and says, "You saw it, didn't you?"

"Yeah. An angel killed a woman in front of me."

I glance at my missing fingers, then to Sasha. Something feels off. She's faster and more capable than I am, but an angel almost killed her. Yet I managed to get away. *Did it spare me?*

Another screech echoes through the air. It's louder than the others. Sasha and I glance around the debris to find an angel and its prey a few feet away. Black tentacles are wrapped around a small girl's neck. Clenching my fists, I take a step forward, lift the other foot and—

"Damnit," I say, loosening my hands.

"What's wrong?"

"I want to save her, but these angels are too dangerous. We need to prioritize finding Melphis and the others. Together maybe, we can fight back," I say, then look into Sasha's eyes. That angel let me get away. I don't know why, but I shouldn't be here right now. For whatever reason, I seem safe, but Sasha isn't. I don't want to risk losing her.

The young girl squeals. Her soul is torn from her body. The angel drops the child, her head splitting atop a sharp metal pole.

I rub my hands together, as if that would relieve agitation. My teeth grit. Sasha slips her palm into mine, squeezing tight.

"I think you're right," she says. "It would be nice to save each person we come across, but what can the two of us do against this legion of angels? Come, let's go find the others."

Melphis conjures a bolt of lightning and grips it with his left hand. Fire bellows from the head of his staff. The flames collide with the angels, their screams fill the air. Melphis waits to hear their bodies hit the ground, but they step through the fire, black with ash, and still alive. He throws the bolt of lightning, piercing the head of the first angel to step through. The electric spear bursts, killing the angel and knocking back the others.

"These creatures are too durable. We cannot handle them all," Adam says, swooping his arms around. The ground bends skyward, circling above and over twelve angels, trapping them in a dome of stone. Eve does the same, but the legion is too large. Trapping them seems to not deplete their numbers. Melphis and the Abysslings huddle together, their backs facing each other. The three of them stare down an ocean of angels. The mass of grotesqueries creep closer, diminishing the room between them and their prey.

An angel amongst the crowd is pinned to the ground as flames overtake its tentacles. The other angels shift away from the fire. Melphis glances over the angelic ocean to see Seth and Sasha standing high atop a collapsed skyscraper. The angels turn toward Seth. Melphis launches a pillar of flames toward their backs. The tenacles melt into tar.

"We need to break through!" Melphis says. "Find a way to them!"

Eve steps forward. She raises her arms, then pulls them away from each other. Stone walls rise upward and outward. A path is created by parting the sea of angels. Melphis darts through the passageway with Adam and Eve close behind. Seth and Sasha run over to meet them. Melphis stares at Seth with dead eyes.

"Melphis," Seth says. "I—"

"Forget it. We don't have time," he says, pointing to the approaching angels. "We need to flee and regroup."

Melphis walks off. Seth and the others follow behind. He looks back at Seth for a moment, expecting his traitorous friend to say something, but nothing comes.

Right. We don't have time to quarrel amongst ourselves. These angels. Hell and Heaven being pulled into view. Something is coming. Melphis scratches the back of his head. Humans scream in the near distance. he scowls. *So, I'm Father's puppet? What if I am? The task he gave me is fulfilled. Now I can become real by finding a new purpose and I can start by defending humanity. They at least may still have a chance.*

A man leading a small army stands at the edge of the George Washington bridge. A violent gust of wind collides with his shaggy brown hair as he stares toward the wreckage of New York City. Clouds rush by in a flash. The sky darkens while the sun passes behind Hell and Heaven.

"These flames. This pressure," he says, scratching his chin. "It's messing with the atmosphere. This wind is unnatural."

"Andes, what is our plan?" a woman asks.

Thousands of screams join the abrasive wind. The Guild is no stranger to humanity's agony, but the carnage was always small and contained. A family at most, being torn apart by an imp. Or like the succubus that consumed his father. *But a whole city plagued by unknown entities?* Andes sighs. *We are up to the task. We must be.*

"There is your answer," Andes says. "Our late patriarch founded the Guild with the protection of humankind as our top priority. We must aid them!"

The women and men cheer and follow Andes into the city. These survivors were fortunate enough to be away on hunts at the time of Magistrum's collapse. *But they may not be fortunate for much longer.* Andes and the Guild march forward, unaware of what is to be found. Andes looks toward the sky. Fire and teal spirits erupt from Hell. Angels descend from Heaven. *I suppose we will not be able to hide ourselves from the world anymore, but to save these poor souls...I know the Matriarch will understand. Sasha, my lady, I hope you are well.*

CHAPTER TWENTY-SEVEN

Six portals surround us. Angels pour out. The collective shimmer produced by their tentacles disorients the surrounding space. My vision appears as if I'm underwater.

Melphis looks toward Heaven and says, "They're gathering here, like they're being drawn to us." More buildings warp and collapse.

"Step back!" Eve says, raising her hands forward. Glimmering light particles converge around us, forming a barrier. Chunks of scrap metal hurtle toward us. The debris ricochets from Eve's defense, slicing off the head of an angel.

"There will be no running. We must fight!" Sasha shouts, conjuring an electrical blast. It wounds the angels, staggering them.

Glancing over the heads of the nearest angels, the horde continues as far as I can see. "Nothing for it then," I say, stepping forward. Wings made from white flames sprout from my back. Hovering over the unbalanced angels, I sweep both my arms around. White fire is conjured above them. The flames are drawn toward the tentacles, as if nothing else could satiate them. Screeching, the angels melt into tar.

Sasha smiles toward me. I smile back.

Melphis shifts his gaze from Seth to Sasha, eyes wide. Eve smiles, then turns to face the angels behind them. She manipulates the water particles in the air, reducing their temperature. The air surrounding the angels freezes, slowing their pace. Melphis raises his staff and conjures a large blast of fire, melting the horde's backsides.

"A good effort, but how long can we keep this up?" Melphis asks, noticing Adam glancing around, making no attempt to fight. The bright teal sheen of his eyes diminishes. A frown overtakes his face.

Smoke rises on all sides. The stench of charred angels fills the air. Others step through the melted corpses of their kin. One rushes at Eve, its tentacles springing toward her—Adam pushes her out of the way. The tentacles wrap around his neck. He becomes woozy. His vision blurs and—he grips the tendrils, pulling them back enough, allowing airflow to return. He says, "Rise."

Stone spikes erupt, severing the tentacles. Melphis knocks the angel away with his staff, then conjures an electrical blast. A downpour of flesh and bloods slathers the three foreign siblings.

The Earth trembles beneath their feet. Adam points toward Heaven, and says, "We cannot keep up. Even if it were possible to defeat them all, the Earth won't last in this state. We must go for the source."

"I assume you have a method of getting there?" Sasha asks.

"Yes, I shall make a path. I just need time, and space."

Melphis notices Eve's moist eyes as she peers upon Adam's gloomy demeanor. Stroking his beard, Melphis loses himself in thought.

"Let's make some room then. Come on now!" Sasha commands. Seth nods his head and readies more flames. Adam kneels and brings his palms together. Fingers hovering an inch apart, tension builds. Light particles slowly converge.

"Brother," Adam says. "Go on, join them in battle, and please watch over my sister."

Melphis's eyes grow wide. His body quakes, hands trembling. "What are you saying?"

❖

"Peculiar," Andes says. "The nearby sensation seems to have moved—no, amassed to a single point."

The Guild wanders the scorched streets of New York City. Collapsed buildings litter the area everywhere they look. The harsh, bellowing wind is all that can be heard. Looking back the way they came, Andes watches as people evacuate the city. Both in vehicles and on foot, they leave behind their burning homes.

"Brace yourselves," he says to the Guild. "Combating whatever caused this will require our full strength and utmost focus."

The women and men of the Guild cheer and march on, ready to act upon any command their temporary leader gives them. Andes smiles, but as he turns away, the grin fades. *I do not want any more deaths, but we must go on.* He lets out a heavy sigh. *What awaits us here?*

"Make some room then. Come on now!" shouts a familiar voice. A bright light engulfs the area just ahead.

Andes's smile returns, now brimming. "Matriarch, we meet again at last!"

Sasha charges toward a group of angels. Seth follows close behind. Melphis and Eve hesitate to leave Adam's side. The light particles amassing before them take the shape of stairs. Step by step, the pathway to Heaven molds into being. The surrounding city seeps into twilight. The area around the stairs is the only spot daylight touches. It's as if Adam is taking the sun itself into his palms.

Melphis asks, "Adam, why would you need me to watch over—"

An angel in the distance swings its tentacles toward the base of a skyscraper. Scraps of metal and glass plunge toward Sasha and Seth. The building collapses, following behind the debris. "Watch out!" Seth yells.

A flame roars overhead, followed by a heavy gust of wind. The building is reduced to ash, then is blown away in a tempest.

Marching into battle is the Guild. Andes's spear is pointed toward the skyscraper. Fire spiraling around the blade dissipates. Behind him is a female member of the Guild with her palms outstretched. The tempest dies down as she lowers her arms.

"Andes!" Sasha shouts. Seeing the surviving Guild members brings the warmth of the sun to her smile. Seth's eyes are tethered to Sasha, sharing her glee.

Andes ignites his spear and charges at the legion. He and seven others plunge their flame-coated spears into the sides of the angels. Black sludge pours out. The tendrils wrap around the spears, yanking them free and snapping the metal poles. A flurry of tentacles swings around, dealing blunt force to Andes. His back hits flat on the ground. Four of the others lay beside him, but the last three are lifted off their feet by a thick tentacle latched around their necks. Andes grinds his teeth. Their souls are siphoned away.

The brunette woman who blew away the ashes joins Andes's side. She conjures another wild tempest, pushing the angels away from Andes. The woman conjures a row of forceful winds, parting the sea of angels in two. Another faction of the Guild stomps the ground. Walls of stone erupt, keeping the angels separate and creating a path through the horde. Andes and the Guild travel between the stone, joining their Matriarch. The sound of angelic tongues slithering around is heard from both sides. Clicking noises emerge as if they are communicating by means of some primitive non-verbal language.

Andes notices the stairs of light forming. Almost high enough to reach Heaven's Gate. He asks, "Matriarch, do you plan to ascend to that dastardly place?"

Sasha nods. Her smile fades into anguish.

"I understand," he says, looking out onto the battlefield. The brave women and men return to fighting the horde of grotesqueries. His hands tremble. He bites his lip. "Go, Matriarch. Leave defending the Earth and humankind to us. Go do what needs be done."

The construction of the stairs finishes. The glimmering, massive staircase made from crystallized light stands before them. They stand in awe at the sublime sight.

"Go, now!" Adam shouts, his voice strained.

"What about you?" Melphis asks.

"I will remain here. I must, to hold its structure firm." Adam coughs up blood. Melphis places a hand on Adam's left shoulder. "I'm fine! Now go. I will hold it long enough for you to enter Heaven. Then I will fight alongside your Guild," Adam says, looking at Sasha.

Melphis hesitates. Eve takes his hand into hers. "Let us go," Eve says, refusing to show Melphis her face. He relents and follows her up the steps.

"Matriarch...come home safe," Andes says, then glares at Seth. At Magistrum, Andes felt an untamable rage inside the young demon. One that led to the deaths of thousands. Andes glances back at Sasha, remembering how volatile she was as a child. The feeling he now senses from Seth strikes him differently than before. Seth was an all-consuming void, but looking upon him now elicits the image of a calm, pensive ocean on a clear and sunny day. An abyssal weight resides beneath, but the surface of this young man is still.

"You," Andes says to Seth. "Take care of our Matriarch."

Seth, awestruck, says, "Of course. Take care, Andes."

Andes smiles, then returns to battle. Seth and Sasha together make the glorious ascent to Heaven.

Adam watches his sister and friends reach the end of the stairs. When they are safely inside, Adam breaks his pose. The crystallized stairs shatter. The glimmering light particles disperse, creating a starlit sky hovering just above the Earth.

His hands drop. Fissures form in his skin. He feels his bones crumbling. As the dispersion of light particles disappears, so does Adam.

1 B.C.

A teal soul floated at the center of Satan's throne room. Its spirit-form bubbled like boiling water. Satan waved His arms around. A composer of souls trying to weave together new life. The soul expanded like yeast in Hell's wretched heat. It exploded into teal light particles and faded away. Satan frowned at the dispersed light.

"Another failure, Lucy?" Yahweh said.

Satan turned to His sister, who was closing the door behind Her, "I asked you not to call me that. I wish to go by Satan now."

"A man picking out his own name. Seems a bit arrogant. You will always be Lucy to me."

"More arrogant than whoring around on Earth and manipulating the minds of men, thinking they belong to you?"

Yahweh glared at Satan. Her eyes were bright with intensity. A crooked smile crept along Her face. Satan's gaze shifted away.

"I would watch your tongue, *Lucy.* Or would you rather I take it from you?"

Satan's mind wandered. In the past, for Yahweh to take His tongue would have meant to feel Her sensual lips against His, but that time has long passed. The phrase had since become more literal. Yahweh seemed to be begging for a reason to act on that impulse.

"I-I am sorry. I have strayed from my position. It will not happen again."

She turned toward the destroyed soul that lingered in the air. She said, "I would hardly call it whoring. Your task here is to create the catalyst from the comfort of your throne room. While you orchestrate a scene here, I am on Earth writing an entire play. It is necessary to manipulate mankind. Religion poisons the soul, crushing the human will alongside it. This makes them easier to control. Not to mention, religious teachings allow us to foster a denial of their world, and a longing for a new one. This is where the creative energy we need stems from."

"I have a question regarding that," Satan said. "I fear that creating a demon born from a human soul may be impossible.

We need a strong will, yes? Then why do we continue to crush their spirits with religion?"

"Be patient. When the White Abyss is strong enough, a disruptive soul will come about. One that can resist religious control. Its ability to rise against the moral path will be proof of its strong will. Give it another two thousand years or so. Try again once our time is almost up."

"But that seems risky," Satan said.

"Perhaps," Yahweh paused. "Call it a hunch, but I fear Father's Abyss might not want us here. The Earth, Heaven, and Hell have grown volatile. I think we have about two millennia before the trinity of realms collide with each other. Shortly before they do, the Abyss will be at its most powerful—and that is when the catalyst will be born. A will strong enough to withstand its profound emptiness. One that possesses both destructive and creative power."

"The Magic of Nil," Satan said, turning to see Yahweh draw a portal into the air. "Leaving already?"

"Yes. One last religion must be born to give way to the power we need. Let us call it...Christianity. Soon the Christian messiah will be born. Then I will descend to Earth one last time to facilitate the religion. Have Gluttony bring extra souls to Heaven to compensate for my absence."

She took one step into the portal, but halted. Turning back toward her brother She said, "And remember, *Lucy*. Have patience. The day will arrive when the one blessed with Nil is born. Our catalyst will come and one way or another, it will show up on *my* doorstep."

Yahweh glared at Satan with grim skepticism, then continued toward Heaven.

Reaching Heaven's Gate, the crystal stairs crumble behind us. Heaven's light is like nothing else on Earth. It pierces my eyes, blurring my vision. The flash reminds me of one other time. Before I died, before I became a demon. Right as I went to take that final step off the cliffside—

Eve weeps to the left of me. Melphis stares at his hands, as if in a trance. Something feels off about those two and the distance between Melphis and I is—well, I wish I could fix it somehow.

Sasha is standing near a bright, golden archway. Past it lays a road of gold bricks. A city is at the other end of the path, with a tall cathedral rising high above the other buildings.

The air here is strange. Hell was full of pain. It's gravity, chaotic. With its demons roaming around, torturing humans, feeding off their souls, in a sick way it felt alive—*but Heaven feels stagnant. It feels...devoid of life.*

CHAPTER TWENTY-EIGHT

Heaven's eerie stillness becomes palpable as we make our way toward the statuesque city that lays beyond the golden brick road. The air is stagnant and cold. No sun hovers above, but harsh rays dart around the sky at illogical angles, like refracted light. Even with the brightness of multiple stars, I can't help but feel that we are venturing into a mass tomb. Empty for now, but ready to contain the corpses of billions.

A burst of teal light blurs overhead. Swirling into Heaven is a tempest of souls, entering from portals. They stretch across the sky, toward the cathedral at Heaven's center. Like fallen fruit being forced down by gravity, they have no choice. Their pained screams tell me so.

Melphis catches me wincing. His mouth gapes, as if he's about to speak, but no words emerge. He turns to Eve, almost like he expects her to take up the mantle of speaking.

The two of them appear to have something dire on their minds. I'd like to ask about it, but I share in their hesitance. I don't know what to say to Melphis anymore. I feel it's too late to salvage the connection. Sasha appears lost in thought as well. She flashes me a brilliant but pensive smile.

Glancing skyward, I can no longer see the tempest of souls, but I can hear them. They must still be above us, but I can't say for sure. Heaven's golden rays have intensified to such a degree that seeing a mere few feet ahead is impossible. We couldn't stop these souls from being siphoned, but the rest of humankind is depending on us. We—*I* need to press on.

◆◇◆

By flashing Seth a smile, Sasha tries to reassure him that everything will be okay. *But what does okay even look like anymore?* Sasha's bright smile descends into stoicism. She turns away from Seth, her mind drifting to the Guild. Her family now scattered and dismantled. *Andes called me Matriarch. He wouldn't have decided that on his own. Is this something father had prepared?*

Her eyes well with tears, but a rising anger pushes them back. The image of Virdeus being sliced in two. Envy, like a pyrographer, had singed the scene into Sasha's memory. She trudges ahead, impatiently waiting for Melphis to lead the way. This is what kept her going while inside the White Abyss. The desire to spill the blood of God.

I will avenge Father, then rebuild the Guild. Euphoric chills surge through her body. Sasha's mouth creeps into a crooked grin. She glances toward the tempest of souls above. A teal blur obscured by Heaven's wretched light. They screech as they are pulled further into Heaven. *They must be headed toward God.*

I will avenge you, Father. I promise. I'll see to it that your dream of humans living in peace without demons becomes a reality. Then, I'll lead the Guild as a God-slayer.

She quivers with anticipation, but on the other side of this curtain of excitement is a worry creeping up a second pole. She can feel it—the trait she and Seth share. The monster she had worked so hard to keep buried, is writhing in the delightful sheen of her want for revenge.

I don't care. I don't care what this does to me. I must see this through. Even if the bloodlust consumes me, I will rid the Earth of this monster. This is my burden to bear.

Sasha sighs heavily, rubbing her temples. *Seth will be fine. He's not the one my smile was trying to reassure.*

Melphis sticks his hands forward, a blind man weeding his way through Heaven's harsh rays. The brightness burns against his skin. The golden light stimulates the feeling of staring into the sun, a mere foot away.

Yahweh—sister, I was always impressed by your magical aptitude, but what do you hope to accomplish by playing the role of God? If what Father said is true, as a child you were presented with the knowledge of your mortality. This instilled fear in you—you, who thought yourself too great to die. You are not a god. You are the inflated ego of a human who would not bear being human, or any of the cruel things that entails.

Andes and the Guild. They're on Earth defending humankind from those monstrous angels. Humans fighting for humanity. They are good, but you—Yahweh? Melphis ponders the creation of Heaven and Hell. These artificial worlds, birthed from the souls of his long-lost siblings. Hell's overwhelming pain and suffering taken from the regret and anguish felt by Satan. *Sister, those grotesqueries you created. Are they an example of what can be found within you? And these blinding rays.* Melphis notices that the brightness is so intense, he can no longer see the sky. *Are they meant to shield you from onlookers who seek the truth about who you are?*

Melphis turns to Seth. He can barely see the young demon, but the close proximity allows him to at least see Seth's shape. A blurred form amidst this oppressive light. Gradually, Seth fades into view, appearing determined. *He has changed, but is it enough?*

Heaven's harsh rays diminish, filtering away as Melphis's hands touch a large stone building. They make their way into the city and—

"What is this?" Melphis shouts.

The golden light dissipates. It's replaced by a thick dark fog. Large black tentacles coil around each building, spiraling toward the sky. Melphis walks forward. Black goop stretches between the ground and his sole. Dark grey particles disperse from the sludge. The fumes cause Melphis, Eve, Seth, and Sasha to cough hoarsely. They have stumbled into a divine bog dense with carcinogens.

"Who cares what it is? Let's get on with it," Sasha says, walking ahead of Melphis. Seth joins her. Melphis and Eve linger behind.

So, this is who you are. You wished to become the sun. But, Yahweh, even you should know that every star will one day burn out.

Melphis turns to Eve. Her eyes have been filled with tears ever since leaving Adam's side.

"Is it too late for me, Melphis?" she asks. "To have a life, a will of my own? I know you think we're just puppets, but—" The dam bursts and the rivers of her eyes disrupts the path of her voice.

Leaving Adam to die brought forth clarity in Melphis. He had lashed out at the Abysslings. Claimed they were puppets with no wills of their own. Mindless drones who could want for nothing more than what Zarathustra demands of them. Melphis realizes that this was an unfair assumption. Maybe his father enslaved them, just as he had been. Perhaps they do want for more, but aren't allowed to have it. *Adam was right. I'm not too different from him and Eve.*

Sasha and Seth are gaining distance from them. "Come on," Melphis says. "Let's work together to aid them. Let's make Adam proud."

Passing Melphis, my eyes drift into his. I want to say something, anything, but after everything I've done, after trying again and again to apologize, what more can I do? Melphis turns to Eve. He appears just as anxious to talk to her as I am to talk to him. I shouldn't bother him with anything more. We can always talk things out later.

The air feels even thicker having ventured in further. It's similar to Hell's supernatural gravity, but far worse. Heaving with every step, even my demonic body is having trouble here. My chest feels as if it's about to cave in. Sasha is also gasping. Large beads of sweat form upon her head. She stops, smiles, and points ahead of us.

"Look," Sasha says. "The cathedral."

A tall church made from black stone stands before us at the center of this treacherous mire. It has a tall wooden double door with a pointed top. Gold outlines its shape. On both sides of the door are stained glass windows. The art branded upon the glass shows the transition of a human in prayer being taken to Heaven by a pair of angels.

Sasha grits her teeth and scowls.

That's right. She has the most stake in all of this. She must have Virdeus on her mind.

Revenge. What good is it? By destroying the one to blame for the loss of someone dear to you...it won't bring them back. I understand her pain better than anyone. I'm here because I vowed to exact revenge on the ones who took Lola away from me. *But I've killed so many innocent people as a result.*

Placing my left palm across my face, tears drip between my fingers. A loud crash of splintering wood grabs my attention. Sasha walks over the shattered door, entering the cathedral. *She was there for me. She forgave me, even though I didn't deserve it. I won't let revenge bring her to ruin like it did to me. I won't let it sour her smile.*

Melphis passes me. Eve places a hand on my left shoulder. She nods and gestures for me to follow.

There are more stained-glass windows on the corridor's sides. Some hold pictures of angels. They're humanoid, with two broad white wings and golden halos above their heads. Even this deep into Heaven, God still has the need to lie. The other windows depict the image of a young girl with blonde hair. Then another of the same girl, but grown up. The next one shows the girl being lifted into the air, sprouting broad golden wings. Sunrays obscure her face.

The room past the entrance is massive. The cathedral's height is profound. Taller than any skyscraper I've seen. My mind goes back to Gluttony. He towered over the tallest building in Dallas. The roof of this cathedral seems high enough to fit even him.

At the end of the large room is a throne. Behind it, a towering menorah-like structure holding seven large black flames.

"Welcome to my divine hall," says a loud, booming voice. Sitting upon the throne is a sight straight from Michelangelo's painting, *The Creation of Adam.* An old man whose hair and beard are flowing and grey, but virile like a lion's mane. Standing up, his long white gown drifts to the floor, covering his feet.

"I am the *Lord thy God*. Not a soul has ever set foot in here. Let alone in Heaven. For thine feet to meet the surface of this holy place, feel honored."

Sasha grips her daggers, electrifying them. I try to follow her lead, but something feels off. To think the God whose existence I had spent my living life denying would be standing before me—but I've been to Hell. I've fought demons and angels alike. Seeing God is no more shocking than the rest of it, but then—*why can't I move!*

A rush of sweet scents flow into me. Forced to my knees, I can no longer breathe. Heart fluttering transmutes into a pounding sensation, as if someone is stomping on my chest. Angelic hymns grace my ears. The combination of this melody and the sweet pheromones stirs a memory. "I've felt this before!" I say, wheezing.

"Seth!" Sasha shouts. "What's wrong?"

Melphis steps forward and says, "You aren't fooling anyone, Yahweh. Show them who you truly are."

Yahweh smirks, and says in a feminine tone, "Good to see you, Abdiel!"

Upon hearing that name, Melphis's face tightens. "You know who I am? Have you always known? But then, why—"

Tremors bombard the cathedral. Black static engulfs Yahweh's body. The face of the old man becomes fluid. His eyes, nose, and mouth sink into his skull. His skin flows like a wave, rising and lowering and mixing. His wrinkles become smooth. New eyes bud in place of the old ones, then grow large, pretty, and blue. A dainty nose and lush pink lips appear. The grey beard is subtracted from his face and added to his scalp. The hair becomes a lush golden blonde, illuminating the room.

The tremors cease. The shapeshifting God's new form, complete. A pristine, beautiful girl stands before us. A slender waist, but with a hiker's legs.

Wait—

Yahweh smiles and says, "I knew you would come for me, Seth."

My eyes spring wide. *Wait, what? No.* "Is that really *you*, Lola?"

CHAPTER TWENTY-NINE

What the fuck is happening?

The pheromonal scent thickens. Its pungency confines me. The angelic melody grinds against my ears. Its volume overshadows all other noise. Sasha glances toward Lola, then to me, concerned. Her lips move, but to my ears, nothing is heard.

In a blurring speed, Sasha throws her electrified daggers. *No, wait!* I want to shout, but no air passes through my mouth. One dagger pierces Lola's heart. The other, Her throat. She stands as a statue. There's no indication of pain. The only reaction is of Lola's rippling skin. A pebble striking a pond. Like quicksand, the blades sink into Her body until even the hilts are consumed.

Sasha forces her arms forward, conjuring a large electrical tempest. The stained-glass windows shatter. Lightning rips into the walls. A cloud of glass and grinded stone disperses into the air. Lola remains still. The electric current cuts lightly into Her skin, but elicits no response. Sasha lunges toward Lola, hand outstretched. *No, stop it!* She reaches for Lola's neck, trying to disrupt the flow of magic—

A black tentacle rips through Lola's upper back. There's no blood. It's like a monster lurking inside a dark obscuring cave. The tendril pounds Sasha, faster than she can react. She crashes into the right wall. *No!* Sasha wheezes, clutching at her ribs with both hands. Blood spills from her mouth.

Dammit! Let me up. Let me speak. Why won't my body move! Come on, damn you! Let me go to her!

My body refuses. As if a boa constrictor is wrapped around me, my struggling seems to increase the pressure. I fall onto my face, scraping against the stone floor upon impact. Eve hurries to Sasha's side.

What is this? Lola, why are you here? Why is this happening? Why are you...

⊰◇⊱

"Yahweh!" Melphis shouts. "Answer me!"

The God of Heaven glares toward Melphis. "Of course, I recognize you, Abdiel. When my son, Greed, found you at Hell's Edge, you reeked of father's influence. I knew that if I let you be, one day you would seek to destroy our brother and me...and I knew that once Lucy was threatened, he would try to use the catalyst against us both."

"Catalyst?" Melphis asks.

Yahweh's eyes lock onto the paralyzed Seth. "I knew that once He had, you would be able to sway Seth to your side, then use him to slay the Archangels—the Sins," She says.

Melphis's eyes widen.

Yahweh smirks. "Lucy constructed the empty vessel, and you delivered him. For that, I thank you, but he was supposed to have arrived alone." Yahweh pauses, glancing toward Eve, then to Sasha. "And you have brought other unexpected faces. That one," She points to Sasha. "Holds an interesting power, but she's still only human. Weak and pathetic."

"Only human?" Eve shouts. "You may be deluded, but even *your* soul is still human!"

"Do not degrade me, spawn of Zarathustra," Yahweh shouts. "I went through my apotheosis long ago. By believing that I alone held the power to lead humankind to salvation, it became Truth. Through Faith, I became God."

Melphis glares inquisitively and says, "Salvation? That new world Satan had spoken about? That's your idea of salvation? Leaving this world and its people to die? Reduced to a state of nothingness?"

"This is what they want," Yahweh says. "To deny their life on Earth in favor of paradise. With hands clasped in prayer, humans are so quick to offer their wills onto me. In exchange for allowing me to feast upon their souls, I offer them an escape from their painful lives. For this, humans should be grateful."

Melphis glances toward the shattered windows. The swarm of teal spirits is circling the cathedral outside. "Is that why you sent your angels to Earth? To extract these souls for you?" he asks.

"Oh, those?" Yahweh says, with a crooked smile. "They're not for me."

Eve closes her eyes, taking a deep breath. She turns to Sasha. *This poor girl. Many of her ribs are broken.* Eve glances toward her hands. This body was gifted to her by Zarathustra. Created to keep him alive and to be an extension of his being. Born from the body of a god, but lacking the regenerative abilities of one. *Adam, are we of no use, after all?*

Turning toward Seth, Eve ponders his motionlessness. *Much like when we first met, but this is different. His eyes were dead back then, but now*—Eve looks closer. Seth's eyes are bright with fury and overwhelmed with tears. *He is not refusing to move.* Eve glares toward Yahweh. *This is because of Her.*

"You say they want this—your salvation," Eve says. "But do you realize just how many lives you have ruined?" Eve takes Sasha by the hand and lowers her to the floor near the cathedral's entrance. Turning to Seth, Eve drags him by the legs, joining him with Sasha. Eve reaches into her robe's pocket. She squeezes Zarathustra's locket, imagining the warmth of her father and brother by her side.

"What gives you the right to toy with the wills of humans?" Eve asks, offering Melphis a soft glance. With a roll of her eyes, she gestures for him to *get back.*

"*I* do," Yahweh says. "It is the right of God to decide the affairs and ultimate fate of humans."

"You are a god? Of what?" Eve asks. "Remember, this *Heaven* is but an extension of your soul, a life created by our father, Zarathustra!"

Eve raises her arms straight, then brings them crashing down. The high walls and ceiling of the cathedral bend and distort. Drooping inward, the building crashes into Yahweh. The giant menorah-like structure behind the throne also distorts, bends, and crashes. High pitched sounds of metal twisting and stone shattering fills the room. The black flames that sat atop the menorah's seven points release themselves from their altars. They dart around the now open air. Heaven's harsh rays beat down on the cathedral's base. The walls and ceiling are no more.

The teal souls circling the cathedral screech, disperse, then reconverge directly above the rubble. Then, silence.

Melphis approaches the high pile of stone and metal beams. Looking back toward Eve, she collapses to her knees. "Eve, are you alri—"

Six thick tentacles ram their way through the mountain of debris. They stretch past Melphis's face, almost tearing off his head.

The sound of blood splattering. Melphis turns to find Eve elevated by a tendril pierced through her chest. The other five tentacles repeatedly stab at her waist, until she's torn in two. Like starved vultures pecking away at carrion. Her upper body is tossed to the right. Her lower, to the left. A geyser of blood sprawls across the air in an arch. The sound of flesh squishing into the floor's hard surface brings Melphis to tears.

The rubble is blown away by a torrent of wind. Melphis conjures a barrier to protect himself from flying stones. With just a few blunt hits, fissures in the barrier form. *Oh, no. I forgot them!* Melphis turns to Seth and Sasha to find them in the protective covering of Yahweh's stretched tentacles. *She really must need him, but for what?*

The explosion of stone and metal slows. Turning to Yahweh, Melphis is struck with horror. An insectile beast stands at the center of the debris. As tall as a giraffe, wide as an elephant. Her prior skin flutters onto the ground. Along with the six tentacles rising from her back, she now has six pincers instead of hands. Enlarged eyes sit sunken in her skull. Loose skin sags from her formless jaw. Six parasitic feelers slither about, dropping steaming piles of tar onto the floor.

"I would be angry about this." Yahweh's voice becomes harsh and guttural. "If the world's end wasn't upon us anyway. Heaven will not be necessary for long." Her deformed fly-like eyes twitch and skitter, then fixate onto the black souls. "Return to me, my children."

The black spirits, the souls of each Sin, come to a halt just above their mother. Each of Yahweh's tentacles snatch one from the air. Her feelers stretch from Her mouth, high enough to reach the seventh. A slit from Her chest down to Her abdomen opens wide, accepting the Sins back into Herself. A large seven-ringed halo appears behind Yahweh. Black static swarms each ring like a horde of wasps. An immense pressure expands outward from Her, like a sudden tempest. Melphis tries to stabilize himself, but feels his feet sliding back.

Yahweh steps forward and says, "You have satisfied my need for you. Begone, Abdiel."

***

The glow of Eve's long teal hair dims. Her eyes, reduced to dull orbs. Unable to move my head, I see Sasha only through the corners of my eyes. She's still clutching her abdomen, struggling to breathe. She's still alive, but—my attention is drawn back to Eve's split corpse. *She was torn apart so easily and Sasha, far more capable than I, was swatted like a fly.*

{Then what do you expect to accomplish? There is nothing you can do.}

Yes, you're ri—no! Shut up. Shut up shut up shut up! I don't care if I'm too weak to do anything. I must at least try.

My rickety arms gradually slide into a push up formation. My elbows shake. The muscles in my neck pinch and tear. My palms slip and my chin slams against the floor.

The beast that emerged from Lola's skin is staring Melphis down. Lola's front remains pristine. Only from the back is her skin torn. The sight is less of a reptile shedding its skin and more of an insect rising from its cocoon. Her large fly-like eyes become tethered to me for a moment, taking notice of my attempt to rise. Her head convulses. Turning back toward Melphis, She rampages toward him, screeching. As if watching me elicited impatience within Her.

Melphis stomps the ground, conjuring a wall of thick stone spikes. He waves his hands around, slowly tightening his fists. The water in the air freezes into sharp lances. The spears launch toward Yahweh, piercing her. Tar oozes from the wounds, but Her momentum doesn't slow. She plows through the stone spikes. Wounding her before shattering.

Melphis picks up his staff, plunging it forward. A flame conjures and—Yahweh brings her pincers down, slicing through the staff. Blood drips from the six bladed arms, having pierced his heart. Melphis stares toward Yahweh's feelers. They slither across his face, plastering him in hot, putrid saliva.

"Receive my salvation," Yahweh says, discharging a pool of steaming tar onto Melphis. It pours into his throat, muffling his screams. The boiling sludge corrodes and consumes his entire body.

My hands quake.

Her mouth makes wet clicking sounds as She walks over to Sasha and me. One of Her tentacles wraps around my feet, pulling me away from Sasha.

"It won't be much longer Seth," Yahweh says, glancing toward the sky. "Once I deal with this troublesome one, the emptiness inside you will be filled with these souls lurking above us. The Abyss within you will speed along the dismantling of the Earth. Then, you shall become a new world for me to inhabit. Isn't that grand? The birth of a universe! You do this for me...and we shall finally be reunited."

A universe without Sasha? Without Melphis? I couldn't bear it!

Yahweh heads toward my last living friend. She's still unable to move, barely holding onto life, but Sasha's intense glare refuses to die.

"I know about you," Yahweh hisses. "The demon huntress of that *Guild* Envy stumbled across. How silly of my daughter to think she could grow strong enough to defy me! And how silly of you, to think you could avenge your fool of a father. Oh, sorry. Not your *real* father."

Sasha's eyes grow wide and furious. Her breathing quick and shallow. Yahweh's tongues caresses Sasha's soft cheeks.

"Receive my salvation," Yahweh says, raising Her pincers.

Father, I'm sorry. I failed you.

Virdeus's face is stirred into Sasha's mind. Andes, too. Even Mikhail. Everyone in the Guild and—the dilapidated shed where she first encountered Seth and Melphis. The passion she felt when looking into Seth's eyes. With her body's last bit of strength, she lets the tears pour.

Lifting her pincers, Yahweh aims to penetrate. Sasha closes her eyes, waiting for her last breath—the sound of heavy footsteps approach quickly. A splattering of warm liquid splashes onto Sasha's face. She opens her eyes to the sound of Yahweh's voice, and Seth standing between them.

"How? No one has ever been able to break that pheromonal spell!" Yahweh shouts, Her voice pained. "Seth, look what you've made me do!"

Seth's hands are gripping two of Yahweh's pincers. His arms shake as he holds them back. The other four arms have pierced through his chest. The tips of Yahweh's blades are protruding from Seth's back, dripping blood onto Sasha.

"You have taken so much from me," Seth says. "*You will not take her, too!*"

White flames erupt from his wounds. The Flames of Nil force Yahweh back. She screeches as they singe Her scaly skin. The same flames curl backward, toward Sasha. Remembering the fate of Magistrum—the screams of all who died there—Sasha winces, closing her eyes.

Calm washes over her. Sasha finds a white barrier enshrouding her. Seth roars in pain. A teal form rises, stretching from his body. As the seams are severed, his spirit rockets toward the upper half of Eve's corpse. His body's voice bellows as his soul clambers for the locket held by Eve's left hand. Seth's body drops to Sasha's side, his lifeless eyes staring into her.

The soul that She waited eons for escapes into the White Abyss. Yahweh screeches. Her agony ripples through the air, causing fissures to form in Heaven's fabric.

CHAPTER THIRTY

Seth's corpse lies near Sasha. She reaches for him, but is denied by the barrier. Her longing hands cannot pass the white flames. "I'm sorry," Sasha says, to ears that can no longer hear her.

You protected me, but what can be done now? Sasha glances around the white capsule, then wails on it with her fists. The flames swirling around her are somehow dense. As if they are made from otherworldly, impenetrable metal—but they also feel gentle, warm. Like cozying up with a loved one near a fire on a cold winter's night.

Her agitation transmutes into tears. *The Earth will die, with the only one left who could do something about it, trapped within your protection.* Heaven's grotesque God approaches. Sasha clutches her broken ribs, as her mind drifts to Melphis and Eve. *No, it wouldn't have mattered. I couldn't do anything before. None of us could, and Seth—I would have done the same for him.*

Yahweh sinks Her pincers into Seth's spinal cord. His body spasms. Blood spurts. His body tears into pieces. "He's useless now," She says.

Sasha's furious glare meets the God's deformed eyes.

"Does this make you angry?" Yahweh asks, like an anthropologist trying to understand the behavior of apes. "Why? He was made for me. To create a new world under my governance. I alone, feel the weight of this loss."

Staring down at Seth's mangled corpse, Yahweh remembers Her failure to consume the White Abyss. Her face scrunches with furious shame. Thinking upon a past trauma. Turning to Sasha, a tentacle slams down—She staggers back, halting the blow. She hisses at the barrier, remembering how the Flames of Nil burnt Her before.

Sasha asks with shallow breath, "Why do you need Seth? You've been eating souls for eons now." Sasha places her head in her palms, almost fainting. "Why not just take the souls into yourself?"

"The catalyst was to birth a new universe, at the cost of his life. What good is a new world, with no God to control it?"

Sasha stares toward Yahweh with dull eyes, unable to speak anymore. *A good world, that's how it would be. No more living and dying, in obedience to gods. We would live for ourselves—for humanity.*

"Besides," Yahweh continues. "His soul was crafted especially for this purpose. Without him, that dream is lost."

Yahweh looks skyward. The mass of teal souls is floating above, patiently awaiting guidance. "If I can't create my new world," She says. "Then I will at least aid in the destruction of Zarathustra's. In my final moments, I will strike the fear of God into the hearts of all humanity!"

Yahweh lifts Her mouth toward the sky. The loose skin around Her jaw stretches, expanding past the width of Her elephant-sized torso. Her tongues stretch above and around the mass of souls, tying them up like fish in a net. Pulling them into Herself, the lives of billions are consumed.

A burst of teal light, and pain as I'm torn from my body. *What is this?* I'm ethereal, translucent. Roaring into Yahweh's face, my eyes turn to the locket in Eve's hand. I had forgotten that Zarathustra took it from me and gave it to her. The teal souls above us appear to be waiting for something—someone to tell them where to go. *Magic does what the mind wills it to do.* The words Melphis once spoke return to me. *The locket, the locket, the locket. I must escape into the locket. I won't let Yahweh have me.* Darting into the air, I spiral toward the locket. A whirlpool of teal light, sinking into another realm.

A strange unfeeling darkness stretches across an unmeasurable space. I hear faint breathing that is like, but still not my own. A chuckle echoes from some unseen place.

"What is this? Who's there?" I ask.

The chuckle evolves into a hoarse chortle. The voice says,

{Civilization has been earned
By a furious power, but can also
At this hour, be brought to
Ashes, and placed within an urn.
Death and Life
One attaches to
As man does his wife
Once he says, "I do."
And who are you
So wretched and entrenched

In destruction, to woo?
Where shall you place your wrench?
You are Flame, and the Abyss
Will destruction, a natural right
Be your aim? Or will you choose creation, amidst
The fire. From whence life can shine bright?}

"Excuse me?" I say.

{Civilization has been earned...} The voice repeats itself word for word.

An imposing white phantom emerges from the darkness. Its lips, outlined by the blackness inside its mouth, morphs into a grin. It stands as tall as I did in my demonic form. With the same long horns.

"Answer my question! I thought I went into the locket. Where is the White Abyss?"

{You shall never grow—never be free. If you do not first understand the monster inside you. You are Flame and the Abyss. Look at what you've done...all of whom you've killed.}

"Is that what you mean by furious power? The Flames of Nil? Power that can kindle civilization, but also destroy it?"

{Yes, destroy. It's all you've ever done. It's all your reckless emotions have ever amounted to.}

Pondering his words, I want to scream, *I never asked for this!* But I hold back. "You're right. I've done terrible things and the regret will stay with me forever, but what's the point of your riddle? Are you telling me to pick one? Stay tethered to destruction? Or choose life instead? Give up my negative emotions, to embrace only positive ones?"

{You will regret these things forever? Convenient, now that you're dead. Is that why you threw yourself in front of Yahweh's blades? To crucify yourself, and wash away your sins within the veil of death?}

"What!" I shout. "No! I came here to seek out Zarathustra! I thought he could help us!"

{Seeking help from a god, to slay God? Pathetic! You're just as worthless as you've ever been! You cannot act for yourself! Melphis, Adam, and Eve, all dead in this pursuit of killing God. This quest has only led to the destruction of everything you hold dear! Yahweh didn't kill them, you did!}

"*Shut up*," I shout. "You're wrong! Melphis, Sasha, Adam, and Eve...we wanted to destroy Yahweh, so life on Earth could flourish! Destruction has its place! As how can a better world be built before first dismantling past structures? Destruction and creation act in tandem. You cannot have one without the other!"

The white phantom's grin diminishes into quiet stoicism.

"The same goes for positive and negative emotions," I say. "Both have their place in this world! Zarathustra taught me that. He never once asked me to give up my anger. No! He told me to make good use of my anger! You think my rage is destructive? Sure, it has been, but I don't care for washing away my sins. Why would I want to? By carrying those mistakes with me, I will learn to be better! It is because of my wrath that Sasha is still alive!" I pause. My mind wanders to the image of Sasha's warm, brilliant smile. Her sharp, perceptive mind and how comforting, nurturing, and forgiving she is. "And my wrath...is also why I wish to go back to her!"

The white phantom offers me its hand, smiling. **{A life beyond good and evil. One that doesn't see negative as bad, positive as good. One who lives above such values. As only they can be a true, full human being. Accepting pain as it comes. As it is neither bad, nor good. It just is. The same is true of you—one who was born into emptiness. For what**

does a painter do with an empty canvas but fill it with their own beauty!}

The phantom's body stretches outward into an all-encompassing whiteness. Grass crunches beneath my feet. A sweet aroma rises from the flower-filled garden.

"Welcome back, my Wrath." Zarathustra says. "I'm impressed. Willing your own soul into the White Abyss. Once someone dies, they become mindless energy, but you remained sentient." Zarathustra lets out a bellowing laugh. "It's finally happening, and I won't live to see it, but that's alright."

"What are you talking about?" I ask. "And what was that strange white phantom?"

"A reflection of yourself, the abyss within you." Zarathustra stares toward the constrictive wood that binds him, his mind adrift. "I did this to them. Melphis, Adam, Eve. With the last of my children gone, no faith in me remains. I will soon disappear. This, I deserve."

"But Sasha and I know you," I say.

"Faith isn't the same as knowing. Faith is born from needfulness, then materializes a solution to that need. This solution—that is what gods are, but you and Sasha have found a greater truth. A world that is built by humans, for humans. One that has no need for gods.

"Seth, imagine if the collective human species retracted their faith in gods. Imagine if they redirected that same unwavering, intense faith—one that creates the very gods they seek help from—back into themselves? Would gods descend into obscurity? Would humanity rise into greater progression? This is the questioning that led me to create the Earth and the White Abyss. I will not live to see the answer, but you and Sasha are fit to lead humanity forward. To a greater, truer strength. A human strength that has no need for gods."

"That's all well and good, but how can I go back? And can we defeat Her? Is there any help you can give us?"

"Oh, you don't need me. You never did, but I can give you a little push, like I have done before," Zarathustra says, gesturing for me to come closer.

He cups my head within his palms. My temples grow hot. His body becomes ethereal, then bursts into teal dust. His voice transcends bodily form, and says, "Thank...you..."

As the old, dying god disappears, the glowing particles left behind flood my eyes.

After consuming the souls, Yahweh's large stature bloats further. The cathedral's broken pieces are pushed back by the supernatural weight of Her increased power. Yahweh walks past Sasha, each step causing a tremor. One foot crushes the remains of Seth's skull.

"The Earth could not hold my brother and me, and that was when my Godhood was young and fresh. I had not yet eaten a single soul. My father's world will surely crumble beneath my feet in an instant, as I am now."

Sasha's labored breathing keeps her from responding. Heaven's parasitic God stomps toward the marsh of tar. The sludge creeps up her legs, latching onto her as a newborn to their mother's teat.

A flash of teal light emerges near Eve's corpse. The sheen, so bright, Heaven's carcinogenic mire is blown away. The sun's morning light, casting off the darkness of the prior night. Yahweh turns to face the brightness that scorches her skin.

It dims and before Her is Zarathustra's locket. Hovering in the air, pulsating a teal glow. The latch bursts open. Out emerges a spirit in the shape of a human man. First his head emerges, then his arms, torso, and legs. He claws his way out of the locket's tiny opening. Expanding as he enters Heaven's open air. His body solidifies.

"You!" Yahweh shouts.

"Recognize me, do you?"

Sasha's eyes light up at the sound of his voice. *Seth?* He stands tall with long, flowing hair and glowing eyes. He glances skyward, noticing that the souls are gone. He squints toward Yahweh's bloated stomach.

"Thank you for returning to me," Yahweh says. "There may be hope for our new world after all! Come here and—"

Seth raises his left hand toward Yahweh, then squeezes it into a fist. Her stomach bursts open, relinquishing the souls. A swirl of teal light rockets toward the sky. The black souls of the Seven Sins are ejected alongside the others. Her seven ringed halo shatters, dispersing into dust. Yahweh screeches. The fissures in Heaven's fabric grow even deeper. The artificial world quakes and crumbles. Seth lifts the locket toward the sky and says, "Do not worry. You may rest now." With furious speed, the souls fly into the locket. Seth crushes Zarathustra's heirloom, tossing the pieces away.

Yahweh's scream bellows as black sludge pours from her stomach wounds. Seth walks over to Sasha, his left hand outstretched. The white orb surrounding her retracts. The flames dance in the air before being absorbed into Seth's palm. He leaves his hand for Sasha to grab, and says, "Would you help me?"

His face is much paler than the dark grey skin of his demonic body. *But there's no doubt. It's really him.* Sasha takes his hand. Teal sparks run down Seth's arm and into Sasha's, like an electrical current shooting through a wire. The creative magic surges up her body, and to her brain. Collecting itself upon Sasha's ribs, she's overcome by a sensation she has never felt before. The bones mend. Her breathing normalizes. She springs to her feet, life ascended.

Hand in hand, they stare toward Yahweh. Their eyes glowing, a brilliant teal sheen. Yahweh wraps Her tentacles around Her stomach, trying to hide the wound. She stares back at Seth and Sasha. Two humans, far smaller than She. They step toward her. She backs away.

The memory of her attempt to eat the White Abyss returns to Yahweh. The death of her human body, so that she could become as she is now. The pain of that failure consumes her.

"How?" she asks. "How could you achieve what I couldn't?"

"I hear him," Seth says. "Zarathustra. His voice is swirling around in my head. He says that you failed because you tried to deny your existence, to become something you weren't—but us?" Seth looks at Sasha. "I am. She is. We are."

"Yes, we are enough." Sasha says. "Humans can find all they need within themselves—and within each other. Monsters like you are no longer needed."

Seth's eyes release a flash of light. Strong vines erupt from the ground. They wrap around Yahweh's arms, tendrils, and legs, anchoring her. Three stalagmites rise from the ground, impaling her core and shoulders.

Yahweh screams. "Seth, it's me! Lola!"

Seth steps forward and whispers, "Flourish."

The stone and vines sprout leaves and flowers. They meld together with Yahweh. A large tree erupts at her core, ripping her flesh asunder. She hangs along the branches, as a cross.

Sasha raises her palms. Teal dust springs into the air. They converge, creating skeletal, winged figures. Black feathers sprout atop newly woven flesh. Broad and feathered beaks form upon the faces of the two giant ravens. Swooping toward Yahweh, they perch on the tree branches made from her flesh. With twitching heads, they glance toward Yahweh's deformed fly-like eyes. Their beaks plunge, blinding the once all-seeing God.

Teal particles converge upon Seth's risen left palm. With them he creates an enormous, blinding sun, made from white flames. Without moving his hand, the sun is launched toward Yahweh. The ravens scatter. The grotesque God of Heaven screams, her body disintegrating under the heat of the white sun. The flames disappear. All that remains is a crater and drifting ashes.

"We did it," Sasha says, "At a great cost, but we did it." She glances toward Eve's corpse. Then at the scorch marks upon the stone floor where Melphis breathed his last.

Seth says, "Yes, we did—"

The ground emits a furious tremble. Seth and Sasha are knocked off balance, into each other's arms.

"It's just like what happened in Hell," Sasha says. "We have to leave. Now!"

The ravens land near their creator. They position themselves low enough to allow Seth and Sasha upon their backs. They climb atop the avian giants and ascend from Heaven.

The ravens perch atop a tall building overlooking Central Park. It, along with rest of the city, are in flames. The angels appear to have stopped moving. The force driving them forward, halted, but the contents of both Hell and Heaven continue to spill onto the Earth. Just like the artificial worlds before it, fissures form within the ground and air.

"What are we to do? We have felled God, but what now?" Sasha asks. Seth's ears twitch, like a dog alerted by a loud noise. A voice whispers inside his head.

"We have to use Zarathustra's power," Seth says, frowning. "I don't know what will happen, but I must release all of his magic onto the Earth. Perhaps that will do...something."

Sasha says, "But what will happen to you?"

Seth pauses, looking over the ruined Earth. Turning toward Sasha, his frown transmutes into a smile. "I'm really happy I met you," he says. "And I'm so glad you're alive."

He lunges his arms forward. His eyes pulsate with light. Teal particles gush from his palms.

"Seth, wait!" Sasha shouts, as the light interrupts her sight. The Earth follows in Seth's disappearance. The world is engulfed in a brilliant, teal shimmer.

EPILOGUE

Sasha makes her way through the streets of Crowley. She passes by a large apartment complex built atop what used to be the large crevasse that she and Virdeus had visited those long three years ago.

The Earth has been mended. Its stability, reinforced for years to come. *As sturdy as the white barrier that he protected me with.* Sasha smiles, warmth overtaking her. She stops to sit for a moment. Walking has become difficult over the last few months. Catching her breath, Sasha stares toward the ground. *Even after all this time, I still can't believe it. He didn't only repair the Earth. I can feel it beneath me—its weight, its essence. The Earth and the White Abyss, wedded into a single form, facilitating new life.*

Walking on, she smiles at a man sitting at ease on his porch. He's holding a laptop, playing a video of a news broadcast.

"It's been three years since the most shocking and catastrophic event in human history. One that many are referring to as the Supernatural Holocaust. Two strange worlds appeared above us—what we are now referring to as Heaven and Hell, terminology provided and popularized by *The Assembly for Human Progression*—and the otherworldly beings that descended to multiple cities around the globe. Led by their leader in Heaven, now known as Yahweh, creator of the angels.

"With the quick destruction of New York City and its sudden repair, even eyewitnesses to the event have found it difficult to accept what happened, but there's no denying the loss we have endured. The millions of lives taken that day. Though we remain thankful to those mysterious heroes who fought back against the angels, saving all they could..."

Sasha smiles, then continues down the road. She reaches an office building, secured behind a steel gate. A sign reads: *Assembly for Human Progression.* Sasha grabs an ID badge from her pocket. It reads *President of the Assembly for Human Progression.* Scanning it at the door, she lets herself in.

Walking into an office, she's greeted by her Vice President. "Ah! Matriarch!" Andes shouts with a wide grin. "It's great to see you!"

His hair has started greying, his skin, wrinkled. Though ever since their victory over the angels, he's been full of life. Looking at him makes Sasha feel as if Virdeus once more walks among them.

"It's great to see you, too, Andes! Though I fear this may be the last time I can make the trip for a while. I'm going to be bedridden soon enough!"

"Things will be in good hands during your absence. I promise," Andes says. "Speaking of which, we may need to rebrand ourselves again. To the Assembly for *Magic Cultivation* and Human Progression.

"Oh? Has something happened?"

Andes shuffles some papers around, then unearths a particular page from his desk. He hands it to Sasha. "It is just as you predicted. The White Abyss really has merged with the Earth."

Sasha glances toward the paper. There are pictures of three newborn babies. Alongside compiled, descriptive notes documenting their date of birth, location, ethnicity, status of parental figures, number of siblings, the symptoms shown...

"These children," Andes says. "Have shown signs of magic. One caused sparks of electricity to rise from its eyes. Another created a flame out of thin air. The last made water spring from a cup and swirled it around. We've been keeping a close eye on them ever since."

"Then it falls to us to guide them along," Sasha says. "If we teach them how to use their magic well, it will be a good thing. For them, and all of humanity."

Pondering the situation, she looks at the large mound of papers on Andes's desk. "I picked a poor time to take a leave of absence, didn't I? Sorry, Andes. I didn't mean to put all this on you."

"Nonsense! You have done enough, and you will do more! But first, please. Take your much needed rest."

She smiles and thanks him, then makes her way home.

She hikes up the mountain path, in the company of the setting sun. After some struggle, Sasha finds herself at the summit. A wooden cabin sits close to the cliffside. There is a gorgeous view overlooking the town of Crowley. Smoke rises from the chimney. The burning smell of a freshly placed log fills her with delight.

To the left of the cabin are four tombstones. The granite has been cut into the shapes of Virdeus, Melphis, Adam, and Eve. Standing near the graves is a tall, bearded man wearing a blue and white plaid shirt, and torn black jeans. Sasha walks to his side.

"Out here again?" she asks.

"Just paying my respects," he says. "How is Andes doing?"

"As jovial as ever, and he had an interesting message."

"Oh?"

"We were right. Humans have started to be born with magic."

He strokes his long, black beard. "Then I suppose we have our work cut out for us."

"Andes says he'll take care of things, so we won't have to worry. To give us our rest for...you know." Sasha smiles. "So, Seth..."

"Yeah?"

"Do you think humans will be alright? With magic, I mean."

"We are. They will be, too. I'm sure of it."

Seth frowns at Melphis's tombstone.

"It wasn't your fault," Sasha says. "You know that, right?"

"I suppose, but I wish I could have made things right. Before it was too late." Seth pauses. He turns toward Sasha, bright-eyed. "Say, we're going to have to be careful. Teaching humans about magic and all. Outing ourselves as having magic, may cause them to think we are gods. We can't have that!"

Sasha chuckles, then takes Seth by the arm. She lays her head on his shoulder. "No, we can't have that. For we are not gods and none exist here anymore. We made sure of that."

"Yes," Seth smiles. "A world led by humans, for humans. A world that has no need for gods. They will find their own way. This world can be whatever they want it to be."

Seth glances back toward the graves. "Thank you, my friends. Thank you...Melphis. For leading me toward this new life." He lays his free hand upon Sasha's rounded belly.

Tears of joy overwhelm him. With Sasha's warmth by his side and his at hers, the world has never felt brighter. The weight of his past persists. His lost friends are on his mind, all the time—and there's the blossoming responsibility of helping Sasha lead humanity toward a new era. Life is hard and far from perfect. They would have it no other way.

Holding Sasha tight, Seth smiles, warm and bright. He feels a kick from Sasha's belly. Having gone through tremendous darkness, they now find themselves cultivating new life. They stand in silence for a moment, within each other's arms. They listen to the wind and the evening's cricket symphony. To Seth, nothing could be more beautiful.

Special Thanks:

I first conceived of "The Monsters Among Us" almost a decade ago, I believe during the spring of 2016. Its early form was vastly different from what has been printed here. That first draft has been thrusted into the Abyss, never to return! But that was when it took its first steps, so to speak, evolving greatly over the course of the following few years when I simply let it linger, marinating inside my mind, growing, festering, into the emotionally charged, multi-epochal epic you've just read. But it took time to become was it is, and I have many to thank for helping shape it into what it needed to be, and for shaping me into the author I am today.

First, I must thank Professor Jordan Bell at Dutchess Community College. I sought career advice from him and had determined that throughout my life, a love for storytelling has always loomed large. So, in lieu of a research paper, he tasked me with writing a short story. I was nervous. It was my first attempt at creative writing, but when giving me his thoughts, he told me it was thoroughly enjoyable, and that contained within the story was the makings of a novel. He suggested I try expanding it. So, I did, and far beyond the scope he foresaw. So, thank you, Jordan Bell. I would not have become an author if not for your guidance, support, and belief in me.

Next, I must thank my advisor at Bard College, author and Professor Joseph O'Neill. The process of writing "The Monsters Among Us" under Joseph O'Neill's tutelage was illuminating and thought-provoking. He helped shape and polish the narrative into being as perfect as it could be. Due to his teaching, I am now a far better writer. He took my talents and sharpened them to a profound edge, and I am forever grateful for it. For that, and for his continued support throughout my career as an author.

I must also thank poet and Professor Cole Heinowitz from Bard College, who in addition to Joseph O'Neill acted as a mentor figure to me. Her support of my writing lifted me into a substan-

tial confidence that has propelled me through the harsh landscape of modern publishing. With the knowledge that my work is good and that with enough persistence, I can and will succeed. In that regard, I must thank the entirety of Bard College. My cherished second home, where I flourished more than I ever had before.

Thank you to Kurt Karlson, my cousin, my first reader, my trusted literary sounding board. I still remember the night we discussed the themes, symbolism, and core philosophy at play within the novel. We chatted for over two hours and barely scratched the surface. It was at that moment that I knew I had created something truly worthwhile and profoundly unique.

Thank you to my publisher Rowan Prose Publishing and my editor Kelly Moran. For through them this special book of mine, after so many years of writing it, has finally been born.

Thank you to the love of my life, Katarina Markota, for without her this book would never have been published. In January of 2024, I was wallowing hard. The death of my grandfather was fresh and had drudged up the painful memories of losing my best friend nine months earlier. I was lost, adrift within the dark sea of my mind, and to make matters worse, failure was looming over me. By then, I had submitted "The Monsters Among Us" to a painfully large number of agents and publishers for over two years. All of whom gave me outright rejections. Mired in despair by the deaths of my grandfather and friend alongside my waning endurance and the crushing fatigue from getting nowhere with my career, I had decided to shelve "The Monsters Among Us" and give up. That is, until expressing my concerns to Katarina Markota, who, in the way she makes me feel perfectly at ease about everything, calmed me down and implored me not to give up on the book, to keep trying—someone will say yes eventually, she told me. Two weeks later, fittingly on Valentine's Day, I signed the publishing contract for "The Monsters Among Us." So, thank you, Katarina, my love, for believing in me, supporting me, and *for being able to see my future more clearly than I can. I'm a published author now thanks to you.*

An extra special thanks to Jacob Lang, my best friend of many years whose belief in this book allowed me to keep going, keep hoping, while the difficulty of getting published weighed heavily upon me. It is with great remorse that I write this, knowing that he'll never get to read it, as we tragically lost Jacob Lang on June 7th, 2023. But his words echo within my mind: keep trying, don't give up. I believe in you and truly believe this book will be published, eventually. How right you were, Jacob, about this and so much more. It embitters me to enjoy the publication of "The Monsters Among Us" without you, for I miss you terribly and your words so perfectly encapsulate the spirit of the book's message: we must keep on and never give up. We must do so with great belief in ourselves and when we do, we shall reach those great heights, eventually—and if we didn't lose you, Jacob, I know you would have also achieved your dreams. For you see, dear reader, Jacob Lang was an amazing, beautiful artist, but he never got to relish getting his art out into the world during his lifetime. So, I'll use my art to benefit his. Please indulge me and check out his memorial website below. Soak up his artwork so that Jacob Lang can live on through us all. Thank you.

Jacob Matthew Lang
July 11th, 1997 – June 7th, 2023
jacoblang.net

CHECK OUT THESE OTHER GREAT READS FROM ROWAN PROSE:

Kent Priore is the debut author of "The Monsters Among Us." He writes dark literature where romanticism meets modern psychology for a macabre but hopeful depiction of inner struggle, and the human ability to endure. He is a fierce advocate for mental health awareness and for greater acceptance of neurodivergence. For this reason, themes of mental health are pronounced and ever present in his work, both the devastating and the hopeful aspects of it. He graduated with honors from Bard College with a BA in the Written Arts, and is a proud marginalized voice in the neurodivergent community.

www.kentpriore.com